Bryony

By Denise M. Baran-Unland

Illustrated by Kathleen R. Van Pelt

This book is lovingly dedicated to the reader, whoever you might be.

Bryony is a rapidly growing, invasive perennial vine, with dark-green, palmate leaves and a thick, extensive rooting system. Its round berries are poisonous to humans and animals.

FOREWARD

Bryony is a cautionary tale replete with all the elements many girls love: fabulous dresses, a mansion, glittering social events, and a handsome man who needs her.

How long, and in what pretty fashion, can we delude ourselves while we are getting what we think we want? Melissa takes a wild risk to experience a life like Bryony's; what young, naive woman wouldn't? When John offers it to her, just a taste and with such a minor commitment, a trifle, really, she leaps right in.

So many recent stories of vampires romanticize the monsters. The angst of the undead, living forever and growing bored, is equated with the angst of young adults. Not so in Bryony. These are not glamorous vampires that dress in the latest leather fashions and have star-crossed love affairs; these are bad, bad people.

Reading this story leads us to ask many questions about John Simons, the "romantic" hero. Why doesn't Melissa ask these questions? What about the other girls who are "saving" vampires? What about the girls who tried and died? What is that concern compared to the romantic haze that Melissa lives in as Bryony?

In her youthful naiveté, Melissa expects romance. She is very clearly not ready for an actual adult relationship. Melissa cannot look at her nocturnal friends out of her peripheral vision for then she sees them as they truly are. She makes a solemn vow before she looks at John Simons from all angles. Is the price of the dream worth what she will find when she learns the whole story?

Bryony is a not a story where love conquers all. It's a tale of appetites, promises, illusions, and lessons. Remember the lessons.

Reverend Sandy D. Costa, editor, artist, teacher, activist, advocate, and mother
April 26, 2011.

TABLE OF CONTENTS

THE PROLOGUE

As the fog rolled inland off the lake, the approaching dusk grew uncommonly gloomy. He sat immobile, brooding and staring out the window overlooking the water. A long-forgotten page flopped over the typewriter. Scattered notes adorned the carpet. His cigar was ashes; the brandy sat untouched. Even the new purple silk tie failed to lift his mood. The fire burned low, but it was light enough. He hadn't the strength to turn up the gas. The scent of roses choked him and mocked the room's glorious memories.

The white Siberian Husky lying by his feet whined. The man started and glanced down. He had forgotten the dog.

"Chinook, hush!"

The husky's head drooped on its paws, and the man closed his eyes. The grandfather clock's metered ticking was intolerable. He clenched the handles of the desk chair, for he refused to fly out of this room like some fool. He'd find out soon enough.

He jerked awake at the familiar rattle, quickly ran a hand through his dark hair, and swerved toward the sound. Another man, tall and broad, stumbled into the room. His long, fair hair hung twisted and wild; his face was red and puffy.

It's over, the man thought, and he swung his chair around to hide his hatred. Not until dusk darkened into night, did the man take a deep breath, stand, and face his enemy.

"John," he said. "I have something to show you."

He strolled out the door, through the hall, and down the back staircase. Without hesitation, the husky followed. Behind him was the satisfying thud of John's footsteps.

The dreaded moment had arrived. Deliverance was denied. He had no choice.

At the bottom, he reached up for the lantern, lit it, and then sharply turned left, away from the main rooms. The husky's toenails clicked on the stone floor, but he no longer cared about the dog, only John.

The corridor ended. The man tapped on a wall, and it noiselessly slid back, revealing a bolted, padlocked door. He produced a set of keys, selected one, unfastened the lock, slid back the bolt, and pushed open the door. The unexpected rush of light visibly shook John. Good. He shoved John into the room and slammed the door.

"What—?"

A knife plunged into John's back. The man slashed, swung, and slashed again, but John was dead long before the man had spent his wrath. As he once more raised the knife, he felt the familiar chest tightness. He struggled against it, then gave up and flung the knife on the floor. Ignoring the dripping sweat, the man braced himself, gasped for breath, and kicked over the corpse. He studied John's twisted face but felt no pity or remorse. He had only a howling emptiness, an aching void time could never heal. The noose beckoned him, but his eyes first swept over rows of easels and the flames of many strategically positioned candles, glad John had seen them, hoping the view haunted him into eternity.

"Forgive me," he said. Then he hanged himself.

CHAPTER 1: WELCOME TO MUNSONVILLE

The old man huddled into the corner of the building and buried his shriveled head into the snarled fur of the sleeping dog. A teen girl in torn jeans held out one thin, blue hand and pleaded silently from sunken, black- rimmed eyes.

Seventeen-year-old Melissa Marchellis slammed the photograph album, ran her fingers over the gilt letters, Frank Marchellis, and blinked back tears. Her father's award-winning pictures of New York's homeless made her feel homeless, too.

"Are you okay, Melissa?" her mother Darlene called from the driver's seat.

"Sure," Melissa answered dully.

"Well, we should be in Munsonville in an hour."

Was it just two weeks ago that her mother had announced "We're moving to Michigan?" Who wanted to live in a fishing village? What a crummy summer 1975 turned out to be!

Melissa slid further into her seat and gazed glumly out the window. After her father had died in June, they learned he had owned a mansion belonging to nineteenth century pianist and composer, John Simons. Her mother had sold it to the village to pay the giant stack of medical bills. The village then hired her to promote the mansion as a tourist attraction and offered, rent-free, the remodeled servant quarters. Melissa tried picturing her new home, but only saw her father in his wheelchair. She squeezed her eyes. If Melissa had been as gutsy as Kimberly, she would have run away. Laura's family sympathized, but had no room for an extra person. Melissa was too afraid to live with her best friend. Shelly's father yelled a lot and sometimes hit Shelly's mother. Melissa couldn't wait until she turned eighteen. Then, no one could tell her what to do.

Melissa replaced the photograph album and slipped a cassette into her tape recorder. They had been driving since dawn. The highway sign announced the next city: Thornton.

"This is where we exit," Darlene called out with forced cheerfulness. Melissa merely flipped back her long, dark hair and inserted an earplug. As a little girl, Melissa escaped troubles by imagining herself in her father's adventures. Now, she only wished to block out the world. She closed her eyes and faded into the music.

When Melissa awoke, the busy highways had vanished into a desolate, two-lane road. She rubbed her eyes and checked her watch. It was almost noon.

Her mother glanced into the rear view window and laughed. "Well, you two aren't much company."

Melissa stretched. Brian slumped in the front seat. On cue, her brother started, sat up, and blinked against the windshield's glare.

"I'm not sleeping." Brian yawned. "I'm thinking."

Her mother smoothed back Brian's hair. "Well, I'm thinking about lunch. You?"

"Heck, yeah!" Brian squirmed away from his mother's hand.

"Sure," Melissa called back. She was surprisingly hungry

"We're almost to Munsonville," Darlene said. "We'll eat there." Half an hour later, they passed a dented sign sporting a large, smiling fish:

Munsonville. Population: 386. Everyone Welcome Here. Only one road led into and through the village: Main Street. How original, Melissa thought wryly.

Munsonville, with its shiny blacktop, plank sidewalks, and weathered brick buildings, seemed frozen in time. Painted wooden signs read: *Village Hall, Joe's General Store, Harper's Grocery, Dalton's Dry Goods, Walker's Apothecary, and Munsonville Public Library. Munsonville Inn* had a three-story turret. A small, cream-colored, clapboard church with arched windows and an ornate steeple sat farther back. A three-story, redbrick school stood near the end. Was that the grade school or the high school? A lake lay beyond one side of the road; a house-lined hill marked the other. Melissa did not see a mansion.

Her mother parked in front of a dingy, squat-looking building, Sue's Diner. Brian turned and rolled his eyes. Melissa mouthed back, *Probably get food poisoning.*

"Let's go, guys!" Darlene peered in the mirror and patted her short hair, the color and texture of corn silk. "Don't judge a book by its cover. I'll bet the food is terrific."

Stiff and cramped from the long ride, Melissa and Brian slowly emerged from the car and entered the dreary building. Brian poked Melissa, and her jaw dropped.

For a small, lakefront village restaurant, throngs of people packed the dining room. There were men in overalls and plaid shirts; women wearing faded, print dresses; and kids in jeans. Darlene asked the gum- cracking, pony-tailed hostess for a table, and the girl led the trio to a booth by the picture window overlooking Main Street. Melissa slid close to the fingerprinted window and glanced down. Clear tape sealed cracks in the vinyl blue-green seats. The table's smooth top was peppered with gold speckles and imbedded with coffee stains.

"How far is it to Simons Mansion?" Darlene said.

The waitress's hand froze in mid-air. "Why?"

"My children and I will be living on the estate in Simons Woods."

The waitress set three sticky, plastic-coated menus in front of them. "You're the writer for the village, aren't ya?"

" Yes," Darlene began. "I'll be...."

"Well, I think you're nuts to live there."

Darlene looked baffled. "Why?"

The waitress huffed in exasperation. "You haven't heard? It's haunted!"

This time, Darlene looked surprised. "Haunted?"

A customer at an adjacent table asked for ketchup, and the waitress left.

"Well," Darlene said, "your father left us with a mansion and a ghost story. Frankly, I prefer the love story."

Melissa bit her lip and opened the menu. Of course, her mother, who once lived a storybook romance, preferred the love story. Brian seemed fine with moving, but, after all, he was only eleven. He'd be okay if a spaceship teleported him to Mars.

"Do you really think the mansion's haunted?" Brian asked eagerly.

Darlene peered up from the menu. "Of course I don't."

"The waitress seemed sure."

"Brian," Darlene turned a page. "I'll bet everyone else does, too."

She gave up and studied the menu. Brian held his hand to the side of his face and mouthed, *Ghost?* His hazel eyes sparked with excitement.

Melissa looked sideways, shook her head, and mouthed back, Not now. So, Brian stuck his tongue at her and picked up his menu, but she knew he wasn't through with ghosts. Then a slim, brown-haired boy about Melissa's age brought three glasses of ice water and set them on the table, and she forgot about Brian.

Why, he's as cute as Jason Frye, Melissa thought. Jason Frye, with his dreamy blue eyes, feathered black hair, and newly developed arm muscles, was the cutest boy in Grover's Park. Melissa often ate at Pizza Express, hoping that, while he was bussing tables, he'd ask her out. Maybe, living in Munsonville wouldn't be so bad.

The boy noticed her looking at him, blushed, and hurried away. Melissa quickly glanced at Brian, expecting a smart aleck comment from him, but Brian's thin face was buried inside his menu. Whew! He hadn't noticed her interest in the boy.

The waitress returned. Her mother ordered the day's special: boiled fish in gravy. "Ma'am, you're in for a real treat," the waitress said, beaming. "That recipe's older than the diner. Everyone likes it."

Brian made a face. "I'll have a cheeseburger and fries."

"Me, too," Melissa hastily added and handed back her menu.

The food was actually good, so they ordered the dessert special, apple pudding.

Brian, still hungry, gobbled his down, but Melissa, now full, slowly picked at hers and noted Main Street's sparse traffic. She counted one car besides theirs. People were walking or biking. Her driver's license would be useless here. The buildings abruptly stopped before the woods.

"Where's Simons Mansion?" Melissa asked.

"On the north end of town," Darlene said, "on its outskirts. The estate is larger than the entire village. It includes most of Lake Munson and much of Simons Woods. The village just opened an additional section for hiking, biking, and fishing."

"What about the mansion part?" Brian said, dropping his spoon with a clank that startled Melissa. Their mother narrowed her eyes at him and then looked to see if anyone heard. Leave it to Brian to embarrass them.

"Sorry," Brian mumbled, picking up his spoon and setting it down with exaggerated quietness. "Where's the mansion?"

"Simons Mansion sits on top of a hill inside the woods and overlooks the property. Beyond the overgrown gardens, the grounds slope to the back of the estate. You can't see the servant's cottage from the main house."

The waitress arrived with the bill. When their mother opened her purse, Melissa glimpsed the book her father had bought during her mother's first signing, his excuse to talk to the petite, recent college graduate. Melissa hadn't seen that book in years.

Brian fidgeted at the cash register. "Look, Mom!" He tugged on her purse and pointed to a flyer on the wall.

"Brian, wait," Darlene said, as the hostess counted back the change.

Melissa followed Brian's gaze. *Coming October 10, 11, 12. Munsonville Centennial Celebration: A Hundred Years of Excellence, 1875-1975.* Her eyes drifted over the events: fishing contest, tours of Simons Mansion, historical displays, vendors, carnival, food. That was the weekend of her eighteenth birthday. Great.

"That's why the village board wanted me here so soon." Darlene stuffed her wallet back inside her purse. "They want help marketing the celebration, especially now that Munsonville owns the mansion."

"Are we going to the carnival?" Brian asked excitedly.

"Actually, you and Melissa are part of the event. The students will create the historical displays and reports."

"We just moved here," Melissa protested. "I don't know anything about Munsonville's history."

"I'm sure you and Brian will get project details once you start school." Melissa looked for Brian's reaction, but he was already out the door. Ever since the waitress had said "haunted," Melissa knew her brother just *had* to see his new home. He hopped into the front seat, before Melissa could claim it.

She fretted about the report all the way past Main Street, which now split in two. One road led into the deeper part of the woods; the other wound up the hill toward their new home. Brian wiggled and bounced to see everything at once. The tops of the lush, profuse trees touched each other, but the sun filtered through the leaves and formed lacy patterns on the asphalt. Lake Munson, full of ducks and geese, rippled a clear blue- green.

Big deal, she thought, catching herself watching them, determined to find nothing redeeming about her new home. Who cares about a bunch of old birds?

Her mother turned left and drove up the hill. At the top, Simons Mansion, tall and majestic, dominated the view. The old, gray, four-story stone building had numerous bay windows and a large porch, wrap-around porch. Green vines covered large portions of the house. Nestling amongst the leaves were pale, pink flowers. Was this bryony?

"It may not be a proper mansion, but the villagers call it Simons Mansion." Her mother slowed to examine the building. "It must seem like a mansion to them."

Brian stretched his neck out the window. "So where is the servant's quarters?"

"Further back."

The road curved past Simons Mansion and beyond its spacious grounds, full of overgrown shrubbery and remnants of trellises and wooden fences, although the grass was neatly trimmed. Winding through the trees were the same vines on Simons Mansion.

In the distance, a shadow flitted through the gazebo. Melissa shaded her eyes, but saw nothing more. The cottage was in sight. Melissa's eyes widened, and her heart sank.

The box-shaped cottage was too flat, too old, too gray, too small, and most of all, too ugly. The Grover's Park ranch, with grey-blue siding, black shutters, and a manicured yard with a few perennials and tomato plants, had been home. This could never be home.

Brian was thrilled. "What if John Simons' ghost haunts the mansion at night? Wouldn't that be awesome?"

His exuberance irritated Melissa. "You're out of your mind!"

Brian ignored Melissa's ill humor and ran to the front stoop. Their mother unlocked the door, and a small brown and white terrier bounded out.

"Meet Scooter," Darlene said. "Steve Barnes, the estate's maintenance man brought him. When I took the job, I asked Steve where I could buy a small dog. Steve found the perfect one."

Brian squealed and threw his arms around his mother's neck.

"Can I take him for a walk? Oh, please, please!"

How could they act so happy? Had her mother and Brian forgotten how long and hard they had cried? Gone forever were the many happy hours in her father's office, listening to his anecdotes of African jungles, circus clowns, and urban life on the streets. Even a hundred dogs could not make up for it.

Her mother stepped inside the house and returned with a blue collar and leash. Brian handed them to Melissa.

"You do it, Liss," Brian said, with unexpected generosity. "He's your dog, too."

10

"Who cares?" Nevertheless, Melissa fastened the collar around the wriggling dog.

"Sit still." Scooter tugged at his leash, and Melissa, vexed, tugged back. "Behave!"

"Hey! Be nice to him."

Brian grabbed the leash and walked Scooter around the yard, letting him sniff at the grass, dandelions, and bushes bordering the house. Melissa stepped through the front door and smelled fresh paint.

"Home," Melissa said aloud. The word sounded hollow.

The living room was half the size of her old bedroom, even with a picture window in front and patio doors in the back, but at least the carpet looked new. A galley kitchen and a small bedroom were on the right; two more bedrooms were on the left. In the kitchen, curtains hung stiff and white. A tiny bathroom, scarcely larger than a closet, was opposite the kitchen sink. Near the end, one door led outside and a second to the basement. She took three steps down the creaking stairs and glimpsed an old furnace and a washer and drier. Melissa couldn't imagine doing laundry in that musty place, where snakes might lurk. She'd let Brian do it. He'd probably find it fun. Melissa returned to the bedroom closest to the kitchen and found piles of boxes with her name in black marker. Her mother draped an arm around Melissa's shoulders.

"I know it's a big change," Darlene said in a soft voice, "but we'll adjust. Steve has offered to build shelves all around the room if you like."

"How did the movers know where to put our stuff?"

"They didn't. Steve sorted it when he brought Scooter. Brian's staying by me, but I thought you'd like more privacy. Steve will be back later to measure for your shelves."

Melissa's spirits rose, a little, at this kindness from a stranger. She climbed over boxes to the window overlooking the back of the estate. Their small yard merged into Simons Woods. A bike path began at the entrance. If Shelly were here, they could....

Brian and Scooter burst into her room. "Do we have to unpack now? Scooter wants to explore!" Scooter yipped to prove Brian's point.

Their mother laughed. "I think the unpacking can wait until later. We've been cooped up for many hours. Perhaps a little exploring is good."

Melissa hesitated, unwilling to meet her new surroundings, but her mother gently pushed her to the door and headed for the typewriter on the living room floor. Death and an eight-hour move did not erase deadlines. Brian and Scooter had already left, so up she trudged to Simons Mansion. Even from a distance, the mansion had an indescribable, intriguing air. Did one maintenance man mow all this grass? She remembered the shadow, so she cut across to the gazebo, a disappointment with its white peeling paint, gaping roof, and broken floorboards. Would the village restore this, too? A sharp scent filled the air. Bryony? Why hadn't her father told them he had owned a mansion?

"Oh, Daddy," Melissa murmured with a hard sigh.

Simons Mansion grew blurry. Forcing back hot tears, Melissa hurried to catch up. Brian and Scooter were speeding downhill toward Lake Munson. They waited for Melissa at the entrance to the deeper part of Simons Woods. The mansion was now out of sight. Adults on bikes and teens on roller skates whizzed past them. The nature center was brand new, the gray-haired, heavy-set woman at the information desk happily said. Village officials would dedicate it during the festivities.

"I've lived here all my life, and I've never seen this kind of change," she said.

Brian gave Melissa a victorious look. "I told *you* it'd be exciting."

Melissa shrugged. She didn't care what he thought.

Brian dawdled on the way back, chattering about the carnival. Melissa plodded beside him, brooding overspending her first adult birthday by eating cotton candy, riding merry-go-rounds, and mourning her father's loss.

Scooter tugged hard.

"Sorry, Liss." Brian drew back on the leash. "He wants to run. Do you mind?"

Melissa shrugged again and watched them dash away. The trail was now empty. Shadows lengthened on the ground; thick clouds masked the sun. The air cooled, and she instinctively shivered. Melissa hugged herself and strained to see Brian and

Scooter. Mist ascended from the lake and hovered on the path directly above Melissa.

What the....?

Her legs wobbled, but she forced them to move faster. The mist thickened and kept pace. Panic surged in her throat, and Melissa swallowed it back. *The mist was following her.* She had to get out, now.

She breathed deeply and blindly tore down the road. The mist pressed into her. The ground disappeared from sight. Melissa stopped short in the swirling haze, wildly shaking her head and panting. *Where was the lake?*

Suddenly, a dim light appeared; the fog gradually lifted. Melissa spotted the entrance. Relief flooded through her. She felt shaky and weak, but who cared? Melissa ran on jelly legs until she was past the trees. Brian and Scooter lingered at the lake's edge. Melissa slowed her pace and panted.

In greeting, Scooter barked three short barks, but Brian merely gaped at her. "What's eating you? You look like you've seen a ghost."

"It's the mist," Melissa said. "I couldn't see."

"Are you nuts?" Brian shaded his eyes and looked past her into the woods.

Turning around, Melissa followed her brother's gaze. The sun radiated through the trees, and the leaves cut patterns on the road. The darkness and mist had vanished.

CHAPTER 2: THERE'S NO SUCH THING AS A GHOST

A lanky man, about forty, in a green pocket T-shirt, faded blue jeans, and threadbare gym shoes, was holding a tape measure against her bedroom wall. He reached behind his ear for his pencil, pulled a wrinkled paper from his pocket, and jotted some figures. Glancing up, he noticed Melissa, and his face broke into a wide grin.

"Howdy!" The man shook Melissa's hand. He had an open, friendly face and a shock of blond hair over his forehead. "I'm Steve. Melissa, right?"

She nodded and limply returned the handshake, feeling a little surprised her mother had become sociable with him. Steve was so different from her father, always sophisticated in pressed pants and collared shirt, even at his sickest.

"Your ma tells me you like to read. Soon, you'll have plenty of bookshelves."

Her mother stuck her head around the door. "Steve, I've got hamburgers and hot dogs. Will you stay for dinner?"

"On one condition," Steve said. "I man the grill."

Brian poked his head past, looking hopeful. Steve grinned. "With Brian's help."

His face lit up as he slipped away. Back home, their mother did the cooking and never allowed Brian near an open flame, despite his loud protests, but Steve seemed relaxed around both Brian and fire. He asked Brian's opinion about the amount of charcoal briquettes and trusted Brian's judgment for when the fire was sufficiently hot. Darlene brought out the meat and a foil pan of frozen French fries.

"Now there's a meal fit for a king," Steve said.

He rumpled Brian's hair. Brian glowed, and Melissa relaxed, a little. Maybe, she could unpack a few boxes. She slipped back inside and surveyed the stacks with despair. Where would she put it all? She slowly peeled tape off the first box. It seemed so final, unpacking her things into a new room in a strange house. So, Melissa set her stereo on top of her dresser, just like in her Grover's Park bedroom, added a stack of 45's, and sang with the music, while she stacked stuffed animals in a corner; hung sweaters; and filled dresser drawers with jeans, T-shirts, and socks. She had just made her bed when her mother's voice startled her.

"Melissa." Darlene opened the door a crack. "Dinner time."

"Already?" Melissa scrambled to her feet. How could two hours have passed?

The makeshift dining room was part of the living room. Brian was actually setting the table, a chore he dodged back home.

"It sure looks good," Melissa said. "The food smells good, too."

"Brian did most of the work." Steve set down a platter of hamburgers.

"I'll take another cook," Darlene said, "especially one that washes dishes."

"Whatever!" Brian twisted his face in disgust.

As they ate, Steve asked Melissa if she had seen the property. Memories of the mist rose in her mind, so she hesitated before answering. It figured Brian would blab.

"Liss saw a ghost." Brian tore apart a French fry. "It chased her down the path."

Melissa glared at Brian, but only because he was too far away for her to stomp on his foot.

"Go on, Liss," Brian said, oblivious to her reaction. "Tell him!"

Steve looked skeptically at Melissa. "A ghost?"

Melissa's face grew hot. "I...I don't know what I saw," she stammered. "I was walking by the lake, and suddenly I was covered with this mist."

"The waitress at Sue's Diner said the mansion was haunted," Darlene said, with a dubious look at Melissa. "My kids have overactive imaginations."

"I'm sure Melissa did see something," Steve said, "but that mist was simply cold and warm air mixing, like how clouds are formed. It's common around here."

"I didn't see it," Brian insisted.

"Were you looking for it?"

Brian shook his head, his eyes on Steve.

"Then it was gone by the time Melissa mentioned it. Now, if you had seen the mist in the mansion...." Steve winked at their mother.

Brian smirked at Melissa, and their mother noticed. "There's no mist inside the mansion, Brian," Darlene said.

Steve's tone grew serious. "Folks here might disagree with you. They tell stories of shadows moving in the house and beautiful piano music at night, but that's all they are, bonfire stories. Naturally, there's no such thing as a ghost." Steve poured another glass of iced tea. "So, don't get ideas about ghost chasing. You could get hurt."

Brian stuck his tongue at Melissa, but she was remembering the shadow in the gazebo.

"Not from a ghost," Steve gave Brian a warning look, "but from playing inside an old, dilapidated house. During some preliminary inspections, a workman was injured. Tell your friends, too. Some kids tried biking up there a few weeks ago, and the project manager had to shoo them away."

Friends, Melissa thought bitterly. My friends are back in Grover's Park. I'll probably never have friends again.

Steve noticed Brian's disappointed look. "Now, now. They're starting work this spring. Maybe, then, we can get you a look around the place."

"Okay," Brian agreed.

16

He nudged Melissa's foot. She peeked underneath. Brian crossed his fingers. How long before Brian stopped thinking about ghosts?

"I know something scarier than ghosts," Darlene said. "School starts next week. We need to go shopping, especially for you, Brian. You've outgrown everything."

Brian made a face and groaned. Melissa said nothing, but she detested shopping more than Brian did. She preferred jeans and only wore dresses when necessary.

Steve asked about her mother's writing, so Brian, restless, walked Scooter behind the cottage. Melissa stretched and followed. Scooter sniffed every blade of grass.

"Maybe the mist was John Simons," Brian said, "pining away for his lost love." He fell to his knees, clasped his hands, and fluttered his lashes, just as Laura did when flirting. Scooter licked his face so hard Brian fell backward, and Melissa laughed. She decided against telling Brian about the shadow in the gazebo. It was probably a raccoon. Why fuel the fire?

"Don't be ridiculous. Look at this place. John Simons got bored, went to Europe, and died there. I'm going back inside. It's too dark to see anymore."

The adults were talking about the village's plans for the Simons estate. The renovation of Simons Mansion might bring significant changes to the village, and that excited Steve.

"People do come here to fish, but that's our only real industry," Steve said. "Opening Simons Mansion to the public would give more people reasons to visit us."

"Classical piano fans are a minority," Darlene said. "That won't bring people in."

"Sure it will, if the village plays up the ghost story," Steve said.

Brian sat up straighter.

"People won't fall for it," Darlene insisted.

"They will, and the village board intends to capitalize on it," Steve said. "Munsonville hasn't progressed much in a century, so you almost can't blame them."

"Why don't you believe the stories?" Brian asked.

"I've worked all over the grounds and have never seen or heard anything."

Brian persisted. "Then why do people say there's a ghost?"

"People invent stories when circumstances are unclear. John Simons abruptly left town, leaving behind a huge estate and no heir, so people speculate. Ghost stories are more fascinating than truth, which, sad to say, can be boring. Of course," Steve winked again at their mother, "the kids can make it exciting for the centennial."

"A ghost is exciting." Brian would not give up.

"The ghost is legendary, not historical. Melissa, maybe you'd like to write about John Simons. He's a significant part of Munsonville's history."

Melissa politely nodded her head. She had no interest in Munsonville history, its dead musician, or the mansion, only her father's connection to them.

"If John Simons didn't leave his estate to anyone," Melissa said, "how did my dad get it?"

Steve corrected her. "Your father had only the mansion and part of the grounds. The village owned the rest. Because of private interest, it was impossible to develop a full-scale tourist plan. It's only recently we discovered the owner." He smiled at her mother. "I'm sure glad we did."

Brian wrinkled his nose and gagged. Melissa nudged him with her elbow, but she glanced at her mother and Steve. That's how her father smiled, and she didn't appreciate it on this man's face. To Melissa's annoyance, her mother smiled back. Melissa shifted uncomfortably. Steve noticed, and his smile faded.

"One last thing," Steve said. "The place is full of bryony. John Simons was a fool to plant that weed all over his house and estate. It's a nuisance for me, but that's an artist for you. In the meantime, stay away from any plant you can't identify."

"Is bryony valuable?" Melissa asked. So, bryony was the vines she had noticed.

"No, it's poisonous." Steve tipped his glass to finish the iced tea, and his eyes fell on his watch. "Gosh, I'm sorry! I didn't realize it was late."

"That's quite all right," Darlene said. "We've enjoyed the company. I'll walk you to your truck. Kids, please clear off the table."

As her mother and Steve moved away, Melissa heard Steve say, "It's not right, you and the kids staying in the woods alone...."

Melissa collected the glasses. Brian stood with his hands in his pockets.

"You could help," Melissa said irritably. "Mom wasn't just talking to me, you know."

"Why not write about the ghost? It's still part of the mansion's history."

"Steve said a ghost is not history. It's legend." Melissa headed for the kitchen. "Can you, at least, open the door?"

Brian absently turned the knob. "It might become history. Look at what you saw."

"Steve told you what I saw: cold and warm air mixing."
"And you believe him?"

"Steve lives here. I guess he knows what's by the lake. Be quiet. Mom's coming."

Her mother moved slowly. Her face looked wan. She had an early morning meeting at Village Hall, too. Melissa hated housework, but she knew what her father would say, so she hugged her mother, forced a smile, and said, "Get some sleep, Mom. I'll clean up."

Her mother, face softening with relief, kissed Melissa on the forehead and headed to her room. Brian darted off before Melissa could order him into duty. Brothers!

Melissa scraped leftover food into the tiny garbage can under the sink. It would need emptying twice a day, but so what? That was Brian's job. She peered through the window, but night shrouded her view. She only saw her mother's wedding ring on the sill. Detergent residue irritated her skin, so her mother always removed her ring before washing dishes. Once, her mother had knocked the ring down the drain, and Laura's dad had spent an entire afternoon fishing it out.

The soap's foam reminded Melissa of mist, and she shook her head to clear the unpleasant memory. As she soaked the silverware and washed the plastic plates, her mind roamed back to the last night at Pizza Express.

"Tell us about your famous musician," Kimberly Whitney had said, her blue eyes gleaming with uncharacteristic interest. She had always claimed not to wear contacts, but Melissa knew she was lying. Nobody's eyes had color that clear.

In hushed, dramatic tones, Shelly Gallagher told how John Simons had fallen in love with seventeen-year-old Bryony Marseilles, daughter of Munsonville's minister, and had built the mansion in the woods as his wedding present to her. John had also covered the house and filled the grounds with pink-flowered bryony, specially bred for his wife.

"Isn't that so romantic?" Shelly had sighed. "She was the same age as us."

Laura Jones had been gawking at Jason, and she blushed and giggled into her pop when he noticed. "Melissa's lucky!" Then she stole another peek at Jason.

Melissa dug through boxes for a towel, still not feeling lucky. She had just dried the last cup when Scooter barked, and she shushed him, wondering what he wanted.

Scooter ran to the living room, so Melissa hung up the towel and followed him to the screen door, where he stood whining. She peered into Brian's room, but her brother was sleeping. Melissa didn't see the leash. Scooter had better not run off.

Melissa opened the patio doors. The overwhelming silence struck her, so different from Grover's Park. There, Melissa often heard cars driving past her house or neighbors talking in their back yards. Here, millions of stars filled the sky, and the moon glowed with golden brilliancy. Her heartbeat fast with indescribable yearning.

Scooter was almost back to the screen door when he stopped, turned around, and froze. His eyes locked onto the woods beyond him. He growled a low, menacing growl. Melissa strained her eyes but saw nothing.

"Silly dog," she scolded him. "It's probably just a rabbit."

Once inside, Melissa refilled Scooter's water and food bowl, then readied for bed, deliberately ignoring the blank walls of her new room. Tomorrow, they would have brand-new shelves, and she would stack all her books. Then would it feel like home?

Melissa switched off the overhead light, felt her way to the nightstand, and groped for her little purple reading light. Propped on her pillow was a ragged, hardbound book, *Nocturnal Lore: The*

Collected Tales of Henry Matthews. Obviously, her mother had found it in the cottage and left it for Melissa.

Burrowing under the covers, Melissa opened the book, wrinkling her nose at its moldy smell. She quickly became engrossed in *Flee Unto Dawn*, a story about a young widow who slept each night on her husband's grave, despite the sexton's persistent warning: *Don't squander it on the dead!*

She blinked several times, but her eyelids grew heavy. She yawned, determined to find out what happened to the woman, and carefully turned a crumbling page. She awoke with her head on the book. In the distance was the faint tinkling of piano music. Melissa slid the book under her pillow and turned off the light. Probably someone's car radio, she thought, as she drifted away to sleep.

CHAPTER 3: THE SCHOOL REPORT

Algebra II had just begun when the ceiling speakers crackled.

"I have an announcement to make," a gruff voice, thick with static, said.

Mrs. Denison set down the attendance book. Melissa heard a cough on her left. A girl with tortoise shell glasses and shoulder-length chestnut hair parted on the side was sliding a note across the floor. Hastily, Melissa retrieved it, placed it on her lap and, eyeing Mrs. Denison, carefully unfolded the note: *It's the principal. Centennial projects.*

"Here is the plan for your centennial projects," the gruff voice continued.

Melissa smothered a laugh at the girl's accuracy.

"Kindergarten through fifth grade will build historical displays, and the junior high school pupils will create art displays. The high school students will write research reports. Judges will review the material and present the awards. Just make sure your English teacher approves your project."

More static, then silence. With only seven seniors, roll call quickly ended. As Mrs. Denison wrote the first problem on the blackboard, the girl coughed again. While watching the teacher, Melissa leaned down to pick up the note. *Ann Dalton.*

Melissa smiled, neatly wrote below, *Melissa Marchellis*, and sent the note back to Ann. Maybe, making new friends would not be so difficult. Melissa began copying equations. The remainder of class quickly passed.

Half an hour later, Melissa walked down the hall, congratulating herself for surviving the first hour in her new school, thanks to Ann's friendly notes. Nevertheless, the backwoods atmosphere baffled her, from the one-piece, wooden desk, and chair sets to having twelve grades contained in one building. Students of all ages passed her.

From Ann's notes, Melissa learned the entire school had less than thirty upperclassmen. The footsteps on the scuffed, wood floors echoed like buffalo, despite the heavy rain pattering above the high ceiling. *Bell bottoms, really?* No one in Grover's Park wore them anymore. A boy, barely twelve, socked the arm of a taller boy, who laughed aloud and lightly thumped back. An algebra classmate, a pretty girl with dark braids, tied the shoe of a tiny, pony-tailed girl carrying an orange, plastic tote bag. Back home, no one her age wore braids. They didn't associate with little kids, either, except during paid babysitting jobs.

In American history, Melissa waited until Mr. Carter, the student teacher, wrote a timeline on the cracked chalkboard before passing a note to Ann. *Where's the gym?*

No gym, Ann wrote back. *The building is too old.*

A scuffle sounded behind her; the squeaking of the chalk stopped. Mr. Carter, tie flapping, swiftly turned around. Silence. He waited, grunted, then returned to the board. Being the new student, Melissa hardly wished to insult the building's lack of modern amenities, so she wrote back, *The narrow windows and high ceilings are charming.*

Mr. Carter paused and leaned to check his book. When he resumed copying, Ann hastily scribbled, *Charm! Wait until you see Mr. Walczak. He's a regular Dr. Moreau.*

Melissa was dying to know why Ann compared that teacher with a macabre scientist, but Mr. Carter was now facing the class. When the second bell rang, Melissa asked, "Who's Mr. Walczak?"

"Biology teacher," Ann said, through the pencil gripped between her teeth.

Melissa removed the pencil and shoved it into Ann's drawstring knapsack. Melissa had rebelled when Darlene had bought one until Melissa learned Munsonville School had no lockers. Once they were in the hall, she asked, "What's so weird about him?"

"He's not weird. Dad said he retired from a real laboratory. He moved here to fish, but someone from the school board persuaded him to teach all the science classes."

"So, why did you call him Dr. Moreau?"

"He brings odd stuff to class, like fifteen species of live spiders, two-headed fish, and vampire bats. I'll bet he does strange experiments in his basement at night."

Ann's dry sense of humor regarding Mr. Walczak surprised and delighted Melissa. She had thought all smart, quiet people were shy and boring. Two boys pushed around them, but Ann ignored them. Obviously, Ann did not share Laura's boy-crazy personality, although later, in the lunchroom, with its wooden tables and folding wooden chairs, Melissa saw her peek at that cute boy from Sue's Diner.

"Who is he?" Melissa set her tray across from Ann's and slid into a seat. Ann glanced furtively around her. "That's Jack Cooper," she said in hushed tones. "His parents own Sue's Diner. He works there every day, even weekends."

Jack walked passed with his tray of food. Ann's eyes followed him. Melissa squirmed, opened a carton of milk, and asked, "What are you researching for the centennial?"

"Owen Munson, the wealthy Scottish mill owner who founded Munsonville in 1835. I'm sure I can get it approved. Your report's about John Simons, right?"

Melissa slowly nodded. Why not? With Steve's help, research would be easy.

Ann sucked a glob of tuna fish from her thumb. "Why is Steve Barnes at your house so much? Is your mom dating him?" Melissa choked on her milk.

"You know about Steve?"

"Nothing and no one's a secret in Munsonville," Ann said.

"Nothing?" Melissa grinned. "Even your crush on Jack Cooper?"

Ann blushed and grinned back. "I'm not trying to be nosy.

It's just that Steve is there so much."

Melissa crumbled crackers into her soup and recalled how Steve had smiled at her mother their first night in Munsonville. Since then, Steve had often stopped at the cottage, but, thankfully, Melissa had not seen another saccharine smile. Steve was equally pleasant to her and Brian, so maybe she had misjudged Steve.

"I don't think they're dating," Melissa said. "They don't go anywhere. Steve spends more time with Brian than with my mom."

"Mom said she's glad Steve found someone nice. He's been alone forever."

Melissa glowed at this compliment to her mother. "Was Steve ever married?"

"No, he took care of his parents, but they died years ago. We've only ever known him as just Steve. It's hard thinking he likes someone."

Especially when that someone is my mother, Melisa thought, then added aloud, "Well, I really think they're just friends."

Besides historical displays and reenactments, her mother, with Steve's help, would lead tours of the Simons estate. The celebration also included food, carnival rides, contests, games, and live entertainment. Best of all, school would close on the Friday of the celebration, so Melissa decided living in Munsonville during its centennial year had one advantage. The library was another story. The small, crate-like, wooden building contained fewer books than the children's section in Grover's Park. Steve probably had more information about John Simons than it did.

"I have a topic," Melissa said Friday night as she scraped mushrooms to the side of her plate. "I'm writing about John Simons."

"That's nice, hon." Darlene unfolded her napkin. "Have you begun any research?"

"Mom, when can I go to Clay's house?" Brian interrupted. Clay was Ann Dalton's younger brother. "His dad's letting us build our display in his basement."

"Tomorrow night," Steve said. "We're having dinner and playing cards there."

"What are you building, Brian?" Darlene asked.

"Main Street, like it looked a hundred years ago."

"I have an old drawing from that time period," Steve said. "I'll bring it for you."

"Thanks, Steve!"

Good. She could count on Steve. "Can you help with my report, too?"

"Well now, Melissa." Steve set down his fork and looked thoughtful. "I've shared what I know. Ask Mrs. Clements at the library. She has access to old newspaper clippings and her great-aunt's diary. She'll have information not everyone has heard."

"Thanks, Steve," Melissa said, trying not to sound disappointed.

Researching the report would not be easy now. She looked sideways at Brian to see if he was gloating and saw Scooter licking chopped steak from Brian's fingers.

She had not often visited a friend by car. Her Grover's Park friends lived in the same neighborhood, but, even so, she did not often see them, although she chatted to and swapped secrets with Shelly every afternoon on the phone. Most evenings and weekends, Melissa hurried through her homework to keep her father company. Her mother worked in the next room, while simultaneously helping Brian with his assignments. This annoyed Kimberly, who scoffed that old, sick people belonged in nursing homes instead of sabotaging people's lives, but Melissa relished those moments with her father. She'd climbed mountains, sailed seas, and soared the skies, all from an armchair.

As they drove downhill, Melissa looked for the mist, but saw nothing. Her mind drifted toward their destination. Melissa had only hung out with Ann at school. What would Ann be like at home? Melissa could not imagine she'd be as easy-going as Shelly.

"Are we almost there?" Brian called out.

"Almost," Steve said, as he turned onto Pike Street.

Clay sat on the front step of the small frame house. When Melissa had first seen him with Brian in the lunchroom, heads bent over a comic book, she decided they could pass for brothers, although Brian had sandy hair, and Clay had chestnut hair and a face full of freckles. Like Brian, Clay ran when he could have walked, talked louder than normal people should, and had the same annoying fascination for the supernatural. To be fair, Clay did live in a village that had a ghost story.

26

Clay jumped to his feet. "Wait till you see the display table my dad built me."

Brian waved his folder at Clay's face. "Wait till you see my picture from Steve!"

The two boys scampered into the house. Mr. Dalton's hair was gray, and he was slightly shorter than Mrs. Dalton, who had Ann's shoulder-length, chestnut hair. Ann hung back and wrung her hands. Why, Melissa thought in astonishment, she's feeling shy, too.

Before Melissa could break the awkward silence, Ann spoke. "Would you like to see my room?"

"Sure!"

Ann's bedroom was smaller than Melissa's was, but she had as many books crammed into it. Melissa glanced at the novel opened, spine up, on Ann's bed and gave a little cry of delight.

"I love that story!" Melissa exclaimed. "I read it this summer. I didn't know you liked mysteries." She had more in common with brainy Ann than she had thought.

"I like all kinds of books," Ann said quietly. "That's why Mom asked Steve to build these shelves."

"Really? Steve built me bookshelves, too."

Melissa scanned the titles. Ann sat on the bed and watched her.

"Have you read," Ann began. Footsteps thudded past her door. "Dinner's ready," she said.

Melissa paused, book in hand. "How do you know?"

Ann smiled. "Because Clay runs past my room like this three times a day."

Melissa picked nervously at the fresh fried fish, but it was almost as good as frozen fish sticks. She and Ann remained quiet while the grownups talked, but Brian and Clay rudely whispered all through dinner. Melissa realized she wasn't paying attention until she heard her father's name.

"Your husband was diabetic?" Mrs. Dalton said. "I hear it's a horrible disease."

"It is," Darlene said. "Frank went blind, lost both legs, and needed dialysis."

"You say Frank had diabetes all his life?"

Melissa winked hard and fast. She would not cry in front of the Daltons.

"Yes, but it wasn't bad until after I had Melissa. Frank cut down on work and watched his blood sugar, but by the time Brian was born...well, he had waited too long."

Her mother's voice quavered a little, so Mr. Dalton, stroking his mustache, changed the subject. "Frank was a photojournalist? How very interesting."

"Oh, it was!" Darlene forced a smile. "When I met Frank after college, he had already traveled all over the world and collected enough stories to fill a library. Before we had children, I accompanied him on some trips. I'm so thankful for those years."

"I've never left Michigan," Mrs. Dalton said, leaning forward with interest and looking very much like Ann had when gazing at Jack. "Was Frank very outgoing?"

"Actually, Frank was terribly bashful, but you wouldn't know it when he looked through a camera lens. Frank could talk to anyone if it guaranteed the perfect shot."

"Was it hard for him to quit photography?" Mr. Dalton said.

"Very," Darlene said. "Frank was twenty years older than me and had always lived by deadlines. He never really adjusted to the slower pace of staying home, although he loved being a father."

A sob escaped Melissa's throat. She quickly turned it into a hiccup.

"He gave us ice cream money when we got good grades," Brian piped up, "and played cards with us in the game room, even when he could hardly see."

Mr. Dalton looked surprised. "You were writing then, too?"

"Yes, thankfully. My portfolio impressed the village. That's why we're here."

Ann nudged Melissa and said, "Mom, we're full. May we be excused?"

"What about the dishes?" Mr. Dalton said, looking stern.

"You go right ahead," Mrs. Dalton said, nodding at the girls. She turned toward her husband. "Rob, Ann has a guest tonight. I can do the dishes."

"I'll help," Darlene said, as the girls walked out the kitchen. "Steve's so helpful, I hardly ever wash...."

With a sigh of relief, Ann shut her bedroom door. "They'll call us when dessert is ready," she said loftily.

Melissa scrutinized Ann's face. Had her friend noticed Melissa's distress?

"Besides," Ann said, "if you write about John Simons, you should see this."

She opened her top dresser drawer and removed a double-sided, cardboard frame.

"I bought it for a quarter last summer at a library sale," Ann said. "Here, look."

Melissa opened it. On the left was an unsmiling man with very long blond hair, almond-shaped blue eyes, and the merest hint of a mustache and beard.

"Is this John Simons?"

Ann nodded. "The other picture is Bryony."

Melissa studied Bryony's small heart-shaped face, big green eyes, and masses of tan hair cascading past her shoulders. If only she could be that beautiful....

She was instantly drawn to this girl, whose life was magically transformed when someone rich, handsome, talented, and famous entered it. To think Bryony had an entire estate created in her honor, from the mansion to the profuse bryony vines! It was as lovely as the fairy tales her father had told Melissa years ago. The story was worthy of a book or, Melissa thought excitedly, a school report.

"Ann, does the library have much information on Bryony Simons?"

"Not sure," Ann said. "Why?"

Bryony's loveliness still mesmerized her. "I think I'll write my report on her."

"Why?" Ann said. "Bryony wasn't famous. John was."

A steady clomping down the hall stopped at Ann's room.

"Hey, you guys," Clay shouted, thumping on the door. "Dessert's ready!"

"Okay," Ann called back. She looked at Melissa. "He won't quit until we come."

Melissa reluctantly returned the frame, but a vision of Bryony's sweet, young face stayed with her. Why didn't Ann understand?

"Because of John Simons, Bryony is also part of Munsonville's history," Melissa said. "I think someone should write her story."

Ann looked doubtful. "Other than marrying someone rich and famous, Bryony didn't do anything interesting. I'll bet you won't find enough facts to fill a page. Besides, you'll need it approved."

Melissa trailed Ann back to the kitchen, but, with each footstep, she resolved to secure that coveted approval. Ann was wrong. Melissa would prove it. She dwelled on Bryony all the way back to the estate, while her mother shared with Steve the latest restoration board meeting.

"It's so frustrating," Darlene said. "Dr. Rothgard opposes every suggestion."

"Do you think he's trying to sabotage the efforts?" Steve said, surprised.

"I don't know," Darlene said. "Why wouldn't he support it? It's a good move for the village."

"If you think he's bad, just wait until Harold Masters returns. I'm surprised the board has gotten this far."

As Steve turned up the drive, Melissa glanced back at the woods. A gauzy film hovered above the trees like a giant spider web, but the sky over the lake was clear. *This was no ordinary fog!*

"Steve!" Melissa cried. "The mist!"

"Where?" Steve said.

"Over there. In the trees."

Brian, who had been dozing next to her, jerked awake, and squinted into the dark.

"Aw, Liss," he said, sounding disappointed. "There's nothing there."

Melissa sat up straighter and strained past Brian's head. The mist was gone.

CHAPTER 4: A TRIP TO THE PAST

"Mom," Melissa asked at breakfast Monday morning. "May I go to the library after school? I'm researching a topic for the centennial report."

"John Simons?" Darlene said, stirring sugar into her coffee.

Melissa shook her head. ", it's Bryony, but Ann thinks I won't find enough information. I'd like to learn more before I decide."

"Don't forget I'm going to Clay's today," Brian yelled from the kitchen where he was making toast.

"Brian don't shout. I didn't forget." Darlene turned to Melissa. "I'll pick you up outside at five o'clock, after my centennial meeting. Is that enough time?"

Brian brought a platter of toast. Melissa picked up a piece and quickly moved it to her plate, but butter dripped anyway. Brian had his own method of making toast: crusts trimmed and buttered on two sides.

Melissa was tired of depending on rides after a whole year of driving her mother's car wherever she needed to go, but she kept quiet. A second vehicle wasn't in the budget, and her mother needed transportation for meetings in town.

Instead, Melissa took a bite and said, "I think so. I'm just getting started."

At lunch, Melissa shared her after-school plans with Ann.

"Good luck," Ann said, unwrapping a sandwich. "And I do mean it. No one knows much about Bryony, except she married John Simons."

"Steve said Mrs. Clements has her great-aunt's diary. Maybe she mentions Bryony." Melissa hated feeling defensive. "Hey, did you research Owen Munson yet?"

"A little," Ann said. "I'll do more today and introduce you to Mrs. Clements."

"That'd be great!"

The library's austere exterior contrasted strongly with the warm atmosphere inside. The dark wood floors and paneled walls gleamed, as if freshly polished. A faint cinnamon scent lingered in the air, reminiscent of her mother's Thanksgiving pumpkin roll. Melissa gazed around the library's single room. Just ten rows of green-painted bookshelves lined one end; several round tables and chairs filled the other. A long, overstuffed couch flanked by floor lamps leaned against the back wall. Two girls Brian's age huddled and whispered over a magazine. Three waist-high bookcases displaying picture books stood near the circulation desk. A pregnant woman sat on the floor and turned the pages of a large board book. A toddler cuddled next to her, sucking his thumb.

As Melissa and Ann approached the counter, a brown-haired woman in a gray-tweed skirt, beige blouse, and glasses hanging on a chain around her neck stepped out, carrying an armful of books.

"Mrs. Clements," Ann said. "This is Melissa Marchellis. She's new in town."

The librarian paused and smiled broadly. "Ah, yes. The family living in the servant's quarters. Welcome to Munsonville, dear."

"Thank you."

Mrs. Clements, Melissa decided, was nice, like Steve.

"Ann, there's a new book about fur trappers on the cart by my desk. It mentions Owen Munson."

"Thanks!" Ann said. "Mrs. Clements, Melissa needs information on Bryony Simons for her centennial report. Can you help her?"

"I might. Melissa, have a seat while I take care of these books. I'll gather some materials and be right back."

Ann went for her book, so Melissa chose a table and rummaged a notebook and pen from her bag. She hoped Mrs. Clements found enough information to get her report approved. A wail rose up from the other end of the library. The toddler had grabbed the book from his mother and had thrown it on the floor. The woman slapped his hand, which made the child howl even louder. She quickly tossed the book on the shelves and carried the little boy, still shrieking, out of the library.

A long line formed at the circulation desk and extended to the front door. Mrs. Clements scurried back to her post. With a sigh of impatience, Melissa glanced at Ann, who sat several tables away and was already copying notes. Melissa turned over her notebook and drew leafy vines on the back, embellishing them with tiny flowers. She had completed an entire border before Mrs. Clements drew up a chair.

"I'm sorry to keep you waiting, dear," Mrs. Clements said. "This might help. My great-aunt was Reverend Marseilles' housekeeper. Here is her diary. It now belongs to the library's historical collection."

"Does your great-aunt mention Bryony?" Melissa asked.

"I'm sure she does. She worked for the reverend after his wife died."

Melissa was stunned. She actually had something in common with Bryony Simons! "Bryony lost a parent?"

"It was very sad," Mrs. Clements said. "Adele Marseilles was not Victorian Munsonville's traditional, hardy wife. She was educated and every bit the reverend's intellectual equal, but she was often ill. She died of pneumonia shortly after Bryony's third birthday."

"Is that when your great-aunt began caring for Bryony?"

"Heavens, no!" Mrs. Clements laughed softly. "The Reverend Galien Marseilles did things his way, and that included raising Bryony. Even after he allowed my aunt to help, the villagers still criticized him."

Melissa jotted that down. "What did he do that was so awful?"

The librarian grew sober. "Because the reverend missed Adele, He tried re-creating her in Bryony. Not physically, mind you, but in personality and intelligence."

"So, why was he criticized? Is that bad?"

"Here's an example. Despite his 'fire and brimstone' sermons at the only church in town, Reverend Marseilles adored art and literature. Every Thursday evening, he hosted a parsonage discussion group, the Munsonville Society for the Humanities. It was mostly an excuse for drinking brandy, smoking cigars, and chatting. The gathering contained all men and…Bryony."

What a boring way to spend an evening! "I still don't see why that's wrong."

Mrs. Clements chuckled. "It wasn't acceptable in nineteenth century Munsonville for a young female child to soak up the conversation of a roomful of men, even if they were sitting in a parsonage parlor."

Melissa couldn't imagine men discussing anything remotely interesting, unless Reverend Marseilles' society was like her mother's writing group. The pieces they shared were interesting, especially when the stories were mysteries.

"Also, Reverend Marseilles was quite overprotective. He was afraid of losing his daughter, too, so he limited Bryony's activities to those he personally supervised."

"Like his society meetings?"

"Yes, like his society meetings."

Mrs. Clements waited until Melissa had finished writing. "I'll bookmark references to Bryony and hunt up newspaper stories on John and Bryony Simons. I know the society page featured some items."

"Is that enough for a report?" Melissa asked, anxiety creeping into her voice.

"Quite possibly, but it might take a few days to find them. Is that okay?"

Melissa nodded and capped her pen. Ann returned, just as Melissa said, "I really appreciate your help, Mrs. Clements."

Mrs. Clements patted her hand and smiled. "That's why I'm here."

After the librarian left, Ann said, "Well?"

Melissa showed Ann her full page of information. "She promised to have more when I come back. What did you learn about Owen Munson?"

Before Ann could answer, Melissa's gaze fell on the wall clock: ten past five.

"Ann, I've got to go." Melissa quickly stuffed her notebook into her book bag. "I promised my mother I'd be waiting outside."

Brian reluctantly moved to the back seat, so Melissa, still excited, could share what she had learned. The words rapidly tumbled from Melissa's mouth, until her mother neared the drive to the Simons estate. As Melissa peered through the twilight into the woods, a chill passed through her, and she didn't know why. There was no mist.

"Can you imagine such a chauvinistic club as the Munsonville Society for the Humanities existing today?" Darlene said.

Melissa turned away from the window, only partially relieved by the lucid sky. "I guess not," she said.

"Make sure you tell Steve tonight. I'm sure he'll be interested."

"He's eating with us again?" Melissa momentarily forgot the mist. Steve had spent the entire weekend at the servant's cottage.

Brian piped up from the back seat. "He's helping me with homework."

Their mother parked in front of the cottage. "He was hoping to cook dinner, too, but he ran errands after work. How about hot dogs? They're fast."

"Okay." Melissa only half-heard her mother. She wondered how soon Mrs. Clements could gather information on Bryony. "When can I go to the library again?"

"Let me check my schedule, but I'm sure any day will be fine."

All week, during lunch hour, Melissa called Mrs. Clements from the school office, but the answer was always, "Not yet." It was hard to wait, especially since Ann, as well as Brian and Clay, were well into their projects. On Friday, Mrs. Clements left a message through the school secretary. She finally had some materials. Melissa hoped she had not been a pest, but her fears

35

quickly vanished. At the library, Mrs. Clements smiled and gestured to Melissa from the copy machine, and Melissa hurried to greet her.

"Thank you for your patience," Mrs. Clements said. "I marked the diary for you, but first, I'll show you some pictures."

Mrs. Clements led Melissa to the oil paintings behind the bookcases. Melissa immediately recognized John and Bryony Simons from Ann's photographs. The rest were men. At each portrait, Mrs. Clements gave Melissa a short biography, but no one sounded familiar, except for Owen Munson, and Melissa wasn't interested in him, either. The men's short dark hair and bushy mustaches clashed with John Simons' nearly invisible beard and abundant fair locks.

"Back then," Mrs. Clements said, "no village man wore hair that long, but you'll quickly see custom meant little to John Simons. For instance, John and Bryony's wedding departed from our tradition of morning receptions and dark fruitcake."

Melissa had fruitcake once, several years ago during a Christmas party at Laura's house, and she had hated it. Good thing no one forced Bryony to eat it at her wedding.

Mrs. Clements held out the diary. "Here, start with this."

Melissa accepted the diary, restraining herself from snatching it out of the librarian's hands. She picked a location far away from the circulation desk, dropped her book bag, and set the diary on the table. An old raffle ticket marked the first entry.

June 5, 1892: A society guest ogled Bryony last evening. I ordered her to withdraw from her father's group but, as usual, the headstrong girl refused. I can't discuss it with her father, for he is more stubborn than she, but I am highly concerned.

That guest must be John, Melissa thought excitedly. She copied the few lines into her notebook and eagerly turned to the next entry.

June 28, 1892: John Simons' actions towards Bryony at this afternoon's ice cream social were so brash that even Reverend can no longer ignore them. I do believe he intends to speak to Mr. Simons this very evening."

I wondered what John did to her, Melissa thought, frustrated at the skimpy detail. She quickly added that passage and turned to the next, hoping it gave the answer.

July 4, 1892: Has everyone gone mad? Reverend is actually allowing Mr. Simons to escort Bryony to the Fourth of July celebration at the lake! I couldn't hold my tongue any further, but Reverend only laughed and said the matter would end when Mr. Simons leaves town. I do hope it's soon. I fear Mr. Simons' notoriety has blinded Reverend's sound judgment.

What a busybody! Melissa briefly wondered what Victorian Munsonville did for the Fourth of July, but the house-keeper didn't mention it.

November 4, 1892: Winter is soon approaching, and that dreadful man is still here. Oh, why won't he leave Bryony alone?

Melissa smiled as she wrote these few words. What had the housekeeper thought when John had proposed? She leafed ahead.

April 18, 1893: Tonight, the hoped-for storm finally broke. John Simons officially announced his intention to marry Bryony, and Reverend exploded. Mr. Simons has been a dreadful influence on Bryony. The child screamed and cried so; it's a wonder she didn't faint. She threatened to leave Munsonville forever, but Reverend didn't acquiesce to her childish tactics.

This time, Melissa almost laughed aloud. Obviously, the reverend had acquiesced to her "childish tactics." Melissa quickly skipped to the final entry.

April 24, 1893: Reverend and Mr. Simons argued for many hours. It appears Mr. Simons won't remove Bryony from Munsonville. He will build a home in the woods and make the village his permanent residence. Perhaps, I have misjudged the man.

That was all. The remaining pages were blank. A movement caught Melissa's attention. Mrs. Clements had returned and was pulling a chair away from the table.

"Does this help with the report, Melissa?" Mrs. Clements eased into the seat.

"Oh yes," Melissa said, "What was your great-aunt's name?"

"Bertha Parks. She wrote it on the very first page."

Melissa flipped back to double-check the spelling of the name, and then returned the diary to the librarian. "I really appreciate all your help."

"It's my pleasure," Mrs. Clements said. "Would you like to look at some newspaper clippings?"

"Yes!" Melissa softly cried. Her mother walked through the front door. "No," she added, her excitement deflated. "I have to go."

She was back on Monday. Luckily, Mrs. Clements was not busy and immediately showed Melissa how to access the microfilm.

"There are few news stories about John Simons before he began courting Bryony," Mrs. Clements said. "Nothing this momentous had ever happened to a villager. Unfortunately, the marriage was short-lived. After Bryony and her baby died in childbirth, John left Munsonville for good. The broken-hearted reverend died a year later." Mrs. Clements paused. "Forgive my rambling. I'll let you read the stories for yourself. Come get me if you need anything."

Melissa was already peering into the projector. She skim-ed too fast and accidentally scrolled past John Simons' name. Quick-ly, Melissa turned back.

JUNE 4, 1892: Renowned concert pianist and composer, John Simons, was the honored guest of the Munsonville Society for the Humanities. Everyone presents enjoyed his stories of music and travel. Mr. Simons, on a respite from his tours to relax in Munsonville, graciously accepted Reverend Marseilles' invitation.

The Reverend Marseilles probably wanted to show him off to everyone, Melissa thought, opening a fresh notebook page. She wondered why John chose Munsonville as a vacation spot. Melissa began writing, and the next couple hours flew past.

A deluge of homework and two tests kept Melissa from the library the rest of the week. Saturday afternoon was warm and sunny, so Melissa coaxed permission to bike there, promising to be on time for dinner. She spent several splendid hours scrolling through microfilm and copying only those passages that referenced Bryony or supported information Mrs. Clements had given her.

The young bride's saga fascinated her. It was romantic, like Shelly had said, except for the strange food the Simons' had served at their wedding reception. Did people back then really eat mushroom catsup and pigeons? Melissa stretched and re-read her entries.

JULY 12, 1892: Legendary composer and pianist John Simons has graciously assumed the position of official pianist at the Munsonville Congregational Church. Mrs. Bertha Parks will continue that role during his absence.

AUGUST 2, 1892: Is your child a budding Mozart? International composer/pianist John Simons is offering private piano consultations and lessons.

MAY 1, 1893: The Reverend Galien Marseilles has officially announced the engagement of his daughter, Miss Bryony Marseilles, to Mr. John Simons, renowned pianist and composer. The wedding will take place 3 p.m., December 24, 1893.

MAY 8, 1893: Construction began last week on Simons Mansion, the very first home in Munsonville to feature indoor plumbing.

JUNE 19, 1893: John Simons has hired an Evansville horticulturist to cross-breed a native Munsonville plant with an English weed, bryony, to honor his bride-to-be. This new plant will also be called bryony.

AUGUST 15, 1893: Today, Reverend Marseilles dispelled a rumor. Mr. John Simons will not play a piece at the wedding he composed specifically for the bride-to-be. "Only sacred music is allowed in my church," the reverend declared.

SEPTEMBER 10, 1893: Reverend Marseilles will limit attendance at the Dec. 24 Marseilles-Simons wedding, fearing Mr. Simons' notoriety might precipitate spectators. However, the entire village of Munsonville is on the guest list for the lavish evening reception at Simons Mansion.

DECEMBER 31, 1893: On December 24, Mr. John Simons and Miss Bryony Marseilles were united in Holy Matrimony. The bride looked lovely in a wedding dress Mr. Simons had ordered from Paris: an ivory satin, floor-length gown, with a lace veil edged in bryony motifs, and a pair of white kid gloves. A gold locket belonging to the bride's mother adorned the outfit. "It's the only jewelry Reverend allows," said Bertha Parks, parsonage housekeeper.

I'll bet that changed after the wedding, Melissa thought, double- checking the description of John's wedding garments. Instead of the traditional black, John wore grey pants, coat, and top hat. His shirt was white, but his cravat and gloves were lavender.

Immediately before the service's commencement, Mr. John Simons played the song he wrote for Miss Marseilles, so Reverend Marseilles refused to attend the reception at Simons Mansion.

The reception featured the following menu items: fish balls, fruit fritters, scalloped oysters, giblet soup with veal, chowder, mushroom catsup, roast wild duck with cranberries and peas, boiled pigeons with turkey stuffing, roast goose with mashed potato stuffing and apple sauce, breaded potatoes, boiled cabbage, winter squash, boiled parsnips and carrots, rice and meat pudding, baked plum pudding, French rolls, jelly tarts, minced pie, and eggnog.

Crowning the occasion was a magnificent twelve-tiered wedding cake, light and white, with scrolls of pink and green frosting, to match the bryony at Simons Mansion. The décor featured lace-covered tabletops decorated with mulberry ribbon, bows, holly, mistletoe, and red roses. For the couple's first dance, a sixteen-piece orchestra played "Bryony." One guest said, "It was like a fairy tale."

Melissa felt a hand lightly touch her arm, bringing her back to reality.

"It's getting late," Mrs. Clements said. "Is someone picking you up?"

Melissa's gaze traveled to the wall clock. Five o'clock! Steve was teaching Brian how to make spaghetti. Melissa, not to be upstaged by her little brother and his new mentor, had promised to make her famous garlic bread, the first time she had done so since moving to Munsonville. Yet, that was not the main reason Melissa wanted to rush home. She did not want to see the mist. She peered anxiously at the window. It was already getting dark.

"Thanks, Mrs. Clements," Melissa said, hastily shoving her supplies into her bag.

"I'm glad to help. Let me know if you need anything else."

She hurried out the door and around the side of the building to the bicycle rack. The small gravel parking lot had room for few cars, but the rack was full. Even Mrs. Clements biked to work, despite her skirt.

Melissa unlocked her bike, more from habit established in Grover's Park after Laura had hers stolen, than from necessity. What was Munsonville's greatest crime? Littering? She crossed Main Street to the path adjacent to Lake Munson. The area was deserted except for two fishermen sitting on the dock. The sun had not set, but it dipped below the horizon line. Drat!

Keeping a wary eye on the lake, Melissa pedaled rapidly down Main Street. The sky above the gently rippling waves was clear; the entrance to the woods was free from haze. Smoke rose from a chimney on Bass Street. No mist, so far. Maybe, she *could* elude it. Was Steve at the cottage yet? How funny Brian enjoyed cooking. So far, he and Steve had made stuffed peppers, roast pork with cabbage and sauerkraut, chicken pot pie, and barbecued ribs. Last weekend, Melissa had leaned against the counter and watched antsy Brian calmly measuring spices. Her mother had always used store-bought sauce. Melissa was amazed this handyman cooked so

41

well. Then again, Steve probably couldn't afford to eat all his meals at Sue's Diner.

Melissa approached the road to Simons Mansion. A gauzy film suspended over the trees, just past the mouth of the woods. It swayed slightly, as if beckoning Melissa to draw near. She swallowed hard and loudly said, "Stupid vapor, I'm not afraid!"

Forcing her quaking legs to pump harder, Melissa headed for the estate's driveway. The mist, she told herself, is a giant cloud. Fear rose a notch. *Stop being a baby!*

The mist thickened and rolled across the road toward the drive. Mist couldn't chase anyone! Her heart pounded, but she shouted to herself, "Scaredy cat!"

The opaque fog engulfed the road. Melissa reluctantly jumped off her bike and pushed it the rest of the way. It was only a short distance, yet Melissa was surprised at how dark it was near the top. At once, the mist vanished.

She wiped her sweaty palms across her jeans, gripped the handlebars with trembling fingers, and remounted her bike. Then, she coasted behind Simons Mansion. The cottage blazed with light; her mother and Steve were talking animatedly in the living room. Her mother punctuated silent words with sweeping hands, but Steve merely stood, arms folded across his chest. Were they arguing? Already? Heart thudding in her chest, Melissa rushed to the back door. Her mother gave a little cry and ran into the kitchen.

"Thank God you're all right!" Darlene plastered Melissa's face with kisses.

Steve leaned against the doorframe, looking highly displeased. "Just where have you been, young lady? Look how you've upset your mother!"

He had never spoken so severely, not even when Brian had lied about cleaning his bedroom. Melissa's eyes widened in shock. She forgot her terrifying ride.

"I was just at the library." Melissa's voice trailed away, as she glanced at the chipped clock hanging above Steve. It was almost midnight.

CHAPTER 5: BLOOD RELATIVES

On Sunday, Melissa welcomed the dreaded drive to Jenson to visit Grandma Marchellis in the nursing home. Her mother had grounded Melissa to her bedroom until she had explained her whereabouts. Of course, Melissa could not. She had mentally reviewed Friday night's events until her brain went numb. Where had she lost so much time? Wasn't it just a few minutes to the top of the hill? She had lain in bed and listened to her mother loudly discuss it with Steve.

"Something's wrong with Melissa!" Darlene's voice choked with tears.

"Darlene, you're overreacting."

"Melissa doesn't behave like this. Now if it had been Brian...."

Steve had said something in a low voice, but her mother was really crying now. "I'm going to lose her, just like I lost Frank. I can't take much more."

"The poor girl's been through a lot. Melissa's a good kid. It'll blow over."

43

Downcast, Melissa watched the autumn landscape roll past her window. Steve, at least, defended her. His presence at the house was now nearly constant, but Brian, especially, enjoyed having him there. He still cried at night, too.

Brian squirmed next to her. "We're here!" He scrambled out of the back seat before anyone could stop him.

"Now, remember...." Darlene began.

"I know. I know," Brian said, mimicking her tone. "Comb my hair; no running in the halls; and speak only when spoken to."

"Come on Melissa, out you go, so I can park the car," Steve said.

Melissa did, while regarding the old one-story, yellow brick building in front of her.

Despite sunny skies, the early afternoon air was lifeless and stale. Dry, bare patches speckled the brown lawn, and the flower beds looked faded and wilted. A row of small, square buildings stood across the street. One read, *Eircheard's Emporium*. Huh?

"It's too bad she had no one to take care of her," Darlene said, "but your father was too sick to help."

"She could've moved in with us," Brian said.

"We tried, but she wanted to stay near Munsonville."

Grandma Marchellis had visited them, once, years ago. Melissa had awakened to hear Grandma chanting and had run to her parents' room for comfort. Her mother had explained how Grandma was only saying her nightly prayers. Melissa was glad she had never seen Grandma again. Those bedtime mutterings were far too bizarre.

"Ready?" Steve held open the front door of the nursing home for Darlene and Melissa, then nodded to Brian. "You too, sport."

Brian assumed his most dignified expression and strutted into the building. Darlene announced their arrival to the receptionist, who smiled and said, "Oh, good. She's been expecting you."

Melissa gazed at the dingy, pale green walls and tried to block out the faint smell of urine. Steve stood near her mother and Brian. They seemed oblivious to the shabby interior. Restless, she wandered to the reception area's magazine rack, selected a ratty gardening magazine dated March 1971, and pretended to read an

44

advertisement for organic plant food. Maybe, Grandma would be sound asleep, or too sick, to visit.

An aide walked into the room. "This way, please," she said in a feeble voice. She was a skeletal woman, as old and shabby as the building, with a thin nose poking out from a pinched face and strategically combed wisps of hair on her pink scalp.

They followed her down a gray, narrow hallway, silent except for the occasional hum of a television set behind a closed door. Grandma's room was last on the left.

"We have visitors today," the aide said, with exaggerated brightness in her voice.

Grandma Marchellis, plump and rosy compared to their pasty- faced usher, was sitting upright in bed, staring at the scuffed wallpaper, and picking at her bed sheet.

"Look who's here, your daughter-in-law and grandchild-ren! Now, I'll leave, so you can have a nice visit." The aide moved close to their mother and dropped her voice. "She has good and bad days. So far, this is a good day. Just ring if you need anything."

Their mother sat by Grandma Marchellis and hugged the elderly woman. The bed sagged and creaked under their combined weight.

"Mother, I am so glad to see you." Darlene even sounded like she meant it. A shadow of recognition passed over Grandma's face, and she smiled weakly.

"Would you like to sit by the window? It's a gorgeous day."

The elderly woman nodded, took a deep breath, and belched. Brian snickered under his breath. Steve eased Grandma into the worn easy chair. Their mother poured a cup of water from the scuffed plastic pitcher on the bedside table and placed a fresh straw in it. Steve tipped the cup to Grandma's lips, and she sipped it, while their mother smoothed the comforter on Grandma's bed and adjusted the pillows.

Grandma looked up at Steve and said, "I'm a big girl now."

Brian yawned and twirled his index finger near his head.

Shh," Melissa said, nudging him. She studied the strange religious pictures hanging around the room, supposing they depicted Jesus and Mary, but, with their large eyes and elongated limbs, the figures resembled praying mantises.

"Mother, I have a surprise for you," Darlene said. "Brian and Melissa are here."

Grandma smiled politely at Brian. Grinning, he poked Melissa in the ribs, but the grin soon faded from Brian's face. Grandma's unsmiling gaze now rested upon Melissa. Instinctively, Melissa stepped backward. Grandma's eyes widened in fright. Melissa's mouth went dry. She peeped at Brian. He stared at Grandma and looked troubled. Grandma glanced fearfully at their mother, then at Steve, then again at their mother. Grandma shrank into the chair. Melissa tugged on Brian's sleeve. He now looked scared, too.

"Mother?" Darlene's gaze anxiously met Steve's. "Should I ring your nurse?"

Grandma struggled to speak.

"There, there." Darlene patted Grandma's back.

Grandma's nose turned crimson. She panted and drove her nails into the chair arms. She tried to speak and choked. Steve rang for the nurse. Grandma locked eyes on Melissa. Grandma's eyes bulged; her face turned blue; and her mouth foamed.

"Kids, get out!" Steve hastily pushed them toward the door.

"Danger...blood!" Grandma gasped. *"Blood! Blood! Blood! Blood! Blood!"* The nurse rushed into the room and shut the door behind her. Melissa and Brian stared ahead and then at each other. They had nothing to say, not until after the ambulance appeared, and Steve had hustled them back to the waiting area.

"Steve, what happened to Grandma?" Brian asked in a shaky voice. Melissa looked at the floor. She knew what had happened to Grandma, and she didn't want to hear it. She closed her eyes against the memory. Something about Melissa had horrified her. Melissa had seen it on her face. Terror and guilt gripped Melissa, as she replayed the macabre scene inside her head. *Blood, blood, blood!* What did it mean?

Even Steve looked pale as he hugged Brian. "I'm sorry, sport," he said. Then he hurried back down the hall to be with their mother.

46

Grandma Marchellis' sudden and unexpected death brought one benefit for Melissa: She was no longer grounded. The funeral was Saturday in Detroit, several hours from home.

"Why so far away?" Brian said at dinner, his mouth half full of food. "There's a church right here in Munsonville."

"Your grandmother belonged to that church. Besides, I promised your father…." Darlene's voice broke.

Melissa brushed a hand across her eyes, then quickly reached over Brian's plate for the ketchup bottle Brian was hoarding. The bottle spluttered red droplets across her plate.

"Don't we have any more?" Melissa asked, crossly.

Her mother wiped her eyes and ran into the kitchen to check. Melissa felt stupid. Steve would have gone for ketchup. Brian whispered to Melissa, "Like Grandma will know the difference."

"Shh! Mom will hear you."

The funeral with its strange church service passed in a blur. The people chanted in an unfamiliar language, adding to Melissa's sense of unreality. Once, her mother leaned close to Melissa, and whispered, "It's Ukrainian." Melissa had nodded, but her head buzzed with a single question. Had she caused Grandma Marchellis' death? Blood!

Afterwards, scores of people hugged her and apologized for her loss. Melissa squirmed inside. What loss? She hadn't known Grandma and did not care she was gone.

"I'm going to belt the next old lady that kisses me." Brian wiped lipstick off his mouth with the back of his hand. "Yuck, yuck, yuck, and super yuck." Their mother accepted everyone's condolences with grace. She spent the afternoon clutching tissue in her left hand and Steve's arm with her right.

That night in bed *blood, blood, blood, blood* echoed in Melissa's head, disturbing her sleep. Grandma was out of her mind, Melissa thought irritably, as she flipped over her pillow. So, why had she recognized Melissa? *Blood!*

The next day, they cleaned out Grandma's room, eerily stark without her in it. They gathered her photo albums, beloved icons, and prayer books into a box to take home. Her mother folded Grandma's few clothes into a garbage bag for charity.

Curious, Melissa removed one of the albums and flipped through the sepia-colored pictures. Melissa didn't recognize anyone, so she skipped to the colored photographs at the back of the book.

Grandma sat on a couch, holding newborn Brian. Melissa, shoulders hunched and head listless, sat stiffly next to her. Melissa flipped to the black and white pictures in the middle. A little boy resembling Brian, except with Melissa's dark hair, stood on a beach holding a pail and shovel. Below, that same boy stood stiffly in sailor suit.

"Is that Daddy?" Melissa held the album up so her mother could see. Her mother paused and nodded. Melissa studied those pictures. Her father looked so young and alive, not gray-haired, sallow, and crouched in a wheelchair. Tears sprang to her eyes. Gently, she closed the book and set it in the box. Her mother taped it shut.

"Melissa, would you please empty the nightstand?"

Glad for something constructive to do, Melissa opened the top drawer. It contained only the nursing home Bible, but the bottom drawer held a pink celluloid brush, comb, and mirror set. A few wisps of white hair clung to the brush.

Her mother tossed a small box on the bed for those last few items. Steve and Brian left with the large box and clothing bag. On impulse, Melissa knelt on the floor and reached to the back of the drawer. Her fingers touched a small, square-shaped object; she pulled out a cherry- wood music box. Tiny, hand-painted, pink flowers poked through the pale green vines winding over it. Melissa raised the lid, and its music sounded vaguely familiar. She rewound it and listened again.

"Mom, do you know the name of this song?"

Her mother shook her head, climbed off the step stool, and, hands on her hips, gave the room one final look.

"Well," Darlene said, with a weary sigh. "I guess that's it."

The music enchanted Melissa, and she only half-heard her mother. She sat on the bed and replayed it. On the third round, her mother joined her.

"I know it's hard," Darlene said, "losing your father, and now your grandmother."

At the mention of her father, Melissa's throat hurt, and she fought back tears. Her mother hugged Melissa tighter, but they both cried anyway. Would life always be so sad?

"We'll get through it," Darlene said, dabbing her eyes with the back of her hand. "Sunshine is just around the corner. I promise you." She absently patted Melissa's back.

"Mom." Melissa wasn't sure how to ask. "Am I the reason Grandma is…."

"Oh, Melissa!" Darlene drew Melissa close. "Is that what's bothering you?"

Melissa nodded, thankful her mother understood without her saying it. She laid Melissa's head on her shoulder and stroked her daughter's hair. "Your grandmother's death is not your fault. It just happened. Try not to think about it."

Melissa looked up at her mother. "But she looked so frightened!"

"The doctor said she often had spells." Darlene lightly touched the music box. "You may keep this, if you like, to remember her always."

Melissa hadn't intended keeping anything belonging to Grandma Marchellis, but the music intrigued her. Where had she heard that song? During the quiet ride home, even Brian didn't stir, except to yank out her earplug and whisper, "I wonder who's next?"

"What do you mean, 'Who's next?' What are you talking about?"

"I wonder who's going to die next."

"Brian Adam Marchellis, what's the matter with you?" Melissa kept her voice soft, but she looked at the front seat. Neither her mother nor Steve appeared to have heard him. "You stop talking like that right now."

"Don't get mad, Liss." Brian's face was earnest. "Remember what Dad always said? Deaths come in threes. Dad was one, and Grandma was two. Who's three?"

"Well, don't ask Mom." Melissa felt better since talking to her mother but thinking about death still unnerved her. She replaced the plug. "She's got enough on her mind without you upsetting her."

Despite Melissa's valiant efforts to catch up on homework, the algebra assignment on her desk made no sense. She strained her eyes until they crossed, but the letters and numbers jumbled together. Melissa sighed and shut the book. She was more tired than she had realized. Too drained for pajamas, teeth brushing, or reading, Melissa kicked off her shoes, slid into bed, and switched off the light. The music box sitting on her nightstand again caught her eye. Melissa wound it up and lay in the dark, listening to its soothing tinkle. Her mind grew fuzzy; her pillow melted, and the music box sped up.

Strange dreams plagued her. Twisted forms called her. White mist enveloped her, strangled her, and drowned her. Shapes whirled around her bed. A piano rapidly plinked the music box's song. Shadows settled onto Melissa's chest, and she heaved and clawed through opaque air.

"Ow!" Her left hand smacked into a plaster wall.

The sound echoed into mist. Bracing against damp walls, Melissa blindly tottered down a long, narrow corridor. A million televisions moaned over the incessant piano. On her left, a bright light seeped through the darkness. Her hand bumped a doorknob; thankful fingers closed around it, and Melissa pushed into Grandma Marchellis' room.

A little girl wearing a dove-colored gown, with a high neck collar and cuffs at her wrists, sat cross-legged on Grandma's bed and sang tunelessly. Between her plump hands was a small, cherry-wood music box decorated with pink, hand-painted flowers and pale green vines. As Melissa entered, the little girl tilted her round face, leered from under blunt-cut, dishwater-colored bangs, and said, "We're blood relatives now, Melissa."

Dread washed over Melissa. She backed away, but the door had dissolved into mist. The little girl chanted, "I'm a big girl now, a big, big girl."

Melissa's head bumped into the wall. The girl sang, "Blood, blood, blood, blood, blood, blood, blood, blood." Melissa covered her ears, screamed, and sped down the hallway. The girl screeched higher: *"Blood! Blood! Blood! Blood! Blood!"*

In terror, Melissa sat straight up in bed and silenced her alarm clock. It had been ringing over five minutes. Bright sunlight poured through the windows and blotted the macabre scene from her immediate memory. It was morning, time for school.

CHAPTER 6: A JOB WELL DONE

Melissa fought back yawns in American History class. Who cared what Sir Francis Drake had claimed for England? She'd bet Ann felt bored, too.

Ann lightly coughed. Glancing at Mr. Carter, Melissa slid her hand under her desk, then stuck her arm into the aisle. She read, *Mr. Masters. Back from vacation.*

Melissa wrinkled her forehead. Who in the heck was Mr. Masters?

She found out last period. Harold Masters was the school's eccentric, middle-aged English teacher, returned from a leave of absence for an illness. Short, dumpy, and bearded, Mr. Masters looked the epitome of the absent-minded professor.

Food stains smeared Mr. Masters' polka-dot shirt, half-tucked into his baggy trousers. With one finger, he slid smudged spectacles back up his nose as he lectured his students. His thick, disheveled, gray-streaked brown hair sorely needed a comb and a bottle of shampoo.

Melissa noticed the change in her English classroom the second she walked into it. The shades were halfway drawn; the lights were off. Mrs. Denison's *Good Grammar* Rules were gone from the bulletin boards. In their place were pen and ink illustrations. Ann whispered, "Mr. Masters says it gives the readings atmosphere."

Mr. Masters collected their homework and launched into a rendition, by heart, of Sir Walter Scott's Lochinvar. When Mr. Masters recited, "The bride kissed the goblet; the knight took it up," Melissa scribbled with haste, *He's our teacher?*

Not just a teacher, Ann wrote back. *He's a famous writer.*

What? Not the Harold Masters, the short story author. His adult horror books always made some bestselling list. *The Eleventh Commandment and Other Tales* sat on the table by her mother's bed. Wow! A famous writer for an English teacher! Who would have guessed it by his appearance?

As overseer for the students' anniversary writing projects. Mr. Masters promised plenty of practice writing assignments to insure the best results.

"I will not tolerate inaccurate or poorly written work," he said.

Ann rolled her eyes and coughed. *He takes MASTERS too far.*

Melissa soon learned Mr. Masters was indeed a master, not only in writing, but in his knowledge of American literature, and he eagerly shared an abundance of that knowledge, whether or not his students liked it. Melissa, however, delighted in Mr. Masters' teaching style and selections, so very different from the teachers at Grover's Park High School.

Mr. Masters didn't follow a set curriculum but assigned several new pieces each day. Over the next few weeks, they studied and analyzed the poems of Henry Wadsworth Longfellow, John Greenleaf Whittier, Emily Dickinson, and Walt Whitman; the essays of Ralph Waldo Emerson and Henry David Thoreau; and selections from F. Scott Fitzgerald, Ernest Hemmingway, James Thurber, and Pearl S. Buck. With his thrilling recitations and vivid descriptions, Melissa could picture herself in every scene. Yet, his open mind with literature did not spill into his students' paltry writings. The voluminous number of practice papers he assigned became the bane of Melissa's existence.

Still, Mr. Masters approved her centennial project, then spoiled it by adding, "I will not accept a paper simply based on folklore and legend, so do not submit one. Research it well and report as truthfully as you can."

Melissa gulped. Everyone who had actually known Bryony was dead. So how could Mr. Masters, or anyone else for that matter, determine fact from fiction? She opened her mouth to protest, but quickly shut it again. Mr. Masters would not welcome her opinion. Mrs. Clements found plenty of information, but Melissa worried it was not enough for Mr. Masters.

Mrs. Clements reassured her. "Just do your best. That's all anybody can ask."

"Even Mr. Masters?"

"Even Mr. Masters. He didn't know Bryony, either."

As the warm fall days merged into chilly fall nights, Melissa now rode a small bus to and from school, and that irritated her. Last spring, Melissa had driven to school, but ever since her midnight escapade, her mother wouldn't even let her start the car. On library days, Steve picked her up and brought her home. Although the sun had always set by the time Steve steered his truck up the hill toward home, they never once encountered the mist. Melissa was tempted to blame it on an inflated imagination, but that didn't explain how she lost seven hours.

Probably, everyone thinks I'm lying, or that I'm nuts, she thought, watching Lake Munson over her shoulder. But I did see it, she silently added. I did see it.

One night after dinner, while Melissa was slouching at the dining room table studying for an American History test, and Brian, with Scooter lying beside his chair, was struggling with fractions, Steve came into the house with something tucked under his arm.

"I have the original floor plans for Simons Mansion. Who wants to see them?"

"Oh, me!" Melissa slammed her notebook and tossed it on the couch. Melissa knocked on her mother's bedroom door and excitedly called, "Mom, Steve's got the floor plans to Simons Mansion!"

Brian cleared the table of all homework, so Steve could carefully unroll the plans and lay them flat. Everyone grabbed a chair and leaned forward to look. Four very large rooms occupied the main floor: the parlor, dining room, library, and another great space for John's music room. The second floor contained six bedrooms, a second dining room, and a morning room. Shelly would love to have seen....

Melissa swallowed hard. Wrinkling his forehead, Brian said, "Steve, what in the heck is a morning room?"

"The Simons' private living room. They only entertained guests in the first-floor parlor. The rooms on the second floor were reserved for the immediate family. The morning room caught the early light, so it was the perfect place to read and plan the day."

Melissa peered at the second floor. "Which room belonged to John and Bryony?"

"These two. Rich couples back then often had separate bedrooms. The others were guest rooms."

"I suppose one was converted into a nursery," Darlene said. Brian studied the plans again. "What's on the third floor?"

"The ballroom," Melissa said, suddenly forgetting her homesickness.

Everyone stared at her, and she blushed. "They had the wedding reception there." Steve grinned. "Well, you have done your homework. You get the first tour just as soon as the workmen declare it's safe."

The lavishness of the mansion impressed Brian. "Wow! Imagine being rich enough to have your own ballroom!" He thought a minute." I guess that means you'd have to dance. Ick! Hey, where's the kitchen?"

Steve chuckled. "In the basement. The cooking and laundry were done there. The servants brought food into the main dining room by the dumbwaiter."

"The what?

"The dumbwaiter. It was like a small elevator."

"Oh."

Melissa tugged a tuft of Brian's hair. "When you and Steve cook dinner, you're our little dumb waiter."

"Stop!" Brian swatted her hand. "Mom!"

Scooter jumped up, barked twice, then laid his head back on his paws.

"The house servants," Steve said, ignoring the commotion, "had living quarters in the attic, but the men who cared for the horses and carriages bunked above the stables. That kept them close to the horses and deterred would-be horse thieves."

"That must have made hot summers and cold winters," Darlene said.

"You bet it did!"

Melissa noted how the grand staircase separated the parlor and dining room from the library and music room. Steve pointed out the adjoining doors dividing the library from the music room.

"If John Simons wanted to entertain many guests, the two rooms could easily become one, great space," Steve rolled up the plans. "I have to return these to Village Hall tomorrow morning. I had just thought you'd like to see them."

"Thanks, Steve," Melissa said. "This will really help my report."

She picked up her notebook and pictured herself climbing that staircase all the way to Bryony's room. Steve promised to help Brian with his fractions, then left to return the plans to his pick-up truck.

"Hey, Mom!" Melissa heard Brian call out. "Your rings on the windowsill!"

Melissa closed her bedroom door and felt warm and glowing inside. It was nice for Steve to share those plans with them. As the days passed, her preoccupation with Bryony increased. Often, Melissa roamed the estate, pretending she was Bryony, with John beside her, who paused now and then to gaze lovingly into her eyes. When Melissa did homework, she was Bryony, writing entries into a diary, her hair flowing down her back, while the sounds of John's piano wafted up to her. Those notes lingered in her mind, filled her dreams, and woke her at night still hearing them before she drifted off to sleep again as they faded.

However, reading and daydreaming about Bryony was much easier than writing a compelling research paper about her. Melissa spent the last weekend writing, and rewriting, her report, until it sounded interesting, even to her ears, leaving no time to type it. Thankfully, her mother did not mind. Melissa marveled at her mother's speedy fingers sprinting over the keys.

"There," Darlene pulled out the last sheet. "Will this do?"

Melissa looked over the pages and then hugged her mother. "Oh, yes! Thank you so much! You are the best mother. How can I ever repay you?"

"You could do the dishes," Steve called from the living room.

He was stretched out on the floor, coffee mug beside him, and playing a board game with Brian. It was a joke, of course. Whenever Steve stayed at the house, he and Brian washed dishes.

Brian drew a card. "Well, she could at least move the laundry."

"It's not my turn," Melissa said loftily. Who knew what creepy things were hiding in that basement.

Melissa brought her report to her bedroom, three-hole punched it, and threaded it into the purple folder her mother had bought to display it. Melissa leafed through it with satisfaction, admiring its layout. It really looked professional. Tomorrow afternoon, she would relinquish it to Mr. Masters. Melissa hoped he liked it.

Humming happily to the music box, yet wistful that her Bryony research had ended, Melissa slipped into pajamas and decided she was too tired even for a new book. With her head feeling stuffed with cotton, Melissa set her alarm clock, and floated to sleep, like mist, she sleepily thought.

Scooter was barking at her bedside. Fighting back sleep with each step, Melissa opened the screen door, and Scooter bounded away toward the distant, dark piano notes.

"Scooter!" she shouted, but the black night swallowed her words. She was inside Simons Woods. The music slowed. Far ahead, Scooter barked. Ice ran through her veins, but how could she leave him alone? He could get hurt or…worse.

Taking a deep breath, Melissa bolted far into the woods, shouting "Scooter!" The dog answered with faint barks. Darkness covered Melissa, but she ran until her legs collapsed. She panted and rubbed the cramp in her side. "Scooter!"

From the distance, he barked short, urgent barks, and the music rose a pitch. A fine, white mist weaved around the trees. How could she find him now?

"Hold on, Scooter!" Her voice was raspy from yelling. "I'm coming for you!"

Melissa stepped forward. *Wham!* She lay for a stunned moment, then cautiously lifted her head. Something latched onto her ankles. She screamed and kicked it away. A bryony vine twisted and curled on the ground. Her face and hands stung. Melissa rubbed her sticky face. Was it sap? Blood? Scooter barked again.

"Scooter!"

She pressed her hands on the ground, painfully stood up against the weight on her chest, and skidded on mud. Melissa teetered, panicked, and clutched the air. *Mud!* She was off the road! Trees enclosed her. An impenetrable mist coated her. Rapid music surrounded her. Scooter barked and barked, close to Melissa, behind a clump of brush.

Melissa clawed with frenzy at the grass. Scooter was not there. He barked again, close to her ear. She spun around. No dog. *Where was he?*

"Scooter!" The barking stopped. "Scooter!"

Melissa held her breath and strained to listen over the pounding in her ears and the low, hard chords. She took a step forward.

Nothing.

She inched deeper into the mist, and it closed around her like a curtain. A large shrub to her left rustled. The music stopped. "Scooter?" Melissa hoped her soft voice would soothe him. "Scooter?"

The bush shook again. Melissa waded through the weeds, farther into the woods. She paused every few paces, listening for a bark, a whimper, something.

A large animal dashed out from behind a tree and rushed past Melissa. She screamed and jumped back. This was no ordinary animal! It wore a full suit of clothes and ran on its hands and feet. The creature's long, golden hair—or was it a mane? — streamed behind it. Far off into the distance, Melissa heard Scooter bark again.

"Melissa!" Darlene yelled.

She startled and sprang to a sitting position. Her alarm clock, still beeping, lay flipped to one side on the floor. Scooter stood on her bed, barking, barking, barking. Melissa twisted over the bedside and pulled up the clock by its cord.

Her mother stuck her head around the door. "Are you okay, Melissa?"

"I'm fine, Mom," Melissa said, in a voice harsher than she had intended.

"I'm not trying to snoop. I didn't know if you had heard the alarm. Breakfast is ready." Her mother shut the door.

Melissa examined her hands. No scratches. She examined her face in the bathroom mirror. No scratches there, either.

All traces of her nightmare melted after she dressed and sat down to breakfast. She now worried about her report. At school, time tricked her. Her classes dragged. The hands on the clocks refused movement. Last period will never come, she thought.

When it did, an anxious Melissa surrendered her report to Mr. Masters. He returned it two days later, and she read his note with pure joy. *A well-researched, well-written paper that provides the reader a fascinating glimpse of Bryony Simons' life.*

Melissa received a B+, the highest grade in the class.
Ann's voiced was tinged with jealousy. "Well, no one ever gets an 'A' from him."

Melissa noticed Mr. Masters hadn't written anything on Ann's report. Melissa lingered after class to thank him for the compliment, but Mr. Masters declined it.

"Your hard work speaks for itself," he said. "The research is thorough, considering the limited amount of available information."

Melissa hadn't thought the information was limited, but if Mr. Masters wished to praise her, who was she to argue? The bus ride home was a bubble of ecstasy. She broadcasted her achievement at dinner, and everyone contributed appropriate lauds.

"It will be the Pulitzer Prize next," Steve teased her.

Melissa threw her paper napkin at his shirt.

"Now she'll act stuck up." Brian knelt beside her chair. "Your autograph, ma'am?"

Melissa raised her hand to whack him, but he ducked out of reach, bumping his head on the chair.

"Ow!" Brian rubbed his temple, but he was grinning when he did it. It was their mother's turn to surprise Melissa. "I invited Shelly, Laura, and Kimberly to the anniversary celebration. They will be here Friday after school. On Sunday, we'll have a festive birthday lunch before they leave."

Steve winked. "Unless eighteen is too old for birthday cake."

Melissa leaped out of her chair and threw her arms around her mother. Her eighteenth birthday would not be dismal, after all.

"Thank you!" she cried. "Now I know everything will be perfect from now on."

CHAPTER 7: THE CENTENNIAL

"Ok, now concentrate this time, Shelly," Melissa guided her friend's right arm.

Shelly blew her bangs out of the way and aimed the dart. "One, two, three, *throw!*"

Pop! The dart landed smack in the middle of an orange balloon.

"Hurray!" Shelly hugged Melissa, then untied her hair. The tapered cut softly framed her shining face.

"It's about time." Kimberly tossed her blonde head and loudly yawned.

Shelly just laughed. "Hey, not everyone's as coordinated as Laura."

Melissa was not as nonchalant as Shelly. She was jealous of Laura's precise aim. Laden with more prizes than she could carry, Laura gave a stuffed leopard and a hard-earned plastic penguin to two crying, little boys who didn't share her luck. Even so, Laura carried a rubber doll in one hand and a brightly colored, plush parrot in the other.

"Well, she can't top our brothers." Ann pointed toward the popcorn machine outside *Dalton's Dry Goods*. Brian and Clay were speeding toward the girls. Each boy held several, large stuffed animals.

"We've already given away five," Brian puffed from behind a giraffe's head.

"No, six." Clay balanced a rhinoceros on his hip and reached into his pocket.

"Five. You dropped the ugly rag doll to that fat girl, and I tossed the bear puppet to the boy who dropped his ice cream cone, and then you handed the squeaking ducks to the girls you thought were cute, and I gave my basketball pillow to my gym teacher, and then you...hey, you're right! That makes six."

"Want some cotton candy?" Clay held out a sticky, blue mass. The girls shook their heads, so he shuffled his back pocket and tried again. "Popcorn, then?" He held up a crumpled, grease-stained bag.

Laura wrinkled her nose and shook out shoulder-length, amber curls. "No!"

"Suit yourself!" Clay shoved the bag into his pocket. "Girls!"

"Come on!" Brian yanked Clay's sleeve and pointed to the roller coaster.

The boys sped toward the ride area, which spanned the entire roadway from the *Welcome to Munsonville* sign to where the shops began.

"Hey!" Melissa yelled after them. "Mom said be at the school by eleven!"

"Yeah, yeah!" Brian turned around and made a face at her.

After buying pink cotton candy and popcorn with extra butter, the girls walked toward the center of town. It had been a great weekend, and Melissa was sorry to see it end, although she had hardly seen her family. For two days, her mother and Steve had hosted formal tours of the mansion's estate. They also distributed an informational brochure Darlene had written. This included the floor plans Steve had shared and parts of Melissa's research paper. Melissa marveled to see her written work in print, but her mother had other thoughts.

"Maybe more outside people will support the restoration," Darlene had said.

A number of contests and activities had punctuated the weekend, like Saturday morning's walleye contest, which had been held at dawn. The competing fishermen heatedly bickered over each fish's weight and debated the integrity of contest guidelines. Judges determined that Bob Cooper had caught the largest fish. It weighed nearly twenty-four and a half pounds and measured just under forty inches long.

"That's one big fish," Laura said, yawning, as Jack's dad lumbered past to claim his prize. She hated waking up early. "How do you even catch something that large?"

"Well, you have to fish in deep, open water," Bob said.

Laura leaned next to Melissa's ear and whispered, "He's huge! No fish would stand a chance. Hey, what are those things hanging from his hat?"

"Lures."

"What?"

"They attract fish."

Melissa's essay did not win first place, although she secretly hoped it might, especially with Mr. Masters' praise written on top. Shelly took credit for inspiring Melissa to write it and admired the blue honorable mention ribbon.

"See, I told you it was a romantic story," Shelly said.

The girls linked arms and wandered amongst the displays in the library's gravel parking lot, but Shelly's remark unsettled Melissa. She felt strangely uncomfortable discussing Bryony in the bright afternoon sunlight, even with Shelly.

"Oh, look," Melissa said to hide her uneasiness. "Ann won third place."

Ann's research highlighted an obscure fact about the village's origins. Nearly two hundred years before Owen Munson visited the area, French fur trapper and fisherman Pierre Sicard had established a small community that had never thrived. During a trip to North America, Owen Munson purchased that land, assumed control, and named it after him.

Kimberly skimmed through the report. "I think Owen Munson still deserves the title of founder. He put the village on the map."

After a lakefront picnic breakfast Steve had packed, Melissa paraded the village's unique features before her friends: Main Street's quaint shops, Lake Munson's blue waters, and

Simons Woods. Laura loitered in Dalton's Dry Goods, admiring its merchandise, the wooden boards creaking under her feet. She held up a beaded necklace. "Who made this?"

"Ann's mother," Melissa said.

"Who's Ann?"

"My friend who won third place. She's stocking in the back room."

Laura bought the necklace and a white, peasant-style blouse, printed in forest green bryony vines and baby pink blossoms.

"To remember our fun this weekend," she said.

Unexpected tears jumped up, and Melissa fought them back. Bryony or no Bryony, Melissa missed Grover's Park and her friends. Life was unfair.

Before lunch, the girls took the official tour of the Simons estate. Her mother began near the mansion's spacious front porch with a brief summary of John Simons' life in Munsonville. Then she walked her group around the mansion's exterior, gesturing to its rooms and adding snippets of the village's restoration plans.

"They intend to use as many of the original furnishings as possible," Darlene said.

She led everyone to the rear grounds, pointing out its former gardens and how much of their spirit village officials might recapture. Only Kimberly lingered near the mansion, while contemplating it with a far-away look in her eyes.

Shelly nudged Melissa. "What's up with her?"

Melissa sighed. "Who knows with Kimberly?"

Kimberly often distanced herself from their group. Despite flawless beauty and near-genius intelligence, Kimberly could be cold, aloof, and restless for something Grover's Park could not offer. Twice Kimberly had run away, and twice the police had brought her home, or so she had claimed. You could never be certain with Kimberly.

"You go ahead," Melissa said. "I'll wait for Kimberly to catch up."

"Are you sure?"

"Sure. It's not like I've never seen the estate."

Shelly darted after the others. Melissa leaned against a tree. For a long time, Kimberly stayed riveted on an upstairs window.

Then, she jerked a little, as if waking from a dream, and shielded her eyes against the sun. Melissa waved at her. Kimberly flashed the peace sign and ran to Melissa.

"What's up?" Melissa said.

"Nothing. I was just thinking."

The girls skipped the food booths in favor of Sue's Diner, which, despite the outdoor activities, overflowed with people. While waiting for a booth, her friends studied the rusty table legs, faded floral curtains, and the stained blond paneling. Just when Melissa opened her mouth to praise the food, Jack rushed past them with a tray full of dirty dishes.

Laura nudged Melissa in the ribs. "Gosh, he's cute. Who is he?"

"Jack Cooper. His family owns the diner. His dad won the fishing contest."

Kimberly overheard them and winked. The next time Jack trotted by them, she ran a finger through her hair and smiled at him. Jack tripped on a hump in the threadbare carpet and almost dropped the water pitcher. Red-faced, he quickly filled the glasses at the table nearest them. Three of the men sitting there wore overalls and the fourth, in a three-piece suit and dark, horn-rimmed glasses, had a briefcase against his chair.

"Wow, that Jack Cooper's really small town, isn't he?" Kimberly said.

Melissa said nothing, embarrassed for Jack. Then, a waitress came
and everyone, except Melissa, forgot about Kimberly's stunt. Most of the girls stuck to cheeseburgers and potato chips, but Kimberly ordered the day's special, lemon chicken with caramelized onions. Shelly shared the latest drama at her house. Melissa absently stirred her ice with a straw. Laura ate breadsticks and eyed Jack. Kimberly placidly watched the crowds from the window.

"Where do people park?" Kimberly asked.

"Are you blind?" Shelly said. "People are parking every-where."

"There are spots behind the buildings," Melissa said, "but unless people are leaving town, hardly anyone drives."

"That's not what I meant," Kimberly said, scanning the dining room.

At sundown, Ann joined Melissa's old group. Melissa screamed herself hoarse on the roller coaster but had as much fun gushing over the attractive band members that played two sets in the school parking lot. Melissa sighed over the blond lead singer, but Shelly insisted the guitar player's large arm muscles were much sexier than any singing.

"Look at the way he moves when he plays," Shelly said. "Isn't he too much?"

"Not as much as the drummer," Ann said.

"You haven't seen Jason Frye," Laura said, but her eyes moved over the bassist.

Only Kimberly abstained from their merriment. She disappeared several times that night, and twice, wandered to the mouth of the woods. The last time Kimberly rejoined the group, Shelly finally asked, "Are you feeling okay? You look a little pale."

"It must be the moonlight." Kimberly's gaze swept over the lake and back to Simons Woods. What did Kimberly find so interesting?

At eleven o'clock, during the band's final song, Steve and her mother drove up in Steve's pick-up truck.

"Hop in," Steve called.

Brian and Clay, laden with more stuffed animals, were lounging in the back. Shelly plopped beside them and eyed their loot. "That is so unfair. How'd you guys do it?" Clay and Brian looked at each other and giggled.

"Trade secret," Clay said. "Superior talent," Brian added.

Shelly and Ann pounced on the boys and pretended to beat them up. The boys giggled some more and hid behind their stuffed animals.

"Hey, cut it out," Clay yelled. "I gotta pee."

Kimberly sat back to back with Laura and silently pondered the night. Steve took Clay home, and then swung the truck onto the hill that led to the Simons estate.

"Why couldn't we go inside the mansion?" Kimberly said.

"People will, someday," Melissa said, "but not until the restoration is complete. It's not safe, I guess."

"Hmm," Kimberly said.

She remained quiet, even after the girls had donned pajamas, brushed their teeth, and settled into sleeping bags. Scooter slipped into the room, as Kimberly shut the door.

"Out!" Melissa collared him and opened the door.

"Oh, let him stay." Kimberly flicked her hair behind her shoulder and watched the gold strands fall perfectly into place. "He's not hurting anybody."

Shelly fumbled with the zipper and complained about her weekend babysitting job for a family of four children.

"They are so adorable, except the three-year-old. The brat picks his nose, and, when I make him go to bed, he spits on me. I'm ready to quit."

Laura was working at Pizza Express, washing dishes. Jason had finally asked her out, but her parents had said no.

"He's only nineteen," an indignant Laura cried. "I don't get it."

"My parents wouldn't care," Shelly said, picking off an imaginary piece of lint from her sleeping bag, "but he didn't ask me. I wish he would."

To Melissa's surprise, she scarcely remembered how Jason looked. She tried picturing him, but only saw Jack Cooper's crew cut and shy smile. Ann changed the subject. "Did you know Simons Mansion is haunted?"

Laura's eyes grew round and large. "Haunted?"

Ann nodded, and her face was so serious Melissa couldn't decide if Ann believed the stories. "They say it's John Simons, roaming the mansion at night and playing piano."

"Wow!" Shelly said, reaching for her brush. "Have you seen the ghost, Melissa?

Melissa shook her head and looked away, but Laura cried, "I don't believe you!"

"I did see something, but it wasn't a ghost."

Melissa explained what happened her first day in Munsonville and the time she stayed too late at the library. Kimberly pensively scratched Scooter's belly.

"I don't believe in ghosts," Kimberly said, "and not I'm scared of any mist, either. People have invented those stories to make their hick, little village seem intriguing. How sad they can only boast about some musician who died a century ago."

Her words ruffled Shelly, and she stopped brushing. "I think Melissa's very brave. You try walking through some mist and finding out hours had passed!"

Kimberly lifted her chin, and her eyes glittered with an unearthly light. "I don't think that Simons Mansion is dangerous; and I *don't* think that old mansion will be restored. It's a publicity ploy to make people come here."

"That's easy to say," Laura said, "because you can't prove it."

"Oh, no? I can prove it, all right. Want to see?"

Kimberly threw off the sleeping bag, grabbed her clothes from Melissa's desk chair, and stalked out of the bedroom. In the distance, the girls heard the bathroom door close. Ann looked quizzically at Melissa, but Melissa merely shrugged.

"Kimberly's just showing off," Melissa said. "She's not going out."

"I sure hope not."

Laura yawned and zipped her sleeping bag. She had just closed her eyes when Kimberly returned to Melissa's room, fully dressed. "Coming?"

"Uh, where?" Shelly said, glancing at Melissa.

"To the mansion." Kimberly sounded impatient. "I'm going after the ghost."

The girls looked at each other and then back at Kimberly. It was past midnight. Although Melissa didn't believe John Simons haunted his mansion, she didn't relish wandering around his estate at night. No one said a word. They never crossed Kimberly.

They simply got dressed, even Ann.

"Thought so," Kimberly said. "Melissa, do you have a flashlight?"

Melissa tiptoed past Steve, who lay snoring on the couch, and into the kitchen. The other girls crept behind her. By the dim light above the kitchen sink, Melissa opened the junk drawer to view its contents, a jumbled mess of masking tape, extension cords, screws, bolts, and way in the back, an old, scuffed, yellow flashlight.

She snapped it on and off and handed it to Kimberly. Then Melissa grabbed her jacket from its hook, steeled herself, and faced Kimberly. "This isn't a good idea."

68

An impish smile danced on Kimberly's lips.

"Come on." Her voice was soft. "Let's go meet John Simons face to face."

Shelly and Laura glanced at each other. Inwardly cursing her timidity, Melissa cracked open the back door. Scooter rushed into the kitchen, whining, wagging his tail, and gazing up at them with pleading eyes.

"Can we take him with us?" Shelly said, hopefully.

"Of course not," Kimberly said. "He'll scare away the ghost."

"That's the point."

Kimberly stared at Shelly with contempt, but Laura still looked grave. "You almost sound as if you believe the ghost is real," Laura said.

"Of course, I don't think the ghost is real," Kimberly rolled her eyes and impatiently shook her head, "but I want to see for myself. Don't you?"

"Why is this so important to you?" Ann's voice was low, but authoritative.

"To prove to you backwoods Munsonvillers there is no such thing as a ghost."

Melissa flushed at this insult toward Ann, who marched right up to Kimberly.

"We backwoods villagers don't believe in ghosts, but we do have enough manners not to let naïve, moronic, city folks hurt themselves over their own stupidity."

Ann stomped out the back door. The other girls slowly followed her. Kimberly's face reddened at Ann's outburst, and, for once, she offered no smart reply. Scooter gave a sharp, little bark at the prospect of a walk, but Melissa shushed him, saying, "Be good, and I'll give you a treat when I get back."

Melissa shut the door, extinguishing the light; Shelly gasped; and Laura squeaked, "I can't do it!"

A beam of light broke the blackness, and the girls relaxed slightly. Kimberly had switched on the flashlight.

Despite her familiarity with the estate by day, the shadows of the tree branches and the unknown sounds of the night toyed with Melissa's sense of direction. She remembered the unexplainable mist and her nightmare of a few days ago, and she wished she had brought Scooter with them. Melissa glanced at Ann. Whether or not her friend believed in ghost tales, Ann was too smart to enter a crumbling building at night. Kimberly held no such reservations and led the little party with quick, confident steps. Shelly's teeth chattered from fright. In the dim light, Laura's face was grim. A twig snapped beneath Shelly's feet, and she squealed. Kimberly whirled around and shone the light in Shelly's face.

"Quiet!" Kimberly hissed.

Shelly whimpered and snuggled into Melissa.

"Your friend is crazy," Ann whispered. "Make her go back."

Melissa took a deep breath and called out, "Kimberly, you win! Let's forget it!"

Kimberly only quickened her pace, and the other girls struggled to keep up.

"Tell her again," Ann said.

Melissa tried once more. "We only have one flashlight! It's too dark too see!"

Kimberly walked faster. Terror plainly showed on Laura's face, so Melissa shouted, "I'll probably get grounded!" That excuse sounded lame even to Melissa's ears, so she tried again. "Someone might get hurt!"

"Why won't she listen?" Shelly clenched her rattling teeth so she could speak.

Simons Mansion loomed ahead of them, distorted and menacing through the flashlight's narrow beam. Shelly shrank closer to Melissa and wailed, "Let's go home!"

Kimberly abruptly stopped and pitched the flashlight to Laura.

"You 'fraidy cats can leave," Kimberly said, "but I'm going in there."

Ann's eyes widened in horror. "You mean, inside Simons Mansion?"

Kimberly smiled a wicked, little smile and tossed her head. "It's the best place to meet up with a ghost." She spun around and fled into the night.

"No!" Laura screamed, dropping the flashlight and plunging them into darkness.

70

Ann groped along the ground. "Got it!" She swerved the light from side to side. Kimberly had disappeared.

"Kimberly! Kimberly!" Melissa yelled, despite her galloping heart.

Shelly clung to Melissa and cried. Steve had warned them about Simons Mansion. Now, Kimberly might be in there, alone, in the secluded, dangerous blackness.

Shelly clutched Melissa's arm. "What if she trips or falls through a hole?"

"We need help." Panic rose in Laura's voice. "Now!"

They ran as fast as the flashlight allowed. The servant's quarters seemed miles away. Melissa's leg muscles burned, and her breath hurt in her throat, but she was too terrified to slow down, even for a second.

"My stomach hurts," Shelly panted. She clutched her side, but continued jogging.

"So does mine," Ann gasped, lagging behind them.

Melissa started to say, "Mine, too," when Laura cried, "Ow!"

Ann stopped and shone the light in the direction of the cry. Laura had tripped on an old tree stump, nearly level with the ground. Melissa and Shelly each grabbed an arm and pulled her up.

"Can you walk?" Ann said.

Laura stepped on her left foot and winced. "I think so. It only hurts a little."

The girls slowed their pace for Laura. Gradually, the stitch in Melissa's side relaxed. The porch light on the cottage's side door welcomed her like a beacon of hope, although Ann would not switch off the flashlight. Melissa dashed for the back door, turned the knob, and her stomach dropped. The door was locked.

CHAPTER 8: THE NIGHT IS DARKEST

It seemed hours before their pounding woke Steve. Finally, the door moved an inch. The girls shoved past him.

Steve stood dazed and unsteady, but he quickly ushered them into the living room. "Sit down." He switched on the table lamp. "What happened?"

Loud, garbled, hysterical words tumbled from their mouths. Disbelief crossed Steve's face, and he ran a hand through his hair.

"One at a time!"

"Kimberly's lost!" Shelly shouted.

"The ghost has her," Laura cried.

"She wouldn't stop!" Ann yelled.

"Steve, you've got to find her!" Melissa said in strained voice.

He rushed to the phone. This was the angriest Melissa had ever seen him, worse than the day she had come home at midnight.

"The police will be here shortly," Steve said. "Why didn't you wake me sooner?"

The girls sobered somewhat at the word "police." Stunned, Melissa stopped talking, but Shelly and Laura frantically babbled about Kimberly. Ann nudged Melissa and whispered, "I'm in big trouble. My uncle's on duty tonight."

Steve banged on her mother's door. "Darlene!"

The knob rattled, and her mother, half-awake, stumbled from the bedroom. She blinked at the light and the loud confusion in the living room.

"Kimberly's lost." Steve turned back. "Quiet!"

She leaned against the wall, yawning, and rubbing her eyes. "What?"

"Apparently, the girls took a midnight exploration of the mansion."

With a little gasp, she covered her mouth, ran into her room, and quickly returned with her personal phone book, the blue corduroy one, the last birthday present from Melissa's father. Melissa, ashamed, closed her eyes. What would he think of her, now?

Steve made a pot of coffee. As he returned, Darlene hung up the phone and said, "Kimberly's parents will be here before morning. How will I face them?"

With half-shut eyes, Brian tripped out of his bedroom. He stopped short at the wailing girls, his mother bracing against Steve for support, the loud knock at the door, and the words, "Munsonville police!" Shocked, he dropped into a chair, not embarrassed by his rumpled pajamas or hair sticking up at gravity-defying angles. He did not mock Kimberly's stupidity or crack blonde jokes. Brian simply sat.

Coffee in hand, Steve strode across the room to open the door. Two officers entered. Melissa started, gave a little cry, and immediately covered her mouth. She recognized the younger one, whom Steve introduced as Officer Will Miller. He had been the cute lead singer in the centennial band. The husky, older man, Sergeant Gabe Swenson, looked just like Ann's mother, except he had a mustache. Melissa turned around to look at her friend, but Ann, still gripping the flashlight, found the patchwork placemats more interesting than the forbidding policemen.

Officer Will slid a notebook from his shirt pocket. "Name of the missing girl?"

Shelly put her face in her hands and sobbed. Laura giggled nervously.

"Well?" asked Sergeant Gabe, but his attention was on Ann.

Melissa looked anxiously at her mother, who nodded with an encouraging smile.

"Kimberly Whitney, sir." Melissa swallowed hard to squelch her trembling voice.

The only sound in the room was the scratching of Officer Will's pen. "Age?"

"Seventeen."

"Town?"

The rapid firing of questions flustered Melissa. Officer Will, pen poised over the notepad, repeated, "Town?"

"Um, Grover's Park, Illinois, sir."

He scribbled it and gazed right at her. Melissa wished he had done so during the concert when circumstances were different.

"What does Kimberly look like?" he asked.

"Like us, I guess, except she has straight blonde hair and blue eyes."

"Long lashes, too," Laura added. "She's really pretty."

Officer Will quickly looked down, but Melissa swore she first saw a glimmer of recognition in his eyes. "She's only seventeen?" His voice shook, but he cleared his throat twice and added, "Was she down on Main Street with you tonight?"

"Yes," Laura said. "Is that important?"

His cheeks turned bright pink, but he only said, "When did you last see her?"

Melissa bit her lip, but it quivered anyway. "In the woods." Her voice sounded small. She closed her eyes against the sight of Kimberly fleeing into the darkness.

"How long ago?"

"I...don't know."

Ann spoke up. "Maybe half an hour? We were near the mansion when she threw the flashlight at us and ran off."

Sergeant Gabe snorted. "And you didn't try looking for her?"

"In the dark?"

The two officers exchanged glances. Melissa shifted her eyes away from the handcuffs hanging from their belts. Would they arrest the girls?

Sergeant Gabe crossed the room and bellowed, "Ann, what in God's name were you doing near the mansion?"

"She wanted to explore it." Ann kept her attention on the placemats.

Shelly glanced up. "We couldn't let her go by herself."

"It wouldn't have been safe," Laura added.

Sergeant Gabe only saw Ann. "Why didn't you get an adult?"

Ann shrugged and set down the flashlight.

Officer Will tapped his pen on the notepad. "Did you girls have an argument?"

"Nooo," Shelly said slowly. "She just left." "Just like that?" Sergeant Gabe mocked her.

"Just like that." Ann twisted a loose thread between her fingers until it snapped.

Panic crossed Shelly's face. "Sir, we're not making it up."

"That's what really happened," echoed Laura. "You do believe us, don't you?"

Melissa looked at Steve for reassurance, but the expression on his face was grim. She wouldn't find any comfort from him.

Officer Will turned a page. "Has Kimberly ever talked about running away?"

Shelly vigorously shook her head and blew hair away from her mouth. "Never!"

Melissa's insides twisted at Shelly's bold lie. She hoped neither officer asked her.

"Did she talk to any strangers at the centennial?"

"She was with us the entire time." Melissa hoped it sounded like the truth.

Sergeant Gabe sighed and scratched under his cap. "How did she behave? Did she do anything out of character?"

"No," Laura said. "She acted like herself."

Officer Will looked at Steve. "Has someone notified Kimberly's parents?"

"I called them," Darlene assured him. "They're on their way."

Sergeant Gabe gave Ann one last withering stare. "If you were my daughter...." he began. "Come on, Will. Let's take a look. She can't have gotten very far."

Steve accompanied them to the door. "You'll keep us posted?"

"We'll probably have her in custody within the hour, scared out of her wits," Sergeant Gabe said, with a curt nod at her mother. "Ma'am."

The police left. Melissa felt too numb to say or do anything. She perched on the edge of the worn seat cushion and wound a strand of hair around her finger. Shelly huddled by Melissa and wept openly on her shoulder. Laura crouched in a corner of the recliner and hugged her knees, tears rolling down her cheeks. Ann rested her face in one hand and gazed into space. Steve paced the floor, pausing only to accept a coffee refill.

"We're really sorry, Mrs. Marchellis," Laura said. "We'll tell Kimberly's parents this was our fault."

At the sound of Laura's voice, Steve stopped pacing and stared at the girls. "Get to bed, now! Not a single peep until morning!"

No one moved. Melissa, who had never received such an order from Steve, appealed to her mother. "Can't we wait until we know she's okay?"

Her mother glanced at Steve, but he remained firm. "The police are handling this," he said to the girls, although he looked at Darlene. She wavered, then sat on the couch between Melissa and Shelly and hugged them both.

"I'm sure she's fine," Darlene said. "The police will probably have her at the station before her parents arrive. She'll be in more trouble when she gets home!"

Since it was pointless to continue arguing, Melissa shuffled to her bedroom, with her friends behind her. No one slept. They whispered in the dark.

"I hope she's okay," Shelly said, "wherever she is."

"I know this sounds crazy," Laura said, "but what if the ghost is real? What if Kimberly met him? What if he....?"

76

No one spoke. Then Ann firmly said, "There's no such thing as a ghost." However, Melissa remembered the dreadful mist and wondered.

Tired from the centennial celebration and their midnight jaunt, one by one, the girls' voices faded into silence, but sleep eluded Melissa. She recalled the questioning.

"Did she do anything out of character?" Sergeant Gabe had asked.
"No," Laura had said. *"She acted like herself."*

Yet, all weekend, Melissa had noticed subtle, disquieting signs: Kimberly's fascination with the mansion's upstairs window and the woods, her disappearances, and her quiet preoccupation all night. Was exploring the mansion a smokescreen for other plans? Kimberly had no reason to run away. The only child of rich parents, Kimberly usually got what she wanted. Melissa hoped vanishing was not one of those things.

Determined to fall asleep, Melissa fluffed up her pillows and rolled onto her side. Soon, she felt hot and kicked off the sheet, and then she was cold and pulled it up again. Now, she was thirsty.

The muffled intonations behind her mother's bedroom door meant she and Steve were still awake, so Melissa tiptoed to the kitchen. Holding her breath, she pried opened the squeaky wooden cabinet near the sink and removed a glass. She ran the water in a trickle. The normalcy of the act relaxed her. As she drank, she glanced at Scooter's food and water bowl. Both were full. How odd. Scooter never left food. That's when Melissa realized she had not seen Scooter since they had left the house with Kimberly.

"Here, boy. Here Scooter," Melissa called softly.

The dog did not respond. She turned off the kitchen light, then wandered to Brian's room and peeked inside. Brian was sleeping. Scooter was not there. He was probably in her mother's bedroom.

Yawning, Melissa crept back to her room. Without a sound, she eased the door shut, tiptoed around the sleeping bags, and climbed into bed. Before drawing up the bedcovers, Melissa took the music box from her nightstand, traced the vines, and then wound it up. She settled into the pillows and floated away on its tinkling.

As Melissa sank into sleep, the faint notes grew loud and incessant, until grand piano sounds filled the concert hall. Melissa, in full evening dress, sat enraptured, face shining with joy, as she clapped long and hard with the rest of the audience. Behind her, the low tones of a man's familiar voice said, "Everyone's asleep. Better not disturb them until morning." Melissa turned to see who was talking. It was Steve, in a green pocket T- shirt with a yellow pencil propped behind his left ear and a lock of hair over his forehead. Kimberly's father knitted his eyebrows together, and Kimberly's mother clenched her hands until her knuckles blanched. Why were they attending the concert? Shouldn't they be searching for Kimberly?

Melissa rolled over in bed and woke up. The hands on her alarm clock pointed to four-thirty. The other girls still slept. She heard the barely audible voices of her mother and Steve talking with Kimberly's parents in the living room. They must have flown here, she thought, her mind fuzzy with sleep. The Whitneys owned a small plane.

The weather was sunny and mild, so she strolled to the middle of Simons Woods. Instantly, the sky blackened; the slight breeze shrieked into a gale and whipped Melissa's hair around her face. She tried to scream, but thick, white mist strangled her. Melissa bolted upright. The mist danced at her window, and hazy moonlight filled the room. Spellbound, Melissa glided over and gazed upward at the gigantic moon, brilliant as noonday. She opened the window, raised the screen, rested her elbows on the ledge, and bathed in the moonlight's splendor. Near the trees, a shadowy figure stretched out his arms, lifted something white, and brought it to his lips. The white was so bright in the darkness that Melissa wondered if the figure was clutching a piece of the moon. The white bled and drenched the figure's arms. Melissa screamed in horror and sat up. Sweat ran down her face. A pair of arms encircled her neck, and Laura cried, "It's okay, Melissa; it's okay."

Still groggy, Melissa dug her face into the pillow and fell back into bottomless, dreamless, endless sleep. When she stirred, sunshine, not moonlight greeted her. She had overslept! Then the

78

previous night's terror flooded her mind. The room was empty. Her friends were awake. Melissa pushed away the sheets.

A tearful Brian tore into the room and jumped on her bed. "Oh, Liss, it's awful!" He threw himself on Melissa and cried hard. "Oh, Scooter!"

Melissa hugged him close, but cold tongues licked up her back. She swallowed twice and said in a low voice, "Brian, where's Scooter?"

Steve dashed into Melissa's bedroom. "Out! I warned you not to bother her."

Brian only burrowed deeper into her shoulder. Melissa turned bewildered eyes at Steve. "Is Scooter okay?"

Steve folded his arms and looked at the floor. "No, Melissa, Scooter is not okay. Brian found him outside this morning."

Melissa leaped out of bed and started for the door, but Steve blocked her way.

"Scooter got out last night and...some animal tore him apart."

The morning passed in a fog. Steve ordered everyone into the house until he buried Scooter in the back yard, underneath a large oak tree that Brian insisted was Scooter's favorite place to squat. Melissa was too heartbroken over the loss of the little dog to make Brian pick a more appropriate site. After a breakfast no one ate, everyone gathered around the fresh mound and offered kind words about Scooter. A desolate Brian scavenged near the woods for wildflowers to stick in the soft earth at Scooter's grave.

"You can get another dog," Shelly said soothingly.

Brian's eyes filled with tears. He stuck out his tongue and ran inside. Shelly's mother arrived after lunch to drive the other two girls back to Grover's Park. Kimberly's parents checked into Munsonville Inn to wait for their daughter. No one mentioned Melissa's birthday. That night, on her way to bed, Melissa heard Steve say, "The poor kid," so she tiptoed to the door.

"I hate to be callous, Steve, but Kimberly's pulled other stunts like this."

"She has? And Melissa associates with her? That doesn't sound like you."

Kimberly had often boasted how hitchhiking was easy if you swindled the right sucker. Could Kimberly have outwitted the wrong person?

Her mother sighed. "They'd been friends since kindergarten, so Frank saw no harm if they stayed in a group. I guess we were wrong."

Melissa stumbled away from the door and into bed, curled into a tight ball, and squeezed the pillow around her head. Too forlorn to cry, she muttered, "Happy Birthday, Melissa," and lay awake a long time.

The week brought no relief. On Saturday, Melissa slumped at her desk and pretended to study. The weather was dull and rainy, but it had been dull and rainy all week, which suited Melissa. The weather perfectly matched her spirits.

Her father was dead; Grandma was dead; Scooter was dead; and Kimberly might very well be dead. The police had still not found her. Where had she gone? Melissa pushed her book away, leaned her elbows on the desk, and cupped her cheeks. She stared blankly through the window and into the gray haze. The police had searched the mansion but had found no evidence of Kimberly. Posters detailing the disappearance hung all over the village, but authorities had no leads. Even a thorough investigation of the estate and woods proved fruitless. Twice, the police had returned and repeated their questioning, but Melissa could add nothing to her original story. Heartbroken and threatening lawsuits, Kimberly's parents returned home. Melissa had cried until she could cry no more, not the way she had planned ending her childhood.

A knock halted Melissa's thoughts. "Like a break?" Her mother held out a steaming mug.

When Melissa was little, a cup of hot chocolate in her favorite purple mug soothed her. When Melissa did not answer, her mother set the drink on the desk, sat on the bed, and motioned. Melissa flew to her side. Her mother kissed the top of her Melissa's head and rubbed Melissa's back. Melissa, feeling little again and liking it, nestled close. No wonder her father had called her mother Florence Nightingale.

"Oh, Melissa," Darlene said. "I wish I could fix it, but everything considered, I think you're handling it well. Your father would be proud of you."

Unbidden tears flowed from Melissa's eyes. She threw her arms around her mother's waist. "I miss him, Mommy! I want him back!"

Her mother wrapped her arms tighter around Melissa. "I do, too, but think of it. He's probably wandering around heaven and taking pictures of everything he sees."

The thought of her father living above the clouds, strolling on golden streets, and snapping his camera strangely cheered Melissa. Her sagging spirits rose high enough for her to settle back at her desk, sip the familiar balm, and muddle through assignments.

That evening, they celebrated Melissa's birthday with a few presents, a cake from Sue's Diner, and a board game. Somewhat consoled, Melissa munched on corn chips dipped in Steve's special corn dip and laughed hard when Brian bought property, developed it, and then watched, chagrined, as the dice rolled everyone past it.

"No fair!" Brian called out more than once. Yet, no one was surprised when he won the game and lorded it over everyone.

"That's enough, young man," Steve said. He began picking up the pieces and setting them back into the box. "No one likes a sore winner."

Melissa's upbeat mood persisted as she dressed for bed. She bundled between the covers with her new mystery book and drowsed over its pages, until she stood outside Simons Mansion. The moonless night was dark and still. No leaves rustled; no crickets chirped; and no owls hooted. Melissa's flashlight penetrated the black shield around her, and she squinted through the waning light. How long since anyone had changed those batteries? Melissa hoped they lasted until she found Kimberly and brought her home.

"Kimberly!"

No answer. Melissa held her breath and listened hard, but she heard nothing except empty silence and the thudding of her heart.

"Kimberly!"

She swung her flashlight from side to side.

"Kimberly!"

The night swallowed up the light. Melissa banged the flashlight on the palm of her hand, but it wouldn't turn on. She banged it again, harder this time. Now what?

Then, out of the blackness, Kimberly appeared.

Gone were the tied blouses and hip hugger jeans. Kimberly wore a fluttering white gown and carried a long, white tapered candle. The melting wax dripped unheeded onto Kimberly's fingers. Her hair, straighter and blonder than ever, hung far past her knees. Kimberly did not speak, and her vacant eyes looked past Melissa, but with a dip of her hand, she summoned Melissa. Not wishing to lose track of Kimberly twice, but scared nonetheless, Melissa took halting steps up the mansion's steep stone stairs to its wide front porch.

Self-composed and self-assured, as if she belonged there, Kimberly swung the front door noiselessly inward. Melissa wavered, but Kimberly twisted her head to see if Melissa had followed. Melissa hesitated again, but only for a second. She entered the chasm-like house, illuminated only by Kimberly's candle.

With quick, light, sure-footed steps, Kimberly steered Melissa to the very back of the mansion. Melissa shuffled after her, groping her way. Every groan of the floorboards jumped-started her heart. The dust watered her eyes. Once, she sneezed.

Kimberly paused before a closet door then, to Melissa's dismay, she opened it and pushed on the back wall. It swung open, revealing a staircase, not a closet. Kimberly descended those stairs as naturally as if she had done it a hundred times. Too frightened to be upstairs alone in the dark, Melissa crept down into the cold, damp basement. At the bottom, she saw a small, square room, almost too small for the rest of the house. A dark, narrow corridor veered to the left, and Kimberly followed it, taking the light with her. Melissa quickened her pace, but the blackness absorbed Kimberly. Melissa was really scared now. What if she lost her way? What if she tripped?

Ahead, the light reappeared. As Melissa walked closer, the light grew steadily larger. Kimberly stood motionless in front of a stone wall. Her back was to Melissa; her outstretched arm held the candle away from her gown. The flame now blazed high, almost to the ceiling, and cast menacing shadows on the wall. How bizarre that the entire passageway led only to a dead end.

She had nearly reached her friend. With slow, jerking motions, Kimberly rotated toward Melissa. Her icy blue eyes widened in fury. She opened her mouth. Her teeth were white and sharp.

"Meow," Kimberly said.

CHAPTER 9: THE MUSIC BOX

"Me-ow," wailed the white cat at the back door. She pressed her little, pink nose against the glass and pleaded to the house's occupants for entrance.

Brian dropped his spoon into the cereal bowl, sloshing milk over the sides. He turned wheedling eyes on his mother, who refused to budge.

"For the hundredth time, no! We are not keeping that cat."

"But Mom, it's freezing outside. Now that Scooter's gone…." Brian's voice broke. "I mean, what if Scooter was cold and hungry and no one let him in?"

Melissa heard the crunch of gravel; Steve's truck had pulled into the yard. Before their mother could answer Brian, Steve had opened the back door. The cat ran inside and hid under the dining room table. Incensed, Darlene threw down her napkin in frustration.

"Thanks a lot, Steve!"

Steve simply opened the cupboard, removed a small tin of tuna, and emptied its contents onto a paper plate, which he set beside the cat. In minutes, the white cat gobbled it up, then sniffed around for more and turned hopeful eyes on Steve. Their mother stomped to her bedroom and slammed the door. Steve rumpled Brian's hair.

"Let me talk to your ma, and then we'll go into the village for real cat food and a litter box. In the meantime, think of names for her. We'll pick the best one."

"How do you know it's a she?"

Steve squatted and reached under the table. He flipped the cat over and then placed it on Brian's lap. "It's a she," he said, grinning. Steve knocked on their mother's door and opened it when she did not respond. Melissa heard him say, "Darlene, don't you think...." before the bedroom door closed.

Consoled, Brian rubbed behind the cat's ears and under her neck. Her snow-white fur was very clean, considering she was a stray. With a regal look on her angelic face, the cat tucked her paws under her stomach and gazed about the room. How did a small cat end up deep in the woods?

"She likes it here," Brian said in awe.

The cat turned its strikingly clear blue eyes on Melissa. Didn't all cats have green eyes? Melissa lightly touched the soft fur, and the cat rewarded her with a loud purr.

"Listen." Brian laid his ear on her back. "It sounds like a motor."

That's when Melissa noticed the odd way the cat held its head, in a cocked position, as if she was listening hard to something. She showed Steve when he came into the dining room. He took the cat from Brian, eased it into the crook of his arm, and felt around her neck. With keen eyes, the cat observed each of Steve's movements.

"She doesn't seem to be hurting." Steve returned the cat to Brian. "I'll talk to the vet. She'll need her shots, anyway." He walked into the bathroom.

Brian stroked the cat's silky fur and stared at the wall, still considering names. Melissa's mind wandered back to her queer dream about Kimberly. Had she really gone into the house as Melissa dreamed? Perhaps, despite a thorough police search, Kimberly was lying inside, hurt, with no one to help her. Maybe, John Simons' ghost really did exist and had captured her. Melissa immediately dismissed the ridiculous idea. Everyone knew ghosts weren't real.

Still petting the cat and on cue, Brian leaned back in the chair. "So, what do you think happened to Kimberly, Liss? Do you think the ghost got her?"

His question surprised Melissa. Brian had never mentioned Kimberly's disappearance, perhaps because, for him, the subsequent loss of Scooter overshadowed it.

Before Melissa could answer, Steve reappeared. "Ready to go?"

Brian nodded and stood up. "Here, Liss, take her while I get my coat." He held the cat out to her, and Melissa cradled it in her arms.

Steve looked at Melissa. "Do you want to come with us?"

Melissa shook her head. "I've got a lot of homework." She hoped it sounded true.

"Why not go to the library for an hour? A change of scenery might be good."

Melissa hurried for her jacket, amazed Steve had discerned her feelings. She almost didn't mind sitting cramped next to Brian. She checked for mist, then she remembered how she had merged her dream of Kimberly with the stray cat and decided she couldn't always trust her senses. Steve and Brian discussed and rejected several cat names.

"Okay, Melissa, out you go," Steve said. "Brian, open the door for your sister."

"Oh!" she said in surprise. "I didn't know we were here already."

Melissa started to crawl over Brian, but he yelled, "Hey, stop!"

Startled, Melissa drew back. Brian shielded the cat with his body and looked at her with cross, accusing eyes. "You almost landed on her!"

"I didn't." Melissa left the truck for real this time. "You're being dramatic."

"It's against the law to hurt defenseless animals, you know!"

"Brian…." Steve began.

Melissa shut the door, cutting off Steve's remark. Mrs. Clements hailed her with a smile and a wave of her hand.

"Here's a brand-new mystery book I saved," Mrs. Clements said, handing it to her. "I haven't seen you since the research paper."

"Thanks!"

Melissa settled into the couch and opened the book. All too soon, she heard Brian's voice at the front desk. She glanced at her watch. An entire hour had passed! Melissa hurried to meet her brother.

"I still have to check out," she told him.

"Okay. I'll tell Steve."

After Mrs. Clements had already returned Melissa's library card, she reached under the counter. "I almost forgot. Here's something else you might like." She handed Melissa a record album. "This just came in."

The top of the cover read, *The Best-Loved Compositions of John Simons*, and featured a picture of the musician sitting at a piano. Melissa turned the album over to the back and blinked in disbelief. She was face to face with her grandmother's music box.

Mrs. Clements smiled wistfully at her. "It's beautiful, isn't it? I suppose you're familiar with its history, from when you wrote your paper?"

Melissa shook her head. Was Mrs. Clements also smitten with the local love legend? Melissa couldn't blame her if she was. Bryony's story was sheer magic.

"John Simons composed a piece for Bryony as a wedding present. He performed it at the end of every concert. It became his signature piece."

Melissa stifled a yawn. She already knew that.

"As part of that wedding present, John Simons ordered this custom music box, so she could always hear that song. After Bryony died, the music box disappeared. Are you sure I didn't mention this to you?"

"The music box isn't gone, it's…."

Melissa stopped herself. Her mother had said the village was seeking original pieces for the restoration. No one must know she owned Bryony's music box. She could not risk losing it.

"I mean, thanks, Mrs. Clements."

Steve and Brian, cat reclining comfortably on his lap, were waiting for her in the truck. Melissa faced the music box picture down and placed her library book on top, but Steve noticed anyway.

"What've you got there, Melissa?"

"Oh, just a book and some new music. Did you name the cat?"

"We sure did," Brian said with enthusiasm. "Her name is Snowbell."

"That's a dumb name for a cat."

"It is not! It's a mix of 'snow,' because she's as white as snow, and 'bell,' like 'blue bells, cockle shells,' because she has blue eyes. It's a good name for a cat, right Steve?"

"Yep." Steve turned up the familiar hill.

At home, Brian buckled a blue collar with a silver bell around the cat's neck and placed the litter box in his bedroom. Ignoring Melissa's enumerations about his past, irresponsible behaviors, Brian filled Snowbell's water bowl and carried it to his bedroom, spilling not one drop.

"Hey, Steve! How much food does she get?"

Steve shouted over the sizzling of the chicken he was frying. "Read the package!"

Brian did and measured the exact amount into Snowbell's bowl. With painstaking care, he arranged Snowbell's other possessions near his bed: a spiky rubber ball and a peculiar-smelling grey cloth mouse.

"Catnip!" Brian waved it in front of Melissa's nose.

Melissa sneezed and brushed it away. How long before Brian tired of the cat and reverted to his old ways? One week? Two?

With everyone occupied, Melissa slipped to her bedroom and removed the album from its hiding place under her bed. The back cover also contained song titles and a profile of the pianist who recorded the pieces. She compared her music box with the album cover's image. They matched. *Bryony* was the last song title. She slid the record onto her turntable, turned the volume low, and listened. There was no doubt about it. Bryony was the music box's tune.

The song had nearly finished when Melissa heard a knock on the door. Quickly, she turned off the sound. Her mother opened the door. "Dinner, Melissa."

"Be right there."

Melissa pulled the record from the stereo. Whew! That was close. Dinner conversation was light and casual, until Brian mentioned
Kimberly.

"What happened to her?" he said, plopping a great spoonful of butter on his mashed potatoes. "Will the police find her?"

"They're working very hard at it," Steve said.

"She'll turn up somewhere," Darlene said. "When she does, well, she'll be in so much trouble, she'll wish she was still gone."

While Melissa scraped the sour cream gravy from her green beans, she saw her mother slip Snowbell a piece of chicken. Snowbell greedily gobbled the meat and licked her mother's fingers. Melissa smiled, knowing the cat's home was secure.

At bedtime, Melissa was still thinking about Grandma and the music box. Humming *Bryony* to herself, Melissa switched off the light and settled into bed. She was almost asleep when she turned on her light to set her alarm clock. Fully awake now, Melissa lay in the dark, picturing Bryony at her dressing table listening to the music box. Switching on her light once more, Melissa retrieved the music box, wound it up, and set it on her nightstand. Drowsiness soon overcame her. The last thing Melissa noticed was mist rising past her bedroom window, but she felt too sleepy to care. The music box's tinkling grew shriller until it stabbed Melissa awake.

Melissa dragged her hand over her night table and groped for the alarm button. Exhausted, she eased her aching head onto her pillow and shut her eyes against the dim light. What was wrong with her? She had slept well enough, more than well enough, Melissa thought, smiling through the pain in her head.

She was Bryony, sitting at the toilet table, brushing that gorgeous hair, and swooning to the music box. From the mirror, she saw John Simons, *her* John Simons, entering her room. He stooped behind her, put a hand on each shoulder, and drew her against him. Willingly, Melissa rested her head on his chest and watched him smile.

"May I?" John held out his hand.

Melissa gave him the brush, daringly skimming her fingertips across his palm. For a time, John pulled the brush through Melissa's hair, then suddenly paused in mid-stroke. He laid the brush on the table and grasped each side of Melissa's head. She closed her eyes and leaned back, weakening at the touch of his fingers as they glided down her face and caressed her neck…until that darned alarm clock spoiled it all!

The alarm clock! Melissa forced open her eyes. She'd hit snooze! She'd miss the bus! She braced her trembling limbs, sat up, then swung her legs over the edge of the bed.

The second Melissa arrived at the breakfast table, her mother dashed for the thermometer. Melissa cradled her head while clenching the probe between shaking lips.

"It's normal," Darlene said, feeling her daughter's forehead and frowning. "Still, I don't like the way you look. I think you need a day off."

Melissa staggered back to the bedroom and let her mother help her back into pajamas before she climbed into bed. Melissa longed to return to the Bryony dream, but sleep was a sinister, ebony hole. She awoke at eleven, no better. Her mother had scheduled an afternoon doctor's appointment in Jenson over Melissa's objections.

"It won't hurt you," Darlene said. "A lot's happened to you lately."

Melissa's symptoms didn't baffle Dr. Anderson. "I just need a blood sample to confirm it," he said.

She detested needles. As a little girl, Melissa cried and screamed at the mere sight of one, so her father never administered insulin in front of her. She still cried and screamed when she needed a shot, but on the inside, because she was, after all, eighteen.

"There, now." Dr. Anderson removed the needle and pressed cotton onto her arm. He winked and twirled a grape lollipop between his fingers. "Too old for this?"

With a grin, Melissa tore off the wrapper, and Dr. Anderson ushered them to the waiting room. "Have a seat. My lab will have your results in a just a few minutes."

The verdict confirmed Dr. Anderson's suspicions. "Anemia. It's very common in girls your age." He scrawled on a piece of paper and handed it to her.

"This is a prescription for an iron supplement. Start these pills, and let's re-check your blood levels in a week. Call me if you don't feel better in a day or two."

Her mother appeared very relieved. Dr. Anderson certainly seemed competent, not the country doctor Melissa had expected. Anyway, anemia couldn't be very serious.

In Munsonville, her mother stopped by the school to save Brian a long ride. The small school bus drove through town first, reserving the outskirts for last. At the bottom of the hill, their mother deposited both Brian and Melissa and instructed them to pick up the mail and bring it home.

"But...." Melissa said, glancing the woods.

"The fresh air might do you good. Besides, Brian will be with you." Her mother waved good-bye and drove up the hill.

The late October wind chilled Melissa inside and out. Feeling forsaken, Melissa hiked up her jacket and shoved her hands inside her pockets. Mothers! Why couldn't they make up their minds? First, she was too sick for school, but now she was well enough for a freezing walk home. Her legs trembled, and she wondered how fast iron supplements worked.

The frosty air didn't bother Brian, but he looked worried. "I'm sorry you're sick, Liss." He meant it; Melissa could tell.

"Thanks, Brian. Just get the mail so we can go home." Her words sounded brisk, even to her ears. Brian's face drooped. She hadn't meant to hurt his feelings. "Sorry, I'm so grouchy."

"It's okay. What else can you expect from a girl?"

With a backward glance and a grin, Brian sped to the mailbox, and then yelled, "Hey, did you see that dog?" He pointed toward the trees.

A man was walking out of the darkening woods toward the lake and holding the leash of a large white husky. The animal sniffed the grass, and a gray squirrel jumped from its hiding place and scampered up a tree. The dog growled but did not move.

"Chinook!"

Melissa knew that voice. She waved. "Mr. Masters!"

He startled slightly, looked for the voice, and then raised a hand in greeting. Forgetting her fear of the mist, Melissa motioned her brother to follow.

"Brian, this is my English teacher, Mr. Masters."

Mr. Masters held out his hand, and Brian shook it. The dog whined, and Brian shuffled his feet. Melissa knew he wanted to touch the dog but didn't dare ask.

"Would you like to pet him?" Mr. Masters said.

"Oh, can I?"

Brian crumpled the mail into his coat pockets, and then stroked the animal's head. The dog wagged his tail in pleasure.

"You sure have a beautiful dog, Mr. Masters." Brian knelt and studied its face. "What kind is it?"

"A Siberian Husky. His name is Chinook."

"Chinook," Brian said. The dog licked his nose. "What does it mean?"

"The Chinook is a type of wind known as a 'snow-eater,' because its warm, dry air scares away Old Man Winter."

"Why did you name your dog that?"

"He had that name when he came to me."

"Nice, Chinook," Brian scratched the husky between his ears. "Good boy."

Melissa fingers prickled with cold, and her head pounded again. She was more than ready to go home. She signaled her feelings to Brian, but he was still crouching beside the dog. Mr. Masters watched her through his dirty glasses.

"I missed you in class today, Melissa. Is something wrong?" He sounded kind, but this was Mr. Masters. Who knew if he meant it?

She told him about the anemia. "I might not be back until the pills start working."

Mr. Masters reached inside his coat, penned something on a small notebook, and handed it to Melissa. "That's the piece we're studying in class. If you're feeling well enough, perhaps, you can read it."

"Thanks, Mr. Masters." The last thing Melissa needed was to fall behind in her schoolwork. She turned toward Brian. "We'd better go. I don't want Mom to worry."

"Okay." Brian stood up. "It was nice meeting you, Mr. Masters. Thank you for letting me pet your dog."

"No problem at all," Mr. Masters said. He shook Brian's hand again, then led the dog into the woods. Melissa, huddled inside her coat, trudged up the hill with Brian.

"He seems like a nice teacher," Brian said. "Maybe, I'll get him in high school, too." He paused. "I hope I have a dog like Chinook one day."

On impulse, Melissa hugged him. Brian squirmed out of reach. "Aw, cut it out!" His irritation faded as quickly as it came, and Brian grew quiet. When he spoke again, he looked troubled. "Did Mr. Masters like talking with us, or was he being polite?"

"I guess he enjoyed it. What difference does it make anyhow?"

"He never acted like he was uncomfortable or anything, but when I shook hands with him…gosh, Liss! They were colder than yours!"

CHAPTER 10: WHEN GOOD DREAMS GO BAD

The iron pills did their job. Within a week, Melissa's iron levels began rising, and she felt healthy again.

"Keep up the good work," Dr. Anderson said. "I'll see you again in three months."

Because it was early afternoon, her mother decided against returning Melissa to school. Instead, she suggested lunch at Sue's Diner.

"Brian can skip the bus today," Darlene said. "We'll collect him when we pick up your assignments."

Melissa had not eaten at Sue's Diner since the centennial celebration. Although Steve had invited them to the Friday fish fries, their mother had always declined, knowing Melissa detested fish. Today, of course, Jack Cooper was in school, a small blight to Melissa's overall sense of contentment, a first since her father's death. Had the iron pills done it, or had good times finally arrived, as her mother had assured her?

They ordered shepherd's pie, the diner's special salad, and freshly baked garlic bread. Then her mother saw Joe Roberts, the project manager for Simons Mansion, talking with someone at another table.

"Do you mind? I'd liked to get an update on the mansion's restoration."

"No, that's fine." Melissa settled into her seat and recalled the conversation her mother and Steve had last night while finishing dishes. Melissa was about to brush her teeth when she heard her mother say, "Kimberly's parents hired a private detective."

"Did you tell the attorney?" Steve said.

"Yes. Apparently, it's the third time Kimberly's gone missing this month. If I had known...." Her mother's voice faded away as she and Steve left the room.

Their food arrived just as her mother returned to the table. She looked disappointed. "He said no work of any kind would be scheduled until spring. He's also afraid the publicity about Kimberly will hurt tourism plans." She tasted a piece of garlic bread. "Yours is better."

"Thanks, Mom."

While they waited outside school for Brian, Ann dashed up. "Mrs. Marchellis, can Melissa come over today? I'll help her with homework."

Melissa understood her friend's hurry. Not everyone in Munsonville had phones. Ann's family had bought one last summer, after her father had chest pains and quickly needed help. Before then, the Daltons recognized no need for a phone, and now that they had one, Ann wasn't allowed to use it. Melissa rarely talked to her Grover's Park friends, either. Long distance phone calls cost too much.

"Melissa," Darlene said, "Do you feel up to it? Steve can pick you up at nine."

"Yes!" Melissa grabbed her book bag and scrambled out of the car. Dinner was pleasant, but Ann's parents argued over the mansion's restoration while the girls worked on homework.

"I don't care, May. I'm completely against it."

"Rob, think what this could mean for our village."

"I did. Traffic. Crowds. Garbage."

"You're just against anything modern."

"Oh, really? Then tell me how that phone got into our kitchen."

As the girls answered the last history question, Julie Drake and Katie Miller entered the kitchen. Katie accentuated her baby face by sweeping her short blonde hair to one side with a pink plastic barrette. She was one of nine children; her brother Will was the cute police officer at Melissa's house. Julie was the pretty girl with braids Melissa noticed the first day of school. Katie carried a beige plastic case and a magazine.

"Feeling brave?" Ann asked.

"Huh," Julie said. "Who cares, as long as Katie's not cutting?"

They walked to Ann's room. Melissa, still shy among these new girls, sat on the bed near Ann. Katie plugged in the rollers, and Julie fiddled with Ann's transistor radio until she found a pop station with reception.

"Still mad about the glasses?" Julie asked.

Ann removed the tortoise shell frames and peered disgustedly through the oval lenses. "They're okay. I wanted wires."

"Wires are out," Julie pulled the rubber bands from her dark braids.

"So are braids." Ann wiped the lenses on her blouse.

"They keep the hair out of my eyes, since Mom won't let me get a page boy. She said it's ridiculous to spend money on fashionable cuts when long hair is always in style. I'm surprised she doesn't make me wear corsets and crinoline, too."

"That's okay," Katie said soothingly. "I can use your hair to practice."

Julie plopped down at Ann's desk. "Which one tonight?"

Katie pointed to the brunette with the puffed-out curls on the cover. "This one."

"Okay." Julie settled back in the chair, ready for the experiment.

"Can I see that, Katie?"

"Sure!" Katie set the magazine near Ann, who centered the magazine so Melissa could see, too, and cupped an ear. "Hark! The parents are silent."

"I can't see why the grown-ups are so bent out of shape," Julie grumbled. "You'd think they'd want Munsonville to progress."

Katie wound a strand of Julie's hair over a roller.

"I don't care," Ann said with a yawn. "I won't be here in a few years."

96

"Me neither," Julie said. "The trouble with Munsonville is that no one thinks past fishing boats. I want something more than night crawlers and dead carp."

"Like what?" Katie reached for the comb.

"Like anything that requires some brain power. Like a car, maybe."

Melissa was surprised at Julie's scornful remarks. She thought all the villagers lived contentedly in Munsonville.

Ann turned a page. "I'll be too busy traveling around the world."

Julie tossed her head and snorted.

"Hold still!" Katie struggled to fasten the roller.

"Not if," Julie snapped her fingers, "Jack Cooper looked twice at you."

Ann blushed, still looking down. "That's not true. I'm marrying someone so rich and ambitious, I'll own homes in three countries and eat gourmet food every night."

"I'd rather get a job and make my own money, thank you."

"Can't you get a job?" Melissa then remembered Munsonville had no industry.

"Not unless you slave for a family business. My mom works the information desk at the nature center, and my dad sells used cars in Jensen. By the time they restore Simons Mansion, I'll be in college, thank God."

Katie rolled another strand and secured it with a pin. "Do you think the ghost will attack once they start fixing it?"

Ann's blue eyes behind the glasses were stern. "There's no ghost. Grow up, Katie."

Julie shook her head in exasperation and a roller fell out. "You've got to keep an open mind. What about the stories?"

"Mass hysteria," Ann said.

"Maybe, except for the evidence backing their claims."

Melissa stiffened and held her breath. Did Julie mean Kimberly? Ann looked down her nose at Julie and snickered. "Not nutty Tina Swanson?"

"Who's she?" Melissa said.

"Last summer," Ann said, "Tina's family rented one of the lakefront fishing cottages. No one liked Tina because she bragged that her red hair made her psychic. After a month, Tina's parents went to Uncle Gabe. Tina had told them a dark man in black had broken into her room while she was sleeping. So, Uncle Gabe posted a guard."

"Did they see anyone?" Melissa asked.

"Of course not," Ann said, giving her a funny look.

"My parents said Tina was just spoiled and looking for attention," Katie said.

"Or maybe she *did* have ESP," Julie said. "Maybe everyone missed what she saw. How do you know nothing comes into your room at night?" "I hope not!" Katie shuddered. "There. You're free for fifteen minutes.

"Here," Ann raised the magazine. "I'm going to wear a wedding dress like this someday. What do you think, Melissa?"

Gold beads ornamented the strapless white dress, and its full skirt spread out several feet. An embroidered, lace veil reached the floor. Was Bryony's gown this pretty?

"It's beautiful," Melissa agreed. She still detested dressing up, but what she would give to wear a dress like that!

"Yeah, your mom will spend two grand on a dress." Julie took the magazine, turned a page, and pointed to a slim satin dress, adorned with just one bow at the waist. "Now that's smart looking. No baubles; no frills."

"But more money," Ann said. "It costs an extra three hundred dollars."

"Who cares?" Julie stretched. "By then, I'll be a successful psychologist."

"Buying your own wedding dress is not very romantic."

"Who says? Anyway, Jack had better save his tips if you want that dress."

Steve arrived promptly at nine. He attempted polite conversation, but her mind, during the way home and while winding up the music box at bedtime, was on romance and wedding gowns. Small wonder Melissa's dreams began by walking into an antiquated parlor with John Simons, who tossed his top hat and cape onto a table, embraced Melissa's waist, and led her to a sofa where they sank into its cushions. Behind them entered Kimberly, with flowing hair, cold eyes, and sharp teeth.

While Melissa praised John for his fine concert performance, Kimberly pranced to the sidebar, poured John a glass of wine, and prepared a cup of hot tea. The look in John's pale, blue eyes suggested a kiss, so Melissa stopped talking and inched forward. Kimberly returned with the drinks, and Melissa stifled a disappointed sigh. Annoyance flickered over John's face, but he leaned back to accept them, and then dismissed Kimberly from the room. She lowered her head and turned to leave. John handed Melissa her tea, so she obediently raised it for a sip. He set down his wine and moved very close.

Kimberly spun around and leaped onto the sofa between them. The hot tea spilled over Melissa's chin and down her neck. Melissa spluttered, recoiled, and dropped the cup. Scowling, John knocked Kimberly onto the floor. The tea seared Melissa's neck; a chunk of flesh dropped onto her lap. Melissa screamed in pain and fright and awoke.

In the luminous glow of the alarm clock, John Simons lay on her chest, thin, sallow, and feral. With a gasp, Melissa switched on the light, but the apparition had vanished. Her heart hammered; she fought for breath. Her eyes flew over the room.

Nothing was there, except for Snowbell contentedly purring at her feet. Melissa touched her chin and her neck. They were whole, untouched, sound.

The cat crept across the bed and nestled into Melissa. Still quaking from the graphic dream, Snowbell's company, a breathing reminder of reality, comforted her. Afraid of what might appear if she turned off the light, Melissa continued petting the cat. Gradually, the terror of her dream waned, and Melissa floated away to undisturbed sleep. She did not stir again until her alarm clock rang.

All day in school, Melissa unsuccessfully forced diligence. Equations baffled her; Jamestown bored her; cell structure escaped her; and diagramming adverbs held no charm. Last night's dream occupied her thoughts. Did her subconscious trick her? Were the village ghost stories true? Was John Simons really in her bedroom?

At lunchtime, Melissa hurried to the school office to telephone her mother.

"What's so urgent?" Darlene sounded wary. "A school project?" Melissa wished her mother would drop the suspicious attitude. "I just have some research to do. It won't take long."

"I'll have Steve pick you up at four-thirty, so please be ready for him."

"Thanks, Mom!"

At the library, Melissa searched up and down the shelves for books about sleep and dreams. She could consult Mrs. Clements, but that might invite questions about why she wanted them. Better safe than sorry, she decided, skimming the titles.

One thick book, *A Complete Guide to Sleep Disorders,* caught Melissa's attention. The listed maladies meant nothing to Melissa, so she flipped through the index until she found, "dreaming while awake," only to read a description of narcolepsy: daytime sleepiness, episodic paralysis, and vivid hallucinations. Even if she had hallucinated, paralysis did not accompany it. The iron supplements cured any sleepiness. She doubted narcolepsy was her problem. Dr. Anderson would have diagnosed it.

Journal Your Dreams offered details for tracking dreams, but Melissa dared not chronicle her adventures, lest prying eyes read them. Finally, she lugged *A Dictionary of Dream Symbolism* to a back table. Melissa skimmed past thunderstorms, illnesses, and journeys, then selected *Supernatural Beings.*

In some dreams, people assume certain, beast-like characteristics, but they may be ghosts, warning the sleeper of impending trouble.

Melissa glanced up at the clock. Only half an hour before Steve arrived. Think, Melissa. She was far past the age for believing in ghosts. Yet, Kimberly had vanished without a trace, in the middle of the night, near Simons Mansion. Did she run off or had a ghost spirited her away? The word "control" caught her attention.

Dreamers have power over their dreams. With practice, one may control the direction of the dream or obey an internal command to awaken.

Was her obsession with Bryony affecting her dreams? Could Melissa cause a Bryony dream by her relentlessly focusing upon the young Mrs. Simons? Had her mind conjured up the image of John in her bedroom last night, while Melissa dwelled in the hazy twilight area between sleep and full alertness? She had to find out.

So that evening, while calculating square roots, Melissa imagined John Simons locking his eyes onto Bryony's the first time he saw her. As she diagrammed gerunds, John played hymns for Sunday services and stole peeks at Bryony from behind the piano. Yet, as bedtime approached, Melissa stalled, afraid of what might happen when she closed her eyes. She carefully soaped her body inch by inch, then shampooed her hair twice and conditioned it three times longer than the bottle recommended. Melissa slowly brushed each tooth and took her time flossing, even behind her molars where wisdom teeth were erupting. She thoroughly dried herself and meticulously wiped puddles from the floor. She stopped in the kitchen to put away the clean dishes, hugged her mother extra hard, and even smoothed the fringe on her throw rug before pulling down the covers.

Finally, Melissa set her alarm for two-thirty, a time for when she ought to be in the middle of a dream. If John Simons materialized in her room, she would trap him in the act. Just the same, she didn't feel very brave.

CHAPTER 11: TRICKS ARE TREATS

"Melissa, hold still," Darlene mumbled through a mouthful of pins.

Anticipating the night's fun, Melissa found it difficult to hold still, at least for very long. She twisted and turned in front of her mother's floor-length mirror.

"Ouch!" she cried, as her mother stuck her backside with a pin.

Darlene only sighed and said, "Now hold still!"

Melissa had not planned on trick or treating. In Grover's Park, kids stopped at age thirteen. Besides, they now lived too far from town. Brian, however, would sooner miss his birthday than Halloween, the one time of the year he freely collected and ate plenty of candy. At the night's end, Brian's pillowcase and pockets overflowed. He would take two pillowcases if he could sneak an extra one.

In Munsonville, trick or treating was popular amongst everyone, even the adults, which Melissa learned on Thursday, when Katie sat next to her at lunch and asked what she was wearing Friday night.

"For what?" Melissa said absently.

"For Halloween," Katie said. "What's your costume?"

Melissa opened her thermos and tore the wrapper off a plastic spoon, wondering if she had heard Katie right. "Aren't we too old for dressing up?"

"My dad dresses as Mr. Peanut every year, just to pass out candy. My mother is making me a Cleopatra costume. I can hardly wait."

Melissa pondered her friend's excitement. Dressing up might be fun, but where would she get a costume this late? Ironically, when Melissa mentioned her plight, her mother suggested Melissa masquerade as Bryony.

"I've got just the dress," Darlene said at dinner. "I saw it over at Village Hall. It wasn't Bryony's, but it's very Victorian-ish, light blue with a scooped neck, puffy sleeves, ruffles, and fake lace. It might be a little big, but we can fix that."

"Oh, Mom!" Melissa flew out of her chair to hug her mother and upset her milk.

"For Pete's sake, Liss!" Brian cried, but it was Steve who ran for a towel.

This was the most thrilling Bryony episode in over a week. Although Melissa had dutifully contemplated Bryony at every bedtime and had set her alarm for two o'clock every single night, she had no further dreams about John Simons. She felt foolish for believing his ghost had visited her room, but missed the Bryony dreams. At least on Halloween, for one night, Melissa could really be Bryony.

They laid their plans. Steve and her mother agreed to drive her and Brian into town. The adults, in costume, would play cards at the Dalton's, while the kids tricked and treated. Afterwards, Mr. Dalton would transport Julie, Katie, and Ann to Melissa's house. Only Ann had spent the night on the Simons estate, so the other girls could not wait.

"This time, no midnight walks around the place," Ann said sternly.

Melissa opened a bag of potato chips and thought about Kimberly. "That's fine with me." Melissa popped a chip into her mouth. She was getting used to the fact that none of her friends drove. She had asked Ann about it once, but her friend had simply said, "Drive where?"

Katie had bought a new ABBA record; Ann promised to bring board games.

"Maybe we'll even tell ghost stories with the lights out." Julie smiled mysteriously.

The next afternoon Steve prepared a big pot of barbecue, so everyone could eat early and have sufficient time to get dressed. Last week, their mother had driven Brian to Dalton's Dry Goods to buy his costume, and he maintained the highest secrecy about it.

"I'm telling you, Melissa, you'll be scared out of your wits," Brian had said, when they had returned from shopping.

Her mother fastened the last pin into Melissa's dress. "There!" She rose from her squatting position and dropped the extra pins into the apron pocket on her maid's costume. "That should do it. Turn around, Melissa, and let's look."

Melissa pirouetted, reveling in the heavenly, blue fabric, as it floated around her. Her mother told her to turn again, a bit slower this time, and Melissa did, flushed and excited. Was this how Bryony had felt when preparing for a ball?

The door burst open, and a young voice shrieked, "I vant to drink your blood!"

Brian leaped out in front of them and froze in a most dramatic pose, while holding his black cape under his nose and fixing sinister eyes on them. He dropped the cape, hissed, and bared white, plastic fangs, the last in stock at Dalton's Dry Goods.

Melissa stopped swaying. "Brian, get out!"

Darlene hugged him. "You're very scary, but wait until I'm done with Melissa."

"Aw, Mom, can't I just have one look?"

"In a minute, after we're finished."

Brian's shoulders sagged, and he shuffled out of the room. "Just because Melissa's a girl," he grumbled.

"Shut the door!" Melissa called after him.

He did, but not until he made a face at Melissa. She did not care, not tonight.

Dreamily, she spun in front of her mother, catching her reflection in the mirror. Why, I'm almost beautiful, Melissa thought, although not as beautiful as Bryony.

Darlene, hands on hips, surveyed her work, pleased to see Melissa in a dress. "You're as pretty as a picture, but you need one more thing." She walked to her closet and reached far into the back. She brought forth the long, hooded, black cloak she once wore for special dates with their father.

"Here," Darlene said. "It will be chilly tonight, and your school jacket doesn't match your costume."

The cloak was perfect. Melissa kept admiring the effect, even after her mother had called Brian into the room. Melissa craned her neck to watch the cape swish behind her, the perfect garment for John's concerts.

"Mom! Melissa's hogging the mirror!"

"Melissa, it's your brother's turn."

"What? Oh, all right. I'll move."

She had scarcely wandered away from the mirror when Brian sprang into her place and studied his appearance with a critical eye. "Mom, can I borrow some lipstick?"

His mother was adjusting Melissa's cloak. "I suppose so."

"Do you have any red?"

She did not reply, and Brian did not wait for her answer. He sauntered to her dresser and slid open the top drawer. He fished around, then cried, "Ick, pink!"

Brian quickly recapped the offending lipstick and tossed it in the drawer. He rummaged again, found another, and twisted its waxy insides to the top. "Yes!"

He carefully drew two heavy, dark lines from the corners of his mouth to the end of his chin. Then, he turned around to face his mother. "Hey, how's this?"

"It's very nice," Darlene looked up. "Brian! My lipstick!"

"What!" Brian's cheeks were now red, too. "You said I could. I didn't use much." He quickly replaced the lid and returned it to the drawer, closing it completely, leaving no gap. "I even put it away."

A scream made them all jump. It was Steve, dressed as an old- fashioned butler, standing in the doorway, grinning and winking at Brian, while trembling violently.

"Oh, it's just you," Steve sighed with relief. "I wondered who let the vampire in."

Steve now gestured toward Melissa. "And who is this beautiful young lady? May I escort the maiden of the house to the Halloween dance?" Steve bowed low.

Melissa, giggling, curtsied back at him. "You may."

With a roll of his hand, Steve offered his arm. "My lady, your chariot awaits."

He drove her mother's car, so they wouldn't sit cramped in his truck. It was only five o'clock, but dark. At the bottom of the drive, Melissa glanced back at the clear woods. Although no one ever again mentioned Melissa's late-night incident, Melissa wished someone else might see the mist, just once. The neighborhoods blazed with porch lights, and the streets were full of costumed people. Brian jiggled with the double anticipation of getting his fair share and scaring an unsuspecting adult or two. Melissa saw Steve nudge her mother and then point at a squad car parked in front of Sue's Diner.

"Gabe's there every Friday night for the fish fry," Steve said. "He can't resist it, especially the tartar sauce. He orders it by the cupful."

He turned right on Pike Street and pulled into Ann's driveway. Clay, in pirate dress, pushed the door open. Brian dashed up the front steps, effectively cutting off an assembly of small ghosts. He pulled his cloak under his eyes. "I vant to drink your blood!"

"Neat-o!" Clay exclaimed.

Brian scooped handfuls of candy and dumped them into the outstretched bags of the costumed children waiting on the stoop. Then he unwrapped a cherry sucker, popped it into his mouth, and distributed another batch. Before he and Clay could get out the door, another group ascended the steps.

"No fair!" Clay said. "Hey, Mom, can't Ann help now?"

With one hand on her witch hat, Mrs. Dalton scurried to relieve Clay. He tore down the hall to his bedroom and returned wearing his pirate's mask. Brian moaned, as two more children mounted the steps.

"Go!" Mrs. Dalton said, pushing them out the door to join the fun. Julie and Katie sat inside Ann's living room waiting for Melissa.

Julie was dressed as a nun; Ann was a clown. Katie, looking svelte and mysterious as Cleopatra, gasped in delight when she saw Melissa's costume. "Melissa, you're beautiful!"

"She's Bryony," Darlene said. "Have fun!"

She lightly kissed her daughter's forehead, and the group of girls trooped into the night. Melissa lifted her chin and surveyed the yard, pretending it was the Simons estate.

"We will!" Melissa called back.

She had no trepidations about walking in the dark with her friends and approaching one welcoming house after another. She glanced back at Lake Munson. She did not see any mist, but she never saw it in town. I'm Bryony, she thought, smiling smugly, and the next two hours raced past.

Soon, everyone was back at the Daltons. The adults set down their cards, and Steve slid aside a plate containing tortilla crumbs and the remains of his avocado dip. One by one, the youth overturned their pillowcases onto the dining room table. No one could sample any treats, until they passed Mr. Dalton's scrutiny.

"Like anyone in Munsonville would put razor blades or poison in candy bars," Clay said scornfully.

"It's just in case," his father reminded him.

Candy inspection passed, Brian and Clay shoveled their stash into their respective pillowcases and lugged the precious loot to Clay's bedroom. They planned to stay up until dawn watching old horror movies and working their way through most of the candy.

"I'm jealous!" Steve hollered after them.

"Don't forget to feed Snowbell!" Brian shouted back.

Once at Melissa's house, Katie placed her record on the turntable, and Ann set up the game. They peeled off costumes, stopping now and then to eat a piece of Halloween candy. Melissa carefully hung the blue dress on the back of her door.

"I'm hungry," Katie announced.

"Have some candy corn." Ann offered a handful from a large package.

"No, I mean for real food."

"I'm hungry, too." Julie buttoned her pajama top.

Food sounded good. It had been a long time since the barbecue. Chocolate bars and candy cigarettes didn't count as food and neither did handfuls of lemon drops.

"Maybe we can make popcorn," Melissa said, with a wistful look at her costume. The night had ended too soon. Would she ever play Bryony again?

Her mother and Steve were holding hands while watching the news. They looked up when Melissa and Katie entered the room.

"Mom, can we make popcorn?" Melissa said

"If you put away the popper when you're done."

Katie trailed Melissa into the kitchen. Melissa crouched before a cabinet, moved aside pots and pans, and pulled out the popcorn popper. The television set droned, "Tonight, in national news...."

"I wish we had one," Katie said. "My mom uses an old pot, and she always burns it." She watched Melissa measure kernels and oil, then plug in the machine.

"Prince Juan Carlos of Spain will become head of state because General Franco's continuing illness prohibits...." The sound of corn popping drowned out the rest.

"How long does it take?" Katie asked.

"Not long. Can you get me a stick of butter?"

Katie plopped it into the saucepan and adjusted the burner to the lowest setting. The popping slowed, then stopped. Melissa found a large plastic bowl, unplugged the machine, and poured out the popcorn. Katie carefully drizzled the butter as Melissa mixed the fluffy kernels with a large spoon.

"Mmm, that smells good," Katie said.

She carried the popcorn into the bedroom. Melissa grabbed napkins and the saltshaker and then quietly walked through the living room.

"A Barnes City, Iowa, teenage girl is still missing...." Melissa shut her bedroom door and glanced back at the gown, hoping Village Hall didn't need it back soon.

During the game, Julie upset her money onto the floor, invoking dirty looks from Ann and snickers from Katie. Everyone howled when

108

Katie, who was losing and pouting about it, had an unexpected stroke of luck and won.

"Cheater!" Julie, laughing, threw her remaining dollars at Katie.

"Shh!" Melissa warned. It was too late.

There was a knock-on Melissa's bedroom door. She shot her friends an "I warned you" look, as she swung her legs over the side of her bed.

Steve looked annoyed. "Your mother and I are going to sleep. If you can't be quiet, then you'll have to do the same."

"We're just putting the game away," Melissa assured him.

Julie suggested they tell ghost stories instead. Ann flicked off the wall switch. The green pallor from Melissa's alarm clock added a satisfying, creepy effect that made everyone, except Melissa, smile with anticipation.

"Only we're not playing Bloody Mary," Katie said.
Bloody Mary was a treasured slumber party ritual. After darkening a room, you looked into a mirror and chanted, "Bloody Mary," thirteen times. If it worked, a ghost would appear over the chanter's shoulder.

"Okay," Ann said, with a nod of her head. "You go first."

In whispered tones, Katie launched into a story about an elderly woman who received mysterious dreams from her long-dead child, summoning her to come out to his grave. When the woman reached his headstone, she saw his stuffed bear and toy truck lying against it.

Melissa shivered, but Ann yawned and said, "That's old. Here's a better one."

She told about a boy whose friends dared him to spend the night in a haunted wax museum. In the morning, the friends found him dead, lying beneath a scythe. A statue of the Grim Reaper had toppled onto the floor, crushing him. This time Katie shivered and snuggled closer to Melissa, but she looked at Julie.

"Your turn," Katie said with a smile.

Julie opened her duffel bag and removed what appeared to be another game.

"What's that?" Katie asked.

"We played it at slumber parties back home," Melissa said. "You ask it questions, and, supposedly, dead spirits answer you."

"Supposedly is right," Ann said. "It's fake. It's how you push it."

Julie set the board on her sleeping bag. It had letters, numbers, and the words *Yes* and *No* written in opposite corners. Katie squealed and scooted away from Melissa. "Oooh, how do we play?"

"Do this," Julie said, as she placed a wooden piece in the middle of the board and rested her fingertips on the wedge. "We take turns asking questions. If a spirit's in the room, it moves the piece to the answer."

The girls knelt around the board and did as Julie said.

"You go first," Katie said to Julie.

Julie thought a minute. "Are there any spirits here?" Nothing happened.

"Ask it again," Katie suggested.

"Are there any spirits here?" Julie said, a little louder this time.

The piece didn't move. Ann made a face. "This is stupid. I think we should...."

Slowly, the piece inched to Yes. The girls raised their eyes and looked at each other. No one said a word, until Katie whispered, "Ask who it is."

"Who is it?" Julie used her sternest voice.

The piece slipped over the letters K...I...M...B...E...

Melissa snatched away her fingers. "Hey! That's not funny!"

The piece stopped. Julie glared at Melissa. "Well, maybe you moved it."

"I didn't touch it!"

Ann looked steadily at Melissa. "Ask Kimberly if she went inside the mansion."

The piece wandered across the board: B...R...O...K...E.

"Broke." Julie gazed across the room. "I wonder what she means."

Melissa grew uncomfortable. One of her new friends was playing a joke at Kimberly's expense, but she wasn't sure how to stop it.

"Ask her if the mansion is really haunted." Katie's eyes sparkled.

110

Julie frowned in deep concentration. "Kimberly, is the mansion haunted?"

The piece quickly slid to *Yes*.

"Is John Simons the ghost?" Ann's voice was low and quiet. Just as quickly, the piece slid to the other side of the board. *No*.

"Then who?" asked Julie, impatiently.

The piece jerked wildly over the letters. The smile fled from Katie's face, and she cried, "I'm scared! I'm scared!"

Without warning, the piece soared off the board into Julie's lap. Ann screamed and then covered her mouth. Snowbell had jumped onto the board, upsetting the piece.

Melissa scooped up the cat and held her close, placing her cheek against the cat's soft fur as she stroked it. Snowbell purred loudly.

"Brian's cat," Melissa explained.

CHAPTER 12: A FAIR TRADE

Melissa flinched and then listened. What woke her up?

Squinting against the early morning light, Melissa glimpsed the sleeping forms of her friends. She must have been dreaming. Melissa snuggled into her pillow.

Bump.

Quietly, Melissa unzipped her sleeping bag, stepped around her friends, and tiptoed out into the living room.

Bump. The kitchen!

Mist rose over the windows. Melissa stumbled through the living room. Her fingers crawled to the kitchen light switch and snapped it on.

The cold tile sent a chill through her bare feet and up her spine, and she gasped.

Kimberly knelt on hands and knees; she cast her eyes around the room. She pounced, missed, and bumped her head into a cabinet door. She drew back, grabbed something, then lay flat on her belly. When had Kimberly returned?

Melissa lightly touched her on the shoulder. "Kimberly?"

Her friend rolled onto her back. A long tail hung out of Kimberly's mouth. Blood oozed onto Kimberly's hands and trickled to her elbows.

Melissa bolted upright. Sweat poured down her face. The first rays of dawn striped across the room. Heart thudding, Melissa picked up her alarm clock: six-thirty. No one was yet awake, but Melissa could not, would not, go back to sleep. So, she washed and repacked the popper back inside the cabinet. She was dressed and eating her second bowl of cereal when her mother stumbled past her into the kitchen.

"Morning," Darlene mumbled, plodding past Melissa to plug in the coffee pot.

Steve stirred on the couch, and his blanket fell off. Her mother tucked it around him on the way to get dressed. One by one, the girls filed into the dining room and poured orange juice and cereal. Katie didn't eat. Her stomach was upset.

"I probably had too much candy last night," Katie groaned.

"And popcorn," Julie added. "Melissa, pass the sugar bowl."

"Too bad Brian isn't here." Ann sipped her juice. "He makes awesome toast."

Snowbell rubbed against Ann's leg. Ann offered the cat a cereal flake, but the cat just sniffed it and stalked away.

Julie grabbed the cereal box. "What's wrong with her neck?"

"We think she sprained it in the woods," Melissa said. "The vet will look at it."

Since he had to pick up Brian and run errands for her mother, Steve drove everyone into Munsonville. The rest of the weekend was quiet, although Brian remained in high spirits, enthusiastically sharing over dinner each detail of the movies he had watched all night with Clay. Only Steve expressed interest for old monster flicks.

"No respect for the little guy." Brian shook his head at his family and buttered both sides of another slice of bread.

Immediately after Sunday dinner, Melissa prepared for bed, too tired for homework, resigned to dealing with the consequences tomorrow. She was even too tired for reading, but not for setting her alarm at two o'clock, just in case. From under the blankets, Melissa heard canned laughter and applause from the variety show Steve and Brian were watching. It grew louder until it deafened Melissa's ears. Nevertheless, she reveled in it, even as she wholeheartedly added to it. John's performance was perfect, and everyone at the concert hall knew it. She was so very proud of him.

Although most of the audience had left their seats, Melissa lingered, basking in the musical strains echoing in her ears. A sea of voices praised John. Since her chaperone had disappeared, Melissa hesitated venturing into the reception area. John disliked her going alone, but she had no choice. She could not stay here. The lingering crowds amazed her. Everyone desired to be near John, and she, Melissa, was a part of it. Her mouth watered at the refreshments: cold meats, pates, cheeses, breads, crisp pickles, jellies in clear glasses, and many delicate pastries. How long had it been since her last meal?

John had not yet arrived, but, just then, a servant girl in a starched white uniform approached her with a note: *Meet me in the dressing room. Love, John.*

"I'll take you there, miss," the girl said.

Lifting the skirts of her plum-colored evening dress, Melissa followed the girl back through the theater and past the curtained area separating the wings from the main stage to the building's rear. The servant knocked at the first door on her left.

"Who is it?"

"It's me, sir. I've brought your wife, sir, as you requested."

After a brief scuffle, the door opened. John, still dressed in his white tails, welcomed Melissa into the dressing room and closed the door. He slowly turned Melissa to face him, looking her up and down and nodding with a smile of approval. She held her breath in blissful anticipation. He put a hand on each side of her neck and bent to kiss her.

In the distance, Melissa heard the faint beep, beep, beep of an alarm clock. As her hand fumbled, a second hand, not hers, switched it off.

114

Squinting in the dark, she barely discerned the figure of John Simons sitting beside her on the bed. Blood, *her blood,* Melissa thought in horror, dripped off his lips and onto his chin.

Melissa swiftly reached for the light, but John, leering, grabbed the lamp and set it on the floor. She opened her mouth to scream, and John clamped his cold hand over it. Keeping his eyes on her, he raised a sleeve to his mouth and wiped away the blood.

"Be a sensible girl, and don't spoil it by yelling," John said.

Her mind whirled at this rapid change of events and at the loathsome creature on her bed. *This couldn't be happening.* Her lips and cheeks smarted from John's cold hand.

"Be assured, Melissa. You are not dreaming. Shall we chat? Promise to be good."

Dazed at John's superior air, Melissa nodded. John removed his hand, rose from the bed, and settled comfortably in Melissa's desk chair. Clutching her bed quilt to her chest, Melissa sat straight and peered through the clock's hazy light for a good look at him. John wore the same white tails from her dream just a few minutes ago, only the threadbare clothes now hung in loose shreds over his gaunt frame. Hollow eyes sank into his skull and wrinkled skin sagged on his pallid face. Bony, gnarled fingers rested on her chair arms. He regarded her with calmness.

He's the very picture of death, Melissa thought, and the thought frightened her. In movies, people pinched themselves when they thought they might be dreaming. Melissa tried, and it hurt.

"Ouch!" she yelped.

John stifled a laugh.

"Who…what are you?" Melissa stammered.

"Who do you think I am?"

She started to say, "vampire," then faltered before John's steady gaze. She imagined how the figure lounging in her chair might hurt her, if he pleased, and her teeth chattered. So, she tightened her grasp on her quilt and said in a shaky voice, "What do you want?"

John, still looking amused, said nothing.

"Are you going to kill me or turn me into a vampire?"

His expression did not change. *What was so funny?*

"But you've been, you've been…." Melissa's voice trailed away.

"Haven't you been drinking my blood?"

"Well, just a little bit. You don't need all of it, and it's a shame to waste it."

His logic baffled her. John still sat there, intently watching her, the same way Snowbell watched mice. Then she remembered what Snowbell did to mice. Melissa shuddered and looked away.

John chuckled at her distress. "Come, let's bargain. I have something you want, and you have something I need. You've enjoyed our time together so far?"

Still wary, Melissa felt unexpected hope rise inside her. This was not what she had expected. Before she quite realized what she was doing, Melissa nodded assent.

"Then let's continue it. You may live part of your life as Bryony, in exchange for some of your blood."

"You *are* going to kill me!"

"Hardly. You'll never miss the small amount I'll take."

"Can you survive on that?"

"I have plenty of food sources. Your blood is not sustenance. It's remedy."

Intense curiosity quelled Melissa's fear of him, and she relaxed slightly.

John's face darkened. "An ancient legend minute says minute amounts of blood consumed from one human source neutralizes vampirism and restores life. For years, I've dreamed of forsaking this wretched, predatory existence." John leaned forward. "You are my redemption."

Was he really speaking the truth, or was this simply a trick? Just how long had John Simons come into her room and, it sickened her to think it, fed on her? Yet, not once had he harmed her. Was it really his intention to spare her? Could it be true this vampire carried goodness within him, enough to start life anew, enough to stop killing innocent people? Could she really help him?

Melissa could not deny it, not to him, much less to herself. She coveted John's passion and fascination for Bryony and longed to change places with her. Now John Simons was offering the chance, as a means of releasing him from a cursed destiny. It was a tantalizing prospect.

116

Sensing his approaching triumph, John rose from the chair and extended his hand.

"Come," he said. "Have a taste of your compensation."

Melissa winced at the word "taste," but, this time, John did not laugh.

"Don't be apprehensive, Melissa. I won't hurt you. You mustn't be afraid."

She made up her mind. Shivering partly from the chilly room, partly from fear, and partly from excitement, Melissa tossed back the bedcovers and stood in front of John. She felt childish and awkward in her old purple flowered pajamas and bare feet.

"What shall I do first?" Melissa whispered.

John reached out his hands. "Touch me," he said in a low, smooth voice.

She hesitated. Even in the dim light, Melissa saw how thin and pale they were. Her insides recoiled at the thought of touching a corpse. Then Melissa remembered how much she wanted to be Bryony. This was nothing new; John had already siphoned blood from her. Could it harm her to continue for a little longer?

Timidly, Melissa stretched out her hands and placed them in John's icy ones. An involuntary shudder ran through her body, but John clasped her hands before she snatched them away. His strength surprised her; his frail appearance did not match his grip. John's other hand trailed up her arm to her shoulder and held it fast. Melissa recoiled from his fetid breath and the musty smell of his clothes, but she remained stoic.

"I'm not afraid," she told herself, but she did not believe it. "I am not afraid. I am not afraid."

"Good," John said, with a smile. "Close your eyes."

She did, but through clenched lids, she sensed acute eyes burning into hers. For a long time, they stood, in silence. Just when Melissa decided nothing would happen, John, still holding her, stepped forward and then back. She felt clumsy and amateurish. Melissa did not know how to dance.

Snubbing her inexperience, John guided her, slowly at first, then, as Melissa matched his steps, with more surety. As they danced, John's hands grew warmer. She squeezed her eyes, shook a little, and John tightened his grasp on her.

"Keep your eyes closed," he hissed in her ear.

Still quaking, Melissa hadn't considered disobeying, but she did detect a faint melody. She tensed her ears. It wasn't Grandma Marchellis' music box playing Bryony, and it wasn't piano music. The song grew louder and more insistent, and, although the composition was unfamiliar, Melissa could not deny the unmistakable sounds of a full-blown orchestra. Was she dreaming? Was she hallucinating? Could one hallucinate and keep time to music?

Suddenly, brightness overwhelmed her eyes, but Melissa resisted the impulse to open them. What was happening? Was it morning, and the light was only the sun at dawn? Maybe, the strange experience was a nightmare, caused by sleeping with a full stomach. Then, John put his lips near her ear, and his warm breath was no longer foul.

"Open your eyes, Melissa," he whispered.

She blinked at the flood of light, and her mouth fell in astonishment. John was waltzing her around a grand ballroom. The wood floor shone like gold, enhancing the gilded ornamentation on the many, crystal chandeliers hanging from the high ceiling. At the far ends of the room, rows of round tables, covered in shimmering, copper fabric, lined the walls. The whirling couples filled the dance floor, men in white tuxedos and women in gay, colorful dresses, intensifying the exhilarating giddiness she now felt.

Melissa caught sight of her reflection on the mirrored walls. She was dressed, from shoulder to toes, in a pale-yellow satin gown, trimmed with lace and pearls. A pearl necklace encircled her throat and matching earrings dangled from her ears. The tight bodice about her waist made deep breaths impossible, but Melissa ignored it. She admired the exquisite whiteness of the gloves, John's and hers. Why, this must have cost a fortune. Entranced, she gazed at her image and thought, I'm beautiful. Never had Melissa dreamed she would bestow that judgment on herself.

"Ravishing, rather," John said.

She glanced up at John, who smiled slyly at her. Melissa quickly averted her gaze.

Why hadn't she noticed in her dreams how tall he was or how broad his shoulders were? She couldn't help stealing another peek. John eyes were still on her. His thick, long hair gleamed in the light. His deep blue eyes bore into hers and warmed her heart.

118

She felt the heat of his hands through their gloves. Was this how Bryony knew him? John pulled her close to him. Melissa nearly burst with happiness.

It was a spectacular evening. Melissa stayed by John's side all night, for he allowed no one else to dance with her. Melissa tingled and flushed when John, full of admiration and pride, introduced her as his beautiful wife, Bryony. John told her this home belonged to Albert Brumfeldt, a publisher of newspapers, books, and sheet music, a devoted admirer of John Simons' compositions, and the host of that evening's concert and subsequent ball in John's honor.

During one such introduction, Melissa accidentally peeped at the guests on her left and almost screamed at the torturous, decaying, writhing individuals in tattered clothes and dripping teeth; they ridiculed Melissa with their eyes. A horrified John was staring at her. With great tact, he guided her through the crowds to an outside balcony. Gently this time, but still firmly, John again placed his hand over her mouth.

"Hush," John said.

"They'll hear you."

"Oh my God! Oh my God! Oh my God!"

John grabbed her shoulders and gave them a little shake, which jolted Melissa into petrified silence. He placed his hands on her cheeks, raised her face, and locked smoldering eyes onto hers.

"Stop," John said, and his voice was very low. "You must understand. I do not proffer the past as it once existed, but the past as it now occurs. Yes, they are all vampires, but as long as you are with me, they dare not harm you."

Melissa started to speak, but John laid a gentle finger on her lips.

"It's quite all right, I assure you. Remember and obey, and you will not be distressed. Always look forward or backward; never allow a peripheral glance, or you will view them in stark reality. Understand?"

John wrapped his arms around Melissa, and all her trepidation melted. He felt so strong, so solid, so protecting. Was this magical moment part of his covenant to her? It was beyond her wildest dreams. How could she ever have mistrusted him? She looked up at John and saw he waited for her answer. Why would a man this talented and wonderful look at her in that way? His face moved closer to hers, and his lips were very near.

There, under the moonlight, John kissed her, with drawn-out tenderness, his soft lips barely meeting hers. Enraptured, Melissa relinquished any lingering doubts. She lifted her chin and willingly offered her neck to him. It was, she decided, a fair trade.

CHAPTER 13: WHO NEEDS CHURCH?

Melissa leaned over her desk, pretending to watch Mrs. Denison demonstrate quadratic equations. Just what happened to her last night? The obvious explanation was too bizarre. John Simons is still alive, she thought. John Simons is a vampire.

In her bedroom, a few hours ago, she believed it. Now, with the autumn sun shining through the window of her algebra classroom, the very premise seemed absurd. *Vampires?* She recalled Brian leaping in that silly cape of his crying, "I vant to drink your blood." John Simons did not fit the category of Easter bunnies, tooth fairies, Santa Claus, and the UFO story she heard on television last week. Vampires were dead people who slept during the day in their coffins and rose at night to drink the blood of sleeping victims. If they didn't get blood, or if someone drove a stake through their hearts, they died. Garlic, crosses, and holy water repelled them. *John Simons is a vampire.* She couldn't swallow it. How convenient for vampires. They could slink around with no one hunting them. *The way John Simons slunk around.*

"You're awfully quiet today," Ann said, sliding beside Melissa.

Yawning, Melissa opened her carton of milk and set it on her lunch tray. "Sorry, Ann. I didn't sleep too well last night."

Julie plunked down across from Melissa. "You're not still freaked out, are you?"

"Oooh, that was pretty freaky," Katie breathed. "We talked to a ghost!"

Ann grimaced. "It's fake. We only spelled 'Kimberly' because we were subconsciously thinking about her."

"Melissa's house was the last place she was seen alive." Julie licked pizza sauce from the back of her hand. "Ghosts like to hang out where they died."

"What do you think, Melissa?" Katie said.

Melissa shrugged and shoved the last piece of crust into her mouth.

"She's tired," Ann said.

"Or maybe daydreaming about Jack Cooper," Katie giggled, glancing at Ann.

Julie looked at Melissa. "So, *do* you think Kimberly's ghost was in your room?"

She closed her eyes and saw a skeletal John Simons sitting in her desk chair, but warmth flowed through her, as she remembered the thrill of dancing close to John and the breathtaking caress of John's lips stroking the side of her neck.

"I thought you guys were mean to spell out Kimberly's name," Melissa said slowly, "but now, I'm not so sure you did."

"Oh, come *on*, Melissa!" Ann gaped at her. "You don't really believe in ghosts!"

"I don't know." Melissa was still thoughtful. "Who can prove ghosts aren't real?"

Julie fired a triumphant smile at Ann. Katie checked her watch and said, "Better hurry." She tossed her wadded napkin on her tray. "Biology starts in five."

"Who thinks earthworm dissections after lunch is a good idea?" Julie groaned.

Melissa picked up her tray and shuffled toward the garbage can. Ann dumped her scraps and looked suspiciously at Melissa.

"Get some sleep tonight, okay?" Ann said.

Before Melissa showered that night, she stood before the bathroom mirror and carefully inspected her body. She scrutinized her arms, spread her fingers to see between each one, and then raised her arms to study underneath. Next, she draped her hair over a shoulder and twisted her trunk to get a good look at her back and down her legs.

Gripping the towel bar with one hand, Melissa set one foot on the sink to check all around the ankle, along the sole, and among her toes, then did the same with the other foot. She tilted her neck from side to side, but didn't see any puncture marks. Wasn't this proof she was only dreaming, that John Simons hadn't bitten her, even after she had raised her neck to him? In movies, vampires left prominent holes in their victims' necks, impressions that vanished after someone killed the vampires. Melissa saw nothing resembling fang marks, not even a mosquito bite. Still, she had to make sure.

After showering and brushing her teeth, Melissa trailed into the living room. "Mom, do you see anything on the back of my neck?"

"Why?"

"I don't know. It just feels like something is there."

Her mother slid a bookmark between the pages of *The Eleventh Commandment* and placed it on the end table. "Turn around. I'll take a look."

Melissa lifted her hair off the nape of her neck and faced Steve, who sat at the dining room table, drilling Brian's spelling. Her mother searched Melissa's neck, then pulled on Melissa's pajama top to peer onto her shoulders and halfway down her back.

"Nope, there's nothing there."

"Oh, well," Melissa dropped her hair. "I guess it's just my imagination."

"Determination," Steve said.

"Hey, maybe a vampire got her the other night!" Brian said.

"Brian," Steve began.

"What if I was the vampire? What if my costume once belonged to a real vampire who put a curse on it? Anyone who wears it becomes a vampire, destined to roam the night and drink people's blood! Boy, wouldn't that be cool?"

"That's stupid." Melissa hugged her mother. "You watch way too many movies."

"Brian," Steve said again.

"Uh, what was the word? Um...d...e...t...e..."

Melissa repressed a smile and shut the bedroom door behind her. Brian had said quite a mouthful. What if she told him about last night? That would trump any Simons Mansion ghost story. She turned back her bedcovers, then reached for her clock, hesitating before setting it to normal wake-up time. If John Simons was real, he should not require an alarm clock to prompt an appearance.

To her great disappointment, Melissa experienced no Bryony dream that night, or the next night, or the next, and she wondered how to fix it. Should she set her alarm clock for the middle of the night or wait for John to visit her? She could not decide.

At dinner Thursday night, her mother announced they were going to church that weekend, in Detroit.

"What!" Brian choked on his milk, and it ran, unheeded, down his nose.

"Brian!" Steve handed Brian a napkin.

"Sorry, Mom, but…church? We never go to church."

"Can't we just go to church in town?" Melissa asked anxiously.

Would John appear to her in Detroit?

"Honestly, I don't see what the big deal is!" Darlene's voice quivered as she spoke, and her lips trembled. "Fr. Alexis called me, and said the church was hosting a memorial service for Grandma Marchellis this Sunday. There's a fellowship dinner in the hall afterwards. Since we're her only living family, the least we could do is show up!"

She threw her fork on her plate, stomped to her bedroom, and slammed the door.

"You know, if I did that," Brian's eyes met Steve's. "I didn't mean to hurt her, but we never go to church. Dad didn't believe in it. I was just surprised."

"Pass the meatloaf, please," Melissa said, "and the gravy, too."

"Gosh, Liss, that's your third helping. What a pig! Save some for us!" Brian glanced again at Steve and stopped.

"I'm glad your appetite is back, Melissa," Steve said. "We were worried."

So, did John visit her every night or only during a Bryony dream, if he came at all, she quickly reminded herself. Had John Simons really defied death? Could Melissa give him a second chance? She doubted her senses. She ached to see him again!

Her mother returned to the table, but Melissa and Brian kept their eyes on their plates, avoiding her swollen eyes and splotchy face.

"Would you like more meatloaf?" Steve said.

With a weary sigh, her mother accepted another slice. "I'm sorry I blew up. I'm just stressed about the memorial service."

Melissa, hoping to appease her mother, said, "When do we pack?" "It can wait until after school tomorrow. Bring bathing suits because we can swim in the hotel pool. On Saturday, we can do sightseeing or shopping, as long as we're back to the hotel fairly early."

"Why?"

"Because Fr. Alexis is taking us to dinner in honor of Melissa's birthday."

Melissa was stunned. "My birthday?"

Her mother patted her hand. "Instead of driving in and out for the service, this can be a mini vacation, to make up for not having a proper birthday celebration. Eighteen is a huge milestone. It should be special."

"Who's Fr. Alexis?" Brian said.

"Don't you remember from the funeral?" Darlene said.

Brian's mouth was full of meatloaf and ketchup, so he shook his head.

"Fr. Alexis Panchuk is the pastor at St. Athanasius Church, where the memorial service will be Sunday morning."

Melissa wished the service happened Friday night, so they could enjoy the rest of the weekend without worrying about it. As Brian methodically cut away a piece of crust, he asked, "What about Snowbell? Can't we take her?"

Their mother clapped a hand to her forehead. "The hotel won't allow animals."

"I'll sneak her inside." "Brian, you can't."

"We're going to let her starve?" Brian was horrified.

"Maybe someone from school could keep her," Steve suggested.

"I don't know anyone," Brian wailed. "Clay's dad is allergic to

Melissa took the last piece of meatloaf. "Maybe Julie can keep her. She already has a cat."

"Go call her, Melissa," Steve said.

Julie agreed to keep Snowbell. With the cat's care arranged, anticipation rose inside Melissa, making it impossible to sleep. She never had a vacation. Her father was too sick for travel. It was midnight when Melissa finally set her book next to the music box on her nightstand.

The music box!

Hadn't she left it hidden inside the drawer? Had someone been snooping in her room? Annoyed, Melissa pushed it to the back and blocked it with her book. She shut her drawer, pulled up the covers, and heard a knock.

"Bryony?"

The Reverend Marseilles poked his head around the door. Tall and thin, with closely cropped gray hair, a long, pointed gray beard, black suit, and white shirt, he looked like an Amish farmer, not a Congregational minister passionate for the arts.

"Yes, Father?"

"John is waiting in the parlor. You have ten minutes."

"Yes, Father."

"Leave the door open." "Yes, Father."

Reverend Marseilles shut the office door. Melissa smiled and closed the ledger. All morning she had counted and recorded the donation change from last Sunday's services. She welcomed the break, made all the more pleasant because she could spend it with John. Why was he calling on her in mid-morning? At the hall mirror, she smoothed her hair and adjusted her salmon-colored day dress, marveling that her father allowed John past the front porch. The reverend had set strict courting rules, even though she and John were engaged, and he did like John.

John stood at the parlor window, gazing into the street. Despite its worn beige carpet and overstuffed pillows and afghans to hide the brown, shabby chairs, the parlor was large enough for entertaining and small enough, especially during long winter nights when the fire was lit, to be cozy. Two walls held bookshelves; several landscape oils hung on the other walls, each with a miniature purple rose painted in the bottom right hand corner. During the warmer months, Melissa arranged vases with fresh flowers from the Betts' garden. It was here Reverend Marseilles often entertained visiting artists and those people, like her father, who shared an observer's interest in art. This room was also where her father allowed her, even from girlhood, to sit and listen, on the stringent condition she remain quiet, so as not to break the stream of sagacious discourse.

She recalled the first night she saw John, or rather, when she noticed him looking at her. She had unintentionally interrupted the meeting with her entrance. The Reverend Marseilles had invited a new young couple from the church to dinner that night. The conversation was lively, and everyone loitered over the meal, until the society men began arriving. Melissa was clearing the table when the couple glanced at the pompous figures strutting into the parlor and quickly declined an invitation to stay. Then Melissa had helped Mrs. Parks wash the dishes, so the housekeeper could hurry home to her sick husband.

The men were discussing Henry James' *Portrait of a Lady,* but when she had entered the parlor, they had all risen with respect. She noticed, with satisfaction, that one of the new men's eyes had riveted toward her and stayed.

"John, I don't believe you have met my daughter," Reverend Marseilles had said. "Bryony, this is Mr. John Simons, international composer and pianist."

Melissa had responded with a courteous smile, which John had returned with a dignified, half-bow. "I am very pleased to make your acquaintance, Miss Marseilles."

He had said no more, but he liked her, Melissa could tell.

Later that evening, after everyone retired, and as Melissa had straightened the cushions, her father had divulged how John had traveled the world with his music and attracted a huge following. John did not seem timid, so why had this famous man waited three whole weeks before requesting her father's permission to court her? Once he received it,

Reverend Marseilles banned his daughter from all society meetings, refusing to taint the purity of the topics discussed with deceptive reasons for attendance. So, under the pretense of reading in her bedroom, Melissa had crouched on the stairs and listened to John's voice.

Melissa had another reason for favoring this parlor, for it was here, last Easter Sunday, that John had proposed marriage. Remembering the brightness in his eyes, as he offered the diamond ring, caused Melissa's own eyes to trail to John's hands, now clasped behind his back. That's when she noticed John clutching another package. She knocked on the open door. John turned at the sound, and Melissa hastened to greet him. His hug, while shooting a glance out the parlor doorway, was brief, but warm.

"Your father's whereabouts?"

"He's making himself scarce. For ten minutes."

Smiling, John shook his head. "He will never survive as number two in your life."

"To him, it's a week away."

"Hmm. Sit. I have something to show you."

He motioned to the sofa before the fire. Wondering, Melissa obeyed. John sat next to her, closer than he would have dared if the Reverend Marseilles had been policing the room. He opened her hand and laid the package in it. Melissa removed the wrapping to reveal a small, carved, highly polished, cherry wood box.

"How lovely!" she breathed.

Painted around its edges were the bryony vines John had bred for her, vines that, by spring, he promised, would bloom pink, shrouding their mansion and bordering their estate grounds. Those words enchanted Melissa. *Their mansion. Their estate.*

John lifted the box's lid. Melissa closed her eyes and listened to the chime of its metallic notes. When the music ceased, Melissa opened her eyes, wrinkled her brow, and looked at John.

"I'm not certain I know that piece."

"You don't," John said. "I composed it just for you, as my wedding gift. We shall dance it together for the first time on Christmas Eve."

"Oh, John!"

"There's more."

John reached inside his pocket and removed a gold pocket watch with an ivory face, black Roman numerals, and silver hands.

128

He gently turned the watch over in his palm. The back's clear glass revealed the inside mechanism. When John pushed a tiny button, the same hypnotizing melody played. A warm, tingling flush spread over Melissa. With the creation of each note, John had thought of her.

He removed the music box from her hand and replaced it with the watch, closing her fingers over the piece and covering them with his warmer, stronger hand. Melissa kept her eyes on the watch. John's unrelenting stare overpowered her.

"Bryony, even when obligations part me from you, these items will…."

"John, how good to see you again."

Melissa started and clutched her throat. John quickly removed the watch and shoved it into his pocket. The Reverend Marseilles strode across the room to embrace John and shake his hand. Melissa sighed and looked at the mantle clock. Exactly ten minutes had passed since the reverend had announced John's arrival. He's certainly punctual, Melissa thought.

"How is my future son-in-law this morning?"

"I merely stopped to check on the young lady's health. She has a big day approaching, you know."

"I do, indeed, and to safeguard that health, excitement should be minimized. Don't you agree?"

"Absolutely." John turned toward Melissa. "A pleasant day to you, Miss Marseilles." He picked up his hat and nodded to her father. "Reverend."

"I'll show you out."

As Reverend Marseilles escorted John to the front door, Melissa raised the music box's lid. No one had ever written a song for her. She rested against the sofa cushion and reveled in the music, a contented smile spreading across her face. She pictured that first dance with John and floated away on the magical strains. She could hardly wait.

Beep, beep, beep. Melissa jumped at the sound. What in the world?

She tipped the music box upside down. Where was the switch? Had she broken it? What if Reverend Marseilles came into the parlor and demanded to know the source of the noise? Melissa reached across her nightstand, turned off the alarm clock, and sat up in bed. She rubbed her eyes, glanced at her nightstand, and blinked in horror.

Bryony's music box sat near the clock, slowly chiming as it wound down.

CHAPTER 14: WEEKEND IN DETROIT

On Friday, time dragged. Detroit will never come, Melissa thought.

She hoped Mr. Masters had planned one of his dramatic recitations. Those never dragged. Instead, Mr. Masters announced a little surprise for them.

"We're going to play a game today," Mr. Masters said. "Boys against the girls. It's called, 'Who Said It Hangman?'"

Melissa and Ann gawked at each other. Seriously?

"Now the rules are quite simple. I will mark a series of dashes on the board, and you shall guess the quote. However, there's a catch. To win, you must also guess what character spoke, the title of the piece, and its author."

Everyone, except Melissa and Ann, groaned in unison. Mr. Masters looked smug. "I knew you'd be excited."

The game was easy, for those who had paid attention in class. Julie guessed the final quote: "'He had loved the princess, and neither he, she, nor anyone else, thought of denying the fact.'"

"The story?" Mr. Masters said

Katie raised her hand. "'The Lady, or the Tiger?'"

"And the author, Ann?"

Ann bit her lip and stared at the ceiling, thinking. "Frank Stockton?"

"Frank R. Stockton," Melissa interrupted, then grinned at Ann.

Mr. Masters frowned at her. "In what year did he die? Julie?"

Julie scrunched her face. "I don't remember."

Jack Cooper raised his hand. "That would be 1902, sir."

Mr. Masters lit up. "Boys win! Class dismissed!"

A chorus of "No fairs!" rang up from the girls, but Mr. Masters was already erasing the chalkboard. Red-headed class clown Dan Walker and his sidekick, stocky, mop-haired Joey Brown, taunted the girls in the hall with broad, victorious smiles.

"Losers!" Dan said, and Joey guffawed on cue.

In vain, the girls protested, but the boys' shouts only grew louder. Jack Cooper, eyes straight ahead, did not join their celebration. Ann solicited Melissa's support, but Melissa merely sprinted to her locker. She cared only about Detroit. Steve had left work early to drive them home, so they could pack their suitcases and prepare a lunchbox dinner to eat during the drive, to beat rush hour traffic.

"When are you dropping off Snowbell?" Julie shifted her books and leaned against the locker adjacent to Melissa's. "I've got a piano lesson tonight in Jenson."

"On the way." Melissa jammed her books inside her locker. "I'll call first."

One would think Brian was abandoning a newborn baby. He brought the cat's blanket, food, water bowl, food dish, litter box, brush, and favorite toys.

"Brian, we're only going for a weekend," Darlene said, as Brian loaded Snowbell's possessions into the car. "Besides, Julie already has everything cats need."

"But, Mom, she's never been away from me." Brian's voice had a catch in it. "I don't want her to miss us." He looked to Steve for assistance, and Steve provided it.

"Nothing worse than a homesick cat." Steve grinned and flicked Brian's nose. "Have we got everything? Yes? Well, everybody, hop in!"

Julie was waiting for them at the front door. Brian handed Julie the box, explained Snowbell's feeding schedule, and provided the hotel telephone number. He hugged Snowbell one last time. "Be a good kitty. I'll see you Sunday."

"For Pete's sake," Melissa fumed from the back seat. "Mom, make him hurry!"

"I promise to take very good care of Snowbell," Julie said.

"Be careful with her neck," Brian added. "We still don't know what's wrong with it."

Julie lingered at the door, waving good-bye. Brian waited until Steve backed out to roll down the window, stick out his head, and yell, "Call if you need anything!" Once on the highway, Brian squirmed and fidgeted in anticipation of the weekend's fun.

"Sit still!" Melissa jabbed his ribs with her elbow. "There's no room." She stretched her feet over her suitcase and massaged a cramp in her calf.

"Well, you're the stupid one for not putting your stuff in the trunk."

"How could I? You had Snowbell's junk in there!" "It's not junk!"

Steve glanced at them from the rear-view mirror. "Brian and Melissa! Any more fighting, and there's no swimming tonight."

The words "no swimming," cast a spell on Brian. He settled into the seat with a new comic book. Melissa set her cassette player on her lap, adjusted the ear plug, and contemplated John Simons' last visit.

At the pool, Steve glided through the water with the skill of a professional swimmer. He demonstrated several impressive dives and taught Melissa and Brian the dead man's float and the dog paddle. Melissa drifted lazily on her back, enjoying the lapping of the water at her ears. Did Bryony ever swim? Brian positioned his hands the way Steve showed him and propelled himself from one side of the deep end to the other.

"Hey, Liss!" his voice echoed off the walls. "I'm Scooter!"

His announcement broke her concentration, and she sank. She bounced her toes off the pool's floor, turned a somersault, then jumped up for air, water trickling water down her forehead, into her eyes, and past her ears. She wiped her face with the backs of her hands, shook her head from side to side, and looked around for Steve. With smooth, easy strokes, Steve was swimming across the far end toward the diving board. Where had he learned to swim so well? Surely, not Lake Munson?

After an hour of splashing, Melissa wearily climbed onto the side of the pool. Her wet suit clung like plastic wrap. Contentedly, she sat on the damp concrete, drew little circles in the water with her feet, and watched Steve show Brian proper diving techniques. A few minutes later, her mother was dangling her feet, too. Strands of wet hair strayed from beneath her mother's rubber swim cap and stuck to her cheeks. She waved and smiled at Brian and Steve, then turned to Melissa. "Having fun?"

Splash! Brian landed on his stomach. He clawed to the top of the water and clutched his ribs. "Ow!"

Steve quickly reached him, looking concerned. "Are you okay?"

Brian managed a weak smile. "I think so. Just knocked the air out of me."

"Rest awhile, and you can try it again."

Within five minutes, Brian was again crouching on the diving board. This time, he completed a successful dive.

"Hurray!" Brian scrambled out of the water. "Did you see that Steve? I did it!"

Steve leaned his elbows outside the pool, looked at their mother, and winked.

"What do you say? Five more minutes?"

"Sounds good to me."

"What! No fair! We're just getting started."

As proof, Brian plunged into the water, flailing arms and legs, and spraying everything within reach. He paused to catch his breath, then he held his nose again and swam to the shallow side.

Steve climbed from the pool and dried his hair. "Brian, if you're up bright and early, I will take you swimming before breakfast."

Brian fired Steve a fiendish grin, but he resignedly climbed the pool's ladder. The next morning, they both arrived at the breakfast table with wet hair. Ordinarily, Melissa might have felt jealous of Brian's extra swim, but today she preferred studying the white tablecloths, the brown-patterned carpet, the dark wood chairs with ruby-cushioned backs, and print wallpaper. Had the dining room inside Simons Mansion looked this elegant?

Her mother leafed through brochures of Detroit's tourist sites, while the fellows ordered their food. After the waitress left, her mother set down a pamphlet about the Detroit Science Center, which Steve immediately scooped up and showed to Brian.

"What do you say, sport?"

Brian quickly scanned it. "Does it have dinosaurs?"

"I was hoping you might like the Art Institute," Darlene said. "I went years ago."

"With Frank?" Steve asked, stirring creamer into his coffee.

Melissa peered closely at him. There was something in his voice that almost sounded mad, but she couldn't tell why. Maybe, Steve simply preferred science to art, and he was afraid her mother would convince him otherwise. Her mother mulled over another brochure and didn't answer him, but, without moving her eyes away from the text, she slid the information across the table. Steve picked it up and carefully studied it.

Brian was annoyed. "Who wants to look at old paintings?"

"I'd like to hear the Detroit Symphony Orchestra," Melissa said. Brian's eyes widened. "I knew it. She's lost her mind."

Steve and her mother exchanged surprised looks, which flustered Melissa. "Can't I expand my musical tastes? I'm eighteen now."

"Honey, you won't get tickets this late," Darlene said. "But it is your birthday celebration. Would you rather we went to the science center with the guys?"

"Nope. I'll go to the Art Institute with you."

Brian looked glum, but he kept his eyes on his plate. Steve noticed and patted her mother's hand. "Are you okay splitting up for the day?"

"I don't mind. Just be sure you and Brian are back by three o'clock to shower and change clothes. We have to meet Fr. Alexis at five."

"Aw, Mom, can't you and Steve just go? Liss and I can order room service."

"No, this is a special dinner for Melissa," Darlene said, "but those who behave get one last swim before bedtime."

Brian flew out of his chair and hugged his mother. She choked and quickly set down her coffee.

"I'll be a perfect angel," Brian said.

"Fallen angel, maybe," Melissa mumbled, so no one could hear.

Melissa didn't find the art museum very interesting, but her mother did, leaving Melissa's mind free to wander back into John's arms at the Brumfeldt ball and to the sofa inside the Reverend Marseilles' parlor, where she sat very close to John, feeling his bare hands. Occasionally, Melissa offered an appropriate remark about this painting or that piece, which seemed to satisfy her mother's desire for conversation.

All too soon, Melissa was sitting in the hotel dining room with the reserved Fr. Alexis. Despite his average height, Melissa felt intimidated by the long white beard on a deeply lined face that didn't know the meaning of a smile. The dinner conversation revolved around their weekend in Detroit, which Melissa didn't find as fascinating as wondering whether or not she was actually reliving Bryony's experiences.

Brian sneezed. Startled into reality, Melissa glanced up. He had scrubbed his face bright pink and appeared very grown-up in his blue and red plaid shirt and black pants. He had draped his napkin over his lap and now, with painstaking care, was cutting roast beef into perfect pieces with a fork *and* a knife. Steve caught his eye and winked, but, when Brian tried to wink back, a piece of roast beef flew off his plate. He sighed in frustration, then lifted the edge of the tablecloth and scoured the carpet for it. Melissa nudged his foot, and Brian's head popped up.

No one saw, Melissa mouthed to him.

Brian relaxed and picked up his fork. Melissa's mind returned to John. The microfilm Melissa had read during her research project never mentioned a musical watch. Had John owned one? Should she ask Mrs. Clements?

"How is the restoration coming on the Simons estate?" Fr. Alexis asked. "It's been many years since I'd been there."

Melissa's ears pricked up.

"You've seen the estate?" Darlene sounded annoyed.

"Well, yes, but, as I said, it's been a long time," Fr. Alexis said.

136

"After Frank died, I wondered what had happened to the mansion until I learned you had sold it to the village."

"For crying out loud! Honestly, it seems nearly everyone knew Frank owned Simons Mansion except us. He never said a single word about it."

Fr. Alexis dusted his beard with his napkin. "I'm really quite surprised. I thought it was fairly common knowledge."

"Do you know why Frank bought it?"

"Not Frank. Peter Marchellis purchased the mansion in 1955 after the death of John Simons. He...."

"That's not true," Melissa objected, breaking into the conversation. "John Simons left town after Bryony and his baby died. No one ever heard from him again."

Her mother gave a cautionary look. "Melissa wrote a report on Bryony Simons for the centennial celebration. Her teacher gave her a high grade for it."

Fr. Alexis dismissed those comments. "Perhaps Melissa should have carefully checked her facts, but, I suppose, legend is considerably more interesting than history."

That's what Steve had said, Melissa thought, which made her look at Steve. He was eating and listening attentively to the conversation with the same odd expression from this morning. What had upset Steve?

"The fact is many people did hear from John Simons. Although rumor states he never returned to Munsonville, the likely truth is he did, because the mansion received basic upkeep and remained in his name, until his death."

Fr. Alexis looked at Melissa. "In 1955."

"What compelled Peter Marchellis to buy it?" Darlene hastily asked.

"His wife's family had often come to Munsonville for the fishing, and she had fond memories of it. So, when the house went to auction after John's death, she persuaded her husband to buy it. She had always intended to restore it to the original condition. Certainly, Peter Marchellis had the money to do it."

"Why didn't they?" Melissa asked.

"Because your grandfather died soon after the purchase, and your grandmother didn't want to tackle the project without him. Even then, village wanted Simons Mansion for a tourist attraction, but your grandmother was against it and refused any offers proposed to her. She maintained the place just enough to keep the village off her back. After your grandmother's first stroke, your father sold most of her assets to pay for her care, but she insisted he take the mansion. He agreed with her decision, to humor her, possibly, although he did manage a special account for the house."

Fr. Alexis leaned slightly forward and looked hard at her mother, who turned as maroon as her sweater.

"Forgive me, if I sound complaining," Darlene stammered. "It's just that...."

Melissa noticed Steve had stopped eating and was monitoring this exchange.

"Personally, I'm convinced if Frank had any interest in the restoration process, they flew out the window when he met and married you," Fr. Alexis said. "Knowing his fragile health, he intended the mansion to be your resource. Fortunately for him, his mother was in no frame of mind to argue with his decision."

Darlene sighed. "I'm certainly grateful. That mansion was a godsend."

"Anyone for dessert?" the waitress said.

The adults declined. Brian, however, ordered a hot fudge sundae.

"Melissa?" Steve asked, eyes twinkling now. "It's your birthday."

She shook her head and said, "I'm too full." The trip, and John, was enough.

Brian dropped his jaw and stared at her with wide eyes. "I don't believe it. You should see her eat at home. She eats like a little pi...."

He stopped. Steve glowered at him, and Fr. Alexis quickly filled the silence.

"Darlene, do you only write children's stories?"

Melissa pretended to listen while Brian ate his ice cream, but her thoughts lingered on Fr. Alexis' words. She did some brisk, mental arithmetic. John must have been nearly ninety when he died. What had transformed him into a vampire?

After Fr. Alexis paid the bill and left, Steve asked, "Who's ready for a swim?"

"Me!" Brian exclaimed, sliding his chair away from the table and jumping to his feet. Steve set a hand on Brian's shoulder and lowered him into the chair. "Melissa?"

"Oh, yes! Are you coming, Mom?"

"I think I'll pass, if you don't mind taking the kids, Steve. I'm a little tired," Darlene said, looking as if she might cry.

Only Brian's heart was in the water. He paddled and thrashed with glee. Steve, while not having a bad time, wasn't as enthusiastic as last night. Spending a day with Brian probably exhausted him. Melissa leisurely moved up and down the pool, picturing John and her swimming in Lake Munson on a summer's day. Steve's voice cut the daydream short. "Last one out is a rotten egg!"

"It's been an hour?" Melissa wiped away water and squinted at the wall clock.

That night, Melissa dreamed she sat in the restaurant with her grandparents. Grandma wore her nightgown from Jenson Nursing Home, but her grandfather was dressed in a brown pin-striped suit and brown bowler hat. While her grandparents talked in low voices, Melissa stabbed at her roast beef, but the meat kept moving to one side. Fr. Alexis watched contemptuously. The beef chuckled.

"You eat like a pig, Melissa," Brian said with a snort.

Melissa opened her mouth to retort, but Brian had changed completely into a little pink pig, who sat on his chair wearing a plaid shirt. She peered over Grandma Marchellis' shoulder. A set of plans for Simons Mansion now lay on the table.

"Hey!" Melissa tugged her grandmother's arm. The misshapen rooms had changed places. "These are wrong!"

Grandpa Marchellis snatched the sheets and rolled them. "Next time, get your facts straight!"

Grandma threw back her head and laughed, shocking Melissa into alertness, but her mother's traveling alarm clock produced no sound. A sliver of light pierced the blackness from the slightly ajar bathroom door. Hot and stifling air gagged Melissa. The clock read three-thirty. Her mother's breathing was soft and light.

Melissa padded to the bathroom for a glass of water, and, while looking in the mirror, leaned her head from side to side. No puncture wounds. Back in the bedroom, she lowered the heat and pulled the curtains aside an inch. The moon above the empty street shone large and full in the calm night. For a long time, Melissa gazed at it, willing John to appear. When she returned to bed, Melissa lay still, staring at the ceiling, but seeing ballroom dancers.

Her mother was ready for church when Melissa woke. "Hello, sleepyhead, hurry and get dressed. We won't order until you come down." She blew a kiss and left.

Breakfast was serene, even with the church service approaching. Brian delighted in the assortment of pancake toppings. "Why don't we buy blueberry syrup?"

"For Pete's sake," Melissa said. "Blueberry syrup! And the science center?"

"It was fun." Brian spelled a cursive "B" on his pancake with thick syrup. "But a guy's got to eat, too. Do you want my stomach to growl in church?"

At church, Brian stood still and remained quiet, but the monotonous chanting bored Melissa. She amused herself by watching the clergy weave in and out among the altar's doors, gazing at the many icons, and listening to Fr. Alexis' sermon about Grandma's devotion to the Holy Mysteries. Afterwards, Melissa endured the same insufferable hugging and kissing by the women of the church, but, this time, her little brother placidly accepted it.

"Boy, oh boy," Brian said, when he joined Melissa, his plate piled high with food. "I can't stand the way all those old ladies smooch on me, but they sure can cook."

Melissa picked at chicken, rolls, and a plain lettuce salad. Still, the large spread in honor of her grandmother impressed her. Fr. Alexis wound through the church hall, shaking hands, offering greetings, and patting small children's heads. Her mother thanked him profusely for his hospitality.

"You're very welcome," Fr. Alexis said. "Perhaps you will visit us again."

"Yes, thank you very much," Brian echoed, looking at Steve.

The priest was moving to the next table when Melissa found her courage. "Fr. Alexis, may I ask you a question? It's about something you said during your talk.

140

Fr. Alexis paused, looking pleased she had paid attention. A satisfied smile spread across her mother's face. Melissa felt proud for detaining him.

"You said Grandma was devoted to, 'The Holy Mysteries.' What are they?"

He stroked his beard. "In the Orthodox Church, we believe the bread and wine we offer and consume is really the body and blood of our Lord and Savior Jesus Christ."

Brian's forkful of carrot cake stopped in mid-air. "You're kidding!"

"Jesus' followers reacted the same way," Fr. Alexis said, "but, as Orthodox Christians, this is the core of our spirituality. I haven't time to speak further, but call me, with your mother's permission, if you have additional questions."

During the drive home, Steve listened to the news; her mother composed a chore list; Brian hummed the opening song from a cartoon show; and Melissa considered Fr. Alexis's words. Orthodox Christians and vampires needed blood to survive. Were the concepts somehow connected? She wanted to discuss it, but the only person available was Brian, and his mind was on Snowbell.

"I sure hope she had a good time, too," he said, between hums.

Snowbell's possessions were packed and waiting at the front door. Julie pushed Snowbell at Brian with such force he almost dropped her. Then she shoved Snowbell's supply box onto the front porch. "Don't ever ask me to watch your creepy cat again!"

"Hey! What's the matter with you? Are you nuts? You could hurt her!"

Julie stormed inside the house and slammed the door. Brian tenderly cuddled Snowbell and murmured, "You're not creepy." Snowbell nestled into his arms and purred. "She is though!" he called after Julie.

Melissa carried Snowbell's box down the stairs. The cat behaved at home. How could Snowbell have made Julie so angry? At home, Brian washed Snowbell's feeding dishes and disinfected the litter box with annoying fastidiousness, to Melissa's annoyance.

"You're being extreme."

Brian snorted. "Liss, who knows what germs are lurking at Julie's house?"

After unpacking and a quick peanut butter sandwich, Melissa climbed into bed.

The music box faintly played while Melissa sat in the Grover's Park basement playing cards with John Simons, now with slicked-back hair, black cape, and Hollywood-style fangs. Kimberly hovered over John's chair and, with unblinking and spiteful eyes, scrutinized her moves.

The airless, yellow-orange room was sweltering. With shaking, slippery hands, Melissa studied the black suits and the demonic faces. John leaned forward, ready to pounce. Melissa slammed down a card.

John leaped at her in a rage, knocking over the game table. His hands tightened around her neck. His hot breath sliced her throat.

Melissa screamed and sat up. Sweat rolled off her face and down her neck. Her heartbeat fast. Breathing was short, quick gasps. She still felt John's arms around her, even as she beat them away.

"Shhh," John murmured, rocking her back and forth. "You're safe with me, Bryony. It was only a dream."

Melissa yanked back, aghast. John's eyes drooped sleepily; his long, tousled hair fell over his eyes and clung to his blue silk pajamas. She blinked against the dim firelight. The low flames cast flickering shadows on the curtains hanging around the four-poster. A long-sleeved pink nightgown had replaced her favorite pajamas. In whose bed had she awakened?

CHAPTER 15: PLAYING BRYONY

Melissa's eyes flew open. The morning sunshine poured into her bedroom. School! She started to throw back the blankets, then stopped, astonished. Melissa didn't own a rosebud quilt. She crawled to the end of the bed and peeked around its curtain. Her room was gone. Last night was not a dream.

Bryony-flecked wallpaper decorated her walls and bryony-patterned curtains fluttered in the chilly, early morning air. A quick survey of the room revealed a washstand with tile on the wall behind it and towel racks on both sides; a tall, ornately carved mirror; a large, beveled wardrobe; a toilet table and chair; a small bookcase; a chest of drawers; a fireplace; and a small couch, all in cherry wood, like Bryony's music box.

Before she could respond to the knock at the door, a slender girl, about Melissa's age, in a black dress entered. Her tawny, corkscrew curls bobbed beneath the white cap, as she carried the silver tray across the room and set it on a small bedside table.

"Good morning, Mrs. John," the girl said. "Mr. John has finished breakfast and is reading the newspaper in the morning room. I'll be back soon to help you dress."

Melissa wasn't sure how to respond. The girl noticed her puzzled expression.

"I'm Trudi, ma'am, remember? I helped you before the wedding." Trudi lifted the bell on the tray. "Just ring if you need anything." She shut the door.

Curious, and hungry, Melissa peeped under the lids: scrambled eggs, sliced pear in syrup, fried potatoes, and puffy-looking bread glistening with sugar. She slid the encrusted ham and fish to the far side of her plate and picked the green pepper from the potatoes. The scrambled eggs had a slightly smoky taste. The bread was good.

The fire crackled, and she looked up to see her music box resting in a prominent place on the toilet table, just like in the dream when John had brushed her hair. Melissa set aside the tray and walked to the table. The rectangular center mirror, which held the beloved music box, had silver edges resembling vines and stood on four, tiny legs. Round silver mirrors held trinket boxes and perfume bottles of colored glass. Matching stones bedecked the bottles under their cloudy glass stoppers. Melissa opened a transparent purple one and smelled the pungent scent she recognized from the estate. Some trinket boxes were oval, but all had either fairy or animal-shaped knobs. One cat resembled Snowbell, for its fur was white; its staring eyes were blue; and its head was cocked to one side. Melissa lifted that lid and revealed a set of silver filigree earrings. She dangled them before her ears and wondered how often Bryony had worn them.

Trudi knocked, startling Melissa into dropping the earrings and scampering to bed, just as the little maid pushed open the door. "All done?"

Melissa nodded. Trudi removed the tray and placed it near the door. "Good. Let's get you ready. It's time to see Mr. John."

The maid opened the wardrobe and selected a cream-colored dress, printed with dainty, blue flowers. Melissa hesitated, looking at the floor. She did not want to undress in front of this strange girl.

"I can do this myself, if you don't mind." Then, her eyes rested on the pile of unfamiliar clothes lying on the bed. "Are those all mine?"

"Of course."

Her mind spun with sudden panic. How would she decipher that stack of garments? Feeling foolish and embarrassed, Melissa raised her arms and submitted to Trudi. White stockings went first, then garters to hold them in place. Cotton drawers followed; these flapped against her legs. Next came a chemise, which resembled the painting smocks she wore in kindergarten. The corset was the worst. Melissa grabbed the bedposts while Trudi pulled the strings. Her ribs cramped, and her lungs constricted.

"I can't breathe!" Melissa cried out in a voice scarcely higher than a whisper.

Trudi relented and loosened the strings.

"More?" Melissa's hopeful smile faded at Trudi's shocked expression.

"It's not proper," Trudi said. "It's just not right, Mrs. John."

The maid slid a camisole over the corset and then two petticoats. Finally, Melissa put on the dress. While Trudi finished dressing Melissa, she reviewed the schedule with her. This morning she would meet with Bryga Czarnecki, the housekeeper, who would familiarize Melissa with the rest of the servants and their duties.

"It's a bit unusual, I know," Trudi said, "but Bryga has worked many years for Mr. John, so he decided this would be good instruction for you."

Mid-morning, John himself would lead Melissa through the stables and grounds. After lunch, Melissa could return to her bedroom to read and nap.

"Mr. John wants you to rest this first week," Trudi said. "However, the ladies of your father's church have a reception for you this afternoon. He said you may attend."

"Mr. John" certainly made many of Bryony's decisions. Perhaps, Bryony, young and innocent, relied on John's wisdom and experience.

Trudi led Melissa to the morning room. At once, Melissa recognized it as the parlor where Kimberly had spilt tea on her, the night she had found a sneering John Simons braced over her chest. However this morning John, dressed in grey striped pants and black vest, sitting at the small table by the large west window, sipping coffee and reading the newspaper, looked anything but vicious. Seeing him in such an unceremonious setting, Melissa suddenly felt inadequate for the grand role she now played. Since escape was impossible, Melissa took a deep breath, lifted her head, walked to her husband, and kissed the top of his head. Was it the right move, consistent with Bryony's actions?

At once, John set the newspaper on the table and drew Melissa onto his lap. "To ensure no more bad dreams," he said, with an inviting smile. He picked up the newspaper, folded it back, and handed it to Melissa.

"Home or abroad, it appears we create quite a stir," he said. "Read it."

Melissa read it. *The Munsonville Times* announced John and Bryony Simons' return from their two month Chicago honeymoon, recapped the wedding celebration, and promised the villagers more festivities at Simons Mansion. More festivities! If Melissa was Bryony, must she now do the planning?

"I think I'll unpack first," Melissa said, too nervous to smile back. She heard a knock on the door.

"Come in," John called from behind her.

Another maid, raven hair piled under her cap, started into the room, until she saw Melissa perched on John's leg.

"Oh, goodness! Pardon me!" The maid ducked her head. "Please forgive the intrusion."

John laughed. "Mrs. Simons will be ready shortly. She is just finishing her tea."

The maid bowed and hastily shut the door. John, still chuckling, shook his head and slid Melissa closer to him. She laid her cheek on his shoulder, exulting in her good fortune of being so close to him. This was much better than Detroit.

"Her little daughter, Anna, is running around somewhere," he said. "You mustn't mind Bryga. She has been with me for years. Her husband worked as my valet before he died. Good people. When you're ready, she'll run you through the house."

Melissa nodded her head in agreement, hoping John wasn't quite ready to leave.

"I have a piece I must complete," he added, and her heart plunged.

Despite her continued shyness in his presence, Melissa longed for him to stay. John must have sensed her feelings, for he leaned back, laid her head on his chest, and stroked her hair. His touch soothed her, but an eerie silence blunted her enjoyment. John had no heartbeat.

"Ma'am?" Bryga's voice made Melissa jump.

John kissed Melissa's forehead and eased her from his lap. "I will see you soon."

"All right."

She could still feel his lips, and the feeling warmed her from head to toe, dispelling her uneasiness. Did Bryga notice she hadn't drunk any tea?

John shut the door behind him. Bryga stared at Melissa, and Melissa reddened. Bryga, just an inch taller than Melissa, was plump, with a round face and bright, black eyes, well suited for supervising a large household. I'll be she doesn't miss a trick, Melissa thought, then noticed Bryga was still watching her.

"Well," Melissa said aloud. "I'm ready when you are."

Bryga led Melissa into the foyer, but before they descended the stairs, Bryga pointed out the bedrooms. Most were unused guest rooms. Melissa wondered which one Bryony had chosen for a nursery, but decided asking would be out of character. The servants, except Anna and Bryga, for they lived in the cottage Melissa now called home, occupied the fourth floor rooms.

"What about this one?" Melissa asked.

She placed her hand on the doorknob of the room closest to hers and turned it.

Bryga covered her mouth and gasped. Melissa dropped her hand as quickly as if she had burned it.

"Begging your pardon, mum," Bryga said, "but that room is Mr. John's. Nobody goes into his sanctuary except for him, Howard, and me when I clean it."

Melissa raised her eyebrows in surprise. "Not even his wife?"

The question distressed Bryga. "No, ma'am. I'm really sorry, ma'am." Melissa sighed, but did not press the issue. Was this part of Victorian society, or simply another of John's quirks? As she walked down the stairs, Melissa wondered if she should make conversation with Bryga. How did one address servants?

"John says you have worked for him a long time," Melissa began, hoping she was observing proper decorum. They had reached the main staircase.

"Only the last five years. My parents had worked for his father." Melissa trailed her fingers along the polished banister and thought about John's family. Would requesting details raise suspicions? Shouldn't Bryony know John's personal history? Lively piano music cut her thoughts short.

"Now it feels like home," Bryga said, smiling. "No matter where we've been, it's never the same without Mr. John's music. I'll introduce the other servants to you."

Melissa's head spun with all the names. She would never match them with the right faces. She learned that, although Bryga supervised the female servants and delegated their duties, Bryga herself reported to Melissa. Gladys oversaw the kitchen and the rest of the cooks. Mildred, the housemaid, took charge of parlor maids and chamber maids, but had the nasty habit of spilling kerosene every time she filled the lamps. Nellie was the scullery maid, and Hattie kept track of the laundry staff. The butler, Morton Brooks, directed the household affairs and managed the footmen, James and Robert, whose main duties appeared to be waiting on tables and opening doors.

"You will probably not have too much to do with them," Bryga said, "although they must obey any orders you give them." Melissa nodded, but thought, Wow!

They had reached the bottom of the stairs. Peeping at Melissa between the railings was a little girl about six years old. A short, blunt haircut framed her large, brown eyes. She wore a faded dove-colored dress with a high neck collar, wide hem at its bottom, and sleeves folded three times at the wrists.

"This is my daughter, Anna," Bryga said, with a stern look at the girl.

Anna curtsied to Melissa, then fled out the back door.

148

"I'm really sorry," Bryga said, as she led Melissa to the cellar. "She knows not to come to the front, but she's bashful. Spying was a safe way to meet you."

"It's quite all right." Melissa hoped Anna wasn't in trouble.

Although she had remembered that the laundry room and kitchen were in the basement, Melissa had not realized what cooking pre-twentieth century meals three times a day and washing the household laundry actually meant. One servant girl was disjointing a chicken; another was chopping a large bowlful of vegetables; and a third, whom Melissa assumed was Nellie, was washing a stack of dishes so large Melissa didn't think she would get done. Nellie already looked tired, and it was only mid-morning. Several limp locks of hair dangled in her face, but she brushed them aside with a soapy hand.

The kitchen was huge and contained several stations. One section had food-preparation tables with drawers; another held several coal stoves; and a third was reserved for dish washing. Shelves for pots, pans, and staples, such as flour and sugar, covered every available wall space. Utensils hung from large hooks on the wall. There was an enormous, walk-in pantry, along with two cellars, one for vegetables and another for wine. Melissa peered inside a large oak cabinet. A block of ice rested on its top shelf; milk, cream, and butter occupied the others. Why it's a refrigerator, Melissa thought. She wiped her damp forehead with her sleeve and flushed at Bryga's shocked look. Had Bryony always acted ladylike?

The adjacent laundry room produced enough steam for a sauna. A stove heated water and irons. Melissa noted several wash tubs and numerous wood frames for drying the clothes. Two more servant girls, their faces pink and damp from effort and heat, scrubbed clothes on long boards. To think she had argued with Brian about moving clothes to the dryer!

As Melissa climbed the last step to the first floor, John walked out of the music room, while pulling on his morning coat. He lightly kissed her forehead and said to Bryga, "I'm taking Mrs. Simons for a tour of the grounds. We shall return by lunch."

Melissa, of course, had already seen the grounds with Brian, but how differently they now looked! Everything seemed fresh, new, and white, from the trellises displaying creeping bryony weed to the distant gazebo. Cobblestone paths, obviously trodden underground ages ago, for Melissa had never seen them, led to different parts of the estate.

Signs of spring had arrived early that year in Munsonville. Red, yellow, and orange buds poked from their hiding places beneath the soil, although Melissa could not identify the flowers. In Grover's Park, her mother had planted mostly tomatoes and impatiens along the sides of the house, but Simons Mansion contained many gardens, each grouped by type or theme. With pride, John showed Melissa the fledgling fruit orchards, the extensive vegetable plots, and the many flowerbeds.

Taking Melissa's hand in his, John led her to his rose garden, the perfect place, he said, for hosting women's teas. Abruptly, he strode to a bush in the middle and bent to examine it. He stood, shook his head in disgust, and scanned the grounds. "Fredericks!"

In the distance, Melissa saw the gardener halt his pruning and tear toward the rose garden. He was already clutching his cap by the time he reached John.

"Begging your pardon, ma'am." Fredericks glanced anxiously at Melissa.

"Never mind!" John thundered. He gestured to the rose bushes. "Look!"

Fredericks ran to the offending bushes and stooped for a close inspection. He moved several plants from side to side. Why, he's stalling, Melissa thought, as Fredericks finally straightened and faced John.

"I don't know how they got there, sir. I assure you I didn't plant them."

"I want them out. *Now.*"

"Yes, sir. I'll get a shovel."

The mortified Fredericks bowed his head at Melissa and began to walk away.

"Wait." To Melissa's wonder, Fredericks waited. She was not accustomed to giving orders, much less having adults obey them. "John, what's wrong with the bushes?"

"Wrong color."

"What color are they?"

"Purple!"

150

"Purple?" Melissa turned to Fredericks for confirmation, and he nodded. "Why, I've never heard of purple roses."

"Well, they do exist, ma'am. Seen 'em myself."

"And you don't know how they got there?"

"No, ma'am."

If she begged, would John allow her to keep them? Just how far would John carry this strange play? Did he really consider her Bryony?

"Oh, John, they're not hurting anything, and I think the other ladies will find them delightful. Please?"

John scowled. Melissa stood on her toes to kiss his cheek, shocked at her boldness. His expression softened, but he only slid his watch from his pocket, checked the time, and said, "I'll show you the carriage house and stables."

So, could she keep them? John closed his watch, and the music stopped.

The carriage house paralleled the mansion in design, down to the bay windows. Another cobblestone path led back to the mansion. John told Melissa only the coachmen stayed in the carriage house. The stable crew lived in the village. John employed two head coachmen, as well as several assistants. Tom Jenkins, first coachman, drove during the day. Alfred Jackson, second coachman, had the misfortune of leading all night trips.

"A fact he reminds me every chance he gets," John said.

Melissa contemplated balls, dinner parties, and festive dress. She sighed with expectancy and wondered why Jackson complained. It seemed he had the better deal.

The carriage house held three covered carriages, two open carriages, and a new sleigh. "We'll take it on its maiden voyage the day of the first snowfall," John promised.

The stables were several paces away. John owned many Arabian horses, which he had ordered during last summer's World's Fair in Chicago. Stable Master Sam Engerson monitored the father/son team of Charlie and Willie Anders, groom and stable boy.

Melissa's experiences with barns were limited to petting zoos. John's stables were larger than her former ranch home, and she marveled that horses required so much space. John handles his horses with the same ease as he did his piano, but Melissa had never touched horses, and she shrank from them. What if one bit her? John lifted Melissa's hand and stroked it against a velvety nose.

"Oh, it's soft!" Melissa said, forgetting her fear.

After lunch, John showed off the spacious music room and its adjoining library, which, because of its proximity to the music room, doubled as John's study. A fireplace graced one end of the room, and his desk sat opposite. Bookshelves lined an entire wall. The room's deep crimson and brown colors appealed to Melissa, as did the thick brass curtain rods and the heavy, gold frames surrounding the large portraits on the wall. She gave them only a quick notice since none were Bryony. Three logs sharpened to a point and a sword with a black handle and silver blade hung over John's desk.

"How odd," Melissa said. "Are they part of a collection?"

John smiled in a mean way. "They keep the vampires away."

"The what?"

"You heard me."

John trotted through the adjoining doors into the music room and shut them. Brisk piano music rent the air. John's abrupt actions confused her. She had not intended to upset him. Was he always so moody?

Melissa ascended the staircase to her bedroom and thought, John is the vampire. When he was married to Bryony, he wasn't a vampire. So, why would John need vampire weapons? Did he have them eighty years ago? Melissa sighed. It was a riddle with no easy solution, and she doubted John would offer answers anytime soon.

The next day, Melissa again awakened in Bryony's room. Although it was only her second day at Simons Mansion, she was learning her routine, which included the necessity of owning a dressing maid to the mechanics of stoking a fire. On this particular morning, Melissa raised the food trays and found potatoes mashed with fish, cottage cheese balls, rice pancakes, and sliced orange in syrup. It was not her typical breakfast back home, but it was surprisingly delicious, except for the potatoes, which she wrapped in her napkin to hide the smell.

The next few weeks passed in a blur. Melissa treasured the early part of the morning, when she and John discussed upcoming plans, for she actually saw very little of John. He mostly occupied the music room, composing or practicing his pieces, and infused the house with poignant melodies. To John, his piano was not simply a functional, music-making device. It was an extension of him.

"It's a Schwechten," John said, the first time he proudly introduced it to Melissa, "a very fine grand piano I special-ordered from an obscure Berlin shop. See the swirls in its finish? Only burr walnut creates those characteristic marks."

It was the one item completely off limits to anyone in the household. No one, but no one, touched that piano, except John and the piano tuner.

Melissa felt she wasted much of her day dressing and undressing. Each activity required a change of clothing: overseeing the household with Bryga, walking or riding in the afternoon, shopping, paying visits, or receiving guests. Melissa owned quite a stock of ball dresses, but John had not yet hosted another ball. Melissa saw more of Trudi than John since she needed help with all those clothes.

Her favorite room, after her bedroom, was the first floor parlor. Light and airy, it contained white curtains, white rugs, and white chair cushions. Deep blue and bright pink accessories accentuated the stark brightness. John certainly had good taste. How could she have managed, had John left her the enormous task of decorating the entire house?

Lunches at Simons Mansion were the not the peanut butter sandwiches, accompanied with a good book, that Melissa ate at home. Pies, such as rice and chicken, mutton and potato, and even venison, were house favorites, although they were quite different from the shepherd's pie Melissa ate at Sue's Diner. Irish soda bread usually accompanied each midday meal. Melissa thought this odd, but since John offered no explanation, she felt uncomfortable asking for one. Every lunch ended with ice cream which, Melissa learned from Bryga, was John's one weakness. Sometimes, other desserts appeared on the table, too, such as nut cake, but it never displaced the ice cream.

In the evening, Melissa and John dined in the spacious dining room, with its gold-speckled, red wallpaper, gleaming wood floors, and Oriental rugs. They rarely ate alone, but, even when they did, in the upstairs dining area, Melissa first changed her clothes. If John didn't invite a client to dinner, then they entertained villagers, who always humbly accepted an invitation to John's table, as if he were their king. Was this how storybook heroines lived after they married the handsome prince? Despite John's unstable temperament, their only real disagreement concerned Melissa's interaction with Anna.

Melissa enjoyed the little girl's company and often engaged her in hopscotch or jump rope. John declared Melissa's fraternization with a servant's child most improper, but Melissa felt sorry for Anna and insisted otherwise.

"I'm sure there's no harm done," Melissa insisted. "Anna has no other playmates, and I promise to be discreet. Please reconsider?"

John did not reply, so Melissa assumed he agreed. Melissa remained true to her word. Every day she reserved some time for Anna, but never in the company of the other servants, except Bryga, or occasionally, Trudi. Sometimes, they played with dolls, Anna's favorite game. Anna owned two, a papier-mâché doll with a stuffed, cloth body and a European doll fashioned from real wax. Bryga said John had given both of them to Anna, which led Melissa to tease John over lunch.

"Fine example you are of proper behavior," she said.

John did not reply.

On other days, Melissa pushed Anna on the garden swing or walked with her through the woods. Inside Simons Mansion, Melissa looked the other way if Anna's hand reached into a dish of candied orange peel. When John was gone, the fun began in earnest. Melissa was not above hijacking the kitchen to whip up a batch of molasses candy with Anna or splitting an entire boiled fruit pudding with the little girl and calling it dinner. However, Anna especially favored bedtime when she bade Melissa goodnight and cradled the coveted music box.

"Bryony, you indulge that child too much," John said one evening.

Melissa and Anna had just finished steamy cups of Bryga's spiced chocolate. Anna telltale smudges around her lips, was snuggling next to Melissa on the couch, holding the little music box on her lap, and singing. At John's voice, Anna looked anxious, until Melissa, her eyes beseeching
John's reassured the girl. John suppressed a smile and left.

As the music box wound down, its notes became less musical, almost shrill. Melissa checked to see if Anna was frightened, but the little girl had disappeared. Melissa snapped the music box closed, but the shrieking continued. Melissa leaned over to switch off her alarm clock. She lay back down, rubbing her eyes and trying to think. Oh, yes, Monday morning. The glorious weekend in Detroit had ended. It was time for school.

CHAPTER 16: SCHOOL DAZE

Despite the narrow rays of sun slipping through the gray, cloudy sky, November's chilly air bit through Melissa's jacket, and she huddled deeper inside it, while waiting on the school steps for Julie. Fifteen minutes ago, Melissa had seen Julie walking down Bass Street and had waved to her from the bus window, but Julie hadn't returned the greeting. Why was Julie so angry about Snowbell?

One by one, students brushed past her, but no Julie. Melissa's eyes strayed to the woods. Had she really dwelled inside John Simons' mansion last night, or was the episode simply another of her outlandish Bryony dreams?

A few minutes later, Julie, nose in the air, silently marched past Melissa. The high spirits Melissa felt upon wakening plummeted. She picked up her book bag and trudged into school. She'd try again, later.

However, when Melissa approached Julie on the way to the cafeteria, Julie "forgot" a book in her locker and sped down the hall. Dejected, Melissa dragged her feet through the food line and over to the table against the wall.

"Did you have a good time in Detroit, Melissa?" Katie said.

Melissa first glanced at Julie, but the other girl merely flipped a braid behind her shoulder and picked up her egg sandwich.

"Oh, yes," Melissa said with significantly less enthusiasm than she felt. She told Katie about the hotel, Brian's diving attempts, and the art museum.

Ann dabbed mayonnaise from her fingers onto her napkin. "What about the memorial service for your Grandma? How did that go?"

"It was okay, I guess," Melissa said, looking again at Julie. "I didn't understand it, but the people were really nice."

"I heard Mr. Walczak has a surprise today," Katie said. "I can only imagine," Ann said with a shudder.

When she entered the classroom, Melissa immediately noticed the large, clear jar on Mr. Walczak's desk. "What's that?"

From under his thinning hair and pince nez, Mr. Walczak smiled serenely and said, "Leeches."

Leeches?

"Cool!" Joey threw his book bag at his desk, where it hit the corner and slid to the floor. He tore to the front and pressed his nose against the glass.

"Yuck!" Katie's hands flew up to her face. "Gross! I'm not going to look." She peeped between her fingers. "Did you collect all these, Mr. Walczak?"

"I certainly did."

"There are plenty more in Lake Munson." Jack yawned, folded his arms, and slouched further into his chair. "Aren't you looking, Melissa?"

"No, thanks." Melissa shuddered. Leeches, ugh! What next?

"Take your seats," Mr. Walczak said. "You can look again at the end of class."

The students quickly opened their book bags and withdrew their biology books.

"A leech," Mr. Walczak began, "is a thirty-two brained, segmented worm. Many are parasites that suck blood, but some are predators that eat fish or earthworms. Blood-sucking species attach to their victims until they are full and then simply drop off."

Katie raised her hand. "Does their sucking hurt?"

"Not at all," Mr. Walczak said, "because of special ingredients inside leech saliva. One is an anesthetic, so the victims, or hosts, cannot feel their skin breaking. An anti-coagulant prevents blood clotting, which prevents premature end to the meal. Some leeches stay with a host for life, while others actually kill the host. Over one thousand different parasites can live in or on the human body. Can you think of some?"

Jack raised his hand and said, "The tapeworm, sir."

Ann coughed.

"And you, Melissa?" Mr. Walczak said.

"Fleas."

When Mr. Walczak resumed his lecture, Melissa retrieved Ann's note. *Mr. Walczak's attempt at humor is pathetic.*

Melissa waited until Dan asked Mr. Walczak, "How big can leeches get?" to scrawl back, *So are Mr. Walczak's attempts at Show and Tell.*

At the end of the day, Melissa finally apologized. "I don't know what happened, Julie, but I'm really sorry."

Julie hugged Melissa, but she still looked grave. "I didn't overreact. Snowbell is definitely weird."

"Like how?" The last few students boarded the bus. "Oh, Julie, I've got to go!"

"I'll call you later, okay?"

After dinner, Melissa joined Steve and Brian's homework club at the dining room table, to Brian's chagrin. "What gives? Don't you have a desk?"

"Don't you?" Melissa shot back.

Steve's coffee mug hit the table with a thump. "Stop bickering!"

"Why does she always butt in?"

Melissa innocently smiled at Brian. "I just felt like company."

Steve glared at them, so Melissa opened her algebra book. Steve was sure cranky tonight. Brian noisily turned pages in his notebook. Melissa worked two equations, while Steve drilled Brian. He excelled with basic terms like *root* and *stem*, but confused *stamen* and *pistil*.

"I just know I'll get those wrong on the test," Brian said.

"We'll take another look at it. Let's review your president facts."

Brian ran to his room. Steve headed into the kitchen for another cup of coffee.

"Hey, Steve," Melissa called after him. "Have you ever heard of purple roses?"

"Yes, I have," Steve called back.

"I heard some grew on our estate."

"I've never seen any. Who told you that?"

"I can't remember."

The phone rang, and Melissa sprang to answer it, saying, "It's probably for me."

It was Julie. After chatting about leeches, Melissa asked about Snowbell. Julie hesitated, then said, "I feel a little silly now, but it sure freaked me out at the time."

"What happened?"

"Every time I turned around, that cat was watching me."

Melissa twirled her fingers around the telephone cord, thinking. Julie had no reason to lie.

"Honestly, Melissa, I'd wake up, and she'd still be staring at me. I was a nervous wreck all weekend."

Melissa hung up the phone, and, deep in thought, returned to the table.

"Brian," she said, "does Snowbell ever stare at you, for no reason, I mean?"

"Of course, she does. She's a cat."

"No, that's not what I meant. Julie said she did it constantly."

"That's because Snowbell's never seen anyone so ugly." Brian glanced up at Steve. "Sorry. Joke."

"And not a very funny one, either," Steve yawned behind his cupped hand.

As she left the room, Melissa heard Brian say, "You don't know what it's like, Steve. You never had a sister."

"Well, now, you do have a point. I was never as lucky as...." Melissa shut her door and readied for bed.

After another night without Bryony dreams, Melissa decided it was time to learn about vampire ways. She couldn't stand not being with John. Her mother, amiable after two cups of coffee, readily gave permission for an after-school library trip, if Steve brought her home.

"I'd do it for you, honey, but I'm on a tight deadline this afternoon."

"Do you think he's awake yet?"

"I'm sure he is."

Although Steve didn't sound quite awake, he agreed with the transportation arrangements. "I'm coming over tonight, anyway. Brian and I are cooking spaghetti."

"I'll make garlic bread, for sure this time," Melissa promised.

Mrs. Clements smiled at the sight of Melissa and walked back to the front desk.

"Some new teen novels arrived," she said. "Here's a couple you might like."

"Thanks!"

Melissa selected two books, then, pretending to browse, scanned the shelves: astral projection, séances, mythology, and *Creatures of the Night: Witches, Werewolves, and Vampires.* Melissa slid the book between the other two and set them on the counter, hoping Mrs. Clements wouldn't notice.

"Oh," Mrs. Clements exclaimed when she came to the middle book. "Well, this is a little different reading for you, Melissa."

"It's for Brian. He and his friend get into that stuff."

At dinner, Melissa wolfed down two plates of Steve's spaghetti, despite Brian's incredulous looks in her direction.

"Can I be excused?" Melissa set down her fork. "I've got tons of homework."

"Sure, dear," Her mother left to refill the spaghetti bowl.

Steve watched her leave. "So, sport, how'd you do on that science test?"

Melissa smuggled a piece of garlic bread and fairly skipped to the bedroom. She placed two books on her desk, ready to swap, if necessary, and flipped to *Vampires.*

A vampire is a former human that relentlessly seeks fresh human blood. Sources include the victim's neck, cheek, thigh, fingers, toes, or below the heart.

Melissa slid her tongue around her cheeks. She hadn't thought of looking there. Was that why John left no marks?

160

Some vampires also force victims to drink blood from their chests or lips.

An early childhood memory flashed: Melissa jumping off a swing too soon, biting the inside of her cheek, and nearly throwing up at the coppery taste. Since John had said nothing about drinking his blood, that couldn't be part of their bargain. She hoped he'd never suggest it.

By day, vampires repose in their burial places; at night, they rise to feed, either to kill or control. Once under the vampire's power, the victim joyfully welcomes the attack. The vampire may now come and go, as he pleases.

The book did not mention the ancient legend of eliminating vampirism with blood from one human source. She scanned the pages. Maybe, she missed it.

Vampires created by murder or suicide retain human traits, most notably a certain passion for life...sharp teeth appear only when feeding...bright red blood may trickle around the mouth...vampires may consume solid food, but must expel it later... experienced vampires tolerate small amounts of sunlight, although it decreases their abilities...vampires travel silently...vampires are expert shape-shifters. Common manifestations include wolves, bats, rats, other humans, and mist.

Melissa's eyes widened. *Mist?* Was John the mist in the woods?

Sometimes, vampires penetrate dreams.

At the knock, Melissa slid the vampire book on her lap and focused on adverbial clauses. "Come in!"

Brian shoved his head around the door. "Mom says come out for dessert."

Reluctantly, Melissa closed the book. Her mother usually reserved dessert for weekends and special occasions. What was up? She resumed her place at the table. "Dessert?"

A proud smile spread across her mother's face. "Brian and Steve made it."

"I only supervised," Steve said with a wink, following closely behind Brian, who slowly walked into the dining room, carefully balancing a chocolate cake.

"Ta da!" Brian set his prize in the middle of the table.

Darlene hugged Brian, but looked up at Steve. "As long as you two are around, we'll never go hungry." Steve blushed harder than Brian did.

Brian wriggled away from Darlene and carefully cut a slice. "Try it, Mom! Steve made it when he was young," Brian slid in his chair. "I'm carrying on the tradition."

Melissa quickly ate the cake and flew back to her room, but waited until she heard the low voice of Steve helping Brian with homework and the faint sound of her mother running dish water before reopening, *Creatures of the Night.*

As predators, vampires possess keen senses, formidable strength, and fantastic speed, enabling them to teleport to other eras and locations.

Melissa grew excited. So, John had sent her back in time to relive Bryony's life.

Vampires are wise...they exude sexual charm, control animals, and read minds... for a reliable slaying, drive an oak stake through a vampire's heart and sever its head with a silver dagger.

Melissa closed the book. A stake of wood and a silver dagger, the very items hanging in John's library. The book confused her more than it helped, but one thing was clear: Melissa believed in John's potential goodness, so why shouldn't he receive a second chance at life? Melissa silently vowed to do everything in her power to insure the famous musician received it.

CHAPTER 17: THAT MYSTERIOUS, HANDSOME MAN

Life, although bizarre, was settling into a predictable pattern. By day, Melissa lived her normal routine under the weight of her secret. By night, nearly every night now, she experienced Munsonville's past as Bryony Simons might have known it.

Melissa now knew almost every inch of the old mansion and its grounds, the little details, the ones not saved on microfilm. She reveled in the blissful scent of the morning air when Trudi opened all the windows and the evening crackle of the fire, as Melissa fell asleep in Bryony's bedroom. Melissa knew how strong John liked his coffee and where he preferred to drink it: at the round table by the far window in the morning room. She knew his arrangement of books in the library, by author, and was positive she could recognize another Schwechten from its distinct sound.

Melissa knew the south window of the parlor was a bit drafty, the stain on the dining room's Oriental rug from where Orville Parks had spilled his goose giblet soup, and which table leg was nicked, because old Clyde Fisher, unsteady on his feet, had tripped over it. Melissa knew Hattie's shrill voice, as she yelled to the other cooks, and the tunes Bessie and Tillie sang while scrubbing laundry. She knew the tone of Morton Brooks' voice, when he announced the guests, and Howard Dobbs' infinite patience, for he labored endless hours for John's comfort and convenience. Melissa could determine by a carriage's speed if Tom Jenkins or Alfred Jackson drove it.

If she closed her eyes, Melissa could hear Anna's feet in the hallways and her uproarious laugh when Melissa pushed her on the swing. She knew Anna was a hellion at bedtime if she could not kiss Melissa goodnight and listen to the music box. Melissa and Anna both knew which stair creaked without fail, the third from the top, and how, when no one was looking, they gleefully jumped over it.

In John's presence, Melissa very naturally played Bryony, almost as if someone scripted her words. Yet, when John deserted Melissa, she stumbled through the stiff and awkward role. Still, no matter how displaced Melissa felt or behaved, the servants, villagers, and even Reverend Marseilles, accepted Melissa as Bryony. Melissa only wished John showed more affection; fleeting moments in John's arms left her desiring more, but John preferred the comfort of the music room to Bryony's bedroom and doted on his piano more than he did Melissa.

Despite her concerns, Melissa adored John's music. Although he tolerated no interruptions when he worked, Melissa could and did, pause in her daily activities to listen. The music bewitched the servants, too, who appeared in better humor when John's music filled the house. Often, the melodies lingered far into the night, and Melissa would waken to hear them as they drifted up the stairs and wafted into her bedroom. She'd lie very still in bed, unwilling to break the enchantment that altered the night. John, for all his distance, must have been in love because the last piece he always played was *Bryony*.

One evening at dinner, John announced he had received an invitation to perform a concert at a brand new venue, Carnegie Hall in New York.

"This is a great honor," John said, with repressed excitement. "Just three years ago, the great composer Pyotr Ilyich Tchaikovsky was the guest conductor at the hall's grand opening. Best of all, you shall accompany me on this trip."

"Father won't like that," Melissa said, knowing John faced a big lecture from Reverend Marseilles if he removed her from Munsonville.

John's face remained impassive. "Father isn't invited."

His performance would be the first weekend in April, which left little time to prepare. There were shopping trips and the packing of trunks, for them, as well as for Trudi and Howard, who would travel with them. Because she had never left Munsonville, save for the honeymoon, John added to the itinerary a steamship ride to Chicago. From there, the little party would board a train to New York.

"We could take the train into the city," John said, "but I thought you might enjoy a boat trip. It will not lengthen our journey much."

As Melissa predicted, Reverend Marseilles exploded when he heard the news.

"John, I won't have it. The girl's health is delicate enough, and you promised to safeguard it. And now, steamboats! Railways! Music halls! It's not right, John; it's not right."

"I beg your pardon, but the Carnegie building is no common music hall. My decision is firm. The girl goes with me."

"I tell you, John, if you persist in this headstrong manner, you'll kill her."

"She's not Adele, Galien. Bryony is stronger than you think she is."

The library door flung open, and Reverend Marseilles stormed out. Melissa feigned surprise at the sight of him. His face softened when he saw Melissa.

"Father, it is good to see you," Melissa said, with a warm hug.

The reverend hastily embraced her in return, then drew back, looking reproachful. "What was I thinking giving that man permission to marry you?"

"Oh, Father, he's not 'that man.' John is kind and good, and you know it."

"Bah!" he said. "Why he...." He stopped, seeing her shocked expression.

"Father, I thought you liked him!"

"I do like him, tremendously, as a gentleman. But as a son-in- law…." He sighed and drew Melissa nearer to him, as he walked to the door. "Most men should marry, but John is not one of them. I should have exercised better judgment."

"John does love me, Father."

"I do not doubt that, child, but still…." He stopped and looked at Melissa with an almost wistful expression. "Are you happy, daughter?"

"Of course. Now, *you* be happy for me. Be assured. John takes good care of me."

The reverend glanced over his shoulder. John was watching from the doorway. The reverend hugged Melissa, but cast a cold eye at John.

"I can show myself out," Reverend Marseilles said. "I'm sure you can," John said.

After Reverend Marseilles' departure, Melissa joined John in the library. He was pouring a drink. Arguments with the reverend always left him tense.

"John, I wish you wouldn't fight with him."

"He's meddling in our lives."

She walked to him, removed the glass, and set it on the sidebar. Then, she put her arms around him and kissed him. John returned the kiss, briefly and without emotion.

"He's just worried for me," Melissa insisted. "Well, he needn't be."

John had reserved private luxury accommodations on both the boat and train. Melissa marveled at the plush carpeting, fine china, and, most importantly, astonishingly good food. In New York City, she and John stayed at the home of piano manufacturer and concert promoter, Herbert Rutherford. His wife, Della, had contrived an entire fortnight of fun for Melissa. A blizzard accompanied by unseasonable freezing temperatures extended winter activities. With glee, Melissa ice skated, ice boated, and tobogganed. Reverend Marseilles would just die if he saw it, Melissa thought.

The Rutherfords concluded each winter event with a party. She marveled at the daily routine of the very rich. In New York, Melissa rarely rose before noon, and the Rutherfords' "dinner parties" often included dances that lingered until dawn. Only rarely

166

did John join the dinner and dancing. However, John's hard work rewarded him. He played to a full house at Carnegie Hall and exited the stage to a standing ovation.

There's no stopping him now, Melissa thought. The sky's the limit for him...and for me, too. She overflowed with happiness for John and grew impatient for the Rutherfords' ball in John's honor.

Each line on her dance card contained a signature, and guests vied for an opportunity to meet John's young bride. She wore a new, pale aquamarine satin gown for the grand occasion and a set of spectacular diamonds from John. At first, Melissa felt uneasy wearing those jewels, and they rattled in her trembling hands. Diamonds didn't impress Trudi, who easily fastened the clasps. Melissa swayed before the mirror, captivated by how her lovely jewelry caught and held the light.

However, the diamonds' magnificence paled when compared to the Rutherfords' ballroom. She had never seen a room so breathtakingly white. Ivory-colored décor accentuated its walls and floors; crystal chandeliers hung from the ceiling. The ball dresses produced the room's only flecks of color.

"Oh, John!" Melissa breathed when she saw it.

John merely squeezed her hand.

After a waltz, John disappeared for a quite a long time, but one dance after another with the gentlemen on her card kept Melissa busy, so the time flew past. As a banker led her from the floor, Melissa felt a tap on her shoulder. It was John.

"Will you do me the honor again?" John was not smiling.

She remembered proper ballroom etiquette. You never danced more than once with your spouse, if at all. Did John ask because he wanted to be with her, or because he enjoyed breaking established traditions? On the other hand, what did it matter? He was so becoming in his white tails, how could she refuse him?

Melissa bowed her head in acknowledgment. John took her hand and led her to the dance floor. John's hands, even though his white dancing gloves, felt warm and strong, not at all like dead man's hands. Was her blood helping him, or was it part of the illusion? He still did not smile or speak, but looked at her with such deep concentration that Melissa's stomach quivered in a most unsteady way. What was he thinking? John was *so* hard to decipher sometimes.

Not once breaking eye contact with her, John eased her around the dance floor. To Melissa, everything merged into one, heavenly existence: the attention from other guests, the beautiful clothes, the setting, and, most importantly, John. To think Melissa could have missed all this, had she not accepted the conditions of John's bargain!

"Thank you," she whispered.

His fingers tightened around her waist.

After the dance, Melissa blithely clung to John's arm, as he walked her from the ballroom into an adjoining room where servants arranged refreshments. He fixed her a plate of baked ham, roast chicken with apple sauce, potato biscuits, and jelly. John passed on the salted beef tongue and the oysters on the half shell, then transported her to a chair against the wall. He left, but soon returned with a glass of punch. Della was with him.

"Bryony, some gentlemen wish to speak to me about a possible contract. I will return shortly." John handed her the glass. "Della will supervise you."

His glance at the sophisticated, burgundy-dressed Della looked more like a command than a question, but if Della felt ordered, she took no notice.

"Of course, John," Della said, with a smile as dazzling as her rubies. "I'll take good care of her."

"Bryony?"

Melissa nodded and watched him withdraw from the refreshment room. She gazed about her, remembering John's warning about peripheral looks at the many guests. How many balls had passed? She had lost count. She was growing accustomed to some the food, too. At one of the Rutherford's buffets, Melissa had devoured a plateful of beef pie, even though it looked different from the frozen ones her mother bought, and had eaten several slices of something called jelly cake. In a brave moment, Melissa had even consumed an entire meatball prepared from veal and was astounded that she liked it. However, the head cheese and pickles had looked disgusting. Back home, dill cucumber pickles were a staple on hot dogs and hamburgers, but Rutherfords pickled anything within their grasp: beef tongue, mushrooms, cabbages, peppers, walnuts, and even peaches! So, Melissa had filled the bare spaces on her plate with sweetened pineapple slices and something that resembled a pear. John later said it was a quince, so Melissa didn't eat that, either.

Once, after a sleighing party, Melissa had poked a suspicious- looking morsel, tasted it, and then hailed a servant on her way to the kitchen.

"Why Mrs. Simons, that's terrapin," the girl said. She smiled at Melissa's blank look. "It's turtle," she added. Horrified, Melissa, retreated to a corner to spit the offending meat into her napkin.

Melissa finished her punch and enjoyed the view, especially the figure of a man at the far end of the room. She guessed his age as similar to John's, but he possessed none of John's height or breadth. He had wavy brown hair, a clean-shaven face, and a slim waist; his casual air of mystery and refinement intrigued her. He's almost as handsome as John, Melissa thought.

She had a second reason for staring at him, a gut sense she knew him. Of course, she had met many people these last few weeks, but something about him triggered a vague familiarity.

The man turned, and his eyes swept the room, as if searching for someone. He caught Melissa gawking at him and grinned broadly at her. Melissa blushed and quickly studied her empty plate.

Why, she thought with sudden pleasure, he's even more forward than John is! She *must* look at him again.

Melissa nonchalantly raised her head, but this time a stout man with a monocle approached the mysterious man and spoke earnestly to him. She seized the opportunity to scrutinize the young man's features. He exuded charm. Melissa was now certain she hadn't met him. She would not have forgotten someone so magnetic.

Della was talking animatedly with another couple, but as Melissa approached her, she abruptly stopped and smiled invitingly. The couple took the cue and moved away. Melissa straightened her shoulders, feeling her importance.

"Della, who is that man, the slim one with the dark hair?"

The woman scanned the area, then turned to Melissa with a bewildered look.

"Goodness, Bryony, that's the short story writer, Henry Matthews. His works are the rage now. Everybody who is anybody reads them." She leaned confidingly into Melissa. "All the women consider him quite handsome, but he never courts anyone, a shame, really. He'd be quite a catch."

The Rutherfords' housekeeper approached Della and mumbled into her ear.

"Excuse me, please, Bryony. I'll return shortly," Della said and left the room.

Melissa searched for a spot to set her empty punch glass, found none, and sneaked it under the refreshment table. She stole a final peek at the sensuous Henry Matthews through the lens of her newfound knowledge. He wore the same white tails as John, but with a casual, offhand manner. True, John always appeared dignified and formal, but this man behaved as if someone had designed the suit with him in mind. Every line of his clothing fit him to perfection.

She started from her reverie. The monocle man had disappeared, and Henry was now walking full speed toward Melissa. Uh, oh, she thought, seeking an easy, accessible exit. Finding none, Melissa raised her fan. Before she quite knew what had happened, Henry was standing beside her at the refreshment table and pouring himself a glass of punch.

"Hello, Melissa," Henry said, with another grin.

Astonished, she almost dropped her fan. *Melissa?* She assumed her most injured demeanor and fluttered her fan, praying it was the correct signal to show displeasure. "Sir, I don't believe we have been properly introduced." Frantically, she searched around the room. Neither John, nor Della, was in sight.

Ignoring her remark and her fan, Henry leaned close to her. "Boring affair, isn't it?" He studied the pale, pink liquid in his glass. "Amazing people actually drink it."

Henry drained the punch and then examined the glass. "This wasn't good eighty years ago." He ducked his glass next to hers, filled another, and handed it to Melissa.

"Well, I…" Melissa stammered, uncertain how to react.

She was not acquainted with Henry; ballroom etiquette prohibited him offering the punch. Melissa felt embarrassed, too, because he had witnessed her ditching the previous glass. How would Bryony handle it? Should she correct Henry's mistake and inform him that her name was Bryony and not Melissa?

Henry guided the fan away from her face.

"Aren't you trotting around the Victorian era rather late on a school night, especially with a literature assignment due for my class tomorrow? I'm loath to bestow a flunking grade, especially after that terrific report on Bryony Simons."

Melissa almost dropped her punch. *His literature class?*

A simpering, blonde woman, in a deep blue ball gown and more diamonds than Melissa had ever seen on any two women, approached Henry. Pressing into him, she whispered something that sent them both laughing. She linked her arm through Henry's to lead him away, but Henry resisted and delivered a final condescending remark.

"Must dash. The lady requires my escort. Heed my words, little one."

Melissa bristled at his rudeness and started to upbraid him, until she saw John approaching them, looking highly displeased. If Henry noticed it, he ignored it.

"Great show as always," he said, shaking John's hand. "You never disappoint."

As the impatient woman yanked on Henry's arm, Henry paused to re-fill his punch glass and raise it toward Melissa in a farewell gesture.

"Pleasant dreams!" he said.

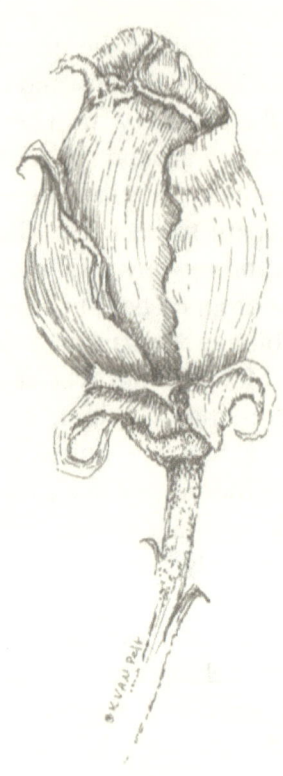

CHAPTER 18: IT COULDN'T BE MASTERS

In English class the next day, Melissa struggled to stay focused on the allegorical interpretation of The Mansion by Henry Van Dyke. Under ordinary circumstances, Mr. Masters' lectures engaged Melissa, but this time the teacher fascinated her more than his material did. Was Mr. Masters a vampire?

With fresh and heightened interest, Melissa watched him push his glasses up his nose every time he turned from the chalkboard. She scrutinized the manner in which he waved his short, fat arms, when he stressed a point. Was this pudgy, homely, little man really the same dashing gentleman she encountered last night?

If Mr. Masters somehow existed as the Henry Matthews of Melissa's dream, he gave no indication of it. He certainly paid her no more attention than he paid the other students, although she now participated frequently in class, causing Ann to stare at her newfound assertiveness. Yet, when she raised her hand to answer, "Who were the only two people John Weightman knew on the road to the Celestial City," Mr. Masters recognized her only with an offhand nod.

"The village doctor who had treated him as a boy and an old bookkeeper who had an insane wife and a crippled daughter," Melissa answered.

"Very good."

Henry Matthews couldn't be Harold Masters, but if he wasn't....

Melissa shook her head in frustration. Mr. Masters noticed it and looked pointedly at her. She blushed, for she hadn't heard him say a word.

"Yes, Melissa?"

"I'm sorry," she said. "I didn't hear the question."

"What! I thought Melissa was the mansion expert." Dan leaned back his head, looked at the ceiling, and chanted: "Melissa Marchellis, mistress of mansions in Munsonville." He sat up straight and nudged Joey. "Hey, say that three times fast."

Dan guffawed, and Joey joined him, but they quickly stopped. Mr. Masters was leaning over his desk and writing out two detention slips.

Jack raised his hand, and Mr. Masters nodded at him. "Because his accomplishments counted only in the world, sir," Jack said.

"Very good."

If John knew Henry, then Henry must be a vampire. So, why should Melissa trust anything Henry had said? Look how he had behaved by the refreshment table, trying to confuse and humiliate her. Why would a vampire tell her the truth?

You trust John to tell the truth, Melissa thought, then quickly halted that thought. John despised being a vampire. Henry Matthews was just plain obnoxious. She hoped their paths never again crossed. Still, she lingered after class.

"Yes, Melissa?" Mr. Masters sounded kind, but indifferent.

"Um," Melissa said. "I wanted to apologize for daydreaming in class."

His expression did not change. "Next time pay more attention. Good day."

She wanted to say more, but Mr. Masters had already turned back to the board.

Mumbling a "Good day, sir," Melissa slipped out of the room. What an odd man, she thought, as she dashed to her locker. She couldn't risk being late for the bus. Her mother would not appreciate an unexpected drive to the school, not on a day she had an article due. Melissa's mind strayed again to Mr. Masters. What a strange, strange little man.

All afternoon, Melissa dwelled on the possible Henry Matthews/Harold Masters connection. Even Brian noticed and made faces at her during dinner when he thought no one was looking. Steve chastised Brian, but her mother looked worried.

"Are you okay, Melissa?"

"I'm fine. I have a big test tomorrow. May I please be excused?"

"Of course, you may. Are you sure nothing is wrong?"

"No, I just want a good grade."

Just before Melissa closed her bedroom door, she heard Brian say, "Well, she's been acting so nutty lately."

Melissa rummaged in her T-shirt drawer for a book, then lay across the bed and re-read:

Vampires are expert shape-shifters. Common manifestations include wolves, bats, rats, other humans, and mist...experienced vampires tolerate small amounts of sunlight, although it decreases their abilities.

Brian said her teacher's hands were cold. Were they as cold as John's hands the first night Melissa held them? Did Mr. Masters need gloves, or was he dead? At bedtime, Melissa checked for bite marks, just in case, but found nothing.

Since his performances at Carnegie Hall, John had received a number of telegrams, either congratulating him or requesting his presence for upcoming engagements. The most esteemed invitation came from a promoter wishing to contract John for a large European tour the following year. With an unusual display of spontaneity, John scooped Melissa in his arms and spun her around the room.

"I have dreamed forever of this opportunity," he said.

Melissa now saw even less of John. He rarely slept, but periodically dozed in a library chair. Brooks brought John's meals, while Mildred complained to Melissa about collecting great stacks of dirty dishes.

"He'll wear himself out, the poor man," Mildred sighed, shaking her head.

Although he left no physical evidence, John must have received his portion of the bargain, because at Melissa's last check-up, Dr. Anderson said her blood count was still low and advised continuing the iron supplements.

"Without the medicine, the anemia will return," he said.

Melissa suspected John took more than he gave. She understood John's music career required hours of practice, but she missed the exhilarating giddiness of being in John's arms. She wound the music box, praying its notes might bring them together.

With a start, Melissa awoke and rubbed her eyes. The heady combination of firewood and roses permeated the air. She propped herself on an elbow and surveyed her surroundings. She was no longer in her bed, nor was she in Bryony's bed. The crimson and gold upholstery of the settee left deep, crisscross marks on her hands. How long had she lain there, in the same sweatshirt and jeans she had removed a few hours ago? Whenever Melissa awakened in a strange place, whether inside Simons Mansion, a concert hall, or a ballroom, she wore Bryony's clothes. Why was tonight different? Was she inside Simons Mansion? Where was John?

The room, although not very large, felt warm and comfortable, with its wine-hued carpeting and wallpaper, overflowing bookshelves, and rich mahogany furniture. Several desks sat at the east end of the room. One held a heavy, black, silver, oddly shaped typewriter, very different from her mother's slim, beige, electric machine. Vases of fragrant, purple roses filled the room. Fully awake now, Melissa rested her head on the back of the settee and blinked in surprise.

By the glow of the firelight from the red-brick hearth, Henry Matthews, dressed in black pants and a red waistcoat, reclined in a leather armchair. His gray cravat draped over the arm of the chair, and he had unfastened the top buttons of his ruffled white shirt. With half-mast eyes, Henry sniffed the cigar he drew under his nose and sighed with pleasure. Chinook lolled on the floor next to Henry's chair. The merest hint of a smile adorned his boyish face.

"Oh, Melissa, why persist in this delusion? John and I exist in such a half-awake state, never knowing the full delights of a good meal, art, architecture, music, or literature, only the memory of them."

Henry sighed again, but not too unhappily it seemed to Melissa. He lightly swept the cigar across his lips and disregarded her silence, while she tried to absorb this turn of events and rack her brain for a comment

"So if being a vampire is so bad, why don't you just...die?" A sardonic smile replaced the melancholy one. "How?"

"Well, in movies, vampires are destroyed if they're pushed into light, or if someone drives a stake through their hearts. Can't someone do that for you?"

Henry chuckled, closed his eyes, stretched, and leaned his head back. "'Death comes in its own time, in its own way. Death is as unique as the individual experiencing it.'" He opened his eyes. "'Gone From My Sight.' Henry Van Dyke."

This time, Melissa sighed, frustrated with his games. "I'm serious."

"So am I. You see, my dear Melissa, the instinct of self-preservation extends beyond the grave, or, at least, it has for me. I died once and landed here. What might happen to me a second time, I can hardly imagine. Why tempt fate? Worse scenarios exist. Given my druthers, I'll take this."

Henry shifted to a more comfortable position. "But you, Melissa, disentangle yourself, while you can. You're young and alive. You belong with the breathing."

He had called her Melissa again. "My name is Bryony."

"Not when you're with me."

With him! She was supposed to be with John.

Henry picked up the glass of brandy on the table next to him and appreciably smelled it. *Vampires!* The real ones were as annoying as Brian in costume. She crossed her arms and glared at him. "So, where am I?"

"Interesting question," Henry said. "Where am I? Who am I, and, perhaps, most importantly, where am I going?"

"No!" Irritation flared into open anger. "Here, this room. What is it?"

"It's my private study."

"Where?"

"Why, Simons Mansion, of course. You mean the mistress of the house is unaware of my presence?"

"You're a guest here?"

"I live here."

What! Why hadn't John mentioned this? Surely, Melissa, as Bryony Simons, should have approved it. Why would John let this disagreeable man...vampire...live at Simons Mansion? When they had met at the Rutherfords' ball, John hadn't seemed to like him.

Henry rose and crossed the room to the sidebar, where he prepared a cup of tea. Melissa brooded on this new development. Since Henry enjoyed talking, she decided to humor him. "So, why am I here, in your study?"

"It's an opportunity to privately chat with you, away from the attentive, and ever so omnipresent, John."

Henry brought Melissa the tea in a beautiful cup and saucer. The background was cobalt blue; the edges were trimmed in gold. The inside of the cup was pure white and boasted one, painted, purple rose near the lip.

"Be careful," Henry said. "It's hot."

Melissa cautiously tasted the foaming tea, nothing like the tea bags her mother used at home, and tried not to make a face. What did Henry put in it? Didn't Victorians make normal food?

"Thank you. It's very good," Melissa lied, pretending to take another sip. "Chat about what?"

Henry sat close to her on the settee. Melissa edged away.

"Tell me, how did John engage your cooperation in this façade, which, I dare say, you play rather badly?"

"He didn't trick me." Melissa set the cup on its saucer. "I wanted to do it."

"You conceived this plan?"

"Um, not exactly."

"Pray, satisfy my curiosity."

A deafening noise filled the room. Melissa jumped in fright and spilled the tea onto the carpet. She quickly set the cup down, then turned   to apologize for the mess, but Henry had vanished. Melissa covered her ears, and a large, ornate clock appeared on the table. Quickly, Melissa closed her hands around it, but she slipped off the settee and onto the floor. She had fallen out of bed holding onto her alarm clock! There was a knock on her door.

"Liss, are you okay?"

Brian? He never wakened early!

"Sure." Melissa replaced the clock and dazedly rubbed her elbow.

"Well, hurry up! Steve made French toast for breakfast, and then he's taking us biking. We're cooking lunch in the woods. He said I can pick the spot!"

As Melissa biked down the trail behind the cottage, her mind wandered to other places and eras. Warm sunshine and a wall of autumn leaves surrounded Melissa, but she saw only darkness, mist and…vampires.

Her mother and Brian pedaled fast, but Steve, who had a small trailer fastened to the back of his bike, dawdled, waiting for her.

"Warm enough?" he asked, matching his pace with her speed.

 "Oh, yes!" Thoughts of John always warmed her.

"You're not tired, are you?"

"No, just thinking. You can go ahead if you want."

With a friendly wave of his hand, Steve sped off.

When they reached the wide, grassy area Brian pronounced as "perfect," he and Steve started the fire. Its smoky scent transported Melissa back to Henry Matthews' study and the perfume of purple roses. Had they grown in the tea garden?

"Lunch is ready!" Steve announced.

Melissa bit into a charred hot dog and ate her mother's potato salad, the one thing, besides desserts, she prepared from scratch.

"Mom," Melissa said. "Have you ever eaten beef tongue?" Her mother looked taken aback.

"Once, why?"

178

"Oh, nothing," Melissa walked to the grill area for another hot dog, but in her mind, she was at a ball, accepting a plate from John. "Just something I read in a book."

"Hey, you two!" Steve called. "Come join Brian and me in croquet."

Her mother crumpled the plate and tossed it into a garbage can, then walked to the hoops. Melissa followed her. Why was she dreaming about Henry Matthews? John controlled her dreams, so had he arranged it? After John's heated reaction about the vampire weapons, Melissa was reluctant to ask more questions. However, she couldn't spend every English class brazenly searching Mr. Masters for clues.

Melissa needn't have worried about upsetting John. He stayed in the music room, alone, leaving Melissa waking in Henry's study. Why had her dreams taken such a curve? For his part, Henry strived to be good company, while beating her at checkers and chasing her off the chessboard. In the morning's dark hours, when Henry worked on a story, Melissa skimmed his vast collection of books and studied his mannerisms. Had Henry Matthews shape-shifted into her teacher?

Melissa waited until Henry took a break to ask him. "I mean, don't vampires ever change into something more regular like, like…." She fumbled for the right words.

Henry set a plate of dainty sandwiches before her. "Like a Newfoundland?"

"Well, yes, like a dog, maybe."

"I could sit on your lap and pant while you scratch behind my…."

Melissa covered her ears. "Stop!"

"….ears," Henry sprawled on the chair opposite her. "It's a joke, Melissa. Have you seen the size of a Newfoundland?"

This unwanted evolution of her dreams made no sense. Why would John bring her to Simons Mansion only to spend the entire night with the odious Henry Matthews?

"Odious. Hmmm," Henry opened the cribbage board and shuffled the cards. "Studied vocabulary words this evening, did we?"

Melissa had forgotten vampires also read minds. "Be serious. Why am I spending so much time with you?"

"It's your dream, Melissa."

"I'm not doing this!"

"Oh no?" Henry stopped shuffling, closed his eyes, and quoted: "'Tell me not, in mournful numbers, life is but an empty dream, for the soul is dead that slumbers, and things are not what they seem.'" He opened his eyes. "Henry Wadsworth Longfellow, A Psalm of Life."

"I don't know that one. Have we studied it?"

Henry grinned. "You tell me. Lately, it seems my persona holds greater charms for you than reading assignments."

He had noticed her staring at him in class! Oh, he was annoying! Yet, far worse than spending time with Henry was the chilling fear the Bryony dreams might disappear.

John's European tour ended years ago. Why was he so persistent in practicing for it now when they could be together?

CHAPTER 19: DARING TO DREAM

"Bryony, are you awake?"

Melissa stirred, excitement mounting. *John had called her Bryony!* She peeped at the curtains around her. She was not in the bedroom at the servant's cottage.

Next to her, propped on an elbow and gazing down on her, lay John Simons, glassy-eyed from many days of lost sleep. His unwashed hair limply hung over his shoulders, and he sorely needed a shave. The waistcoat was gone; the cravat was untied; and his shirt was completely unbuttoned.

"Bryony," he whispered again. *"Are you awake?"*

How could she not be when he sounded like that? Heart pounding, barely breathing, she lay immobile, while John lightly stroked her hair with a warm, strong hand, so different form the icy, skeletal one that clutched her weeks ago. He glided his palm along her face until he closed around her neck; he brushed his other hand across her face to her lips and lightly traced them. Melissa dared not move, afraid to break the delectable spell. Then, with the utmost gentleness, John cupped her face between those musical hands, bent down, and kissed her.

John Simons kissed her! Oh, how long since the last time, in the morning room, when she first woke inside Simons Mansion, and here he was, kissing her over and again. He took a deep breath, pressed her close, and bit her lip. *Hard.*

Melissa flinched, recoiled from the pain, and awoke. The moonlight streaming through the curtains shed only a dusky light in her bedroom, but Melissa could see John Simons reclining next to her, exactly as he had in her dream. She tasted blood, which John methodically licked from her lips with his tongue.

John looked as haggard as he had that first night in her bedroom, but his face looked fuller, younger. She ran her hands over his taut trunk, amazed at her audacity. His abundant hair shone in the room's dim light. He did not repel her anymore. She had to get closer. She had not forgotten he was a vampire. She knew what she must do.

Still lapping her blood, John lifted his eyes and noticed she was awake. He drew back slightly and studied her expression, contemplating this new development. A cunning look crept over his face, and his eyes irresistibly wandered down to Melissa's lips, while he tasted his own. John glanced back up at Melissa and saw she had observed him.

"Go to sleep," John whispered, and his words rolled into waves of slumber that lulled her into its comforting warmth.

"No!" Melissa jerked away from his touch.

Her boldness surprised them both. The guile faded from John's face, and the barest hint of vexation replaced it. "You don't recall our bargain?"

"Yes," Melissa said, "but I want to watch."

"Absolutely not!"

John bounded off the bed, but Melissa quickly grabbed his sleeve.

"Please," Melissa said and sat up. "Don't go. I only want to see you do it."

He hesitated. "That's not part of the deal."

"You never said it wasn't."

She slid her hand down to his and brought his fingertips to her lips. John's eyes turned stony cold, but he straddled Melissa

182

and eased her back onto her pillow. He wound one hand around her neck, fastened the other onto her chin, and held her face steady. Deftly, John licked the last dribbles. Every flicker of his tongue captivated her.

"Will it hurt?"

He did not look at her. "A bit."

"Will it make me sick, like before?"

"No."

"You don't take that much?"

"I dine later."

John prodded his face inside her neck, until he located a spot on the left that particularly fascinated him. He outlined it with his finger, and then tapped it with his tongue. The area grew warm and numb.

"Does it....?"

John tilted up her head up, fully exposing her throat. The mild countenance left his face. His eyes blazed; his lips parted; and for the first time, Melissa saw how sharp and pointed his teeth really were. His fingers tore into her back, and, with controlled frenzy, John crushed her against him and buried his face. Fangs tore into soft flesh, but Melissa winced back tears and stifled the moan in her throat. The ache went to her toes. She panicked, momentarily regretting her decision, but only for a moment.

Warmth oozed onto her neck. John fastened his mouth around it and grazed his tongue over it, taking his time, savoring it. Melissa put her hands on John's head and held him there, marveling. This was not what she had expected. Her head whirled. Was it from bleeding or the dangerous excitement of what she was allowing him to do? Dazed, Melissa floated away to euphoric sleep. Once in the night, when Melissa changed positions, a sobering thought struck her. John said he would dine later. That meant someone, somewhere, lost a life tonight. Had she passively helped John take it?

Steve arrived at the house early the next morning. Melissa looked up from her homework, the question forming on lips as raw as the weather. Before she asked it, Steve answered her. "Snowbell has a check- up for her neck. Want to come along for the ride?"

"Okay." Melissa closed her book.

Dr. Samuelson kept a small office in the back of Walker's Apothecary. It was a jumble of filing cabinets and cages for any stray dogs and cats he encountered.

"Steve, is this where you got Scooter?" Brian's voice caught, but he covered it by clucking his tongue at Snowbell.

"Yep." Steve gave Brian's shoulder a quick pat.

Melissa walked among the pens. All sat empty except one at the end, which contained one large, black, shaggy puppy that regarded her with sad, brown eyes.

"Can I pet him?" Melissa begged.

The phone rang, and the receptionist reached for it. "Sure," she said absently.

Melissa stroked the dog's silky fur and scratched him behind his ears. He nudged his head into Melissa's hand for more attention. The receptionist hung up the phone and leaned forward on her desk, watching her.

"You sure have a way with animals," she said.

"Maybe," Melissa said, "but I don't have much luck with them." She had a brief image of Scooter sniffing around the back yard her first night in Munsonville. "What kind of dog is this? He seems sweet."

"A Newfoundland. I'm surprised Doc found him. I've never seen one around here."

A Newfoundland! Melissa snatched away her hand and peered into its eyes. The dog panted in near ecstasy and slung great slobs of saliva across the cage. Henry?

"Snowbell," the technician announced.

She led them into the examining room. Snowbell nestled into Brian's arms.

"She's just scared. Snowbell doesn't like doctors...or mean people." Brian looked at Melissa, and she knew he meant Julie.

"Oh, we're not going to hurt you, Snowbell," the technician said, opening the chart and studying it. She looked at Steve. "How is she doing?"

"No problems at all, except the head tilt."

"Any pain, lack of appetite, or vomiting?"

Brian shook his head.

"She's not falling?"

"No," Steve said. "Except for her neck, she seems perfectly healthy."

The technician jotted that down. "Dr. Samuelson will see you shortly."

As she left the room, Dr. Samuelson entered, looking like Santa Claus, with his balding head, round belly, and long white beard under fat, rosy cheeks. He studied the cat's chart and then placed his soft, pudgy hands on her neck to examine her.

"Snowbell's torticollis stumps me," he said. "Her tests are normal, no infections or tumors. The only other possible cause is a past head trauma. Bring her back if you notice other symptoms, but, otherwise, don't worry. She seems to have adjusted to it."

"Okay," Steve said, with a nod at Brian, who was nuzzling Snowbell's cheek. "Brian, are you ready?"

The Newfoundland had tucked his head into his paws, but his ears pricked up when Melissa walked past. It panted so loudly that Brian said, "Hey, Liss, that dog sure likes you."

"I guess," Melissa averted her eyes away from the cage.

"Mom let me keep Snowbell. Maybe, she'll let you have this dog."

"Keep your voice down." Melissa looked to see if Steve had heard, but he was standing by the cash register and opening his wallet. "I don't want a dog."

"Well, this one really wants you."

The dog turned large, hopeful eyes on Melissa.

"See? He's saying, 'Take me home.'"

"I don't want any stupid dog."

"Okay, okay, settle down. It was just an idea."

Melissa resisted a backward glance. Oh, how she detested Henry Matthews! If she really had been Bryony, she would've kicked him out of Simons Mansion a long time ago.

While Steve and Brian prepared lunch, Melissa tackled homework, but the fire in John's eyes before he bit her swept away all concentration on American settlements. She slammed her history book shut, retrieved her precious music maker, and hugged it, all the while dreaming of life once John was again human. Would he be famous? Would they tour the world together? Would he write her a special song, present her with a music box that played it, and humbly thank her for the wonderful gift of new life she had given him, declare his enormous love for her, and look at her the way he once looked at Bryony?

A knock on the door chased away the daydream. Melissa returned the music box and dashed to her desk chair, just as her mother opened the door.

"Dinner's ready." She paused. "Are you okay?"

"Sure, why?"

"Because you're concentrating on a closed book."

Melissa had a Bryony dream every night that week, without Henry, but without John, too. He stayed inside the music room, and she attended teas, but her bubble of rapture continued to swell as she dreamed of her next encounter with John. Her bottom lip still felt wonderfully tender. Wasn't this proof of John's existence?

When Melissa entered her English classroom on Friday afternoon, Mr. Masters had left a note on the chalkboard: *Open literature books to page ninety-eight.*

Pages rustled, but Mr. Masters waited until the room was deathly silent.

"I'm sure you recall, our thorough study of 'Hiawatha's Childhood,'" he said. "Tell me about its author."

Katie raised her hand. "Henry Wadsworth Longfellow was a poet." "And he often wrote about legends," Julie burst out, then slapped her hand over her mouth. "Sorry."

Surprisingly, Mr. Masters let it pass. "Any boys? Jack?"

"He wrote a poem about Paul Revere's famous ride," Jack said.

"Very good," Mr. Masters said. "Today, I will share one of Mr. Longfellow's early, lesser known poems, and then we shall analyze its meaning."

He cleared his throat with a dramatic, "Ahem!" which made everyone giggle, then tucked his hands behind his back and announced in a clear voice, "A Psalm of Life."

What the heart of the young man said to the psalmist.
Tell me not, in mournful numbers, life is
but an empty dream,
For the soul is dead that slumbers
And things are not what they seem.

Melissa's eyes widened at the familiar words. Where had she heard them? She chewed her pen cap, thinking.

> *Life is real! Life is earnest!*
> *And the grave is not its goal!*
> *Dust thou art, to dust returnest,*
> *Was not spoken of the soul.*
> *Not enjoyment and not sorrow,*
> *Is our destined end or way;*
> *But to act, that each tomorrow*
> *Find us farther than today.*

Now, Melissa knew. Henry had quote from this poem in his study. She rested her elbows on her desk and leaned forward, fascinated.

> *Art is long and time is fleeting,*
> *And our hearts, though stout and brave,*
> *Still, like muffled drums, are beating*
> *Funeral marches to the grave.*
> *In the world's broad field of battle,*
> *In the bivouac of life,*
> *Be not dumb, like driven cattle.*
> *Be a hero in the strife!*
> "

Mr. Masters closed his eyes, and his voice boomed with emotion. *A hero?* Melissa could not reconcile that term with the comical figure at the head of the room. She sat on the edge of her seat. No one spoke, not even Dan.

> *Trust no future, however pleasant.*
> *Let the dead past bury its dead.*
> *Act, act in the living present,*
> *Hearts within and God o'er head.*
> *Lives of great men all remind us*
> *We can make our lives sublime.*
> *And, departing, leave behind us*
> *Footprints on the sands of time.*

Melissa, too, closed her eyes. The fireplace logs snapped; the heavenly aroma of many purple roses hung in the air. Mr. Masters had to be Henry.

Footprints, that perhaps another,
 Sailing o'er life's solemn main,
 Forlorn and shipwrecked brother,
Seeing, shall take heart again.
With a heart, for any fate;
Still achieving, still pursing,
Learn to labor and to wait.

Mr. Masters bowed his head and spoke no more. Then, with a pirouette, he picked up a piece of chalk and turned to face the class.

"What is Mr. Longfellow communicating in that poem?" he asked.

Dan, of all people, raised his hand. "That death is not an end to   life, sir."

Mr. Masters wrote that on the blackboard. "What lines support your statement?"

On the bus, Ann chattered about Mr. Masters. "He's awesome, even though he's strange," she said. "I wish he would always teach here."

"Doesn't he?" Melissa said, surprised.

"No, he comes and goes, probably because he's a famous writer, so the school hires a sub. I've waited a long time to have him for a teacher."

Was Henry laboring and waiting for real death to come or was it, as he said, only instinct preserving him from the grave? Maybe, with nothing except music and Henry for company, John had no reason to live, until now. No one had ever witnessed a vampire in action and lived, but John had openly shared it with Melissa. That made her special.

Her mother was opening a can of spaghetti sauce. "How was your day," Darlene began, then peered closely at Melissa. "Ouch! I'll bet that hurts!"

"What hurts?" Melissa reached into the fruit bowl for a banana.

"You can't feel the giant cold sore on your bottom lip?"

CHAPTER 20: CONFUSION IN THE CLOSET

Because another thrilling night with John was slow to arrive, Melissa decided to create one, the next time she woke inside Simons Mansion. John might be unrelenting in practicing, but, certainly, he would welcome a romantic break from it.

Yet, when the coveted time materialized, Melissa's resolve fled, and she floundered outside the music room. Once John closed the doors and began pounding the keys, he loathed interruptions, but Melissa couldn't imagine his rule applied to Bryony. She closed her eyes and visualized Bryony sneaking into the music room, placing her hands on John's shoulders, and leaning down to kiss his cheek. Delighted to see her, John would immediately cease playing and draw Bryony into his arms.

So, Melissa counted to ten, then twenty, and then a hundred before she summoned enough courage to enter the music room. John was so absorbed in his piano he did not notice her. She stood motionless, silently pleading for him to sense her presence and kiss her, but the room resonated with his music.

She was just about to touch him when John, still playing, said,

"Melissa, I don't have time tonight."

He had called her Melissa! She glanced at her coral gown. No, she was Bryony. She smoothed her skirt and sat on the bench beside him. "John...."

John struck a wrong note. The music stopped. He turned brutal eyes at her. Melissa's heart sank like lead. She had not expected this reaction. What should she say to him now?

"The other night...." she began.

"Thank you," John said. "Truly."

"No, that's not it, it's...it's...didn't it mean *anything* to you?"

"Very much, but not exactly, I'm afraid, what it meant to you. You enjoyed a small sign of affection. I sampled an appetizer before the banquet."

Melissa wrinkled her nose. "That's disgusting."

"You asked."

"I wanted it to be special."

"I quite assure you it was." "Not like that."

The music resumed. Melissa laid a light hand on John's arm, one not hard enough to halt his practice and invoke his wrath.

"You said we could be like you and Bryony."

"I did not. You get to play Bryony, while I harvest blood samples. If our bargain is no longer palatable, I'll release...." John paused, hands dangling in mid-key.

Melissa vehemently shook her head. "No!"

"Then stop this childish whining. You don't hunt by night with me, but I'm not crying over it."

John had played only five chords, when Henry Matthews strolled in, leaned his arm on the piano ledge, and said, "John, I need a word with you about the mansion's restoration."

"I told you the restoration is dead," John said, head back, eyes closed, and fingers flying over the keys. "I refuse to allow it."

Henry frowned. "Well, whether you approve or not, the village's plans are in place. Work will begin once the ground thaws unless we can...."

"Stop," John closed the piano lid. "Go back to sleep, Melissa. Nothing will happen tonight."

He walked into the library with Henry, shutting the double doors behind him.

"Melissa!"

Her bedroom door banged open, and her mother marched across the room. Melissa rapidly regained consciousness and silenced her clock. It had rung half an hour.

"I've got it, Mom," she said. "I'm getting up."

"Well, hurry up, or you'll be late for school. Brian's already dressed and eating breakfast." She stayed until Melissa sat up. "Your cold sore looks better."

Within minutes, Melissa had joined Brian at the breakfast table. She dumped cereal into her bowl and looked with disdain at the kaleidoscope of sugary slop Brian was stirring, as he read the back of the box.

"How can you eat such revolting stuff?" She reached for the milk.

"Plenty of sugar." Brian smuggled another tablespoon into his bowl before their mother saw him do it.

Today, Melissa's favorite cereal tasted like cardboard. Why had John evaded her? He acted as if Melissa meant nothing. She needed to share how much she liked it and to find out if he liked it, too. Was that such a crime? She worried about John all day.

Ann noticed her listlessness in algebra and passed a note. *Are you okay?*

Didn't sleep well, Melissa scrawled back.

Her brain felt as thick as Gladys' pea soup. Melissa muddled through her classes. Ann must have alerted Julie and Katie, because they all tried cheering her up at lunch.

"Knock, knock," Katie said, nudging Julie.

"Who's there?" Julie said.

"A little old lady."

"A little old lady who?"

"I didn't know...." Katie erupted into giggles. "I didn't know you could yodel."

Julie poked Katie with her straw. Jack Cooper walked past their table with his lunch tray. Melissa only gave him a fleeting glance. She took a bite from her bologna sandwich, then set it on her tray. Eyes down, she chewed for a long time.

"I love the way his butt moves," Katie said. "Don't you, Ann?"

Julie leaned forward. "I know something about Jack."

"Oooh, what?" Katie said.

"He likes a junior."

Ann sighed in exasperation. "How's that going to make Melissa feel better?" She cast a worried look in Jack's direction.

Katie disregarded Ann's remark. "How do you know?"

"Because he's sitting with her." Julie jerked her head at Jack's table. Melissa briefly noted a slender girl with short jet-black hair and wide smile.

"Who is that?" Katie said.

"I think her name is Sandy...something," Ann said. "Do you know, Melissa?"

"No," she mumbled, looking up to see Julie grinning at Ann's discomfort.

"Biology starts in three minutes," Katie said.

Shuffling like a sleepwalker, Melissa carried her tray to the garbage can. She felt like crying. She didn't want John to be mad at her. She hoped his coldness soon thawed. Melissa looked so miserable at bedtime that her mother set aside her file when Melissa kissed her goodnight.

"Sit down," Darlene said, patting her lap.

With a heavy heart, Melissa sat. She stared at her mother's keyboard, which was heavily speckled with liquid correction fluid.

Her mother smoothed Melissa's hair from her eyes. "What's wrong, honey?"

"Nothing," Melissa said. "Nothing at all."

"Would you like to talk to someone?"

She vigorously shook her head.

"Melissa," Darlene said, drawing her back and looking at her with a face full of concern, "don't feel ashamed if you need help. Promise if whatever is troubling you grows too big to handle, you'll come to me."

She started to move, but her mother held her fast. "Promise?"

"I promise."

Melissa mentally crossed her fingers. Her father had adored her mother, and Steve treated her like a queen. What would her mother know about vampires?

John's aloof manner persisted for days, even at the Harrington's ball. She found it stifling to be physically close to John while he maintained such a vast emotional distance. Could she slip outside, away from the crowds, just to clear her head?

She waited until John was engaged in conversation with Marshall Harrington before attempting retreat. The Harringtons must be important in the music world, or John would not be trying so hard to impress them. Hoping no one was watching her, Melissa edged toward the exit and glided out of the ballroom. She was free!

Melissa discreetly headed for the back staircase, then fled down the stairs and smacked directly into a man racing up them. His sleek hair and goatee were blacker than his coat and tails. He appeared unruffled by their collision.

"Excuse me, ma'am," he said, hastening past her and up the stairs.

Not a single guest occupied the women's spacious dressing room; even the servants had departed. Melissa opened the closet, the first Victorian home she had encountered with one, and rummaged amongst the guests' outerwear for her cloak. Her fingers soon found it, but before she could grab it, the door shut and latched behind her. She whirled to face the intruder. Squinting through the darkness, Melissa glimpsed a man's form.

"John?"

Unseen hands pushed Melissa against the rear wall. Henry Matthews! Rage replaced her fear. How dare he?

"Just what do you think you're doing?" she demanded.

"Shh," Henry grazed a finger across her lips. "Do you crave attention? What might John say if he found us here?"

"He'd be furious with you!"

"Do you really think so?"

Her eyes had adjusted to the dark. Henry looked so amused that Melissa wished she could slap him. Instead, she tried pushing him away, but Henry's hands slid down her arms and encircled her wrists.

"No need to get fiery, my dear. I merely wish to finish our conversation."

"We did finish it. Let me go."

Melissa struggled to free herself, but Henry strengthened his grip. "Go ahead. Shout out for John to save you."

At the mention of John's name, Melissa's face softened. Henry must have noticed because his voice lowered and filled with disgust.

"Ah, I thought so. Our John wants to be a real boy. Have you realized the price for your folly, or is the truth of the little arrangement greater than your heart could bear?"

How dare he mock her?

"Stop it!" she cried under her breath. "I won't hear anymore. This is not an 'arrangement.' I'm making a huge sacrifice for John. He will love me some day for it, just you wait and see!"

Henry laughed heartily at her outburst, but he did not loosen his hold.

"Listen to me," he hissed. "Don't discard your life for him. Possibly John was capable of love before he died, but he is now purely a creature of the flesh, anyone's flesh, not just yours. He's a predator, bent on survival."

Dropping a wrist, Henry gently grasped Melissa's cheeks and guided her face to him. His brown eyes, no longer soft, smoldered with fury.

"It matters not how freely you give your blood," Henry said. "He can seize it from you, anyway, should you refuse him. He has no soul. He does not love you. You will not make him love you."

If Henry had spoken those words to her in his study, he would have angered her, but now, in the closet, with his face inches away, Melissa was no longer mad, not even mildly annoyed. Why must he be so close? Electricity tingled through her entire body; every nerve quickened; and each sense crackled with fresh life. Had Henry noticed, for he pressed closer to her, cutting off air, arresting her next breath. Fearing the worst, Melissa closed her eyes. Henry still held her face, although now he lifted it slightly. She felt his lips at the base of her throat.

"Melissa," he whispered.

She waited, heart pounding, for the inevitable prick of needle- sharp teeth. How much blood would he take, enough to kill her, or just enough to taunt her and blunt his appetite, until the next victim?

Abruptly, almost disappointingly, he let her go.

"Forget this madness," Henry said. "Forget John. Go back to your life. You are playing with fire."

Henry unlocked the door and flung it open. The door banged on its hinges. He was gone.

Melissa stood there, uncertain of her next move. She no longer wanted to step outside. She drifted out of the closet and onto the toilet table chair. She thought for a long time. Why should Henry care about Melissa's bargain with John?

As she neared the ballroom, Melissa saw John pacing before it. At her approach, he pulled his watch from his pocket and frowned. That act could have warmed Melissa's heart, if only his face had not been so grim.

"Where have you been?" John demanded. "They're serving refreshments."

Melissa groped for an explanation, but John interrupted her. "Forget it," he said, relenting, "Shall we eat?"

He offered Melissa his arm, which she blissfully received, relieved John was not upset with her anymore. Why did Henry say such dreadful things? Evil people didn't compose and play beautiful music. They passed Henry, leaning against a wall, while a young woman, yellow ringlets bobbing, enticed him with a strip of pickled herring.

John tapped Henry's cravat. "I prefer the blue silk," he said, leading Melissa into the refreshment room.

"That's not funny, John!" Henry called after him.

An older couple stopped and stared at Henry. Melissa turned questioning eyes on John, but he stared coolly ahead. She soon forgot about Henry and his tie at the sight of the bountiful refreshment table. She wouldn't go hungry tonight. John placed a glass of punch into Melissa's hand and piled her plate with slices of cold beef, several tiny biscuits, miniature lemon and coconut cakes, and a mound of plum preserves. He ignored the beef tongue.

A voice behind Melissa startled her. "John! I don't believe I've met your bride."

196

Melissa almost dropped her glass. Standing next to her was a gray- haired and gray-bearded, bespectacled, pot-bellied man of average height. He was dressed in a plaid kilt, matching cap, and gold and bronze wristies. She looked at John, but John's expression was noncommittal.

"Bryony," he said. "This is Ed Calkins, Steward of Tara."

"Tara?"

"It's the holy seat of the High King of Ireland," Ed Calkins said.

"Oh," Melissa said.

A servant approached John and whispered into his ear. Before John could reply, Ed said, "Go, John. I'll look after…uh…."

"Bryony," John said.

"Yes, of course, Bryony."

Ed accepted Melissa's plate and conducted her to a small, round table at the far end of the room. He sat opposite, then leaned his elbows on the table and cupped his cheeks. Melissa had no idea what to say to him, but his pensive stare unnerved her. She broke a piece of biscuit and put it into her mouth. Ed did not eat.

"Will you marry me?" Ed said.

Melissa choked, spluttered, and grabbed her napkin. "I'm sorry?"

His face remained placid. "Will you marry me?"

"Um…I'm already married, remember?"

"Oh, there's no ceremony," Ed said, "and no sex. I couldn't be unfaithful to Colpa. I just appreciate beautiful women, and being a vampire doesn't change that. You only verbally agree to join my harem. This way, I make wives left and right."

Melissa's eyes flew over the room. Where was John? She looked back at Ed, who gazed at her with composed expectation. How well did John know this man? Would John be upset if she declined Ed's offer? Would that insult Ed? Perhaps, she could distract him until John returned.

"Uh, Colpa?"

"She is my favorite wife. Can I tell you how we met?"

Melissa scanned the room again, but still no John.

"Before I had much power, I was in a terrible battle and, consequently, hadn't bathed in days. Despite my poor appearance and weakened state, I managed to take possession of a well. Five De Danann maidens wanted to drink from it, but they had to kiss me first. Only Colpa would do it. After she kissed me, I revealed my true, handsome identity and made her a wife. She had only one request: to be my only lover. Because I loved her so much, I respected her desire. In fact, her love is why I became so ruthless."

He waited for Melissa's reaction, but she merely cut into a plum with her fork.

"You see, I behaved as if I was a frog that eats flies. Colpa recognized the poet in me, so she enchanted me, empowered me, and taught me to be a prince."

Ed sighed and looked so lost, that Melissa interjected, "What's a De Danann?"

"Have you ever heard of a leprechaun?" "Everyone's heard of leprechauns."

"That's what the De Dannans eventually became. The De Dananns were Ireland's rulers, before the Milesians, later called the Celts, were shipwrecked there. Now the De Dananns were wiser and far more powerful. They had better warriors and craftsmen, yet the Milesians smote the De Dananns in a single battle."

"How?"

"Well, that's the legend," Ed winked at her. "As an Irishman, it's my right to create myth. That way, you don't bother about the facts, only what you imagined happened. I know all this because I was there. I didn't kill anyone. I subdued the De Dananns through verse."

"Verse?"

"The power of poetry. I had a very great poet, Amerigian, working for me. Now, his poetry was not the high art, high-minded poetry of the De Dannans who were tremendous poets. It was vulgar poetry, the precursor to the limerick, the most superior kind of poem. Why is it superior, you ask? Well, because people can pronounce it. They can remember it, and it flows freely from the tongue."

Incredulous, Melissa said, "You conquered the De Danann's through poems?"

"Of course," Ed said. "My words created fear in the warriors, but not fear of death. You see, the wise know they will die, so they fear how others will remember them. All it takes is one good poem to turn your victories into treachery and your missteps and misfortunes into epic blunders. This fear creates willingness in your enemy to compromise, to confront you in more friendly terms, or maybe to ally with you. That's why my poet was extremely important. He was like the minstrels of the Middle Ages. People got their news from him. As my poet, he was careful to legitimize some news, reject others, and elevate my status. There was no need to be bloody. I was very effective at praise, condemnation, mockery, and most importantly of all, at being ruthless."

Melissa felt movement near her elbow and looked up. John was back! She breathed a sigh of relief. Ed Calkins jumped to his feet.

"If you will excuse me," he said. "I have some ruthless business to conduct."

Despite his earlier, mild demeanor, John had little to say during their ride back to Simons Mansion. Why wasn't she surprised? She tried not to think about the silent man sitting opposite her. Even the dark night could not completely hide his hard features beneath the magnificent top hat. She closed her eyes, settled into the cushion, and reflected upon Ed Calkins and the fantastic stories of love, power, and verse he had openly told her. Then she considered what John had done to her in the bedroom and his reaction when she tried to discuss it with him in the music room. She never imagined a vampire attack could be so wonderful. Better yet, John Simons, the vampire, was beginning to look like the John Simons of her dreams, even when she wasn't dreaming. Could that mean her blood was helping him?

Maybe Ed Calkins is right, Melissa thought. Maybe, John seems handsome, now, because I kissed him. Maybe, it's because I made a deal with him that someone else, seeing only his vampire side, would not have made.

The carriage lurched, and Melissa's eyes flew open, but John's countenance remained frigid and impassive, causing her to shiver. She took one wistful look at John, hoping he might warm her under the folds of his cloak, since she dared not ask him. She much preferred a substantial bleeding than his continued contempt.

When John did not move, Melissa resignedly closed her eyes and contemplated Henry's confrontation. He was mistaken about John and her, despite John's present detachment. Like Colpa, she thought, I do see the potential in John, and, once he is human again, he'll come around. It will just take some time, that's all.

CHAPTER 21: FETES AND FEASTS

John Simons entered the morning room, where Melissa sipped her tea and attended to household concerns with Bryga. He nodded to Bryga who, without saying a word, immediately rose and departed. Melissa, too, stood to greet John, but said nothing. These days, she hardly knew how to address him. She did not need to speak after all. John handed Melissa a card.

"For you," he said. "Please forgive my rudeness of late."
Melissa accepted the card from him and read:

Mr. and Mrs. John Simons
Request the pleasure of your company
4:00 p.m. Monday, May 30.
Garden Party, Simons Mansion, Munsonville.

"Oh, John!" She looked up at him with shining eyes. "Happy?"
John stood immobile, waiting for her response, and Melissa did not disappoint him. She threw her arms around his neck and

brought his lips down to hers. She paused, eyes closed, heart thumping, wishing. Oh, please, kiss me back, she thought. *Please!*

She felt John rest a light hand on each side of her head, not her neck. He kissed her softly, barely touching his lips against hers. Melissa opened her eyes. John's eyes were the deepest blue she had ever seen, and they looked straight at her.

"I love you, Bryony," was all he said.

One day, Melissa vowed, John will say those words to me.

Over the next few weeks, with Bryga's help, Melissa actually composed an attendance list and planned the menu and games. Guests could play croquet on the main grounds and archery on the back lawn beyond the gazebo. John informed Jackson, a skilled boatman, to be available if someone wished to venture onto the lake. Jackson objected strenuously and, cap in hand, appealed to Melissa, whom, he said, was much more reasonable than Mr. John.

"I'm a second coachman, mum, not a ship's captain," he said. "It's not my job."

"Your job is whatever Mr. Simons orders," Melissa dismissed him. How easy life would be at home, if only she could manage Brian the same way.

On the big day, Melissa flitted about the estate with Bryga, who insured every little detail met with Melissa's approval. Everything, Melissa noted with immense satisfaction, was beautiful. Large tables scattered the grounds, with smaller tables on the porch for those who preferred privacy and shade. Glassware and silverware, along with fresh white linen napkins, lined the buffet tables. Baskets lay waiting for servants to haul dirty items down to the kitchen. The food smelled delicious, even that detestable tongue. The kitchen staff had prepared chicken salad with crackers, thick bologna sausage sandwiches, bread and butter, crisp salads, wild strawberries and blueberries from Simons Woods, and peaches from John's orchards. There were also cakes and ices, along with real and mock champagne. One drink, which Bryga called sarsaparilla mead, tasted like the cold, bottled root beer Melissa had often split with her father.

At the rumble of carriage wheels, Melissa hurried to help John greet their first guests. There was the short and stocky Mayor James Fisher, his equally short and stocky wife Maybelle, and their two daughters, whose names Melissa did not catch, and who resembled a female version of Tweedledum and Tweedledee. The fair-haired, pink- cheeked Susan Betts, Bryony's best friend, came with her parents and brothers. Stretching her neck to see past the Betts family was the matriarchal town gossip, Bertha Parks, followed by her husband Orville.

Bertha Parks? Reverend Marseilles' housekeeper?

Bertha was a large woman who stood a full head and shoulders taller than Orville, not including the tall mass of thick gray hair that easily added another foot to her height. Orville was nearly as wide as he was tall and was panting and mopping his face against the heat.

The men walked directly to the grounds, while the women, laughing and chatting, dispersed to dressing rooms. For the next hour, a sea of faces blurred by Melissa, and she gave up trying to remember names. She would never meet most of them again.

When the last guest had filed passed, Melissa strolled to the lawns, astonished at the many people occupying them. Women were carrying parasols over wide-brimmed hats to shield their fair skin against the sun, and men were dressed in fine clothing, unlike the jeans and T-shirts guys wore to Grover's Park picnics. She couldn't wait for croquet to begin, because that game, thanks to Steve, was familiar to her. However, some of her enthusiasm ebbed when Henry Matthews, light and cool in his cream- colored suit, black bow tie, and straw hat, set his ball alongside Melissa's.

"You! Why do you keep following me?"

"As Bryony, you would know that."

She would not allow that obnoxious man to spoil her day. Melissa took careful aim and hit her ball straight through the first two hoops. Henry clapped, so Melissa shot him an evil glance, which he calmly disregarded.

"A regular Mrs. Joad," he said admiringly.

A regular *who?* She swung her mallet again and sent her ball a few feet away from the next hoop. In two shots, Henry's ball lay against Melissa's.

"I must say, Mrs. Simons, I was extremely touched when I received your invitation. I feared our last meeting had not transpired well, but I can now see that…."

How could she not invite him? He lived here! Melissa glowered at him. "Don't you ever shut up?"

Henry ran his finger across his lips and remained silent, but stayed under Melissa's feet like a stray Newfoundland. The sun shone with unusual brightness for so late in the afternoon, casting a glare on the wickets and obscuring Melissa's view. She shaded her eyes and found the next hoop. If only she might trade Bryony's heavy skirt for shorts and a halter top. Henry seemed unmindful of the heat, despite his full suit of clothes. He stood at Melissa's elbow, placidly waiting for her next swing. Someone, she silently raged, should permanently send him back to the grave.

"I thought vampires couldn't go out in the sun," Melissa said scornfully.

Henry looked up at the sky, then quizzically at Melissa. "What sun?"

Angrily, she turned her back on him, but he persisted. "My dear, Melissa, it's only two o'clock in the morning."

Melissa wiped her dripping forehead with her sleeve, glad Trudi or Bryga didn't see her. *Two o'clock in the morning!* What did Henry mean? She assumed her most disdainful look, adjusted her mallet, tossed him an offhand, "You're crazy," and then hit the ball. It landed in front of the wicket. One more blow would carry it to the other side, a long distance from Henry. He merely swung his mallet, smacking his ball into the side of Melissa's, and sending it bounding toward the gazebo and the archers. His, of course, sailed straight through the hoop.

"Am I really crazy?" Henry aligned his mallet for the bonus shot. "You are the one playing croquet in your bedroom."

Very funny! Melissa lifted her skirts high above her ankles and marched after her ball. She thoroughly searched the area, even the bushes, and then found it, huddled in a small hollow, on a slight decline, a few yards past the gazebo. Still seething, Melissa raised her mallet, gleefully picturing Henry's face on the ball. She glanced sideways at the cavorting groups of guests; the scene instantly darkened, and the refined figures on the lawn began decaying before her eyes. She gasped, dropped her mallet, and spun around, panting hard to catch her breath. For weeks, under the Cinderella-like banner of Bryony's life, Melissa had quite forgotten John's warning.

Her racing heart slowed to normal. She reclaimed her mallet and bent over the ball, guarding her eyes from the grisly view. Actually, the other vampires disturbed her less than Henry Matthews did, but maybe she could prod an answer or two out of him, since she shrank from asking   John further questions. Her opportunity soon arrived.

John was filling Melissa's plate when a tall man approached them and insisted he immediately speak to John. *It was the man on the stairs!*

Melissa bowed her head, but peeked at him from under her hat. So, he *did* know John. The other men sensibly wore light colored suits to deflect the sun's heat, but this man dressed in black from head to toe and looked sinister to match.

John motioned for Henry, who was sitting at nearby table and chatting to a pretty young brunette, to relieve him of Melissa's plate. Without a word to Melissa, John and the man in black trotted towards the house. Melissa watched them leave, feeling like an abandoned child.

"Henry," she said, too upset over John's disappearance to be annoyed with him. "Who is that man with John?"

"That is Kellen Wechsler." Henry spat on the ground. "John's manager."

"I didn't know John had a manager," she said in surprise. "Does he need one?"

"This depends. If you ask me, no, John capably manages himself. Nonetheless, John believes Kellen is essential to his success."

"You don't like him?"

"No, I don't. If I had any authority in the matter, he'd be terminated."

"I wish you did. He seems evil." Melissa watched the vanishing figures.

"You will never convince John. In his mind, only one opinion is valid: John's."

Henry carried Melissa's plate to the side porch, retreated to the refreshment table, and returned in short time with a heaping plate, which he daintily devoured.

Fascinated, Melissa blurted out, "Can vampires eat real food?"

"Who's eating?"

Melissa's patience was ebbing. "Why won't you answer any of my questions?"

"What questions?" Henry wiped his lips with his napkin.

"Like, why you are at my heels every single second?"

"My sincerest apologies to the hostess. Shall we find a closet and chat?"

That did it. Melissa snatched her plate and started to rise, but Henry placed a firm hand on her arm. "You must stay. I promised John."

"That's your problem."

Clutching her skirts, Melissa stalked away. Several older ladies from church were discussing the latest corsets, so Melissa decided to join them. Henry Matthews, plate in hand, followed like an obedient puppy. He placed her food before her, sat beside her, and offered a glass. "I brought you an ice."

With a frustrated sigh, Melissa accepted it, took a taste, then pointed her spoon at his nose.

"Can't you take a hint?"

"Tsk, tsk. I had hoped you approved."

"Approved what?"

"Why, my fine job with you."

"I'm John's wife. You're not responsible for me."

"Wrong again. I'm your chaperone."

She dropped her spoon on the table, and Maybelle Fisher stopped in shocked mid-sentence. Melissa's cheeks grew warm, as she hissed, "My *what?*"

"Your chaperone." Still seated, Henry gave a mock bow. "The odious Henry Matthews, at your service." He waited for Melissa's response, but none came, so he leaned forward and smiled. "Feeling more secure now?"

"Get lost!"

Melissa jumped up, shoved her chair from the table, and walked away as briskly as her skirts allowed, leaving behind her

206

plate, the ice, her toppled chair, and the loathsome Henry Matthews. She felt too angry to worry what he, or anyone else, including John, thought about her behavior. The afternoon merged into dusk, but Melissa saw neither John nor the disagreeable Kellen Wechsler. Luckily, she also saw no more of Henry. Instead, Melissa mingled with her many grateful guests, all eagerly waiting to talk with her. At twilight, an apologetic John returned alone. She quickly scanned the grounds. Kellen Wechsler was nowhere in sight.

"I'm terribly sorry, Bryony." John kissed her cheek in greeting. "It's business."

"Say no more." Melissa touched a finger to his lips. "You're here now."

For the next hour, she and John relaxed near the gazebo, where John spun enthralling stories about his travels and performances across Europe. Bertha Parks raised her eyeglass and gasped.

"Good heavens, Mr. Simons! You've been to Austria?"

"Yes, twice."

Was this the woman who had objected so strenuously to Bryony's association with John? She certainly seemed impressed with the musician.

John stopped speaking. Henry had approached the table and was now laying a gentle hand on his shoulder.

"I'll be in my study," Henry said. "Please join me for a nightcap after your party." He motioned toward Melissa. "Your wife is rather good with a mallet. Perhaps, someday, she may beat me at croquet."

"I should like to see that," John said, smiling.

"Tell me, John," one of the men interrupted. "Were you ever in the mountains?"

Melissa ignored the lingering Henry and placed her full attention on John's answer. Henry bent near Melissa's ear. She swatted him away, but he clasped her hand against his chest and murmured, "You've chosen to play a dangerous game, my dear. Too bad, it's not your game."

The garden party initiated a series of outdoor repasts at Simons Mansion that extended throughout the summer: concerts, plays, teas, masquerade balls, bicycle trips, and boat outings. In

August, the villagers reciprocated the Simons' generosity by hosting an event. James Fisher's Uncle Clyde had died, leaving the farmhouse abandoned. James offered it as a wedding present to one of his daughters, but the ceremony was a year away. In the meantime, James offered it as a party venue.

On the invitations, the Fishers instructed guests to don floral-print clothes and decorate their carriages with native flowers and greenery. The Fishers did likewise to the barn, which they transformed into a concert hall, and arranged the farmhouse for dressing rooms and a buffet supper. The countrified invitation highly amused John when he read it, but panic gripped Melissa's heart. Would he attend such a provincial event?

"We'll go, won't we John?"

"We must." John set the invitation on the sideboard and poured a drink. "I'm the entertainment."

Whew! The event was not beneath his dignity; success had not spoiled him. If the summer fete appeared substandard in any way, it was not the villagers' fault. They showcased their best food, finest clothes, and most aristocratic manners for Munsonville's first couple. In return, John prepared several original pieces, which touched everyone within Melissa's hearing.

"He's a regular Beethoven," Mrs. Parks sighed, wiping her eyes.

As much as she enjoyed John's playing, Melissa nearly cheered when John broke for intermission. The open doors did little to remove the hot, stale air. As she moved through the crowd, a large boot crushed the hem of her dress and ripped it at the waist.

"Drat!"

Melissa hastily looked around. Had anyone heard?

She assessed the ragged tear. The gap, although not large, definitely needed repair. If the Fishers could not spare a servant, Melissa hoped to find a safety pin in the dressing room. Choosing modesty over propriety, Melissa spurned the escort, gathered the folds of her dress, and rushed to the farmhouse.

Once inside, she discovered the Fishers were indeed short on servants, even with Bryga and Mildred helping. The Fishers' housemaid panicked at Melissa's request for an escort, rattled directions, and scurried away. Melissa climbed to the second floor, but found one closed door after another. The farmhouse was too small for a wrong turn.

Ahead on her left, Melissa heard feminine laughter. Was that the dressing room? Should she knock? Remembering she was Bryony Simons, Melissa started to enter, felt sheepish, and knocked. A woman's voice called out, "Come in!"

Melissa opened the door. Henry Matthews was reclining on an ornately carved chaise lounge. Three women, clad in brightly colored dresses in various states of disarray, knelt before him. In unison, they turned from Henry to gawk at Melissa.

On a table beside the lounge sat a tray of melon slices, which Henry fed to the women, one bite at a time. After each morsel, they licked his fingers and squealed. The woman in the middle whispered something to her companion, inducing raucous laughter from them both. Henry positioned a watermelon chunk in the middle of his hand and offered it to Melissa, a sardonic grin spreading across his face.

"Mrs. Simons, pray, come join us!" Henry called out to her. The women inched closer to him. Melissa's face burned. This was worse than the embarrassing gap in her skirt. Quickly, she turned and fled.

Her mind wandered during the second half of John's concert. Never mind the dress. Who were those women with Henry? Villagers? Vampires? James Fisher would not like it. How could John and Henry be friends? They seemed too different to be compatible. She started at the familiar notes. John had begun *Bryony.*

After the party, the guests strayed toward the house. Servants hustled about the lower level, dishing up roasted rabbits and opossums, potatoes in herb gravy, cold fish salads, melon slices, and cake. The maids poured coffee and tea and refilled glasses of wine. Melissa bumped into Bryga as she scuttled past. She sympathized with Melissa's plight of the torn dress.

"Oh, you poor thing," Bryga said. "Come with me. I'll fix you up." Bryga handed the coffee pot to the serving girl, then motioned to Melissa.

"There's a small dressing room upstairs," she said. "I'm sure we'll find something."

The first door to the left stood wide open and contained all manner of toilette items, including a couple of safety pins. Melissa really felt foolish. If she only had known the dressing room's location, she could have remedied it herself.

Downstairs, John had disappeared with some of the men into the makeshift drawing room to talk, drink, and smoke. In the parlor, the women flocked around Melissa and rattled about John's performance. Melissa flushed happily at their words. She never tired of the attention. Then Henry entered the room and spoiled it.

"Let's go, Mrs. Simons." Henry was buttoning his coat and heading for the front door. A maid handed him his hat, and he nodded to her. "Bring Mrs. Simons' cloak."

"Go?" Melissa said, gazing at her garment in the maid's hands. "Go, where?"

"I'm taking you home."

Melissa picked up her skirts, without her cloak, and walked ahead of him. "I shall leave with my husband."

"It was your husband who petitioned me to fetch you."

Fetch her? Like a dog? Melissa spun around and glared at him with all the hatred she could muster. "Stop following me! Don't you have your own life?"

"Not when I'm with you."

"I'm still not going."

"Suit yourself. It's you who will answer to him."

Henry stepped onto the front porch. Melissa, still boiling, did too, and watched him put on gloves. Dumbfounded, he turned toward her. "I thought you were staying."

"I am!"

He looked left and right for Jackson, while Melissa stirred up the courage to ask him something. "Those women, in that room with you, were they vampires?"

"Vampires?" Henry threw back his head and heartily laughed aloud. "When flesh and blood women are so freely available?" He removed his hat, rested it on his chest, and bowed his head. "God rest their souls."

His answer appalled her. "You didn't, I mean, you wouldn't...all three of them? Oh, those poor, poor women!"

210

"Not at all. They enjoyed it to the end, well, almost to the end." He contemplated the night sky and quoted, "'Come loving and soothing death. Undulate 'round the world, serenely arriving, arriving. In the day, in the night, to all, to each, sooner or later, delicate death.'" Henry winked at the open-mouthed Melissa. "Walt Whitman."

How could he be so callous? Words failed her, or she would have delivered the lecture he so well deserved. As Jackson and the carriage drove up to the porch, Henry blew a light kiss at Melissa.

"Now, Melissa, none of your maudlin sentimentality. There are worse ways to go." He climbed into the waiting vehicle. "You sure you won't come along? No? Well, then, you should go back inside the house. You know better than to be alone. Ta!"

Subdued, Melissa stood on the porch and watched until the carriage rolled from view. Playing Bryony wasn't fun anymore. As she stepped back inside, John walked from the drawing room and saw her.

"Has Henry gone?" John said, looking perplexed.

"Yes, he has, but...."

"You aren't with him, why?"

"Well, I wanted to stay with you and...."

"That's not your decision."

Melissa bristled at his response. "Wait a minute," she said. "Don't I....?"

John hailed a housemaid carrying a tray. "Excuse me, could you please collect Mrs. Simons' wraps? She is leaving now. And tell Bryga to come here, too."

"Yes, Mr. Simons."

Melissa burned inside. The idea! She wasn't going to take orders from him, either. Before she could fire a fitting retort, Bryga appeared.

"Yes, Mr. Simons?"

"Mrs. Simons has a headache. Please accompany her home." "Of course, sir."

"Locate a quiet room, so she can rest until Jackson returns."

"Immediately, sir."

Bryga hastened away. When the foyer was empty, John stepped close to Melissa and embraced her. He lightly brushed his lips across her forehead, then swept them down to her ear. Melissa relaxed at his touch and instantly forgave him. From over John's shoulder, Melissa saw Kellen Wechsler standing in the drawing room's doorway. He coolly held a glass of brandy, but his jubilant air nettled her.

"Play the part, or our deal ends," John hissed.

He turned on his heel, strode into the drawing room, and shut the door with a firm click. Melissa reeled from John's cold-hearted desertion and almost broke down, but Bryga's reappearance saved her.

"Come this way, Mrs. Simons," the housekeeper said in her kindly way. "I'm sorry you're feeling peaked. I sure hope you're better soon."

"Me, too. Bryga," Melissa said, looking dejectedly over her shoulder at the closed door, a tangible symbol of the growing rift between them. "Me, too."

The next day, an air of despairing gloom hung over Melissa. Outwardly, she mechanically moved from class to class, jotting notes, and answering questions. Inwardly, Melissa agonized over her deteriorating relationship with John.

"Are you ready for Monday's biology test?" Ann said on the way
home.

"No, I'm not ready for the test. There are too many definitions. I'm like Brian. I can get a few straight, and then I mix up the rest." "Me, too. Let's drill each other until my stop."

"Ann Dalton!" Mr. Carlson shouted.

"Never mind." Ann grabbed her book bag. "I'll talk to you tomorrow, okay?"

That evening, Melissa spent more time moping about John than having to study biology over the weekend. Forcing aside thoughts of John, Melissa reviewed her notes, until her head ached, and stomach knotted. Disheartened and frustrated, Melissa threw the book on the floor. Tomorrow was Saturday; she had an entire weekend to prepare. Sleep only brought an apathetic John Simons, despite the new green-trimmed pink dress Melissa wore at John's reception for his newest acquaintances and colleagues in the music field. Promoters, sponsors, and even a few fellow artists flocked to John, but the women accompanying them were more attentive.

They hung on his arm, flattered him, and swooned at every word. To Melissa's chagrin, John did little to discourage it. One young woman, with yards of glistening, blonde hair, one shade lighter than her bright yellow dress, fastened herself to John's side all night. How had she escaped the scrutiny of Kellen Wechsler, John's human shield and regulator of the admirers? Henry's obvious dislike for Kellen brought little consolation, for John's disinterest toward Melissa continued during refreshments. Henry brought Melissa a plate of food, and she would have refused it, too, if John had not been within hearing range.

"Thank you very kindly, Mr. Matthews," Melissa lowered her voice, "but unlike the women you gobbled in the farmhouse, I can feed myself."

"Ahem," said a man, very close to her ear.

It was Ed Calkins. Melissa quickly scanned the room for John. Henry was already flirting with a young woman more appreciative of his solicitations, but she only cared that John was gone.

"I'm sorry he's such a jerk," Ed said.

"It's okay." The woman in the yellow dress had left, too.

"You should recite one of my open-ended limericks to him. The punch line is blank, so you can personalize the insult."

John walked past the parlor window. Melissa handed Ed Calkins her plate and rushed from the room, bumping into Mildred on the way out.

"Sorry!" Melissa muttered, as she fled through the door.

She stepped into the silent and starry night, never minding whom she offended. John occupied those grounds with another woman. Remembering to lift her skirts, Melissa trotted down the porch steps and whisked to the back of the house where, just a few, short weeks ago, they held the garden picnic. Skidding on satin slippers, Melissa fled past the croquet grounds and then the tea garden, in full bloom with Henry's forbidden purple roses. In the distance, John and that horrible woman strolled toward the gazebo. Her dress shimmered like gauze under the moonlight.

"John!"

A gloved hand clapped over her mouth. Henry Matthews again! "I wouldn't go there if I were you," he said gravely.

Melissa clawed her nails into his hand and peeled it from her mouth. "Stop telling me what to do! You're not my boss."

Henry started to object, then shrugged and stepped aside. That was easy. She should tell him off more often. Melissa again collected her skirts and hurried away through the damp grass. Who was that woman? A former lover, perhaps?

"John!"

Melissa cursed her youth, unable to compete with glamour, and then she cursed her Victorian garments. She could have run there if she had worn jeans and sneakers. Melissa stepped through the bushes. John was crouched on the gazebo floor.

"John?"

He leaped out and sprinted into the night.

"John!" She stepped inside.

The woman who, just minutes ago, had wandered the estate with John now lay, lifeless and blue, in a tumbled heap on the floor. The shredded remains of her dress barely concealed the gashes and bruises covering her battered body. Her head bent at an odd angle, and her sightless eyes stared past Melissa. Something had slit her chin to the base of her throat. The little blood left hadn't begun coagulating.

CHAPTER 22: LISA HARDING

Melissa began her day in the hour before dawn by vomiting all over her bed. Her mother rushed into the room, helped Melissa to the desk chair, and then changed the sheets, while she took Melissa's temperature.

"101.4," she said. "Well, I know someone who's staying in bed today."

Groaning, Melissa slumped further into her chair. "The biology test is Monday."

"That's two days away," Darlene reassured her. "You get some rest. I'll bring something to drink."

Sleep was gray loneliness without John. Being awake was no better, for she only saw the grotesque form on the gazebo floor. Twice, Melissa ran to the bathroom and threw up. After the second trip, her sheets lay smooth and folded back. Fluffed pillows rested against her headboard. Her mother held a glass of ginger ale with a straw in it.

"Try this," she said. "Let's see if we can't keep something in your stomach."

Melissa crawled into bed. Her mother tucked the sheets and handed her the glass.

"Just sip," Darlene said. "Don't try drinking it all at once."

Despite her shivering body and chattering teeth, Melissa managed a few swallows, until her stomach rebelled. She set down the glass and leaned against cool pillows.

Her mother gently kissed Melissa's forehead, whispered, "Just yell if you need something, hon," and left the door ajar.

Melissa closed her eyes. Her head pounded a hole into the pillow. She reopened them, but the room tilted, and her stomach heaved. She rolled onto her side and began sinking into queasy sleep, when a voice quite near Melissa's ear said, "Hi."

She turned to see a red-haired girl, about her age.

"Hello," Melissa said, as she handed her cloak to the dressing room maid. The girl's stared. Her nearly colorless green eyes were almost devoid of lashes; her dry lips faded into her thin, white face; and the short sleeves on her emerald gown overemphasized her skinny arms.

She inched closer to Melissa. "What's your name?"

"Bryony."

"No, your real name."

"I just *told* you. I'm Bryony Simons, John Simons' wife."

The girl gazed condescendingly at her, and that annoyed Melissa who, as Bryony, had been accustomed to deference and respect. She smoothed her skirts, adjusted her brooch, and started to leave.

"Everyone here tonight will call me Imelda," the girl said, "but my real name is Lisa Harding. I'm a host, too, from Barnes City."

Melissa stopped short. *"What?"*

"Barnes City. It's in Iowa."

"No, what did you call yourself?"

"A host, like you. My vampire, Kellen, a poor German farmer from the seventeenth century, died from bubonic plague. I'm giving him a second chance at life."

Kellen...Wechsler? What did Lisa mean by host? Leeches had hosts, not vampires. She wished this girl would leave. She made Melissa uneasy.

"That's ridiculous!" Melissa tried pushing past, but Lisa blocked her way.

"Don't be angry," Lisa said. "I meant no harm. I've never seen another host. Everyone I meet is dead."

Melissa slept most of Saturday into Sunday morning, sipping ginger ale between naps and progressing to canned chicken noodle soup, apple juice, and dry toast. Around noon on Sunday, her mother cheerfully announced Melissa's temperature was normal.

"Feeling well enough to try some real food?"

"Yes! I'm starving!"

"You can eat on the couch, if you're careful."

Melissa dragged her blanket and pillow into the living room to watch television reruns. Snowbell jumped next to her and curled into a ball on Melissa's blanket. Her mother brought a toasted cheese sandwich and a bowl of applesauce.

"If you keep that down," Darlene said, "you may try dinner tonight."

Snowbell roused only to sniff Melissa's bread. Melissa bit the corner of her sandwich. She felt ravenous. At dinner, Melissa joined her family at the table.

"Welcome back to the fold." Steve, smiling, passed her the mashed potatoes.

She gave him a weak smile in return. "Thanks."

"Mom," Brian said. "Steve needs my help picking out a turkey. Can I go to Jenson after school tomorrow, please, Mom?"

While they talked about Thanksgiving, Melissa made up her mind, but she waited until Brian and Steve began dinner dishes, and her mother retreated to the bedroom. When Melissa heard the sounds of her mother's typewriter, the running of tap water, and Steve and Brian's lively conversation about turkeys, she tiptoed to the telephone table and picked up the receiver. The dial tone sounded like a foghorn in the quiet room.

Prrrpp! Snowbell leaped onto the table.

"Shhh," Melissa warned the cat.

She quickly dialed "0." Snowbell watched the wheel as it spun.

"Operator."

"Barnes City, Iowa," Melissa whispered.

"I'm sorry?"

"Barnes City, Iowa," Melissa said, raising her voice a small notch.

"Name?"

"Harding."

Silence, except for the clatter of dishes.

"There are two listings for that number. Do you want them both?"

"Yes, please." Melissa held her breath.

The operator recited the telephone numbers. As Melissa wrote them down, the sink water gurgled. She quickly replaced the receiver and tucked the numbers into her pajama top, then tiptoed back to the couch, picked up her book, and nestled amongst the pillows. Steve entered, carrying his coffee mug and the newspaper.

"Don't forget the garbage, sport! Then, we'll start on homework."

Melissa slept poorly that night and woke up cranky. Even Trudi noticed.

"Are you ill, Mrs. Simons?" "No. Just grouchy."

"Well, maybe the Smythes' dinner party tonight will put you in better humor."

The wealthy and music-loving Bartholomew and Edwina Smythe had just bought a second home in Munsonville. At the Harrington ball, where Henry had trapped Melissa in the closet, John had so impressed Bartholomew, a former banker with exquisite taste in art and strong connections in the music world. that the couple invited John to their first Munsonville affair. They also extended an invitation to a well-known concert promoter and insisted John perform for their guests that evening. Naturally, John agreed.

For two weeks, John had secluded himself in the music room. The glow of Carnegie Hall had diminished long ago and fantasies of conquering the next musical plateau consumed him, but Europe was still a year way. John intended to present an unforgettable impression on the Smythes, the concert promoter, and any guests who had the ability to further his career. Day and night, John's music thundered throughout the house, hindering the daily routine and prohibiting both the entertaining of guests and sound sleep. He stopped only to yell shocking curses at his mistakes. Mildred and Howard trotted back and forth, adding and removing dishes and chamber pots, while Melissa hung back, yearning to encourage him. How unlike John to have such little confidence in himself!

Bryga disagreed. John needed no coddling and suffered no lack of self-esteem. To him, anything short of a flawless performance equaled failure; he must play to perfection.

"It's best not to go near him when he's in a mood," Bryga said.

So Melissa instead fretted about the upcoming event. Although excited about such a grand affair in Munsonville, she dreaded John's unpredictable emotions and his easy penchant of dismissing her to the care of Henry Matthews. The less she saw of John, the more Melissa desired him, but she had no idea how to facilitate more time together.

As the great day approached, Melissa's apprehension increased, but she kept hope in check. Despite her good intentions, when John sent word through Bryga that he would be ready for departure in exactly thirty minutes, Melissa's longing for John and anticipation for the affair leaped into her throat.

"Oh Trudi, hurry, please!"

She stood wiggling in corsets and placing her faith in the new orchid party dress Trudi had spread over her bed. Maybe, tonight would be their night, John's and hers. As soon as the maid fastened the last earring, Melissa rushed down the stairs to the waiting carriage. Henry Matthews held his hand toward Melissa. *No!* Not tonight!

Melissa whirled back to the house. "I'm not going with you!"

"Please forgive the inconvenience, Mrs. Simons. John will join us later. Until then, he appointed me as your escort."

Still suspicious, Melissa slowly turned to face him. "John will attend the dinner? He's not just coming to play?"

Henry bowed in affirmation. "You're sure?"

"My honor as a gentleman."

Bristling with resentment, Melissa accepted Henry's hand, even though she wished she had stayed home. She brooded all the way to the peak of Bass Street, close to the cemetery entrance. The tops of Munsonville's streets featured the largest houses; their sizes gradually diminished as one approached the fishing cottages near Lake Munson.

However, the outside of the Smythe's spacious, three-story abode was misleading, for the rooms were all small and crammed with furniture. The chair arms touched, so bumping elbows was unavoidable.

"How fortunate they stopped the guest list at fourteen," Henry murmured.

Once settled, Melissa anxiously monitored the front door. One decrepit couple, then a second, entered the room, the women's satin gowns swishing loudly. A pretty, young woman at the far end of the room whispered something at the equally lovely young lady on her right. Henry said they were the Smythes' granddaughters.

The clock loudly ticked each agonizing minute, but John did not appear. What delayed him? Surely, not one last practice? The clock chimed six times and now seven, with no sign of John. Melissa's heart fluttered with each knock. The butler greeted another guest, but anticipation crashed into despair when she saw Ed Calkins. How did he get away with wearing a kilt and cap to a formal dinner party?

When the butler announced dinner, Henry offered Melissa his arm. She hesitated then, feeling utterly dejected, reluctantly accepted it. Henry sputtered with choked laughter at the fourteen table settings jammed together, and he whipped out his handkerchief to conceal his mirth. Ed Calkins sat across from Melissa. Kellen Wechsler slid into the room at the last minute, flung her a scornful look, and stole the antique chair on Melissa's right. So, he didn't like her either? Good, she hoped he ignored her. The frightful pallor of the other guests unsettled her, so she read her dinner card. Suckling pig seemed palatable, and so did turkey drawn with butter, but boiled calves head?

"Don't worry," Henry said in a low voice. "You needn't accept everything. The menu is a guide so guests can plan their eating, more of what they like, less, or none, of what they do not."

220

"You may have my mashed turnips, too," Melissa said, very much relieved. She peeped into her bowl and nudged Henry. "Hey, what's in the soup?"

Through rattling teeth between gaunt lips, Mr. Smythe chose that very moment to praise Henry's latest story, so Melissa ate the potatoes and carrots out of the broth and ignored the unfamiliar meat. The formality of Victorian dinner parties mystified Melissa. Servants brought the food to the table, one item at a time, then removed all traces of it, before they served the next dish. Henry handed her the appropriate utensils. She marveled at each bite he ate.

"So vampires can eat anything they want?"

"No. Depending upon the source, sometimes even blood doesn't...take."

"What happens?"

"Our bodies eliminate it."

Melissa started to ask how vampires disposed of blood, but Kellen Wechsler was staring at her with unconcealed malice.

"Don't you feel conspicuous, the only human among vampires?" Rancor gleamed in Kellen's coal-black eyes.

Melissa glanced at Lisa Harding. Didn't she count?

"Don't you miss being human?" Melissa snapped back at him.

"Not at all," Kellen broke a piece of bread and dipped it into the sauce that was once the brains of a little calf. "When I was a man, the ground fought me; the wife fought me; and the nobility fought me. Every year, the good Lord sent another mouth to feed. Now, no one fights me. I have so much more power."

Kellen moved his frigid lips close to her ear.

"Most importantly, one act satisfies all the appetites," His breath chilled her neck. "It's so efficient. I quite prefer it."

She wished he would leave her alone. He made her skin crawl.

"Well, Mr. Wechsler," Melissa said in her most dignified voice, as she accepted a slice of turkey. "I think I prefer a human existence."

"Have you ever died of the bubonic plague, Mrs. Simons?"

"Well, I can't say that...."

"Your head hurts, your body aches, and feverish chills overtake you. Your lymph nodes swell in your neck, armpits, and groin. Shall I continue, Mrs. Simons?"

Melissa turned to Henry for help, but he was flirting with the Smythes' oldest granddaughter. Some chaperone he turned out to be!

What should she do? She didn't like Kellen, but neither could she insult him and incur John's wrath.

"Please do," Melissa said. "It's most fascinating."

"Soon those swollen lymph nodes leak pus and blood. Red spots break through your skin and turn black. You vomit blood. There is unbearable, wracking pain. Do you know why, Mrs. Simons?"

Melissa swallowed hard. "Um, no I...."

"You've begun decomposing. Are you still finding this fascinating, Mrs. Simons? Then there is the persistent coughing, rapid heart rate, delirium, and crushing spasms, all before merciful death finally descends."

"So, you died of the bubonic plague?"

"Actually, no. I was ...."

She followed Kellen's gaze. He was looking past her at Henry. To Melissa's surprise, Henry had also stopped talking and was glowering at Kellen. How much of the conversation had Henry actually heard?

Feeling supported now, Melissa smiled sweetly at Kellen. "Yes, Mr. Wechsler?"

"I, uh, died from something else." Kellen rose from his seat and bumped the table so hard, the silverware jangled. "Excuse me please, Mrs. Simons." He sped away.

"I took an arrow in my back."

Melissa startled at the sound of that voice. She had forgotten about Ed Calkins.

"It was an act of treachery by Amerigian. He hated that too many of his poems were associated more with me, the ruthless dictator, and not with him. Still, I don't think I would have received an arrow if my wife was alive. Either she wasn't there to protect me, or I had lost the will to live and had let my guard down."

"How very thrilling, Mr. Calkins," With a clawed, emaciated hand, Mrs. Smythe raised her wine glass to blue lips and glanced warningly at her husband.

Ed Calkins sighed with deep unhappiness. "Without her, I preferred to die. Still, being a vampire has its advantages. I never kill my victims, you know. That way, they can remember how ruthless I am."

The clock struck nine, jarring Ed from his musings. He checked the time on his wristwatch and rose. "I must go. I have ruthless business in 2008."

"As Steward of Tara?" Melissa asked.

"There is still a need for a ruthless dictator in Tara," Ed said, "but I also supervise a news agency by night. If you ever need a job, come see me. It's a profitable business, especially since I print my own currency. To amuse the peasants, I grill steaks on the Fourth of July, host a Queen of Christmas contest where I distribute candy canes and presents, and organize a pallet jack race for Labor Day."

"I'm sure they appreciate your concessions," Mr. Smythe's cheeks collapsed as he said it, but he rolled his hollow eyes helplessly at Mrs. Smythe.

"Of course, the highlight of the year is the Calkins Day parade on February thirteenth, my birthday. In fact, I have a petition circulating to make February twelfth through the fourteenth a three-day national holiday. Would you care to sign it?"

"I, uh...." Melissa began.

Ed unsuccessfully searched his kilt. "Next time," he promised with a hearty smile and a farewell nod.

Henry was not the only one eavesdropping. A contemptuous Lisa Harding watched Melissa's every forkful. The girl was crazy. Kellen meant nothing to Melissa.

"Good evening, Imelda."

"Good evening." Lisa's voice was crisp.

"Your husband tells such interesting stories."

"Yes."

"So, Mr. Wechsler was a German farmer?"

"Yes."

"A peasant?"

"Yes."

"Seventeenth?"

"Yes."

Melissa gritted her teeth. What was this girl's problem anyway? "So, what is he doing in Victorian America? Isn't he out of time frame?" When Lisa said nothing, Melissa added, "And his league?"

"Not really," Lisa sniffed her pudding. "You'll see lots of strange things now."

John Simons briskly entered the dining room and assumed Kellen's vacant seat. Because it was John, Mrs. Smythe ignored his breach of etiquette, rang a bell, and ordered the servant who responded to serve him.

"Forgive the delay," John muttered to Melissa. He looked exhausted.

"Forget it."

Melissa had no reason to look at him. She was certain another disappointment from John was not far away. Would her anger bother John? Melissa hoped it did, but doubted it could.

The concert promoter arrived at dessert. John's after-dinner performance passed without blemish, no surprise there. The promoter extolled John's talent, so Melissa knew more bookings were in John's immediate future. In the past, such knowledge would have filled her heart with pride, admiration, and love. Tonight, realizing John would intensify his practices, the news only saddened her.

Yet, as he accepted his well-earned congratulations, John's eyes skimmed the over the guests, seeking her approval. On impulse, Melissa avoided his gaze. John could stew tonight. He well deserved it.

When the men adjourned to the library, Melissa dashed into the parlor to join the other ladies, before John could approach her. She feigned delight at the Smythes' imported coffee, but otherwise ignored the conversation floating around her ears. What might happen when she and John went home? She buried her earlier hopes. The night did not look promising for them.

From her parlor chair, Melissa saw Henry standing in the hallway, wearing his coat and putting on gloves. He stopped a maid, laden with a tray full of glasses, and said something

224

inaudible, although Melissa suspected what it was. Leave without me, Melissa silently begged him. *Leave, leave, leave.*

"Fetch Mrs. Simons' cloak," Henry said. "I'm overseeing her safe journey home."

Melissa sighed in resignation. Why argue anymore? As Henry once said, John saw only one perspective, and that was his. So, why had he sought her approval tonight? Did that mean something to him, or did he only want additional validation for his performance? Was her adulation equal to everyone else's?

Henry attempted light conversation on the way home, but Melissa was in no mood. He even apologized for Kellen's rudeness, but Melissa didn't care for that, either.

"I'm surprised you're sorry, considering you're one of them!"

His frosty reply astonished her. "Mrs. Simons, you insult me. I was charged with your care!"

Melissa dropped her mouth. Had she really insulted him? Melissa scrutinized his face, but in the dark, with Henry on the opposite seat, she wasn't certain. Henry Matthews wasn't the type to be easily grieved, yet he ignored her for the remainder of the ride home.

Gloomily, Melissa stared out her window, mystified at the Victorian vampire mind. Henry could tear apart a woman for a midnight snack and be okay with it, but then take offense if someone attacked his fine manners.

A loud beeping filled the carriage, but Henry did not move. As Melissa sat up in bed to switch off her alarm clock, she realized Henry had called her Mrs. Simons. Didn't he once tell her that, in private, he would refer to her only as Melissa?

After school that afternoon, Steve waited patiently for Brian, who, with Clay, took the stairs by twos. Melissa gaped at the sight of Steve in work clothes: green-checked jacket over black coveralls and a gray cap buttoned over his ears. Steve always showered and changed into fresh blue jeans before he came to their house. What work had Steve done outside today? Clearly, there was no grass to cut until spring.

"Sure you won't change your mind and come with us, Melissa?" Steve said, leaning out the truck window.

It was tempting. Her mother always cooked simple Thanksgiving dinners and turned down help. It would be fun to participate this year. Then she saw Brian mouthing the word, *No.*

"Thanks anyway, Steve. I have a lot of homework to make up."

From the rapid clacking of her mother's typewriter behind the bedroom door, Melissa knew she was safe until dinnertime. She would worry about the long distance phone bill later. Instead, she knocked and called, "Mom, I'm home!"

"Come in."

Melissa peeped around the corner. Her mother was typing with gusto, glancing back and forth from her notes to the machine.

"How are you feeling, dear?" Darlene said, still typing. "Stomach better?"

"Sure. I'm going to start homework." "How about the biology test?"

"I passed it, barely. Who's cooking tonight?"

No answer, so Melissa scampered to the telephone, picked up the receiver, wavered, then set it down again, and scolded her timidity. If no Lisa Harding existed, she would just apologize for calling the wrong number. With trembling fingers, Melissa dialed the first number on her sheet. It was busy. She hung up and dialed the second one. A woman responded, "Hello?" on the third ring.

"May I please speak to Lisa Harding?"

Pause. "Who is this?"

"A friend, from school."

Melissa heard sobbing in the background, and then a man's voice said, "This is Lisa's father. You say you're her friend?"

"That's right." Melissa grew uncomfortable. "And when did you last see her?"

"Um, a couple of days ago?"

"I don't know what game you're playing, but it's not funny. You didn't talk to Lisa. If you were really Lisa's friend, then you'd know she was murdered over a month ago."

Melissa heard a sharp click and then a dial tone. Murdered? Now what?

The next afternoon Steve was again sitting outside the school and looking embarrassed.

"Brian and I forgot some things."

"You're not going back to Jenson?" Melissa asked.

"No, just to Harper's Grocery."

"Can I get a ride home from the library?"

"Sure!"

Near the door was a new teen mystery series, but Melissa walked straight to the circulation desk. "Mrs. Clements, how do I look up a newspaper article?"

"How old is it?"

"About a month. Someone I met at camp was killed. She lived in Iowa."

"Oh, the Harding girl. I remember that story. It's not on microfilm yet."

Melissa trailed Mrs. Clements to the reference section. The librarian pulled out a drawer and flipped through the newspapers.

"Here." Mrs. Clements left a stack on the table. "I have to check out someone's books. You may go ahead and look for yourself. Just be very careful with them, okay?"

"Okay."

Melissa picked up *The Munsonville Times*. The national news was on the back page of the first section. She only scanned three newspapers before she found the story in the November tenth issue.

Newspaper Boy Finds Body Of Missing Teen

A 12-year-old boy delivering newspapers early Sunday morning stumbled upon the dismembered and badly decomposed body of a 16-year- old girl, who had been missing for more than a month.

Police identified the remains as Lisa Harding of Barnes City, Iowa. Her mother reported the disappearance when the girl failed to come home from school. Funeral arrangements are pending.

Melissa brought the newspaper to the circulation desk. "May I copy this?"

"Certainly, you may. That will be ten cents."

An elderly woman in a purple skirt and sweater rushed past Melissa far too fast for someone with a hunched back. Her purse strap caught on the door handle, and the woman paused to yank it off. *On the side of the handbag was a large rose motif.* Henry!

"Melissa, ten cents, please."

"What?" Melissa said, startled. "I'm sorry.

She was too late. The woman was gone. Melissa had given Mrs. Clements her dime and was heading for the door when her eyes rested on a book sitting on the shelving cart: *An Encyclopedia of American Authors.* Melissa flipped to the index and found the entry:

Henry Matthews (1866-1932). A writer of short stories, mostly supernatural and sensational fiction. Works include, *The Demonic Ride, Calling Down the Moon, and Werewolf!* Died of pneumonia at age 66."

Soberly, Melissa walked outside the library, shoving the story into her coat pocket. Steve noticed her somber expression, while she struggled to find the latch.

"Everything okay?" He fastened her seatbelt.

"Sure," Melissa said, but her mind still saw the woman in purple.

She tossed all night, twisting the covers around her. Instead of leaving the Smythe party with Henry, she swiftly turned right, to the cemetery, the uppermost of Munsonville, overlooking the entire village. The night was eerily quiet and as still as the death lying below the crooked fieldstone markers dotting the wooded graveyard. Melissa glided through the weeds and read the names chiseled into them: James Fisher, Owen Munson, Orville Parks, and Susan Betts. Far in the back, close to where the cemetery merged with the thicker woods, and tilted to one side, was the headstone of Reverend Galien Marseilles. The one beside it had toppled onto its back. Melissa squatted down, brushed away leaves, and read, *Adele Marseilles.* Layers of dirt filled the birth year, but the last date read, *1875.* A third, smaller headstone, rested behind them.

"Go on," Henry said, suddenly beside her. "Read it. She's dead, you know."

"She can't be," Melissa said, glancing at her long skirts, suddenly confused. *"I'm* Bryony."

Henry's face was expressionless. "You're food."

228

Melissa covered her ears and angrily stomped her foot. "I'm not! Those are the others! I'm special! John needs my blood. He won't hurt me!"

"A trussed-up turkey nicely adorned with apples and berries on a platter is a splendid sight to behold, but it's still dead," Henry said. "And it's still dinner."

His words unexpectedly chilled her to the core, and she shivered. She kept her eyes on Henry, but took a hesitant step backward.

"And dead is what you'll be, if you persist in this charade."

Melissa started. She had fallen asleep in the library! She returned to her biology test, while Lisa Harding hovered over her, copying the answers.

"Go away, Lisa! You're not anyone's host. You're dead!"

"I'm not." Lisa glared at Melissa and sat on her test. "Don't say that about me."

"You *are* dead. Your parents said so. I called them, and they told me. Then I read it in the newspaper. The paperboy found you lying in a ditch. You're dead, dead, dead!"

"It's a lie!"

With clawed fingers, Lisa lunged at Melissa's face and passed through her. Melissa spun around. Lisa bowed her head and cried very softly.

"It was an accident," Lisa said in a faint voice. "Kellen didn't mean it. He was in love with me. He got carried away. It wasn't supposed to happen. He wanted to marry me and have a farm. We're going to…."

Melissa blinked awake, sweaty pajamas clinging to her skin, her heart wildly pounding. Hadn't Henry said it all along? Melissa was playing with fire; Melissa was playing a dangerous game. Was she nuts, making pacts with vampires, even in her sleep? What if they were real? What if they weren't? Melissa knew just one person who understood a vampire's incessant need for blood, the one person who might help her.

Her mother shuffled into the kitchen to start the coffee, then jumped at the sight of Melissa leaning against the counter, fully dressed for school, book bag at her feet.

"Oh, you startled me!" She gave Melissa a brief hug, then opened a cabinet door and groped for the canister. "You're up early. Big day today?"

"Mom," Melissa said. "You're right. I should talk to someone. Can we see Fr. Alexis?

CHAPTER 23: WHAT MELISSA LEARNED FROM FR. ALEXIS

Steve arrived at the cottage early Thanksgiving morning, and Brian was up to meet him. Together, they babysat the turkey and prepared side dishes. Brian even set the table.

Melissa spent the morning reading and trying not to think about vampires. Her mother finished a story. The smell of food reached Melissa's nose long before Brian announced dinner. In amazement, Melissa gazed at the festive table Brian had laid: lace tablecloth, her mother's real silverware, and even a centerpiece of autumn leaves. Just last summer Brian had scorned napkins. Gracing the table, in addition to the turkey, was a medley of roasted vegetables that included regular and sweet potatoes, cornbread, baking powder biscuits, and a salad Brian had tossed with a special dressing he had made. Yesterday, her mother had prepared trifle and her traditional pumpkin log with cream cheese filling. The table looked so good no one wanted to touch it.

No one, that is, except Brian. "I mean, we made all this food to eat, right?"

"Right!" Steve lightly socked Brian's arm.

Brian narrowed his eyes and whispered, "Do I have to?"

Steve whispered back, "Yes, you have to."

Then Steve pulled out a chair for her mother, and she sat, cheeks pinking. Brian sucked in his breath, walked to the opposite chair, and slid it away from the table.

"Hey, Liss, aren't you going to sit down?" He glanced at Steve. "Uh, I mean, Happy Thanksgiving."

Touched at this unexpected chivalry from her little brother, Melissa threw her arms around him. Brian gagged and attempted to pull away, but Melissa held him fast.

"Happy Thanksgiving to you, too, Brian!" she exclaimed.

After passing the serving dishes around the table, her mother said, "Let's take turns giving thanks. I'll go first. I'm thankful for all the wonderful years with Frank, our family and how, even in death, Frank has continued to provide for us."

She smiled shyly at Steve and added. "Also, I'm very thankful that, coming into a new place and not knowing anyone, our new, good friend Steve has made us feel so welcomed and accepted."

Steve was helping himself to more turkey and a generous helping of potatoes, but, when her mother mentioned his name, he missed the turkey with the gravy boat and poured the brown liquid onto the table.

"Shoot!"

He leaped up and ran for a rag, calling back, "Sorry guys." Red-faced, Steve mopped the mess and grinned. "I'm thankful for my new, understanding family."

Were they family to him? Steve did spend large amounts of time at their house, time he might spend elsewhere. Except for telling Brian he didn't have a sister, Steve had never mentioned his family. Had he ever had a girlfriend or a wife? How had Steve celebrated holidays before the Marchellises moved to Munsonville?

Brian waved his hand in the air. "My turn, my turn! I'm thankful for my friends, for Snowbell, and for Steve, who teaches me cooking and helps me with my homework. And, for second helpings, or maybe even thirds." He looked hopefully at his mother.

Melissa smiled sweetly. "I'm thankful for new experiences!" Well, it was true.

232

Steve raised his wine glass and beamed, but he winked at her mother. "Here, here!" he said.

The next morning dawned cold and gray. Melissa and her mother packed overnight bags, gulped quick bowls of cereal, and left before Steve and Brian stirred. They took their time and talked the entire length of the trip, their first extended conversation since Melissa's father had died. Ignoring occasional sparks of anxiety and any mention for the visit to Detroit, Melissa chatted about her new friends and updated her mother on school projects. Her mother shared the details of a new children's book and two story assignments for a parenting magazine.

"What are Steve and Brian doing today?" Melissa said.

Her mother signaled left to pass a large van. "He's taking Brian into Simons Woods to pick out a Christmas tree."

"Is that legal?" Melissa remembered the big fuss last Christmas when someone in Grover's Park had cut and removed a giant spruce on park district property.

Her mother chuckled and glanced in the mirror, then moved back into the right lane. "I suppose it is. Steve said he always chops down his Christmas tree."

"I hope he does the chopping. I can just see Brian cutting off his leg."

They didn't stop for lunch until Detroit. Melissa dawdled over her choices at the family-style buffet, but her meeting with Fr. Alexis rapidly approached anyway. Had she made the wrong decision in coming here? What if he considered her a complete loon?

The rectory was a large, two-story bungalow house, next door to the church.

Her mother touched her arm. "Well, here we are."

Melissa forced a smile. Her fears about vampires now seemed fanciful and unreal.

She slowly left the car, then stood on the sidewalk and looked at the short flight of steps leading to the front door. Could she really climb them, all the way to the top? She looked away and shoved her hands into her pockets.

Her mother lightly stroked Melissa's cheek. "You don't have to go in there."

"No, it's okay. I'm just cold."

A small, stout woman with wiry, gray hair twisted into a bun greeted them with a friendly smile.

"Come right in," she said, wiping her hands on her apron. "I'm Mary Lister, Father's housekeeper. He's just finishing lunch."

She led Melissa and her mother into a pleasant living room. Mismatched, floral, upholstered chairs formed a semi-circle. A coffee table held several, large books, all related to Eastern Orthodoxy. Darlene reached for a spiral-bound anthology of the saints and surfed through its pages. Melissa studied the wall pictures: two boys fishing at a pond, assorted tulips standing "at attention" in a vase, and a barn sitting on top of a hill.

"Good afternoon."

Fr. Alexis walked through the doorway. Her mother rose and accepted his hand.

"Father, thank you for seeing us on short notice," Darlene said.

"My pleasure," Fr. Alexis said with a smile.

"You remember my daughter Melissa?"

"I certainly do. She asked questions about the Holy Mysteries. If only my people would be so inquisitive."

Melissa was glad Fr. Alexis remembered her in a positive way and hoped this meant he wouldn't trivialize her concerns.

"Shall we stay here, or would you prefer my office?"

Although Melissa longed for moral support, she could not freely speak with her mother sitting next to her. She wavered, helpless.

Her mother noticed the dilemma. "Melissa, why don't you go ahead? I'd like to rest and browse through this book."

Melissa gave her mother a quick, grateful hug.

"Ready?" Fr. Alexis said.

Melissa nodded and followed him to his office. One glance and Melissa knew this was where Fr. Alexis spent the most time. Icons of all sizes hung on every wall, and stacks of paper were everywhere. Even Henry's desk wasn't this bad.

Fr. Alexis motioned Melisa to an armchair in front of his desk. One large icon on the wall behind him intrigued her: a man on a white horse, thrusting a spear into the side of a dragon. Fr. Alexis noticed her interest.

234

"You have good taste, Melissa," he said. "That is one of my favorites, St. George, slaying the dragon. A friend who is a monk painted it for me years ago, when we were in seminary. So, how is school?"

Melissa shared the results of her latest report card, which prompted questions about her friends and whether or not she liked her new home. He seemed much nicer than the Fr. Alexis who had treated them to dinner earlier in the month. She told him about Mr. Walczak's collections, Mr. Masters' dramatic recitations, her first research paper, Kimberly's disappearance, Snowbell's crooked neck, and finally her obsession with Bryony and Grandma Marchellis' music box.

"Your friend," Fr. Alexis said. "Is that the reason for your visit today?"

"No." Melissa was no longer afraid of him. "It's because of my strange dreams."

"Dreams?"

"Well, that's why I thought you would understand, because of your beliefs about drinking blood. I'm dreaming about," she hesitated, then blurted out, "vampires."

Fr. Alexis's countenance did not change. "Is that all?"

"That's not a problem?"

He stroked his chin. "It depends, Melissa. Can you tell me about the dreams?"

"How much?"

"As much as you wish."

Taking a deep breath, Melissa told him about the ghost stories surrounding Simons Mansion, the mysterious mist that stalked her, and the pact she had made with John Simons. Fr. Alexis listened in silence, until she finished.

"As I see it, Melissa," he said, "the problem is not the dreams, but why they are bothering you."

He stunned her. "But...," she began.

"They seem to be a natural outgrowth of some very emotional and trying events: the death of your father, your move to an unfamiliar area, the tragic disappearance of a friend, and the fact that you are growing up and testing a few boundaries."

She hedged. "That's not all."

Fr. Alexis leaned back in his chair. "Well?" he said.

She took a deep breath. "I'm not sure they're dreams. I think they're real."

"What makes you say that?"

"I met someone in my dream who was real, who I didn't know existed."

"So, how do you know she was real?"

"She told me her name and where she lived. I called the operator for her phone number. Then, I called her house, and her dad got mad at me because she had been murdered, and, Fr. Alexis, she really was. I looked her up in the library."

"You don't mean the Harding girl?"

Her jaw flew open. "How do you know?"

"Melissa, it's been on the news. You must have heard it and then dreamed it."

She vehemently shook her head. "No, I would have remembered."

"Not necessarily. Our minds gather, process, and store information in our subconscious mind that spills out at the most random times, especially during dreaming."

Melissa was unconvinced. "I feel pretty awake when these things happen."

"So, you're in school or talking to a friend, and suddenly you see vampires?"

"No, it's always after I've fallen asleep at night." "Never at any other time?"

"No, never."

"I still think you're dreaming. People often vividly dream they have awakened when they are still soundly asleep. Did you know your grandmother once used her imagination to cope with grief?"

Melissa's ears perked up. "Grandma Marchellis? How do you know?"

"Because she was my babysitter. My parents ran a grocery store and, like many people of that era, worked long, hard hours. So they hired a local girl, your grandmother, to oversee part of my care. Oh, how I tormented her with my tantrums. One day, I created quite a scene. I threw my dinner plate across the room and obstinately refused to take my bath and go to bed. I remember how patient she was, while I pounded the mattress in my fury and

236

shouted at the top of my lungs. When I exhausted myself, she shut off the light and sat at the edge of my bed. She told me it was a shame I didn't have a special friend, like her imaginary playmate, who would come to her whenever she played her magic music box."

Melissa's eyes opened wide.

"I'm assuming it's the very same music box you now own. And no, I don't think it's Bryony Simons' music box. There must be hundreds of replications out there. Given John Simons' enormous popularity of the day, the story of the music box must have leaked out, and a few, savvy individuals made some easy money.

"The point here, Melissa, is that your grandmother saw no one, just as you are not seeing vampires. Because it comforted her, she used it to entertain me. Your mind merely connected your grandmother's Eucharistic beliefs and your friend's death into some logical sense."

"But…"

"Let me finish. Furthermore, it's natural for you to dwell on Bryony Simons. She was similar in age, had a tragic past, and you are now living on her property, which comes attached with a few legends of its own. Anyone with some imagination can see how you conjured up some vampire dreams."

Listening to his calm, logical explanations, Melissa wondered if he might be right.

"Does this help you at all?"

"I think so," Melissa said, slowly. "Will the dreams go away?"

Fr. Alexis chuckled. "In time when you don't need them for coping. I wouldn't let them distress you. You're a sensible girl, or you wouldn't have asked to talk with me. I'm confident your judicious side will always prevail. Any more questions?"

She did have one. "What happened to Grandma's parents?"

"I know little. Her real father died when she was a baby, and her mother later abandoned her. I assume that, in her grief, she panicked. It was hard for women, in those days, to support a family. Another couple raised her. My point, Melissa, is that one can overcome adversity and thrive. Your grandmother did, and you can, too. She was a devout member of this church, a good friend of mine, and a spiritual mother to many who attended St. Athanasius. She is sorely missed."

When Melissa and Fr. Alexis returned to the waiting room, her mother shut the book and stood, looking apprehensive and relieved. "All done? How did it go?"

"Good," Fr. Alexis said, with a smile and a nod. "You should be proud of your daughter. She has quite the head on her shoulders." To Melissa, he added, "Please contact me again if you have further concerns. However, I think you will be fine."

As Melissa walked out to the car, her heart felt lighter than it had   in weeks, and she felt thankful Fr. Alexis had put her dreams into perspective. She resolved to let the phantoms of the night be just that, nocturnal hallucinations that vanished with the morning light and her alarm clock. It would be a long time before the Bryony fantasy lost its allure, and an even longer time before she could forget the intoxicating rush of merely thinking about John Simons, let alone remembering the incomparable ecstasy of dancing close to him at a grand ball.

Nevertheless, she would stop allowing her imagination to interfere with the more relevant parts of her life, like wondering if she could make cute Jack Cooper look her way.

CHAPTER 24: IT'S NO USE

As summer ended, Melissa vainly tried amusing herself with the remaining outdoor frolics. She hated to admit it, but the repetitive nature of these events bored her, especially when hostesses outdid each other in food, atmosphere, and noteworthy guests.

One afternoon, as Melissa stepped into the hallway following another dreadful tea, John strolled from the music room and ordered Bryga to pack a supper basket.

"I'm taking Mrs. Simons on a picnic," he said. "We won't return for dinner."

Melissa's pulse quickened. She would be alone with John, their first intimate moment since he had condescendingly let Melissa witness a feeding.

"Yes sir," Bryga said.

Melissa heard a rustle and glimpsed Anna, peeping around the parlor doors. Anna wanted to go, too, but wouldn't dare say it.

"Send word to Jackson to prepare a boat."

"Yes, sir."

The blow crashed Melissa's hopes. So, Jackson would be there, too. Anna hung back, looking longingly at Melissa, and then traipsed after her mother to the kitchen.

John was halfway into the music room. "Be at the dock in thirty minutes," he called over his shoulder, then closed the door behind him.

Melissa lifted her skirts and flew up the stairs, two at a time. Trudi, armed with a shrewd smile, was waiting for her. Word certainly traveled fast at Simons Mansion.

"Oh, Trudi! Please help me look pretty."

Trudi selected a white afternoon dress, printed with tiny red roses. Flustered, Melissa tugged her grey visiting dress up and over her head. Trudi flapped her arms.

"Wait, Mrs. Simons! You'll tear it."

Just as Trudi fastened the last button, Anna plopped on the bed and watched Melissa swish before the mirror. The corners of Anna's mouth turned down and her lips trembled. Melissa smoothed her hair into place and pretended she hadn't noticed.

"Why can't I go, too?" Anna whined, tugging at Melissa's dress.

Melissa knelt and hugged the little girl. "Oh darling, you can't this time."

Anna started to protest, but Melissa quickly added, "Tell your mother Mrs. John says to fix you something special for dinner tonight and a basket for us tomorrow. We'll have our lunch outside, under any tree you like."

"No! I want to go now!"

Melissa glanced at the mantle clock. She had to hurry. John hated waiting, and she feared angering him with her tardiness and spoiling the trip. She started to leave, but Anna clung to her skirts.

"Don't go," she wailed. "Take me too!"

"Anna, I can't!"

In desperation, Melissa wound up the music box and led Anna to the little couch under the window. The music distracted Anna long enough for Melissa to sneak out the door. She flew down the hill to where John was checking his watch and patrolling the dock. He noted Melissa dashing down the hill, but did not otherwise acknowledge her. Preparations appeared complete. Melissa saw no sign of the second coachman.

"Where's Jackson?" She looked around her for the hulking figure.

"Not coming."

"Jackson's not rowing?"

"No."

Melissa's heart skipped a beat at this unexpected news, but she had no chance to react any further, for John was extending his hand, and she happily took it, allowing him to ease her into the little rowboat and onto the wooden bench opposite the oars. The picnic basket, topped with a folded blanket, rested at her feet. Before entering the boat, John removed his coat and tossed it onto the blanket. He unbuttoned his cuffs and rolled his sleeves to the elbow, then untied the rope and lifted the anchor. With smooth, confident strokes, John rowed the small boat into the middle of Lake Munson.

Although late in the day, the sun beat warm on Melissa's face, and the sky boasted the same clear blue it had at noon. As the boat moved away from the estate, Melissa felt the slightest wisp of a breeze across her face. In silence, she and John drifted north of the mansion, farther into the woods than Melissa had yet explored with Brian. Surrounding her on all sides was Munsonville in full August splendor, the way Melissa might have remembered it when she first came to the village a few, short months ago, if she had paid attention. The grasses lining the bank stood proud and unmoving in the heat and formed a thick barrier to the lush trees behind them. The air buzzed with the singing of thousands of grasshoppers calling their mates; an occasional fish splashed near the boat and vanished again before Melissa saw it. When the wind shifted, Melissa caught a faint whiff of the wildflowers that hid in those weeds, but decided from their perfume bryony was not among them. For a fleeting moment, she wondered if John had any particular destination in mind, then decided it was pointless to ask. She'd find out soon enough. John did nothing without a purpose.

"Would you like to row?"

The unexpected sound of his voice startled her.

"I've never rowed a boat," she said, hoping her inexperience would cause him to change his mind. She did not want to appear stupid before John.

"Come here."

Melissa hesitated, stalling. "I don't want to tip the boat."

"You won't. Don't stand. Keep low to the floor."

Gripping the sides of the boat with shaky hands, Melissa followed John's instructions; nevertheless, she cringed every time the boat rocked, so he shifted position to adjust their combined weight. John rested his right hand on his oar and took Melissa's left hand. He held it while she turned herself around to sit next to him.

It was a snug fit. Even after Melissa smoothed her dress flat, her right knee still pressed against John's hard and unyielding leg, but Melissa liked the way it felt. She had not expected such strength from a man who spent his days sitting at a piano. Did John notice that they touched? If so, he gave no sign. Instead, he reached across her, raised her hand from her lap, and placed it on the abandoned oar. He closed her fingers around it and said, "You hold the oar like this."

John leaned so near, she could smell the salt on his skin, so different from the stench that had clung to him that first night. A breeze brushed his hair across her cheek, and Melissa had to squash the urge to reach up and touch it. He tightened his fingers over Melissa's hand and guided her. The oar was heavier than she had expected, still, with John's hand maneuvering hers, Melissa caught onto the rhythm of the strokes she needed to help propel the boat. For a long, rapturous time, she enjoyed the circular up and down motions their hands made, and she couldn't tell if he naturally felt this warm, or if the sun was causing the heat. All too soon, John removed his hand, settled back, and said, "Now you try."

She needed two hands to John's one, and it was a lot of work. She gripped the oars so tightly her knuckles blanched, and her fingers ached. Sweat beaded on her forehead and rolled into her eyes, but she would not remove a hand to wipe it away. John effortlessly moved his oar. After monitoring Melissa for a few minutes, he draped one arm across the back of the boat and gazed out across the water. Had she ever seen him so relaxed, almost carefree? He seemed like a brand-new John. Melissa could not dwell on it long because rowing required her entire concentration. The only sound she heard for a long time was dip and splash, as she and John dragged the oars in and out of the blue-green Lake Munson water. They rowed for quite some time before John spoke.

"Hungry?"

She was, but she could not catch her breath long enough to answer him. He pointed toward a cove. "Steer that way."

"How do I turn it?" she asked, still panting.

"Just row. I'll stop."

John lifted his oar out of the water, while Melissa struggled to manipulate hers. Bit by bit, the boat swerved in the direction John had indicated. Brian would never believe it.

When they reached land, John anchored the boat and grasped Melissa's hand. She gratefully accepted it and stepped onto the ground. John carried the picnic supplies. As he spread the blanket on the grass, Melissa sat on a stump, opened the basket, and peeked inside. Bryga had packed cold beef and lamb, bread and cheese, cucumbers and tomatoes, stewed fruit with cream, an entire cheesecake, butter, horseradish, lemonade, and champagne. She had tucked plates, silverware, linen napkins, tumblers, and wine glasses amongst the food. How romantic! It was all for John and her to enjoy together. Melissa couldn't wait.

John sat on the blanket, and Melissa cuddled quite close beside him. He opened the basket, and his eyes widened. "Good heavens! We've enough food for a week!"

His words popped the filmy bubble that had floated around her all afternoon and destroyed any amorous hopes she had nourished. Still, it wasn't a bad picnic, especially since John insisted on laying out the table settings and serving the food. Melissa ate everything except the cold lamb and horseradish, proud she had expanded her narrow food likes. She even drank the lemonade, despite its bitter taste and lavender scent. Only John's silence unnerved her. To fill the void, Melissa repeated the latest gossip the ladies had dished out at Mabel Elliot's tea party earlier this afternoon. Someone had caught Mrs. Parks' daughter-in-law riding late at night with a man who was not Mrs. Parks' son. Mrs. Parks, of course, heatedly denied it.

"Did you ever!" Melissa exclaimed.

John admitted he had not, but his tone was flat, and Melissa wondered if he had really heard her. The more Melissa talked, the less John heeded her words. Several times, John's eyes drifted away from Melissa's face and roamed the rest of her in a manner that caught her breath and halted her speech. His smiles grew less bright and more distracted. Finally, Melissa's voice trailed into nothingness. John brought forth his watch, noted the time, and repacked the remains. Melissa bit her lip, but what could she do?

Instead of lugging the basket to the boat, John pushed it to the edge of the blanket. With a brief stretch, John lay down, looked at Melissa, and patted a spot on the blanket next to him. His face appeared tranquil, but his eyes held a yearning, almost hungry, look that nearly smothered her. She didn't move. She couldn't move. Should she move?

John was waiting for her. This was it. She couldn't refuse him now.

Despite her trembling, Melissa inched away from her place on the blanket and lay next to him. John covered her hand with his, but he did not speak or glance at her. Neither one moved, but every so often, John's fingertips caressed her skin. They lay there in silence, watching the shadows of the trees lengthen, and the sun dip lower in the sky, exploding into vibrant reds, yellows, and oranges. Gradually, night settled over Lake Munson, and the brilliant colors darkened into purples and blues, but still Melissa felt no urge to leave for Simons Mansion. She only wished this moment would last forever because, although John still did not talk, neither did he release her hand. Feeling more serene than she had in a long time, Melissa closed her eyes and allowed the approaching night to wrap her into its comforting cocoon. She was afraid to respond; she was unwilling to break its magic. Instead, Melissa listened to the lake dashing itself against the shore. She heard the distant call of an unknown bird. John's breathing sounded steady and rhythmical. She wondered if he had fallen asleep.

Without warning, John's fingers traveled up her arm, past her shoulder, and to her neck. They stopped at the base of her throat and rested there, warm, unmoving. Melissa melted into his touch, unable to tell where she began, and his fingers ended.

"Bryony, look at me."

John's words cut through the air. Melissa obediently opened her eyes. John's nostrils flared; his lips parted; he searched her face with wild and restless eyes. The waves crashed on the shore and pounded in her ears. Sliding his body onto hers, John slipped both hands under her head, wrapped his fingers around her hair, and pulled her up. His lips touched hers for a fleeting kiss,

244

then traveled to the base of her neck. Melissa sighed in delight and wrapped her arms around John; razor-sharp pain sliced through her throat. A gull shrieked in agony. The waterfront scene vanished. Melissa bolted awake. Her bedroom felt as icy cold as the unyielding hands pressing against each side of her head, its fingers still clutching great handfuls of her hair. With exaggerated greed, John Simons vigorously sucked and lapped the blood from Melissa's neck, grunting between swallows and gasping hard and fast for air. A vision of Lisa Harding's dismembered body rose before her. Lisa had said Kellen had accidentally lost control. What if John lost control and killed her?

John loosened his grip and raised himself slightly to lick the overflow. Melissa stretched out her arm, switched on the lamp, and blinked against the sudden rush of brightness. The room was empty. Her heart was racing. Her neck was wet and tacky. Angry scratches crisscrossed her left arm, from her shoulder to back of her hand. Snowbell jumped off the bed. *Darned cat!*

Melissa tossed Snowbell out of her room and tottered to the bathroom. She pulled the light chain, looked into the mirror, and leaned her neck to one side. Two tiny puncture marks marred her neck, and blood streaked into her pajama top. Melissa sank onto the edge of the bathtub. *Snowbell?* The answer really did not matter. Whether these were dreams, delusions, or vampire's hypnotic spell, Melissa was deeply in love with John and did not want this bizarre affair to end, ever, no matter what.

Brian pounded on her bedroom door. "Get up! We're decorating the tree!"

She rubbed her eyes. Hazy pink streaks were breaking through the night sky. Was he kidding? She folded her pillow over her head. In the distance, Melissa heard more banging. "Morning, Mom! Time to decorate the tree!"

Brian was back and steadily rapping at her door. Melissa rolled over in frustration, and Snowbell nipped her ear. Melissa threw down the pillow and weakly tossed back the bedcovers. Snowbell sat beside her, merrily licking her paws. Melissa eyed her with suspicion. "Didn't I put you out last night?"

Snowbell stared at her, then jumped off the bed. Melissa fumbled for slippers and tried to ignore the insistent pounding in her head and on her door.

"Knock it off, Brian!"

She grabbed her robe from her desk chair and trudged out. Her mother's door was closed. Steve was snoring.

"Come on!" Brian shouted in Steve's ear.

Steve threw an arm over his face and rolled onto his back.

"We're putting up the Christmas tree today. You promised."

Brian pulled Steve's arm away. Steve cracked open an eye.

"Yay! He's up! He's up! He's up!"

"Minus an eardrum," Steve groaned, rubbing the side of his head.

While Steve scrambled eggs and fried bacon, Brian lugged every box from the basement labeled *Christmas*. Their mother, coffee in hand, sniffed the tree on her way to get dressed. As Melissa and Steve brought out the food, she sank gratefully into her chair and handed Steve her mug.

"Can I get a refill?"

"Sure," Steve said, with a sympathetic smile. "How late did you work last night?"

"You don't want to know. Tomorrow is deadline, but I wanted to help decorate."

Steve soon returned with her coffee mug and placed her wedding ring beside it.

"Sorry," Darlene said, blushing.

"Darlene, I know you don't want to hear it, but I think the village owes you a higher…."

Her mother scowled. A strange look passed over Steve's face, but he only said, "Melissa, please pass the toast."

Melissa did, wondering why grown-ups, including John, always changed the subject after introducing a juicy topic. She searched Steve's face for clues, but Steve buttered his toast with the same unwavering concentration he used when nailing bookshelves. So, instead, she said, "I didn't know you could cut down trees here."

"I always have," Steve said. "I'm not one for new-fangled, plastic trees. The real thing is good enough for me. I'm just grateful that, this year, I can share it with others."

"Like me." Brian spooned eggs onto his toast.

"Like you, sport," Steve said, but he looked at their mother, who yawned between bites and struggled to lift her fork.

Steve and Brian strung lights and hung ornaments, while Melissa and her mother offered hints. Melissa was dangling a piece of gold garland above Snowbell's head and watching her swipe it, when Brian peeled the tape off the box of her father's collectibles.

"No!" Melissa ran to her room, slamming the door and crying scalding tears of fresh grief. *Daddy don't leave us! Please, please come back!* She moped all afternoon, until the tempting smell of Steve's vegetarian chili, along with his sweet, almost bashful request to come to dinner, finally coaxed Melissa away from her bed. The Christmas tree, minus her father's ornaments, cast a hazy glow over the room. After a hasty meal, Melissa, drained, crept back to bed, ripped away the detested afghan, stomped to the door, and screamed, "I'm not staying here tonight! I'm not!"

She rushed to the stairs, stopped at the boisterous laughter, and spun around. Henry stood in the doorway, laughing so hard his slender form shook.

"You'll go where? Out into the nineteenth century night?"

"You said it's my dream. So, I'll go home."

"Do it. I wouldn't miss this exhibition."

He leaned against the frame, prepared for more entertainment. Melissa floundered. She had no desire to amuse Henry at her expense. Grudgingly, Melissa slunk back into Henry's study, but, too agitated to sit, she paced and ranted while Henry lounged in the recliner, clasped his hands behind his neck, and watched her.

"I just don't get him!" Melissa finally dropped onto the settee. "Where is he?"

"Our John is attending to other matters tonight."

"Like what?"

Henry pretended to be shocked. "Melissa, really! There are some things a man won't bring into his home."

"You mean, like other women?"

He laughed again, less heartily this time, almost as if he sympathized with her. "Is that what you think, Melissa?"

"I don't know what to think. Why orchestrate all this, if he doesn't...."

"Doesn't want to be with you? You're not the meal, remember?"

Melissa did not say a word. She sure felt like the meal last night.

"Now, if you're talking about delicate matters of the heart, then you surprise me."

"Stop making fun of me!"

"I'm not teasing you, Melissa. Women are the fickle ones. They profess undying affection for a man today and fall in love with another tomorrow. Men are different. We love only once, for life, and close our hearts to other women."

"What a lie!"

"I said 'hearts,' not other parts. There was only one woman for John. You're deluding yourself by thinking otherwise."

"He wants a second chance!"

"At music, nothing more. John would rather touch a piano than a woman."

"You're lying. John's music was an enormous success when he was alive."

"Not by his own merit." "I don't believe you!"

"Hmm," Henry looked thoughtful. "Melissa, did John ever tell you *why* Kellen Wechsler is his manager?"

"No. John doesn't like questions."

Henry raised an eyebrow and lowered his hand to stroke Chinook's head. "In my opinion, John's career officially ended the day he met Kellen Wechsler."

"Why?"

"I knew you'd beg me to tell."

Melissa threw a pillow, but Henry ducked, and it hit the dog. Chinook growled, eliciting a "Behave!" from Henry, but she couldn't tell if he meant her or the dog. Henry loosened his tie, propped his feet, and reached for his cigar.

"John's father, Abbott Simons, was a New York banker," Henry said, "shrewd at making money and fully expecting John to assume control of his business, but John instead possessed a natural, almost intuitive, disposition toward music. As a boy, he not only taught himself to play piano by ear, he composed quite complex pieces and amused his parents' guests with concerts at their dinner parties.

248

"Although Abbott viewed this talent as drawing room entertainment, John's mother, Lucetta, understood how music affected her son. Against her husband's wishes, she arranged tutors in John's early years and attendance at a conservatory when he was older. Abbott opposed it all and urged John to consider finance. John vowed to only play and compose or die, and he meant it, eventually refusing to remain at home in his mother's sheltering arms if it also meant embracing his father's scorn. Fortunately, the social climate was ripe for John's experiment. Classical music had regained popularity, and John found a few audiences receptive enough to hire him, which kept bread in his mouth and lodgings in a garret apartment. This, instead of discouraging him, only magnified his thirst for glory and wealth. Then he met Kellen Wechsler.

"One late night, John exited the backstage door to find a man standing in the shadows, waiting for him. John was surprised, but unafraid. He had little money left; the rent was due; and no further concerts were scheduled. If this stranger should accost and kill him, so be it. John had played.

"'Who is it?' John called.

"'I am the devil,' Kellen calmly replied.

"Well, John wished him a pleasant evening and started for home, but Kellen stepped in front of him, said he was a well-connected concert promoter acquainted with John's reputation, and would John care to dine with him that evening? John decided he had nothing to lose and accompanied Kellen to a local pub.

"The snake ordered more forbidden fruit than John had eaten since his parents' home. As he devoured it, John noticed his host did not also partake. Kellen said he had feasted earlier, then leaned forward and asked, 'Mr. Simons, how would you like to be the premiere musical artist throughout all western civilization?'

"'Like it?' John said. 'I'd die for it.'

"Kellen assured him those terms were not in the contact. He dropped his voice and told John he was a vampire, eager to barter. The exchange was simple. John would regularly supply blood for Kellen, much as you do for John, and Kellen, in return, would arrange circumstances for John's success. To prove his earnestness, Kellen offered the first three concerts unconditionally.

If John was dissatisfied, Kellen would not bind him. If, however, John was pleased, they would seal their pact in John's blood.

"The concerts were scheduled at noteworthy venues where, in ordinary circumstances, John could only have fantasized playing. Needless to say, the performances were overwhelmingly successful; John was now on the road to the proverbial fame and fortune; and Kellen became known as John's manager. John relinquished the garret and rented an apartment suite in New York, since Kellen had engaged several months of concerts there. Of course, John spurned his parents' home, taking especial pleasure in declining invitations to play for their events, but that was the least of his concerns. The time had arrived, my dear, for him to pay his piper.

"One night, after another championship performance, John accompanied Kellen to his abode. Kellen intended to prolong the festivities, but John, impatient to complete the act, seated himself in an armchair, closed his eyes, and waited. Kellen had long anticipated this moment, and he relished it. Gleefully, he hopped around the chair, rubbing his hands together, fondling John's neck, and licking his chops. The actual deed, John said, was not as repulsive as he had feared. He did not flinch when Kellen sank his fangs into his neck. He did not recoil from Kellen's slithering tongue, when he gulped John's life-blood right out of him. John merely sat and took it.

"John had quite a run that summer. I stayed in London for the season, but read of his good fortune in the local newspapers. Toward fall, he came to London for a fortnight, and he enthusiastically shared with me the dark secret of his prosperity. He had succeeded beyond his wildest dreams and wished the same for me. I did not partake in his excitement or his deeds, and not because I disbelieved him. I feared what I might lose in the process, should I join him. I feared what John had already lost."

Henry smiled weakly, but his voice was acerbic. "Ironic, now isn't it?"

He set down the cigar, picked up the brandy, and appreciably sniffed it, waiting for Melissa's reply. Henry's stark depiction of John's compromise, when it suited him, reminded Melissa of John's identity. Kellen had planted the initial seed long ago. She looked at the carpet and said nothing.

"For some time John lived his ideal life, which was literally wine, women, and his original songs, with Kellen as his constant companion. This caused some people to whisper that Kellen was, perhaps, in addition to John's manager, John's lover. John did not dispel that rumor, since it made women quite fancy him."

Henry looked straight at Melissa. "It seems what's most attractive to a woman, my dear, is a man who needs saving."

She blushed right to the roots of her hair and kept her eyes on the floor, too mortified to face Henry. He really had known since the beginning.

"Now, John had considered himself immune to love, until he met Bryony. John would have laid down his life for her, if he already not laid it down for Kellen. When John announced his upcoming marriage, Kellen threatened John with the loss of his career, should he renege on their deal. John assured Kellen their covenant was indissoluble. Nevertheless, Kellen remained quite jealous of John's relationship with Bryony. Her presence spoiled his exclusive bond with John."

"I don't see how." Melissa slowing lifted her eyes to him. "It's not the same."

"My dear Melissa, Kellen's dominion over John must not be diluted by anyone, especially a woman. Fortunately, John never revealed to Bryony his exact relationship with Kellen, who intended to beget John as a vampire, but someone else beat him to it, making John his manager's equal, which infuriates Kellen. Today, Kellen's hosts are young girls he entices with false promises and then devours, as he did with Lisa.

"So, if they're equals, why does John keep Kellen hanging around?"

Henry regarded her in silence for a long moment. "Melissa, did John ever give you a time frame for your little arrangement?"

"I've already told you. It's not 'an arrangement,' and, no, he did not."

"Do you know what a parasite is?"

"Of course I do. We studied it in school. A parasite lives off its host until it is full. Later, it either returns to the host for more food or kills it and finds a new host."

Realization of what Henry had attempted to explain these last weeks finally tumbled onto Melissa like a stack of bricks.

"So you're telling me to have no hope at all, that John and I won't...."

Flustered, Melissa tripped over her words. She didn't know how to say it. She only knew Henry was very, very wrong.

"John is *not* a common parasite, like Kellen! Maybe John has no soul now, but he'll be human again. Are you saying that means nothing to John, *nothing?*"

Henry sighed and set down the brandy glass.

"Melissa, you are such a child. Just whose memories did you think you were reliving?"

CHAPTER 25: A LESSON IN LOVE

Melissa sighed as the grandfather clock in Henry's study chimed three times. More than half the night had passed, and still no John. Even before Melissa had opened her eyes, she had felt the heavy brocade of the dress, and her hopes had soared, until she smelled the conspicuous fragrance of many lavish bouquets of roses. It wasn't fair.

Merely playing Bryony had lost its sheen. She wanted more. She needed John. Why couldn't he understand that?

Stretching full length across the settee, Melissa dropped *Emerson's Essays* onto the floor, raised herself on an elbow, and glanced to see if Henry had noticed. Bored and restless, Melissa wished Henry might humor her with a game of checkers, even if he rapidly and shamelessly annihilated her feeble attempts to conquer him. However, his story consumed him, and he paid no attention to Melissa, which did not surprise her. He had paid little attention to her all night, save for some caustic remarks at being stuck with her company again. Well, she could try.

Melissa cleared her throat. Henry continued typing. She walked to the sidebar, poured a glass of water, and glanced at

Henry. He didn't yield. Still looking at him, she set the glass on the edge of the tea tray and upset   a vase of purple roses.

"Shoot!"

He didn't notice.

She reached for a towel and then wiped the water, gathered the roses, and tossed them into the garbage. Was he watching her? No! Melissa threw the towel on the sidebar, which tipped the vase onto the floor. She squatted to retrieve it and bumped her head on the table on the way back up.

"Ow!" Melissa cried, rubbing her head.

The typing ceased. Melissa looked hopefully at him, but Henry was checking his notes. The typing resumed.

"Melissa, I have no tolerance for your histrionics tonight," Henry said over the clatter of the keys.

Hands clasped behind her back, Melissa sauntered to the desk and peered over his shoulder. "Are you almost done?"

He did not answer.

"I was wondering if we perhaps could play….?"

 "I'm not a nursemaid."

Why was he acting like that? Was it her fault John thrust them together night after blasted night?

"You know, if you didn't want to be my chaperone, you should never…."

Tap. Tap. Tap.

Melissa ripped the sheet of paper from the machine. Henry spun around in his chair and regarded her with an amused expression. That did it.

"I'm so sick of you! You can't feel love, and you can't stand it when someone else, like John, does! You hide behind books and make fun of everything beautiful, everything! You're cold, selfish, and heartless! No woman would want you!"

Her voice faded away. Henry had stopped smiling. His cheeks flushed; his eyes narrowed; and his jaw hardened. She had roused him from his poised and arrogant complacency, and liked how powerful it made her feel. With a dramatic flounce, Melissa nearly skipped to the exit, but Henry was already there blocking the door. He grabbed her arm and held it fast behind her.

"So, I know nothing about love?" he said in a low, hoarse voice.

254

Melissa looked away, but Henry grasped her cheeks and wrenched her back.

"How dare you upbraid me when you're engaging in a deadly fantasy you call love? Perhaps you need another lesson."

Henry would not intimidate her, *not this time.*

"You have a lot of nerve! You're the pretender, Mr. Masters, English teacher! You can't teach me anything about love!"

"Oh, but perhaps, I shall." Henry's fingers tightened on her arm. His voice was controlled, but his eyes were stony. "Yes, perhaps, I shall."

With a hard yank, Henry dragged Melissa toward the back staircase and down the stairs, all the way to the rear door Kimberly had opened, and through the corridor to the dead end. Henry thumped a stone, and it noiselessly moved aside, revealing the secured door. Henry rapidly unlocked it, pushed Melissa inside, and banged the door behind them. The sound bounced and echoed away as Melissa, open-mouthed, blinked at the vision before her.

Bryony stared at her from every direction, amidst the glow from a sea of candles. Dozens upon dozens of exquisite oil paintings, all Bryony, filled the large cellar. Bryony sat at her dressing table brushing her hair, her dreamy eyes half-closed. Bryony, face propped and framed with bryony vines, gazed out of the window and over the mansion's spacious grounds. Bryony held the music box. Bryony played dolls with Anna. Bryony sipped tea.

"…and there he kept her very well," Henry muttered. Melissa started at his voice, but Henry averted his eyes and said no more.

Awed, Melissa weaved among the art. Bryony stretched high to pick a ripe, red apple from one of John's prized trees. Beyond it, Bryony sat in full concert dress, her excited face shining, her eyes on John's performance. Bryony paused in a half-twist before a full-length mirror, admiring her Parisian wedding gown. Bryony stroked the nose of one of John's Arabian horses. Bryony stood poised with a croquet mallet. In an aquamarine ball dress and diamonds, Bryony checked her dance card. A single, painted purple rose lay at the right-hand base of each image.

Marveling, Melissa faced Henry. Listless, he leaned against the wall by the door, all passion drained from his face.

"Henry, I...."

"Yes, I painted them," Henry said softly. "I loved her from the first moment I saw her, but she wanted only John, not that the stupid fool deserved her. Had she given me the chance, I would have worshipped at her feet and dedicated my life to her happiness."

Melissa's eyes swerved to the paintings. "Did she know your feelings for her?"

"No, but John did. I killed him here."

Her stomach lurched; her legs buckled to the cold floor; and her mind whirled with this sudden knowledge. Henry wasn't just a vampire; he was a murderer, and he had trapped Melissa in the basement. Just how angry was Henry with her? Melissa hadn't cared earlier, but she cared now.

However, Henry, slouched and eyes closed, appeared anything but dangerous. Melissa gazed about the room, seeking an alternative exit, but there wasn't one.

Henry opened dull eyes. "Melissa, look at me."

John had spoken those words to her, the night she had lain with him by the lake. Melissa's mouth went dry. This new side of Henry frightened her.

"I'm going to tell you something, and, for once, you will be quiet and listen."

Melissa opened her mouth to object, noticed the desolation on Henry's face, and quickly shut it again.

"Bryony adored John," Henry said, "and while he returned that adoration to a degree, he loved himself, and his music, more. When he toured, I knew he had others, but we never spoke about them. Bryony sensed his divided affection, and it depressed her, for she never fully grasped his ardor for music, and she found the days without him long and hard to fill, for how could parsonage clerical work fulfill a young, beautiful girl longing for romance? John, robust, strong, and built for adventure, had promised Bryony's father he would not push the limits of her resistance, but he was reluctant to let her out of his sight, even for a moment. Oh, he trusted her, but he didn't trust other men around her, except me. So, he invited me to reside at the mansion for free, if I oversaw and managed his affairs, including Bryony, while he was gone. It was a delicious offer, since I could pursue my writing, free from other occupation. Bryony knew the reason for my presence and resented my intrusion into her household, and, perhaps, rightly so. Unless strictly necessary, I had no contact with her, which was best for both of us. Nevertheless, John's frequent absences were miserable for her. Often, she sought reassurance of John's absolute faithfulness. This, I gave her. It was not my place to say differently."

Henry again closed his eyes and remained silent for an eternity, or so it seemed to Melissa. When he reopened them, their expression remained flat.

"One rainy afternoon at dusk, she came to my study, crying and demanding the truth. John had been absent many weeks, longer than usual, and she terribly missed him. I quickly, possibly too quickly, reassured her John would not, could not, love any other woman; it was just not possible. That answer no longer satisfied her."

Henry paused, and Melissa shivered. She knew what was coming.

"Did she feel some small affection for me, or had she secretly desired revenge? Either way, I was quite unprepared for it when it happened, for she suddenly threw both arms around my neck, lifted her tear-stained face, and kissed me, sealing our fate." Henry slumped further. "What followed was inexcusable, and I knew it, but I did not care. In that moment, she ceased to be John's wife."

Melissa longed to offer words of comfort, a hug, anything, but she did not budge. She knew Henry well enough to know he would never welcome, nor tolerate, her pity.

"Ironically, John came home the next day, and Bryony, in her typical fashion, joyfully rushed out to meet him. He stayed only a brief time before departing again for another tour. This time, Bryony was not sad. I often caught her smiling to herself and humming little songs. Knowing Bryony, I had my suspicions, but I wisely avoided her by shutting myself in my study. I needn't have worried. She had no interest in me.

"When John returned home, Bryony obviously shared with him the source of her happiness. I will never forget the elation and pride in John's voice when he made the announcement, and the hopeless despair I felt in my heart that his child might be mine.

Even as I congratulated them, my eyes sought Bryony's, but she saw only John.

"Sadly for her, for all of us, it was not to be. She died giving birth and took her infant son with her. I blamed John for her death then, and I blame him today. He made her unhappy, and this I could not bear. Why should he breathe when she could not? So, I killed him in the presence of her image and hanged myself. When everything turned thankfully black, I thought my misery had ended, but I was wrong. Death was not the easy finale I had anticipated.

"I felt a tug at my bonds and fell to the floor. John had cut the rope. I shook my head in disbelief, at the hard truth of legend. Our sudden, violent deaths had transformed us into vampires, and I was doomed to spend an eternity in his loathsome presence; our mutual survival depended upon it. None of that mattered then. I had an intense, nearly maniacal hunger for blood. I swung the door hard, and there stood my faithful dog Chinook, who had followed me to my gallows. Smelling death, he inched away, but I tackled him, strangled him, and gorged on his blood and raw flesh until I nearly burst. John dashed upstairs. Bryga screamed. John had found his first meal and was searching for more."

Melissa shuddered, glanced at the door, and then looked away before Henry noticed. Would he harm her if she attempted escape?

"Lamentably, another person was on the premises, the housekeeper's daughter, Anna, your grandmother, who was nearly six years old at the time. John had given the other servants a holiday, to ensure Bryony's privacy."

"Anna was Grandma Marchellis?" Melissa said, startled, "but how....?"

"With my appetite temporarily assuaged, my thirst for blood mellowed. I flew up the stairs, amazed at my lightning speed. Dashing from room to room, I shouted John's name, until I heard voices from Bryony's chamber. Bryony and her baby still lay on the bed, covered, but there. Anna was crouching in the corner and clutching Bryony's music box.

John sat next to her, winding it, and saying, 'You're a big girl, now.'

258

"I can still see Anna looking up at John and crying, 'Oh, Mr. John, I'm so scared.'

John removed his handkerchief, dried her eyes, and told her she must be brave, for she was going to have a new home, and he was going away. If she ever needed him, she should play the music box, and he would come to her. Then he kissed her forehead, nodded to me, and I took the cue. Leaving Anna on the floor, I went to her room, packed some belongings, and gathered her wraps. I carried her to the carriage house where I hitched the horse; she clung fearfully to me.

"The parsonage housekeeper broke down when I informed her about Bryony's death, how it had terribly shocked Anna, and that Bryga, half-crazed in her own grief, had temporarily fled. The minister, overhearing, shut himself in his office. Sobbing, the housekeeper promised to care for Anna until her mother returned home. At that moment, John was digging a grave for Bryga. Then John wrote orders for the undertaker, apologizing for not overseeing the matter of his wife and begging forgiveness for his distressed state. He composed another note informing the servants of their permanent dismissal. Then, we left."

"Left where?" Melissa asked.

A cunning expression flickered over Henry's face.

"Just left," he said, shortly.

Melissa fell silent. Henry was right. She didn't know anything about love. Repressed doubts about John's truthfulness and sincerity rose to the surface of her heart.

"So, why live like this? Stop hurting people and be with Bryony forever."

"Be with her forever?" Henry's voice was bitter. "Even in death, she loves only John." His voice dropped a notch. "Besides, Melissa, I'm a coward, content to stay imprisoned in this rotting shell that once was me."

Without warning, Henry jerked upwards. Violent rivers of blood poured from his mouth, nostrils, pupils, ears, and the very pores of his skin. Melissa covered her eyes and screamed. Henry gagged and sputtered, but blood still flowed. She ran to the door, to blessed freedom, then stopped, convicted. She could not, would not leave him there, drenched in other people's blood, not now, not after he'd spoken so candidly to her. Melissa steeled herself for the disagreeable task, wrapped her arms around Henry, and attempted to lift him, but her arms slid off. She gagged and tried again. The metallic stench choked her. His face was ashen; he feebly resisted. She tugged again and prevailed, despite his weak attempts to overthrow her.

"You're sick." Melissa hoped she sounded casual. "I'm taking you upstairs."

Pale as death and too debilitated to protest any more, Henry allowed Melissa to pull him to his feet and upstairs to his study. He faltered every few paces, and Melissa steadied him, occasionally wiping slippery hands across a dry spot on her undergarments and trying not think why they were wet. Henry's pallor frightened her. Henry could not die on the stairs. He was not her chaperone; he was her bulwark. When John neglected Melissa, Henry stayed, shielding her from harm, steering her through unfamiliar territory, occupying her lonely hours, and chastising her illusory notions. Melissa cringed at the many times she had wished Henry would disown her and realized, with a despairing heart, she might now get her wish. Should John completely withdraw from her, Henry forged the only real link to John she possessed. How could she have been so blind? *Henry must not die,* but he needed blood to survive, and he was too weak to hunt for it tonight, without fortification. She knew where he could get it.

Melissa hauled him into the study they had vacated with such passion only a short time ago and tried stalling the inevitable. She helped Henry to the sofa, slipped off his shoes, and loosened his shirt, hoping her efforts soothed him. Henry lay, breathing hard. Between half-closed eyes in a face gray from effort, he steadily watched each movement.

She sat on the sofa next to him. With trembling fingers, Melissa unbuttoned the top of the dress and pretended not to hear Henry's objections. She leaned very close to him.

"Drink," she said.

Then, she cupped her hands on his sticky face and pressed his lips into her neck.

CHAPTER 26: SICK AND TIRED

The approaching daybreak was filtering into Melissa's room, but even that dim light was too bright for her pounding head. She switched off the alarm before it could ring, her muscles throbbing from the effort, but last night was worth it. She had saved Henry's life.

Melissa shuddered and painfully pulled the quilt up to her chin, remembering how she had closed her eyes to avoid Henry's transformed look. He had drunk with tensed body and clenched fists, with ravenous, yet curtailed, vigor. Even in desperate need, Henry held back. He could have drained her of all blood, and then....

She eased onto her back and cautiously stretched her cramped legs. How much blood had Henry taken, or would the iron pills compensate the extra loss?

If Melissa had felt this ill on any other day, she might have begged her mother for permission to stay home. Today, she did not have to suggest it.

"Melissa!" Darlene stopped in the doorway, coffee mug in mid-air, watching Melissa lumber from the bedroom. "What's wrong? Are you sick?"

"Just tired." Melissa dropped into her place at the dining room table.

"You look more than tired," Darlene felt Melissa's forehead.

"Would you like to stay home?"

"No!"

Startled, her mother jumped back.

"I mean, I've got a test today."

Her mother tightly pressed her lips and looked hard at Melissa.

"If I feel worse, I'll call for a ride home. Okay?"

"Okay," Darlene said slowly then gave Melissa a long, warm hug.

That anxious look bothered Melissa, but she couldn't forsake school today, not after what happened in Henry's study. She had to see for herself that Henry was okay. However, Harold Masters was absent that day. Instead, they had the morning kindergarten teacher, Miss Elbert, a tall, thin woman with gray hair, gray beady eyes, and a nose like a bird's beak. Melissa, along with the entire class, moaned aloud when Miss Elbert announced the day's essay: *My Dream Vacation.*

"Wherever Mr. Masters is, I sure hope he gets back here soon," Ann mumbled.

Dan raised his hand. "Can it include naked girls?"

Joey tittered on cue. Miss Elbert blushed and cleared her throat. "Keep it clean."

"Won't be much of an ideal vacation for him then," Ann whispered.

Melissa only gave her a distracted nod, since she was already writing. *I've always wished my parents would take me to Disneyland, but to my father, who had traveled in African jungles, Disneyland was boring."* With haste, she scrawled some lame reasons why Disneyland appealed to her, but her mind was inside Henry's study.

By the time the final bell had rung, Melissa had already packed her book bag and was moving out of her seat.

262

"Do me a favor, please," she said to Ann. "Tell the bus driver I stopped at the office and to wait for me, okay?"

"Sure, no problem," Ann said.

The first student in line brandished a doctor's note. The second had instructions to pick up the homework for a sick, younger brother. The old- fashioned wall clock ticked off the minutes, and Melissa felt smug for remembering Roman numerals. The door to the principal's office was slightly ajar, and the voices on the other side sounded stern. Oh, please hurry, she silently begged the other kids.

She set down her book bag and leaned against the rusty filing cabinets. Five minutes passed. She crossed her arms and almost stomped her foot with impatience. The black specks in the green linoleum hid the dirt, but the floor was still ugly. Whose idea was it to paint the walls a light blue?

The last child moved away from the desk. Finally!

"Yes, Melissa?" Mrs. Joyce, the office secretary, said, smiling. "Um, I was wondering if you knew what happened to Mr. Masters."

"He'll be back Monday. He had a mild case of food poisoning."

Food poisoning?

"Do you, um, have an address for him? I thought I could, maybe, well, you know, send him a 'Get Well' card."

"That's very nice of you, Melissa, but I can't give out his address. It's against school policy. Wait until he returns and then present the card. I'm sure he'll appreciate it just as much."

"Okay," Melissa said, feeling deflated. "Thanks."

Melissa hurried to the bus. Mr. Carlson glared at her tardiness and shut the door the second she cleared it. He was already in traffic when Melissa tumbled next to Ann.

"What gives?" Ann said. "Everything all right?"

"Sure. I forgot to turn in my lunch money."

In bed that night, Melissa's mind was still on Henry. He had urged Melissa to abandon her bargain with John, and now she knew why. John had forced him to chaperone Melissa, the pseudo-reincarnated Bryony. How painful for Henry! She had considered

Henry obnoxious and revolting, and he certainly could be, yet how had she missed his suffering?

Melissa dreamed no Bryony dreams that night and woke before dawn in a panic. She had not skipped a night in a long time. At breakfast, Melissa told her mother she really did feel sick, her excuse for spending most of the next two days in her room, brooding over John and Henry, participating little in family activities, and scarcely completing her homework. Limp and listless, less from blood loss and more from lack of continued and persistent contact with the objects of her obsessions, she lay on her bed, repeatedly listening to Grandma Marchellis' music box, no, *Anna's* music box, and remembering the bittersweet past few weeks, the past she now shared with Bryony.

Once again, she waltzed with John on filmy clouds of bliss at the Rutherfords' ball. She sank into John's lap in the sunny morning room, and faded into the grassy bank by Lake Munson, while the sun bid the world good-night, and John let loose his passions.

Only by the cessation of the music box and the time it took for Melissa to rewind it arrested her thoughts. The visions that followed assumed a different shape, for Henry broke into her trance, and, to Melissa's great surprise, she welcomed him, for these new imaginings showcased not Henry the nuisance, but Henry the love-sick suitor, who, with sorrowful eyes, watched every move that transpired between John and Melissa.

"Melissa?" Darlene called through the door.

Annoyed, she closed the lid. "What?"

"Dinner's ready."

"I'm not hungry."

"It's an easy meal. Steve and Brian made club sandwiches. Please come join us, even if you only feel like eating a little bit."

What could she say? She had to come out.

"Okay!" she called.

Melissa pushed the music box to the back of her nightstand. Surely tonight she'd see John! However, neither John nor Henry came to her that weekend.

Harold Masters returned to class on Monday, appearing wan, but otherwise his normal, eccentric self. Today, instead of reciting sections of Macbeth for the class as he had promised, he divided the parts among the students.

"You should have some feel for the dramatic by now," Mr. Masters said in a feeble voice. For the next fifty-five minutes, Melissa scrutinized each motion, unsuccessfully seeking signs of Henry.

"Leave your essays from Miss Elbert on my desk, as you leave," Mr. Masters said when he dismissed class. "Miss Marchellis, please see me on the way out."

Dan pulled a length of Melissa's hair, sang, "Melissa's in trouble," then scampered away.

Ann whispered, "What'd you do?" but when Melissa shrugged and looked away, Ann hurried to catch up with Katie and Julie. Melissa slung her book bag over her shoulder and plodded to Mr. Masters' desk. He was stacking their assignments and did not look up.

"Miss Marchellis," he said. "I understand you inquired about me at the office."

An uncomfortable flush spread across her face.

"I, I hope you didn't mind," she stammered. "I heard you were sick, and I, uh...."

He snapped the briefcase closed, then peered at her so keenly she grew uneasy and flustered. He was Henry, wasn't he? Feeling very foolish, Melissa studied the floor tile, the same hideous pattern as in the school office.

"Your concern for my health is appreciated," he said. "Thank you, for...."

Mr. Masters looked beyond Melissa, then and over the entire room,
as if he sought something. Melissa held her breath and waited, the ticking of the clock matching each heartbeat. His eyes, when they returned to her, looked sad.

"....for everything." He picked up his briefcase and walked past Melissa.

The after-school trek up the hill seemed longer today without Brian, who had gone with Steve to a dentist appointment in Jenson. The woods drew her like a magnet. The mist might be a vampire, but was it John? She quickened her steps.

The scent of vanilla hit Melissa outside the back door. Her mother pulled a baking tray out of the oven and hailed Melissa with a warm smile.

"Cookies!" Melissa tossed her book bag on the kitchen floor. "Oh, can I help?"

"I was hoping you'd say that," Darlene said, smiling. "Go put your school things away and wash up. Too bad Brian isn't here. We'll have to eat the mistakes."

"Oh, darn!" Melissa pecked her mother's cheek, then hurried to obey. Her mother poured another cup of coffee and a glass of milk for Melissa.

"These don't have to be perfect," Darlene said, bringing a chilled ball of dough to the dining room table. "I'm taking them to the nursing home tomorrow. The residents are appreciative of everything."

"That's nice of you, Mom," Melissa said.

Her mother's thumbprint cookies at Christmas cookies were a cherished holiday tradition. Melissa spooned up raspberry jam and began to fill the indentations.

"How was school today, hon?"

"Fine."

Darlene drizzled icing over a baked cookie, split it, and, with dancing eyes, gave half to Melissa. "Can't really give them away, until we know they're good to eat."

Thinking, Melissa bit into her cookie. "Mom, can I ask you something?"

"Sure."

"Can you be in love with two guys at the same time?"

"You're not still mooning over Jason? Aren't there cute boys at school?"

"I want to know how could you be in love with Daddy, but like Steve, too."

"Melissa," Darlene said, as she set a cookie on a tray, "there are many kinds of love. You don't love your friends as you love Brian, do you?"

"That's different."

"The human heart is amazing," she said. "We love, hurt, heal, and love again. I loved, still love, your father very much.

Steve is not your father, but he is a very nice man, and I like being near him. Does that answer your question?"

"What if you had met Steve when Dad was still alive?"

"Honey, I can't answer that question. I didn't meet Steve then."

"You *did* love Daddy, didn't you?" A lump blocked Melissa's throat.

"Oh, Melissa!" Her mother set aside the cookies and held out her arms.

Melissa leaped from her chair and fairly jumped onto Darlene's lap. When she was a very little girl, all problems vanished under her mother's embrace. Why couldn't life still be that simple?

"*Of course* I loved your father. Why are you bringing this up?"

Melissa sniffed back tears. "You miss Daddy, right?"

"Every day." Her mother's voice broke.

"Well, do you love Steve?" When her mother did not reply, Melissa pulled away to look at her. "Do you?"

Her mother gently brushed the hair off Melissa's wet cheek. "Love is such a big word. Let's just say Steve and I are good friends."

Melissa was unconvinced. "So, you can't love two guys at the same time?"

Her mother chuckled. "Melissa, when the time comes for you to worry about it, let your heart decide."

"But...."

"You'll know what's right for you."

Melissa fretted that night in bed. How do people know? How do they decide? She was in love with John; there was no doubt about it. So why was she obsessing over Henry? Melissa rolled onto her side to turn off her light, then heard a voice from the opposite end of the room. "....the restoration and all it entails." Melissa's eyes flew open. Where was she? She raised herself on one arm and saw the familiar settee. Henry! Was he okay?

Henry was leaning back in his desk chair, calmly regarding Melissa, and patiently waiting her response. She brushed the afghan onto the floor and sat up, rubbing her eyes.

"I'm sorry," she stammered. "I was asleep."

Unruffled by the delay, Henry continued. "Well, Melissa, now you see why the restoration shall not occur. It's a safety matter for John and me. We are in that basement."

Henry's voice quavered, but he covered it by picking up his notes and running a hand through his hair. Here was her chance. Melissa stood, stretched, and walked to his desk. He had notes strewn everywhere. She wondered how difficult clerical work was.

A small sheet, ragged at the edges, caught Melissa's attention. Scrawled on the paper, in Henry's old-fashioned script, were the words, *There is a time for departure, even when there's no certain place to go.* After it, he had written, *Tennessee Williams.*

Alarmed by those words, Melissa scrutinized his appearance. Henry looked pale, even for a vampire. Nevertheless, if something really was wrong with him, Melissa was fairly certain he would not share it with her.

"Are you all right? You know, from the other night."

He turned a page. "Good as new."

"Well, you don't look like it. Have you had dinner?"

"Not yet."

Something in Henry's tone startled Melissa. "What do you mean, 'Not yet?' You're going out, aren't you?"

"Eventually."

"Why not now?"

Exasperated, Henry threw down his notes. "See here, Melissa, nothing's wrong! Nothing's changed. I'm just tired tonight, that's all, tired of feigning an imitation life. I died eighty years ago. My existence depends upon prolonging the inevitable. I don't expect you to understand, and I don't care to discuss it."

"So you're going to starve yourself?"

A retort formed on Henry's lips, which he immediately stifled. A bit of the old swagger returned, as he said, "Of course not. What kind of repayment would that be, after you so generously shared with me your, ahem, elixir of life?"

He waited for her heated reaction, ready to pounce, but none came.

"Just don't do anything foolish," Melissa said.

"That has been accomplished."

"What do you mean?"

"The other night should not have happened."

"What are you talking about? You were dying. I saved your life!"

"With John's blood."

"What do you mean, *'John's blood?'* That was my blood!"

"You are mistaken. You gave it to John. Remember your bargain with him? Melissa, know this. John does not take kindly to betrayal."

Melissa shook her head in what she hoped was a reassuring manner.

"I think you're exaggerating. There was no betrayal. The bargain is still on. You're John's best friend, despite what happened years ago. You've seen a lot together. You've been through a lot together. He wouldn't want you to perish."

Henry retrieved the fallen notes and said nothing, but this time, Melissa let it go. She had something else on her mind and pondered how to say it.

"Soooo," she said slowly. "There's a repayment for the other night?"

A flicker of surprise passed over Henry's face, but his voice remained steady.

"Of course," he said, but his eyes scanned his notes. "What would you have, Melissa? Gold? Diamonds? Pearls? A new ball dress?"

Melissa leaned her elbows on Henry's desk, bringing her face close to his.

"A date," she said, "with you."

Henry smothered a grin, but he still did not look up. "Ah, so the fictitious wife of John Simons is still in a swoon over the transfusion."

"No, that's not it." "Then what?"

"I told you. I want a real date. With *you.*"

Henry swerved his chair to the typewriter.

"Unlike our good friend John, I refuse to sully Bryony's memory with cheap theatrics. The answer is, 'No.'"

"I'm not talking about Bryony. I want you to date, me, Melissa."

"Oh, ho!" he laughed, as he typed. "Do I understand correctly?

The twentieth century adolescent girl wants a modern date with an old, nineteenth century dandy, who just happens to be a vampire."

"You're not old."

Still chuckling, Henry shook his head. "No, Melissa."

"Why not? You asked me what I wanted. Well, I told you. I want this."

Henry sighed. Melissa crossed her fingers and silently begged Henry to say yes.

He spoke with hesitation. "Fair enough. Since I introduced the subject, why not? I will take you on a real date, if that is what you wish." Henry turned to look at her, but his face bore the oddest expression. "Will dinner and a show be satisfactory for the lady?"

Melissa's heart skipped a beat. Henry called her a lady. "You'll really take me?"

"Yes, really."

"Oh, when?" The excitement was uncontainable. How would she wait?

"I will let you know," Henry said, returning to his typing.

"Promise? You're not just saying it?"

"Promise. I am not just saying it."

Melissa spent the next day at school walking on air. Yet, if Henry intended to keep his promise, he took his time doing it, for several days passed with no date. A week elapsed, and he did not refer to it again. Melissa recalled Henry's hesitation when he consented, but she swept it from her mind. Henry *had* agreed to it. The last fall days merged into the dreary, cold nights of early December, and still Henry said not a word, but Melissa hadn't the courage to ask him again.

One chilly night, Melissa's mother distributed extra blankets, and Melissa nestled under the warm layers, pondering the future sleigh ride and wondering if it was cold enough to snow, her last thought until the first blush of dawn appeared in the gray-black sky. The old staircase squeaked, a sure sign Reverend Marseilles had completed his early morning prayers and was heading downstairs for his first cup of coffee.

John had sent Trudi to the parsonage to assist Melissa with her garments. Melissa had thought it unnecessary and had told John so, but he staunchly insisted otherwise.

"Once we're married, Trudi becomes responsible for dressing you," John had told her. "She may as well begin with your wedding preparations."

Now, Melissa smoothed the folds of the lovely gown spread across her bed. She couldn't wait to wear it. John had custom-ordered the ivory satin from Paris. It had a floor length, lace veil edged with bryony motifs; white silk stockings; satin slippers; and a pair of white kid gloves.

As Trudi adjusted the veil, someone knocked on the door. Trudi waited until Melissa nodded assent, then cracked the door to reveal Reverend Marseilles.

"Come in, Father!"

Reverend Marseilles hesitated, then slowly stepped into Melissa's bedroom.

"Trudi, please leave us a moment," Melissa said.

The second Trudi left, Melissa strode across the floor, embraced him with gentleness, and kissed his cheek; the reverend gratefully returned her greeting with a quick hug. He laid a hand on each of her shoulders, eased her slightly away from him, and studied her from the veil to the dainty slippers.

"You look just like your mother," he said in a low, gruff voice.

"Oh, Father, do you really think so?"

He took a deep breath. "Do you need anything before I leave for church?"

She shook her head.

"Has Mrs. Parks had that little talk with you?"

Melissa turned pink and looked at her slippers. "Yes, Father."

"Bryony, it's not too late to...."

"Father, thank you, but I want this." She took his hand in hers. "Really."

He quickly withdrew it. "Well, then, I must go. John is sending a carriage?"

"Yes, Father."

"Well, then remember, no one else sees you until the ceremony."

Melissa gave her bedroom a final glance. Tomorrow, she would wake up inside Simons Mansion. The following day, she and John would embark for Chicago on a two-month trip. What would it be like? She had never been outside Munsonville. Then Melissa heard the pounding of hooves and forgot everything, except meeting John at the altar.

It was a short downhill trot to the parish temple, certainly not sufficient time for Melissa to dwell on the inevitable conclusion of her journey, her marriage to John Simons. Would she stay asleep long enough to experience it? Tom Jenkins stopped the carriage in front of the church.

She detected a hint of familiar piano music, which grew louder whenever someone opened the front doors. Reverend Marseilles must be livid, although John technically obeyed him, by playing Bryony before the official ceremony.

Jenkins helped her from the carriage just as Orville Parks reached the church. He hastened Melissa inside and led her into Reverend Marseilles' private office.

"You stay there until you're called." Orville closed the door behind him, then reopened it a sliver. "Golly, Bryony, you sure look pretty."

The starkness of the reverend's church office greatly clashed with the warm tones of his home one, replete with books, oil paintings, and lavishly upholstered furniture. He had furnished this room with only the barest necessities: a weather-beaten desk holding a lone Bible, whitewashed walls, and a single rag rug covering the unfinished boards that served as a floor.

Melissa flipped through the pages of the good book, pretending to be interested in its pious words, but she saw only John's face, and her pulse beat hard and fast with the excitement of becoming John's wife. So what if it was only in his memory, as Henry alluded? For now, that was good enough for her. Why was it taking so long to begin? Don't wake up, Melissa told herself.

The piano music stopped. Melissa heard a scuffle, then the familiar sounds of the traditional wedding march. Susan Betts, her best friend since childhood and the only bridesmaid, flung open the door. "Come *on,* Bryony! We're starting."

272

Susan wore a simple lavender dress and a short veil, but her face was rosy, and her eyes were bright. Why, Melissa thought, she's almost as excited as I am.

The Reverend Marseilles was waited in the back of the church for Melissa and offering his arm. "Ready, daughter?"

Melissa nodded, suddenly overwhelmed by the crowds that craned their necks around their neighbors, poised on tiptoe to peek at her. Did the whole village attend this wedding? Near the altar, Bertha Parks sat at the piano, playing *The Wedding March* and hitting only a few wrong notes. Henry stood beside John. Both wore grey suits with lavender cravats, boutonnières, and gloves. When they reached the front, Reverend Marseilles picked up his service book, turned to her, and motioned John to join them.

"Dearly beloved, we are gathered here this day...." he intoned.

Through her lacy veil, Melissa stole a glimpse at John and stifled a gasp. Who was this man standing next to her and displaying such naked emotion? He appeared calm, but his eyes shone with pure love for her.

No, not for me, Melissa silently corrected herself, heart sinking. For Bryony.

"John, repeat after me...."

All at once, Melissa felt uneasy. This moment belonged to someone else. She should not hear these words or receive those adoring looks from John.

"....in the presence of God, our family, and our friends."

Melissa closed her eyes. She could not do it.

The Reverend Marseilles said, "I offer you my solemn vow to be your faithful partner."

"I offer you my solemn vow to be your faithful partner."

John's voice shook a little, and Melissa insides quivered. How would she say those words to John and then wake up for school, as if nothing had happened?

"....and to cherish you for as long as we both shall live."

"....and to cherish you for as long as we both shall live."

The Reverend Marseilles faced Melissa. "Bryony, repeat after me."

She had to look at John. His ardor and passion overwhelmed her. Even mental escape was impossible, for John's eyes hypnotically captured hers and held them. He waited, expectantly, eagerly, for her to repeat those exact words back to him.

Reverend Marseilles, oblivious to Melissa's storm, proceeded with the ceremony and Melissa, haltingly, parroted every word.

"….and to cherish you, for as long as we both shall live."

"….and to cherish you…." Melissa hesitated, blinked, and swallowed hard. Were these her emotions, or were they Bryony's?

…" for as long as we both shall live."

John looked calm, but his fingers trembled as he slid the ring onto Melissa's finger. She gazed down. This was not the gold band with the large, solitary diamond her mother wore. A scattering of diamonds, interspersed with pearls, ornamented the silver lattice. John removed his hand, and Melissa heard him take a deep, quiet breath. He was nervous, she thought. The great John Simons was actually nervous.

Weeks before the ceremony, when Reverend Marseilles had clearly stated to John the traditional, "Now, you may kiss the bride," would not be part of the ceremony, John had merely smiled. Melissa held her breath at the uneasy silence because Reverend Marseilles did not say those words now. As the minister opened his mouth to conclude the service, John slowly raised the veil over Melissa's head. His eyes met her eyes, and nothing mattered, except his great love for her. His gaze wove down her face to her lips and back again. The dark blue in his eyes reflected the high energy of his desires.

The Reverend Marseilles stood motionless. She recalled Henry saying that John recognized only one opinion, his own. Did that mean he would insist on his way, even in Reverend Marseilles' church, in front of the entire village?

John bent down and placed one light, small kiss on Melissa's forehead. Then, he replaced the veil.

Such an enthusiastic reception awaited John and her outside the church! Rice rained on them from every direction and competed with the hugs and kisses from family and friends. Jenkins sat in the carriage and patiently waited for the festivities' conclusion. Sorrowfully, Melissa watched the disgusted minister walk toward the parsonage. She knew he would not attend the reception.

Henry Matthews kissed her cheek and quietly wished her many happy years with John. Melissa lowered her head. She could not bear the longing in Henry's eyes. Bryony must have known how he felt about her, Melissa thought. It's all too obvious.

John guided Melissa into the carriage, shut the door, and closed the curtains. He did not speak, but wound his arms around Melissa, pulled her very close to him, and said in a low, controlled voice, "Congratulations, Mrs. Simons."

He closed his eyes and kissed her, with the utmost tenderness at first and then roughly, hungrily, until Melissa thought she would faint. His lips pressed so insistently that when she parted her lips to take a breath, John's tongue was inside it, exploring every crevice of her mouth. He had never kissed her like this, not in her dreams and certainly not in real life, where every contact ended with a chomp to her neck. His intensity frightened her and intoxicated her. She wished he would stop; she hoped he did not.

Jenkins slowed the horses to a walk. They had arrived at Simons Mansion.

Even before they reached the ballroom, Melissa felt the house buzzing with anticipation and excitement. The servants had decorated the room in white with splashes of mulberry. The tables were bedecked in lace, mulberry ribbon bows, holly and mistletoe, and red, not purple, roses. A Christmas tree of grandiose proportions graced the corner of the room, adorned with homemade candies, gingerbread men, nuts, and berries. Servants were lighting its white, hand-dipped candles.

Large amounts of food filled the buffet tables, just as *The Munsonville Times* had said. There were fish balls, fruit fritters, scalloped oysters, giblet soup with veal, chowder, mushroom catsup, roast duck with cranberries and peas, boiled pigeons with turkey stuffing, roast goose with mashed potato stuffing and apple sauce, breaded potatoes, boiled cabbage, winter squash, boiled parsnips and carrots, rice and meat pudding, plum pudding, French rolls, and minced meat pie. One section held a bowl of Bryga's special eggnog, sprinkled with nutmeg; a magnificent, twelve-tiered wedding cake, one layer for each month of their anticipated first year of marriage, graced the center of the dessert table.

John only left Melissa when a servant required John's attention. Melissa seized one of those opportunities to approach Henry, who stood near the Christmas tree conversing with a group of men. She couldn't bypass this chance to flaunt.

"Look at him, how happy he is," Melissa said, nudging him and speaking close to his ear. "Do you still think John would rather touch a piano than a woman?"

"Not on this night," Henry agreed.

The orchestra was ready, but Melissa was watching the window, where steady, silent snow fell. Mesmerized, Melissa watched the pirouetting flecks of white in the approaching twilight, even as she heard the first notes of *Bryony*. She turned to see John, holding out his hand for her, and with a heart spilling over with passion and rapture, Melissa followed him onto the dance floor. Again, he did not speak to her, and Melissa felt glad of it, for joy rushed into her throat and left no room for words. She wondered if John felt the same way.

As they stepped to the magical music, Melissa discerned yet another sound, a very faint tinkle, far away in the background. She ignored the muffled voices surrounding her on all sides and concentrated on the distant music. It couldn't be, not here, not in this place, but she knew too well the sounds of Bryony's music box to mistake it. Did John hear it, too? Melissa thought he might have sensed it, for the expression had changed in his eyes. He no longer smiled. He was miles away.

"John?" Melissa asked softly.

He did not answer her. John paused, swaying and looking lost. His eyes were full. His lashes were wet.

"Bryony?" he asked with uncertainty. "I'm here, John," Melissa said.

She put her arms around him and tightly held him. John hesitated a moment, then wrapped his arms about her waist and rested his cheek on her head. They stood there, unmoving, as the orchestra's music faded into the walls. Even after it stopped, Melissa continued rocking on her bedroom floor. The only sound in the room was Bryony's music box on Melissa's nightstand, as it gradually wound down.

Dawn had not yet broken when Melissa popped open her eyes. She switched off her alarm before it rang, then leaned onto the pillows and reclosed her eyes. She clasped the music box to her breast, as she drifted away on a sea of wistful yearnings. She loved John, but John loved Bryony and only wanted Melissa's blood. Yet, Bryony was dead and so was her baby. Could Melissa ever take her place? At school, she moved with languor, as if still living inside the dream, which triggered the drill sergeant in Ann. Frustrated by her inability to motivate her friend, Ann took notes for Melissa in history, passed algebra answers to her, and kept pace with her friend, as they ran laps around the school.

"Snap out of it already," Ann barked more than once.

At lunch, Ann brazenly waved her hands before Melissa's face, but "Hmm?" was all Melissa said before drifting back into her reverie.

"That was rude," Julie said, brushing cookie crumbs off her hands.

"Well, she's been like this all day," Ann said with exasperation.

"Maybe, it's her blood sickness," Katie said. "Maybe, she needs more sleep."

Ann sniffed. "I think she is asleep."

"I am *not* asleep," Melissa protested. "I heard every word you guys said."

When they entered English class, Mr. Masters was writing a note on the chalkboard: *No talking. Quiz today.*

Over their united groans, Mr. Masters calmly informed them the quiz was merely a practice test for the semester's final exam. The grade would not count.

"If you do poorly today, you can study hard and repair the damage," he said.

Melissa moved aimlessly from one question to another, then lagged behind Ann after class, hoping Mr. Masters might initiate some conversation with her. Ann noticed, marched right into the classroom, and tugged Melissa's arm.

"Come on! You're going to be late for the bus."

Melissa plodded down the hallway after Ann. Dan threw a paper airplane, which bounced off a locker and landed on Julie's head. That act caused Melissa's eyes to travel past it to the clock on the wall. It was after three o'clock.

"Oh, gosh!" Melissa gasped, reality finally sinking into her. "The bus!"

Melissa sprang ahead to her locker, spun the combination lock, and flung open the door, then shoved her books on the locker's top shelf. The abrupt movement sent her art case tumbling to the floor, spilling its contents.

"Shoot!"

Melissa knelt to collect her things. As she did so, one last item dropped from the top shelf and landed beside her. It was a purple rose.

CHAPTER 27: A REAL DATE?

Wrapped around the stem was a piece of paper, yellow and brittle with age, fastened with a bit of purple ribbon. Melissa untied the ribbon and gently unwound the paper. The edges crumbled in her hands. Its quaint handwriting simply read: *Simons Mansion. Porch. Midnight.*

These last months of living a double life never included a set of instructions. Melissa had asked Henry to date her, in person, and it seemed he planned to do exactly that, except first, Henry wanted her to walk to Simons' Mansion, by herself, at midnight. She couldn't!

It was too dangerous. She could get hurt. The police might catch her. Steve would never let her past the back door. Maybe, Henry's message was for her dreams. He was a vampire. Did he mean harm? On the other hand....

"Come on, Melissa!"

Melissa had forgotten about Ann. With a disgusted grunt, Ann tore down the hall. Melissa shoved her art supplies into her locker, slammed the door before they fell, and scrambled to her feet. She must conquer her fear. She really wanted this date with

Henry. Melissa had felt differently about him, ever since the night he confessed his love for Bryony to her, the night she learned he had tender feelings inside him. She opened her bag and laid the rose on top of her books. It would prevent questions from Ann she was unprepared to hear. Students still boarded the bus, so she took her time. Melissa's conflicting feelings for Henry confused her. He annoyed her, and he charmed her. She definitely didn't love him like John, but....

Someone bumped into her, momentarily jarring Melissa to reality. She quickly slipped back into her musings. Anyway, Henry accepted her, as she was. He didn't pretend she was someone else, like John did. Yes, Henry was a royal pain in the neck. The thought made her giggle, and Ann tossed her a withering look. Henry had a heart, or at least the memory of a heart. Thinking about meeting Henry at midnight in the dark and in front of Simons Mansion excited her and frightened her at the same time. She was excited because it was her first real date, and she did not know what to expect. She felt frightened, because her date was a vampire, and she did not know what to expect. Henry was not the appointed chaperone tonight.

Ann took out her science notebook and began the weekend's homework.

How quickly might Melissa walk to Simons Mansion in the dark? During the day, she and Brian trekked there in ten minutes. To be safe, Melissa decided to set her alarm clock for eleven-thirty. She hoped her mother and Steve would be sleeping. To save time, Melissa would stay dressed. She would also need a flashlight. She hoped she could find one without raising suspicions. Unfortunately, her mother was cooking dinner when Melissa trooped into the kitchen.

"Hi, Mom, how was your day?" Melissa cracked open the utility drawer and rummaged inside.

"Fine, Melissa, how was yours?" Her mother slid a pan of plain pork chops into the oven. "What are you looking for, hon?'"

"Tape. I ripped my notes in class and need to fix them."

"Check with Brian. He borrowed it last."

"Okay." Luck was with Melissa. She had spied the flashlight near the back.

That evening, while Steve and her mother were watching television, Melissa sneaked the flashlight into the bathroom. Yes, it worked! Holding it behind her back and sipping a glass of water, Melissa walked nonchalantly to the bedroom. She unzipped her book bag and examined the rose. It was still fresh and intact, but too tall for the glass.

Both Steve and her mother looked up when Melissa returned to the kitchen with her empty glass of water. She ran the water full blast as she opened the utility drawer for the scissors. They, too, went behind her. Melissa carried the glass of water back to her bedroom. She saw Steve and her mother glance at each other.

"Boy, am I thirsty tonight," Melissa said.

To insure sufficient rest, Melissa went to bed extra early that night, far too excited to fall asleep. She read the clock at nine and then at ten. Eleven-thirty would never come.

Beep! Beep! Beep!

Melissa's hand fumbled for the switch. The alarm clock? Then, thoughts of her impending date rushed into her brain. She snatched the flashlight from under the pillow, scrambled out of bed, and slipped on her shoes. Cautiously, Melissa opened her door.

Creak!

She held her breath. Why wasn't the door noisy in the daytime? Steve stirred on the couch and mumbled something in his sleep, but he did not wake up. She tiptoed across the floor; the boards under the carpet groaned with her weight. She stopped and waited, but Steve lay still.

By the light above the sink, Melissa sprinted on tiptoe across the kitchen toward the back door. She snatched her winter jacket off its hook, zipped it, and stepped outside. The black night smothered her, and Melissa wasted no time switching on the flashlight. Its beam threw the only sliver of light. She again considered her last midnight walk, just two short months ago, and the fact that Kimberly remained lost. Melissa wavered with

281

indecision. What should she do? She really wanted to see Henry. Shoving doubts away, Melissa plunged into her nocturnal adventure.

How creepy are the woods at night! The entire area had come alive since sunset. The cold December wind, barely perceptible yesterday, now squealed through the trees and sliced through Melissa's coat. Leafless branches creaked to, fro, up and down and tried to catch Melissa with its spindly arms. Unseen objects cast unearthly shadows. Tiny feet scuttled past her. Somewhere, an owl hooted. Melissa mentally kicked away her uneasiness, for it slowed her progress. She wouldn't, couldn't miss her one, paradisiacal chance with Henry. Panicking, Melissa broke into a run. Her feet slipped, then skidded and, before she realized what happened, she was lying on a bare patch of muddy ground. Leave it to her to hit the only place not frozen!

Stunned, Melissa slowly sat up and surveyed her filthy clothes. If she went home to change clothes, she might miss Henry. Besides, why would a vampire mind a little dirt? Melissa brushed aside her misgivings, renewed her determination, and turned resolute steps toward Simons Mansion.

With its shabby exterior spotlighted under moonlight, the great house less resembled the stately home of a world-famous musician and more the classic haunted house. Again Melissa wavered, and again she pointed her flashlight on the mansion and marched forward, lauding her daring behavior, so different from several weeks ago. Nevertheless, her courage waned as she rounded the corner toward the front porch. Her heart beat hard as she imagined a ghoulish Henry Matthews stepping out from the trees.

A far-off rumble and the pounding of hoof beats made Melissa jump and drop her flashlight, extinguishing it's comforting beam. With a cry of fright, Melissa dropped to the ground and clawed for the flashlight. She picked it up and banged it hard.

A shaft of light illuminated the immediate darkness. The roaring grew until two very familiar Arabian horses, drawing an equally familiar carriage, stopped in front of Simons Mansion. Its driver leaned forward.

"'Ere miss, are you Miss Marchellis?"

Jackson!

"Yes, Jackson, it's me, Melissa!"

"I don't know any 'Melissa.' Your Uncle 'Enry sent me here to fetch you."

"My what?"

Jackson disgustedly shook his head, and an eyeball popped out. He swung from the seat and limped toward her. She shrank from his rotted form and disapproving look, as he contemptuously inspected her dirty clothes. With another shake of his head, Jackson leaned into the carriage, shook out a piece of burlap and laid it on the rear seat.

"A man works 'ard all 'is life, and then does he get to rest in peace? No, I'm summoned at all hours of the night to give some young girl, without a chaperone, mind you, a ride to Chicago."

Melissa switched off her flashlight, grinned, and accepted the second coachman's moldy hand. "It's okay, Jackson, if you don't know me," she said, scrambling onto her seat. "I know you."

"Your Uncle 'henry said to keep the curtains shut."

Resisting a powerful urge to peek into forbidden territory, Melissa settled back and glanced down. Even in the dark, she smelled the damp earth. *This was no dream!*

The carriage lurched. Melissa bumped her head against the carriage wall. The horses increased speed as they moved away from Simons Mansion. Melissa rubbed the side of her head, wondering where Jackson was taking her.

They rode so long Melissa began worrying if they would ever stop. Tired from her tramp in the woods and the frightening walk on John's estate, the carriage's vibration lulled her to sleep. With a jerk, Melissa awakened and groped for the seat's rough cloth. The carriage had stopped. How much time had elapsed?

She waited and waited, but Jackson did not appear. Deciding she had nothing to lose, except Henry's scorn, which was nothing new, Melissa slid to the end of the carriage and lifted the latch. She opened the door, eased her stiff legs to a standing position, and looked outside into the night.

Beside the carriage stood Henry, but, oh, what a different Henry! He seemed as young as Jason Frye and was dressed in midnight blue, from his top of his hat to the tips of his shoes. His shirt was white; his tie and waistcoat were gray. The sight of him was intoxicating, and it took her breath away, just as it had the first time she had seen him, at the Rutherford's, before his obnoxious side made her forget how attractive he really was. Flustered, Melissa began climbing out of the carriage.

"Wait," Henry said. " Watch your step."

He spoke too late. Melissa tripped in the folds of her gown and would have fallen if two hands hadn't encircled her waist. Her cheeks burned, but she managed a timorous smile at Henry, as he lithely swung her to the ground. She turned at the sound of hoof beats. Jackson had driven away. She retied the strings of her dark blue bonnet and gazed around her. A succession of horse-drawn carriages unloaded person after person, all dressed in Victorian clothes. She gazed up at the ornate six- story building. Its sign read, *McVickers Theatre*. She looked at Henry with large, questioning eyes.

"Dinner and a show, remember?" Henry's face was deadpan, but his eyes danced with merriment.

"Matthews!"

It was the monocle man from Della's party, rushing to greet Henry. "Brumfeldt, I'd like to present to you my niece, Miss Marchellis," Henry said. "Melissa, this is my publisher, Mr. Albert Brumfeldt."

He was the host of the first ball she had attended with John, the night she had made her bargain with him. Melissa remembered his name, but she had not met him before tonight.

The man raised an eyebrow, and the glass fell. "Good Lord!" he said. "This one is the spitting image of you. It's quite the family you have." To Melissa he added, "Pleased to meet you, my dear."

His *niece?* Melissa turned accusing eyes at the sheepish Henry, who self-consciously patted her hand.

"Have you read the reviews?" Brumfeldt said. "Boucicault missed the mark."

"I read that, too," Henry said, "but I'm curious to see it, just the same."

Brumfeldt tipped his hat at Melissa, and walked into the theatre.

Melissa still stared at Henry. He pretended not to notice.

"Now, shall we go inside?" he said, offering his arm. "We mustn't miss the start of the play."

Melissa conceded, but only because he looked so handsome. "Onward to a perfect evening!"

"Two souls with but a single thought."

Melissa playfully slapped Henry's arm.

Henry beamed at her. "Friedrich Halm."

Joy and anticipation bubbling inside her, Melissa happily linked arms with Henry and walked inside the theatre. While waiting for the usher, Melissa gazed in awe around the crowded lobby. Her previous show background was limited to the Grover's Park's movie theater and the occasional drive-in with Laura's family. She had never seen plays, except for school plays, or had entered such an old-fashioned building. She admired its many rectangular windows, arched doorways, tall columns, and flowery stenciling.

"Old-fashioned?" Henry stared at her in disbelief. "I assure you it's utterly contemporary in design and concept and only recently rebuilt after a fire destroyed it."

Henry's telepathy made her nervous. Did he also know her feelings for him?

"So," Melissa said, hoping to sidetrack him. "What are we seeing tonight?"

"Dion Boucicault's 'Robert Emmet.'" Melissa looked blank.

"The play revolves around the leader of an Irish rebellion against the British in 1803," Henry said.

"Oh," Melissa said. "Does he win?"

"No, he is convicted and hanged."

Melissa fell silent. It didn't sound very interesting, but she wouldn't tell him. After all, Henry had arranged this night at her request. Again, he read her mind.

"I am rather in the mood for Boucicault, tonight," Henry said. "Perhaps, you would prefer, 'The Vampire, A Phantasm in Three Dramas'? Say the word, Melissa. It's your night."

She looked up at Henry. The corner of his eyes barely crinkled. Vampires, again! Was he making fun of her?

He leaned close to Melissa's ear. "Robert Emmett has quite a nice love story attached to it, which you might find poetic. He was so passionately in love with Sarah Curran that, although he was in jail and at the expense of her safety, he wrote one final letter to her. The authorities intercepted it."

Henry grinned and raised an eyebrow. Melissa relaxed into her seat and decided whatever else happened this evening, it would not be boring.

He never moved during the entire play. Although its political storyline was dull, and she caught herself fidgeting more than once, Henry was right about one thing. She immensely enjoyed the quaint love story between Robert Emmet and Sarah Curran, especially the poignant, final meeting where Robert hid at Sarah's house before his capture. She told Henry so when they were back inside the carriage.

"It was beautiful," Melissa said. "Thank you so much for taking me."

She wondered what she would tell her children years from now when they asked her about her first date, then brushed the thought aside. Melissa could not imagine having children with anyone except John. At any rate, her remarks pleased Henry, she could tell.

"I thought you might appreciate it," Henry said. "Moreover, I enjoyed experiencing it again from another perspective."

"Again?"

"I first saw it here in 1884, when I was 18."

"Oh." So that's why he looked so young. What niece accompanied him that time, Melissa briefly wondered, with a tinge of jealousy.

In time, the carriage turned off the busy streets and onto a small dusty road. Henry drew the curtains. Was this so Melissa couldn't see where they were going, or did he have something else in mind?

However, if Henry had amorous ideas, he gave no indication of it. He was engaging company, nonetheless, for he inquired about Melissa's interests and the circumstances surrounding her move to Munsonville. He sympathized at the loss of her father. Henry did not share John's brooding nature; he was appreciably, delightfully, present to the moment and all it

286

contained. Yet, while Henry talked, Melissa felt increasingly troubled.

"Out with it, Melissa."

"When we were playing croquet," Melissa said haltingly, "you said I never left my bedroom. Is that true?"

"Perhaps."

"The other night," Melissa persisted, "in the basement of Simons Mansion. Was that my bedroom, too?"

Henry pulled the curtain aside and stared out the window. "No."

"So, I have really been inside the mansion? Or was I just dreaming it?"

Henry didn't answer.

"Are we in my bedroom now?"

He sighed in irritation, closed the curtain, and faced Melissa.

"Dearest Melissa, you ask far too many questions. You chose this night, so please don't keep me from enjoying it, because I have very much, up until this moment."

"Okay," Melissa conceded.

"One more thing." Henry leaned close. "Forbidden conversation for the remainder of this evening is John Simons and anything peripheral to him. That includes his mansion. Agreed?"

Henry's request tickled Melissa. He's jealous, she thought. Henry Matthews is jealous of John Simons. The night ripened with untold, delicious possibilities.

"Agreed!" she cried.

Jackson slowed the carriage. Henry gestured at the window. "Look, Melissa!"

She followed Henry's gaze. In the distance, on a tall hill, stood the ruins of a large building.

"Is that a real castle?" Melissa said, excitedly.

"It is," Henry said, smiling at her.

"Castle Dracula?"

"Most certainly not," Henry cried with indignation. "That is Khust Castle, an edifice impervious to human hands."

Just like vampires, Melissa thought. No wonder he likes it. She couldn't help smiling, and Henry took that as a sign she wanted to hear more.

"Its origins are obscure. Some say robbers built the castle to protect the salt route near the Tysa River. Others claim St. Ladislaus used it as a fortress from the Cumans. Either way, The Mongols demolished it in 1241, but, a century later, it was once again standing. Then King Matthias restrained his defiant uncle inside its walls, but, in 1514, the local peasants captured it. When the Tartars destroyed the town, they failed to claim this magnificent castle."

She sat up straighter at the fire in Henry's voice, trying to glimpse Henry's face. He sounded exactly like Mr. Masters.

"...through the years, many more armies assaulted it, but Khust Castle prevailed against them all. No mortal man, Melissa, has ever defeated it, only violent acts of nature and even then, as you see, not completely. In 1766, lightning struck it and in several years, a storm annihilated its tower. It remains, ruined, but it remains."

Melissa was unaware of the eroding castle or its history, but it sounded exhilarating, especially the way Henry told it. She wished Harold Masters taught history, too.

The countryside rolled past Melissa's eyes, but she strained for one last view of the romantic edifice. They traveled only a short way before Jackson halted the carriage beside a row of low stone buildings.

"Where are we?" Melissa asked.

"Why, the second part of our date. I believe we agreed on dinner, too."

Henry helped her from the carriage and opened the thick wooden door of one of the buildings. Looking around her, Melissa felt she had stepped onto the set of a very old movie. Gone was the refined, Victorian society to which John had introduced her. This place was noisy and raw, and Melissa was not sure if she liked it or not. Its only light shone from a fireplace at its far end and from many candles poking through crevices in the stone walls. Unruly laughter bordered every side and from the rows of the long wooden tables and benches that ran down the middle and against the edges of the immense room. Beside her, one man in rust-colored breeches slapped the back of the man in front of him, spilling his beer down his calico homespun shirt and narrowly missing

Melissa's dress. Someone shouted a loud greeting, and a voice in the background bellowed a response.

A woman wearing colorful peasant dress, white apron and matching headdress, dashed up to Henry and threw herself at him with an exuberant hug.

"Henry, you naughty boy," she said in a thick accent. "You've stayed away far too long. Come, sit down, and order what you like. It's all on the house."

Before Henry answered her, the woman noticed Melissa standing next to him.

"Your niece?" she said.

Melissa frowned and looked away.

"Yes, yes," Henry said with animation. "Danika, this is my niece, Miss Melissa Marchellis. Melissa, this is Danika Burundukov. She and her husband Sergei own this pub, which, I daresay, serves the most remarkable food this side of the Danube."

"Oh, go on with you!" Danika flushed with pride and embarrassment. She led them to a table near the fireplace, away from the rowdy activity of the main room. "The usual, I suppose?" she asked.

"Why, of course," he said, with a warm, open smile and a slight nod of his head, but his attention was already on a certain young woman, her long, tawny braids reaching the end of her bright green skirt, as she scurried past carrying two red-clay bowls. Behind, a small boy struggled with a water jar half the size as he. As Henry seated her, Melissa saw a woman at the far end of the room slide two long broom handles into a stone oven. Soon, the yeasty smell of fresh bread reached her nose. Unfamiliar food still made Melissa uncomfortable, but, if anyone understood her quirks, Henry did. She hoped he chose something delicious. She was starving.

"Psst," Henry said, lowering his voice. "Here comes your friend."

Ed Calkins approached the table and shook Henry's hand, asking him the state of his health and commenting on the night air, which Ed said was bad for his constitution. He did not wait for Henry's answer, for he leaned forward slightly and peered at Melissa, as if he knew her from somewhere, but couldn't quite place it.

"My niece, Miss Melissa Marchellis," Henry said.

Ed Calkins stared at Melissa for a very long moment, then back at Henry.

"Have I met her?" he said with uncertainty.

"Doubtful," Henry said.

"A pleasure to meet you, sir," Melissa said, smothering a grin.

Ed Calkins turned toward Henry. "I've recently expanded my harem. I married the waitress tonight."

A large, beefy woman, carrying two mugs of beer into the dining room, turned her head and smiled a broad, toothy grin at Ed. He blew her a kiss and waved.

"Let's see, does that make four?" Henry said, with a sidelong glance at Melissa.

"No, indeed!" Ed Calkins puffed out his chest and smiled cheerfully through the hole in his beard. "That makes five." He simpered at the waitress on her way back to the kitchen and she, in return, blew him a lip-smacking kiss. "Actually, that might make six." He held up both hands. "I've lost count."

"Given her size, I'd say she's both five and six," Henry murmured to Melissa, and she quickly covered her mouth to choke down a laugh.

Henry picked up the clay pitcher, poured Melissa a mug of water, and set it down in front of her. Melissa took a grateful sip.

"The night air is also bad for my niece," Henry said. "She's not been well."

Ed Calkins clucked his tongue in sympathy. "Well, I must get going. I'm having a policewoman for dinner tonight."

Henry's glance at Melissa was a solemn one, but Ed missed Henry's jolly wink. Melissa nearly exploded with restrained laughter.

"It's a very special dinner," he said. "I've even written a limerick for her, so she will remember how ruthless I am."

Ed Calkins strutted through the crowds, and Melissa marveled that none of the patrons or staff had noticed the kilt. Danika returned with a loaf of rye bread and a bowl of deep, brown liquid, which she placed before Melissa.

Melissa peered into her bowl. "What is this?"

"It's tripe soup," Henry said.

"What's tripe? Is it gross?"

"I should say not!"

Melissa still felt leery. "So, what's in it?" she said.

"Will you just try it?" Henry lifted her spoon and handed it to her. "Unless you would prefer *turtle* soup."

She recalled the tortoise she had sampled at one of the Rutherfords parties and quickly looked up. Was Henry making fun of her? She noticed him watching her and said, "Aren't you getting anything to eat?

"I've had a little something."

Didn't Henry mean, "a little someone?" Melissa could not think about it long, for Henry's keen eyes remained on her. She accepted the spoon, dipped up a small amount of the soup, and cautiously tasted it. The flavor was strong, but not entirely disagreeable. Buoyed by this unexpected knowledge, Melissa heartily devoured the remainder of the meal: lentils in sour gravy; pork with kohlrabi; potato dumplings; fritters that Henry said were made from kale; and biscuits topped with jam, cottage cheese, and cream. Henry watched each bite with amusement. She refused his offer for dessert.

"If I eat anymore, I'll burst."

"We'll wait to dance," Henry said. "Open your mouth."

Wondering, Melissa obeyed. Henry popped a cinnamon lozenge inside.

"Call that dessert," he said.

Henry could not be serious about dancing. The only dances Melissa knew were the steps John had taught her. A group of men wearing black pants, white shirts, and vests embroidered in blue, purple, and red, filed into the room. Each carried a stringed instrument. It took them several minutes to prepare, which only expanded Melissa's apprehensions about joining them, but when the rollicking music began, Melissa's foot uncontrollably tapped to the music.

Henry grinned at her movements. "Ready?"

Melissa studied the gyrating the figures on the dance floor and hedged. "I don't think I can dance that."

"It's not difficult. Come, I'll show you."

Henry stretched out his hand so invitingly, Melissa decided making a fool of herself wasn't nearly as bad as passing up the opportunity to see Henry polka. Not only did he dance well, Melissa had almost mastered the moves he taught her by the time the band had finished playing for the night.

"I have to stop, anyway," Melissa said, huffing, puffing, and rubbing her side.

Jackson was waiting outside for them. Henry assisted Melissa into the carriage, then walked to the front and muttered something unintelligible to the second coachman. Now, Melissa wondered, what was that all about? She didn't speculate too much because Henry climbed into the carriage and sat opposite Melissa. *It was now or never.*

As the carriage pulled away from the inn, Melissa tumbled across the seat and squeezed next to Henry. He inched away from her and said, "Did you have a nice time?"

"Oh yes!" Melissa exclaimed, looking at him with round, shining eyes.

"Look, Melissa…"

Melissa flung her arms around his neck and started to kiss him, but Henry unwound her arms and set them on her lap.

"Melissa, we can't," he said with uncharacteristic gentleness. "I can't."

She smiled wickedly at him, "Yes, we can," and tried a second time. Henry again clasped her hands together and securely held them. Melissa ignored the faint chill seeping through Henry's gloves.

"No, we can't," he repeated.

Hurt by his stern voice, Melissa struggled to free herself, but Henry tightly gripped them.

"Why not?" she asked, almost petulantly, abashed now at her boldness, but clinging to the faint hope he might change his mind. That hope quickly dissipated when she saw the way he looked at her. The expression on his face was not encouraging.

"Melissa, you are still a child, and you're not Bryony, no matter how much you, or I in this moment, would like to pretend otherwise." He put a finger to her lips when she opened her mouth to interrupt. "I'm no longer a man. I'm a vampire, remember?" He moved closer to Melissa, locking her eyes in his. "I can't."

"So, you won't kiss me? Not even once?" Her heartbeat fast, and her cheeks grew hot with anticipation. Henry just had to kiss her, even if he pretended she was Bryony, but Henry's face remained grave.

"Do you really want me to kiss you?" he said, still unsmiling.

"Yes!"

Henry cupped Melissa's face in his hands and closed his eyes. For a long while, he did not move. Just when Melissa wondered if she should initiate it, he brushed his lips across hers, but only for a moment. Why, Henry gave cigars more attention! He drew away from her and stared ahead. His distance and silence confused Melissa.

"You didn't...you didn't like that?" Melissa asked.

He did not respond.

"Not even a little bit?"

Henry sighed, draped his arm around her shoulder, and pulled her close to him.

"You're very sweet," he said, then dropped his voice. "Melissa, I crave only blood. It's the only thing that satisfies me, the only thing here on earth I need."

"But you agreed to a date!"

"Mere semantics."

"Semantics?"

"Date...meeting...field trip."

Field trip! Melissa knew Henry was cold-hearted, but this was cruel! Why was he doing this to her? Melissa pulled away his arm and scooted closer to the window just in case she started crying.

"Listen to me, Melissa," Henry's voice sounded urgent. "Tonight's engagement was for your benefit only. Hence, I must apologize for becoming ensnared in my own arrangement. I should not have kissed you. *You are not Bryony.*"

The last of her romantic illusions crashed to earth with a bang. Memory flashed, and she was in the second grade, standing in line with the rest of her class outside the Shedd Aquarium in Chicago. Is that what their date meant to Henry, displays and reports?

"Your trip through time was too restricted. I wanted to show you a larger world of possibilities, which was impossible to view through the narrow lens of John's memories."

Why couldn't Henry understand her world was now bigger and more vibrant because of John and his glorious memories with Bryony? Besides, what was wrong with memories? Frank had a roomful of memories; he made even the recounting of safaris feel exhilarating. Unless, Melissa thought, spirits rising, Henry meant something else. Just why had Henry shown her a piece his life? Was it because he wanted her there, too, and he just didn't know how to say it? She brushed a hand across her eyes and faced him.

"What kind of possibilities?" Melissa asked, trying not to sound too expectant.

"Not the kind you're envisioning," Henry said.

Henry's tone was curt, but she was close enough to see his eyes were sad. The detestable Henry was easier to read than this one, yet Melissa had the uncomfortable feeling he was also starkly honest with her. It reminded her of the night he opened up, after he dragged her to the cellar. Melissa searched her brain for answers. What was Henry trying to tell her? Was he missing Bryony? Was that why he kissed her? Did that mean he would not kiss her again? *Ever?*

"Remember when I said you're playing with fire? Tonight proves it," Henry said. "You're too young and far too idealistic. Don't squander it on the dead."

The words jolted her memory, but at last, Melissa understood. It bothered Henry that he was still a vampire.

"I'm not squandering it," she said softly. "Don't worry. John won't be dead much longer. He won't need a host anymore and then...."

Melissa hoped she would not have to say it. Once John was alive, why should he care if Melissa helped Henry become human, too?

"Melissa!" Henry roughly shook her shoulder. "Step away from Bryony's shadow. She lost her life to John. Don't repeat her fatal error. Life is full of exquisite opportunities. Choose yours well."

Melissa was silent. So, Henry only took her out to preach. She had hoped for romance and received a classroom lecture. What a wasted night!

"Thank you for suggesting tonight, really," he said, in a kinder tone that made Melissa's heart once again leap with anticipation. Henry was right. Life still held possibilities, and John caring for her was one of them. Tonight was bad timing. She would not give up on John or Henry. She needed them both very much alive.

"Tonight was not a waste," Henry continued, "at least, not for me. It was a pleasant distraction, I assure you, and one I badly needed. Thank you for your company and delightful conversation, for it certainly clarified something for me."

Melissa still stared at him, perplexed. What was Henry talking about?

"Nevertheless, it's time you went home. You need sleep and I have…." he paused, then added, "another engagement."

The scene faded. *No!* Her words floated up and away like the soap bubbles of her childhood. *Stop, oh, stop!* The carriage was gone, and Henry was gone. Melissa rolled over, and she was inside a florist's shop, a shop that sold only bryony vines and purple roses. John was examining the profuse weeds, but his watch kept playing *Bryony*. Melissa crossed her fingers and hoped John would notice her, but the flowers absorbed his interest. Henry selected a dozen purple roses, which he brought to the counter for wrapping. Whether it was because John was ignoring her or Henry had rejected her, Melissa did not know, but she ducked around a corner. As she peeped around the wall, John snatched a bunch of vines. Melissa started to warn him they were poisonous, and then stopped herself from going any further. What if they saw her? Hadn't Henry sent her home?

John and Henry left together, laughing as they talked, leaving Melissa alone. Huge waves of sadness engulfed Melissa, and she bit her lip, afraid she might cry in the store. The fire alarm sounded. Melissa turned to quiet it and bumped into Fr. Alexis.

"See?" Fr. Alexis said. "You don't need vampires anymore."

Melissa reached behind the counter and silenced her alarm clock. She switched on her light and rubbed her eyes, trying to clear the fuzziness from her head. Why had she set the alarm? It was Saturday. Remembrances of last night leaped into her mind. How had she returned home and turned on the alarm? She did not recall walking back or changing into pajamas. Was it only a dream after all?

Half-blind with sleep, she started to crawl out of the bed, then saw her shoes and the pile of clothes lying beside them. They were packed with mud.

CHAPTER 28: GONE

Harold Masters was gone.

The principal announced over the intercom on Monday morning that the English teacher had a family emergency and could not return for the spring semester. Miss Elbert would finish the last week of school for him, with another teacher replacing him after Christmas break.

"I'm sure we all hope everything goes well for him," the principal said.

Melissa sat in stunned disbelief. How could Mr. Masters be gone? Did that mean Henry was gone, too? How could he do this to her? Did he regret last night? And where did that leave her with John?

She brooded on this new development all morning. Henry lived inside Simons Mansion, because he must, for survival. How likely was it, really, that he would leave forever? Mr. Masters might be gone, but Melissa would see Henry in her dreams tonight. Cheered by her logic, Melissa vigorously tackled her lessons. At lunchtime, her friends discussed Harold Masters' departure.

"I hope he's not sick again." Julie opened a bag of potato chips and scattered some on Katie's plate.

"The principal said it was a family emergency." Ann reached for a chip. "Maybe, he has an elderly mother."

"Or a secret lover," Katie added, with a giggle.

Ann twisted her face in disgust, while Julie twirled a braid and pretended to retch.

"I don't think you should judge a book by its cover," Melissa said. In unison, the girls dropped their mouths.

"You're kidding!" Ann said.

"People are not always what they seem to be," Melissa said. "You just never know. There's probably more to Mr. Masters than we'll ever see."

Katie stared at Melissa.

"Yeah, right," Julie said. "Are you eating that last cookie, Melissa?"

Melissa tossed the peanut butter cookie onto Julie's tray.

"I can't imagine English without him," Ann said.

It sickened Melissa to see Miss Elbert standing where Harold Masters always recited. Her only comfort was that the teaching part of the semester had ended.

"Use this week to study for Friday's final exam," Miss Elbert said. "Also, don't think you can cut any corners. Mr. Masters has already prepared your test, and I have it."

Dan poked Joey. "Talk about haunting us from the grave."

Melissa shot him a mean look.

Coming home did not improve her mood. Her mother had bad news, too. Steve was gone.

"At least for a few weeks," Darlene said, with a little sigh. "He's temporarily taken a night cleaning job in Jenson. He's sorry, but he needs the extra money."

Brian slumped at her words. Suddenly, Melissa realized how much she, too, depended upon Steve's enduring presence. The house seemed vacant without him.

Her mother hugged Brian and said, "How about helping me make dinner?"

Brian jerked away from her. "No! I don't want to make any stupid dinner. I don't want to eat ever again!"

"Brian!" Melissa yelled, surprised at his outburst.

He threw his books on the floor, stomped to his room, and slammed the door.

Melissa started after him, but her mother stopped her.

"Let him go," Darlene said, stooping to pick up the books.

She sounded drained. Steve always said she worked too hard, but Melissa had ignored it, for her mother had always worked hard.

"I'll help with dinner, Mom." Melissa opened the refrigerator door. "What did you want to make?" Steve was eventually coming back, but what about John and Henry?

Melissa opened cans of condensed soup and tuna. Her mother boiled water for macaroni and crushed a small bag of potato chips for a casserole topping. With a tight throat, Melissa set only three plates at the dining room table instead of the usual four. She hoped Steve wasn't making excuses to stay away.

Even Snowbell sensed their mood. With drooping tail and ears, the cat hunched on the couch and watched dinner preparations with dull eyes. Melissa straightened the napkins one last time and joined her. Snowbell did not move closer, but Melissa absently scratched the cat's neck, anyway.

When her mother listlessly announced dinner, Melissa gave Snowbell one final, half-hearted pat, then plodded to her brother's room and knocked on his door.

"Go away!" came the muffled voice behind it.

Melissa tried the door handle, and, surprisingly, it turned. Brian was leaning against the headboard and reading a comic book. His face was red and puffy.

"Hey, doofus, can't you understand English?" Brian said.

The word "English," reminded Melissa of Mr. Masters. She blinked hard, then sat on her brother's bed and stroked his hair.

He pulled away from her. "Beat it."

"I'm sorry about Steve."

Brian only settled deeper into his pillow.

"I know how much you're going to miss him."

He yawned and turned a page.

"It's only for a little while."

His silence irritated her, so she grabbed Brian's book.

"Hey, give it back!" Brian cried.

He lunged for it, but Melissa shoved it under his bed. With all the junk he stashed there, he'd need weeks to find it. "You're being very selfish."

Brian crossed his arms and looked away.

"What about Mom? She lost a sick husband and now someone nice who helps her out has left! Do you care about her feelings? No! You are such a jerk."

She stomped her feet all the way to the door, hoping Brian felt guilty. Brian not only joined them for dinner, he offered to wash the dishes and take out the garbage, too, which only slightly stirred their mother from her gloom.

"I'll help," Darlene said with a gaiety Melissa knew she did not feel.

Melissa grabbed the broom and reflected on Harold Masters' departure. As she reached for the dustpan, Melissa heard her mother say, "How odd."

"What?" Melissa swept up the dirt.

"My ring is gone. I could have sworn I left it on the sill last night."

Melissa set aside the broom and looked anxiously around the sink. "Did it fall?"

"I don't think so," Darlene said, looking puzzled. "I must have just misplaced it."

Melissa felt unconvinced. Her mother noticed and hugged her. "Don't look so glum. It will turn up."

Although she hated waking up in Henry Matthews' study, tonight Melissa actually looked forward to it. She needed to talk with him about why he left her school. She hoped it had nothing to do with their date. She prayed they were still friends.

That night, for the first time in many weeks, Melissa's sleep was uneventful. She had no Bryony dream, nor did she spend any part of the night in Henry Matthews' study. She woke up rested and refreshed, but very sad. What had happened to John and Henry?

Filled with unbearable grief, Melissa went through the motions of readying for school. When she reached the dining room, Brian was already at the table and fixing his eyes on his untouched cereal bowl. Their mother sat next to him, looking dazed, her coffee untouched. She forced a frail smile, as they walked out the door.

"Have a good day at school," Darlene said.

The entire day limped along minute by tormenting minute, making it impossible to concentrate on schoolwork. Her friends, remembering Melissa's quiet spells of the past, gave her plenty of space. Melissa barely noticed. The world, once again, had become a miserably, lonely place.

They ate canned stew in silence that evening, and she and Brian worked on homework in equal silence. He did not object to her presence in the dining room. Melissa watched the clock, impatient for bedtime, and decided to quit early anyway, crossing her fingers, as she set her alarm clock. She climbed into bed and leaned to switch off the light, and then remembered the music box. In the past, it had brought John Simons to her bedroom and to her dreams. Maybe, it would tonight, too.

Restraining eagerness the best she could, Melissa wound up the box and paused to listen to, *Bryony.* She traced a finger along a vine and waited for the music's magic to work tonight, then, PING! The music stopped.

No!

Melissa tried winding it again, but nothing turned. She stared in horrified disbelief at the silent box resting in her lap. Cradling her talisman between shaking hands, Melissa trudged back to the living room where her mother was pretending to watch television. Her book sat untouched on the table next to her, and she glanced up in surprise when she saw Melissa.

"Honey, I thought you went to bed."

Melissa, still trembling, sat on the couch next to her mother. "I did, but this broke. Can you fix it?"

Her mother examined the music box and shook her head. "It's so old, I doubt even Steve can fix it."

"Then, who can?"

"Honey, I don't know who," Darlene said, irritably. "I'm not sure anyone in Munsonville could work on it. I can ask Steve when I talk to him. Maybe, he knows someone in Jenson. I do know it can't be repaired tonight."

"Okay, okay."

Clasping the beloved music box near her heart, Melissa returned to her room. She wavered, then opened the nightstand drawer, pushed the music box to the back, and placed a book in front of it. Since she could not bear to look at it, there was nothing else to do, except climb into bed and turn off the light. She lay awake thinking about John and Henry long after her mother had shut off the television and gone to her room.

She had no dreams that night, or the next, or the one after that. All week Melissa dutifully, automatically, studied for final exams. When she walked out the door Friday morning, her mother reminded Melissa she had an after-school appointment with Dr. Anderson. Melissa limped through her tests. After school, her mother was waiting. She had wanted Steve to get Brian, but Steve had his second job. So, Brian went scowling to the doctor's office.

"The sacrifices I make for people," Brian mumbled out his window.

"I know someone who's staying in the waiting room," Darlene warned.

"Fine!" Brian retorted.

The only smiling person that afternoon was Dr. Anderson.

"Well, Melissa, I have some very good news for you," he said. "Your blood levels look good. I think the anemia is about gone. Let's consider discontinuing the iron supplements after the first of the year."

Melissa forced a return smile, but her insides felt dried and shriveled. Did John no longer need her blood? Had he found a new host, or was he cured, ready to begin his brand-new human life without her?

It was a quiet ride back to the Simons estate. In the old days, her mother would have drawn Melissa into a conversation. Today, she left her alone. When they turned onto the hill leading to the estate, Melissa abruptly asked to get out.

"What in the world?" Darlene braked hard. "Are you going to be sick?

"I just feel like walking," Melissa said. "Please, Mom."

"Me, too!" Brian's words stunned both Melissa and his mother, so he added, "What's the big deal? Can't a guy walk with his sister?"

302

Brian opened the door and leaped out before anyone could stop him. Melissa gave her mother a quick peck on her cheek. Not to be outdone, Brian walked to the car window and, unexpectedly, hugged his mother, too. Looking bewildered and waving a hesitant good-bye, their mother drove from sight.

Brian stared at Melissa. "Okay, what gives?"

"Nothing." Melissa looked towards the woods and shaded her eyes. The cold air promised snow, but so far, none came. The sun had begun to set, but the sky was otherwise clear. "I just feel like walking." She started toward the trail.

Brian caught her jacket sleeve. "I thought you were afraid of the mist."

"I am," Melissa said. "Well, I was. I always wanted to test Steve's theory about warm air and cool air, but never had a chance to do it, until today."

"Well, you're not going alone."

Melissa and Brian had not gone far before darkness descended. Still, nothing hazy hampered their way. There was no mist on the trail, no mist on the lake, and no mist at any point during their walk up the hill toward home.

"Maybe you imagined it," Brian said.

It was not what Melissa wanted to hear.

Her throat closed when they passed Simons Mansion. It seemed so empty, so desolate. Just a couple short weeks ago, it was paradise. Were John and Henry still in that basement, had they gone somewhere else, or was it only a dream, as Fr. Alexis suggested, a dream Melissa no longer needed?

"Did you have a nice walk?" Darlene asked when Melissa and Brian stepped through the back door.

She turned down the burner and placed a lid on a saucepan. An open can of spaghetti sauce sat on the counter.

"Sure," Melissa said, continuing past her mother and into her bedroom.

After dinner, Melissa was at odds with herself. Except for test results and the school party on Monday, school was finished until after the first of the year. She did not feel like reading, and she certainly did not feel like thinking. Instead, Melissa sat limply on the couch with Brian and her mother. After its opening credits, her mother left to make popcorn. The bowl sat untouched on

Brian's lap, even with extra butter. Melissa ditched the small group one hour into the movie, giving the excuse she was tired from final exams. Maybe tonight would be the long-awaited night.

With a jolt, she sat up. The room was dark. She did not remember switching off the light. Had her mother done it? Her clock said almost two in the morning, the same time she had first seen John Simons in her room, many weeks ago. Yet, tonight her room was empty. She could sense it. The outside was probably empty, too, but she had to be sure.

Fearing the worse and hoping for John, Melissa flung aside the covers. Her shaking hand slid between the window curtains, and she peered outside, but the night was clear and full of stars. She opened the curtains wide and looked around the yard. Not the tiniest wisp of mist. The cloud of disappointment hanging over Melissa burst. She crawled into bed, curled into a ball, pulled the covers over her head, and cried until dawn.

At breakfast, her mother said they were going Christmas shopping in Jenson.

"It's like a funeral around here." She looked at Melissa and Brian's dismal faces and tried to sound upbeat. "Heaven knows we've certainly had enough of those."

"I don't feel like Christmas shopping." Head in hand, Brian stirred his cereal around in his bowl, but he ate very little of it. Some of it sloshed over the sides, but no one said anything.

"Me, neither," Melissa said.

"We need to get out of the house," Darlene said. "We can mope in Jenson."

Back in Grover's Park, one couldn't miss the start of the holiday season. Garland angels topped streetlights, store windows delivered Christmas surprises with every glimpse, and a giant tree graced the center of town, which the mayor dedicated and lit with grand solemnity each Thanksgiving weekend at the conclusion of the annual Step Into Christmas parade. Munsonville's Main Street showcased none of that glamour. There was no elaborate décor and no signs advertising sale items for those special Christmas gifts.

True, someone ran a strand of blinking lights around the perimeter of the picture window of Sue's Diner, and Ann's mother hung a wreath on the front door of Dalton's Dry Goods, but those flaccid decorating attempts scarcely hinted that Christmas was fast approaching, which suited Melissa, for she felt no holiday spirit. She gazed at the tiny tree flaunting the front porch of the general store, then realized, with sudden astonishment, in all these months she had lived in Munsonville, she had never gone inside that building.

When Melissa's father was alive, her mother shopped and ran errands once a week, while Melissa and Brian completed their homework under their father's watchful eye. Shopping, for Melissa, meant going to the Grover's Park mall with her friends, so even accompanying her mother to the supermarket had never entered Melissa's mind.

Here, she was so engrossed in John that mundane, daily tasks escaped her. Did her mother shop in town while Melissa and Brian were in school, or had Steve, who did most of the cooking, buy their food?

Melissa wished that, with Munsonville behind them, she could banish depressing thoughts for an afternoon, but driving through the desolate countryside reminded Melissa of her carriage ride with Henry, only a week ago. The barren landscape intensified Melissa's ache for roses and firewood, the delicate fragrance of wildflowers on a summer afternoon, and the mouthwatering smells of a Simons Mansion dinner.

Thirty minutes later, Melissa was amidst the crowds who packed downtown Jenson seeking last minute bargains. Her mother rode around the block searching for a parking place. After the third trip, she squeezed the station wagon between two pick-up trucks. The car behind her blasted its horn.

"I think that man wanted your space, Mom," Brian said.

"Tough!" Darlene said, with uncharacteristic sharpness. "Remind me to come back in two hours," she added, softening. "I'll have to put more change in the meter."

While waiting for the traffic light to change, their mother put her arms around Melissa and Brian and hugged them.

"I'm really sorry I spoke that way, kids," Darlene said. "It wasn't a very good example. I know we're not in the Christmas mood, but let's have a good time anyway."

No one answered her.

Store windows boasted colorful Christmas decorations, more like Grover's Park than Munsonville, but to Melissa, they were hardly worth a second glance. One store featured eight, very tiny reindeer pulling a sleigh filled with toys, while Santa waved a mechanical arm at shoppers. Another window offered a winter wonderland of snowflakes, snowmen, snowwomen, and mitten-clad dolls engaged in a mock snowball fight. A third was full of games, trucks, and dolls, flanked by colorful packages tied with shiny bows and stacked in groups of threes, fours, and fives.

On nearly every street corner, a Santa Claus rang a bell, and shoppers dropped coins into his bucket.

"Merry Christmas!" Santa called to each one, as he distributed candy canes.

"It's to help the poor people," Melissa said to Brian.

"I know," Brian said.

They weaved aimlessly through the mob. The cold and gray stamped out hope. At first, Melissa wished it would snow, for flurries would mask the dreary sky, until she recalled the eighty-year-old carriage house lodging, somewhere in the past, a brand-new, eighty-year-old sleigh. John had pledged a sleigh ride through the woods on the day of the first snow. Would he still keep that promise?

"Wait!" Brian said.

He stopped outside a large window. An electric train ran around the tracks of a North Pole scene. He stood there, mesmerized by the sleek cars winding up hills, through tunnels, and around lakes.

"Boy, Steve and I could have some fun with this," Brian said, then stopped. He turned away from the window, and Melissa avoided his crestfallen face.

"Let's go inside," Darlene said, putting her arm around his shoulders and drawing him close to her. To Melissa's surprise, Brian let her.

They meandered up and down the aisles, pretending to look at rows of toys. Melissa ignored the collector Victorian dolls. Her mother did not have to tell Brian to keep his hands to himself.

"I want to go home," Brian whined.

"Let's get some hot chocolate," Darlene quickly said.

They left the store and trudged to a small restaurant. Although not yet lunchtime, shoppers filled the dining area. They found a table in the back, near the kitchen, amidst the banging of

306

frying pans. Her mother ordered three hot chocolates topped with mounds of whipped cream. In the past, pausing in their holiday activities to get warm and drink hot chocolate was a cherished tradition. Now, no one cared.

"This isn't very good hot chocolate," Melissa said, to no one in particular.

The speakers in the diner played a children's chorus singing, *Jingle Bells,* mocking Melissa with the thrill of horse-drawn sleigh rides. Brian didn't eat the whipped cream with his fingers. Darlene paid the bill, and they left half-full cups.

As they plodded along the sidewalk, Melissa had an idea that cheered her slightly. She fell behind her mother and poked Brian in the ribs.

"We should get Mom something," she said, "for Christmas."

Brian perked up. "I have some allowance money left."

Her mother's face brightened when Melissa suggested stopping at the bookstore. Inside, Brian scoured a new comic book, and Melissa lingered by an exhibit of hardcover books. Darlene browsed the shelves.

"What are you looking at, Liss?" Brian asked, the crook of a candy cane hanging from his mouth.

"Where'd you get that?"

"Santa," he said and pointed to the red-suited man standing outside the door. "I dropped a quarter in the bucket."

Under *New Releases,* Melissa pointed to the title capturing her attention: *The Prosecutor Rests and Other Short Stories* by Harold Masters.

"Doesn't he teach at our school?" Brian licked his sticky fingers.

"He did, until last week. Mom likes to read his books, and she doesn't have this one. Maybe, a good book would get her mind off stuff."

"Okay, let's get it."

She mostly wanted to distract her mother, and yet, Melissa found herself stroking the book jacket. She knew Henry hadn't touched it, but somehow, holding the words he wrote made her feel closer to him. When she stopped, Melisa noticed Brian's queer stare.

While they stood in line to pay for the book, Brian picked out a large piece of foil-wrapped chocolate, decorated like a tree ornament, to accompany the gift. "We can tape it on the book when we wrap it," he said.

The clerk handed Melissa the bag, just as their mother approached the front of the store. Brian waved at her, and she wound her way through the crowds to reach them.

"Well," Darlene said, with an exuberance Melissa suspected she did not feel. "I'm glad to see you have a dash of Christmas spirit in you, after all.

"No peeking," Brian warned her.

They left Jenson before the meter time expired. When they returned home, Brian insisted on grabbing the bag. Melissa didn't argue with him. She was in no mood for wrapping Christmas presents. They had driven past Simons Mansion twice that day, and twice Melissa had closed her eyes against the royal, old building, once full of future assurance. How could she tolerate living here? Why had her vampires forsaken her? Sleep that night was hollow and restless. Twice, Melissa woke and checked her clock. She flipped over her pillow, and sleep dragged her into a woozy, ghastly marsh of silhouettes spewing unintelligible wails until they became barks. Scooter!

Melissa rose to let him outside, but when she opened the patio door, Scooter was a Newfoundland. His face twisted in demonic fury, and he growled and bared his fangs at her before disappearing among the naked trees and into the chilly night. Melissa grabbed a flashlight and her heavy coat, then stepped outside.

"Scooter!"

A faint, screeching bark answered her, and the landscape changed. Simons Mansion reached to the moon, and its warped, grotesque stones jeered at Melissa when she hurried past it. Nearing hysteria, Melissa swung her flashlight back and found herself near the woods' entrance. She heard Scooter inside, barking for her to come and find him. She wiped her palms on her jeans and swallowed hard.

"It's now or never!" she shouted

Melissa dashed into Simons Woods and shouted Scooter's name, but only silence answered back. She choked down panic and continued running and shouting, "Scooter!"

The flashlight flickered and went out. Solid blackness closed around Melissa. The sky and earth, foliage and pathway vanished under its cover of nothing. She banged her flashlight on her leg and flipped the switch on and off. There was only impenetrable night and the barely perceptible sound of rustling leaves. A spiraling mist encircled Melissa; she jumped at a swish on her right, whirled toward it, and softly called, "Scooter?" hoping it was the dog, and hoping it wasn't.

Silence.

"John?" she called, in her softest, most optimistic whisper.

Out of the grayish gloom, a cloaked figure appeared. It was Kellen Wechsler.

CHAPTER 29: UP IN SMOKE

Instinctively, Melissa stepped backward, away from the dark, rigid figure, who gazed at Melissa with deep hatred.

"Do I intimidate you?" Kellen said.

Incredulous, Melissa stared back. Kellen was the mist?

"I won't harm you. On the contrary, I have come to give you immortal life." Kellen's voice was silky, but, through the haze, his eyes blazed red with malevolence.

He's pure venom, Melissa thought. She wouldn't have liked him even when he was alive.

"He's done with you, Melissa," Kellen continued. "It is acceptable, now, to call you 'Melissa?'"

She said nothing.

"If you choose to remain with John, he will destroy you. Do you comprehend?"

Afraid now, Melissa squeezed her eyes shut, willing to awaken in her own bed, but solid ground remained beneath her feet. She counted to ten, but the wind still whistled through the trees, and the mist's cool film settled on her throat. She opened her eyes and steeled herself for the inevitable. How ironic that, after all the times she had feared John might hurt her, she would face death at the hands of his enemy.

"Do not despond, fair maiden. Kellen has come to save you. You can flee with me and live well." He took a step forward.

A strong desire to defend John against his nefarious manager diminished her mounting terror.

"That's a lie! John wouldn't hurt me, but you killed Lisa Harding." "Yes, that's true, but Lisa was a silly fool. You, Melissa, are an intelligent young woman. You outwitted John at his own game, no mean accomplishment. You will be a more fitting...." Kellen stopped and smiled, drawing out the moment. "....assistant."

Assistant? Whatever did he mean by that? Her eyes zipped around her, seeking escape. If she could ever voluntarily arise from a dream, now would be a good time.

"I forget my manners. This is no place to converse with a damsel.

We need something more suitable. Something like...."

A thoughtful look replaced the diabolical one. "Something like this!" Kellen snapped his fingers, and the woods vanished.

A giant, ceramic bathtub sat in the center of a spacious domed room. Tunic-clad women bathed Kellen with large sponges. He closed his eyes, reclined his head, and luxuriously stretched out his arms, as he lounged in the tub and purred.

"Oh, much better." Kellen opened his eyes. "Care to join me, Melissa?"

One of the women snickered. Kellen's smile fled. "Silence!"

The women vanished.

"Where was I? Oh yes, eternal life." He reached for a bathrobe and batted his eyes. "Turn around."

Stupefied, Melissa could only gawk at Kellen. He made circular motions with his hands and added, "Go on, turn, turn."

Melissa obediently faced the wall. Kellen snapped his fingers, and she sank into an oversized chair in a large hotel suite. Kellen wore so many gold chains around his neck, Melissa wondered how he managed to hold his head upright. Kellen poured himself a drink and dropped onto the plush sofa opposite Melissa.

"I sense your curiosity about my vampire roots." He tipped the glass to his lips, took a swig, and waited for her response.

Melissa sighed loud and hard. "Can I go home now?"

Kellen tipped his head and pretended to blush. "Oh, Melissa, how you tease!"

Melissa looked down, more annoyed now than afraid. Kellen seemed too unstable for rational conversation. Was he always like this, even with John?

"As I was saying, like you, I did not seek eternal life. Instead, it followed me until it offered itself, much as I now offer it to you."

She pretended to examine the checkered pattern on the sofa.

"Pay attention to me!" Kellen threw the glass over her head. It hit the wall, shattered into a thousand pieces, and dribbled amber liquid to the carpet. "Will hamburger and fries do?"

"What?" said Melissa.

She and Kellen were sitting inside a convertible at an old-fashioned drive-through restaurant. Melissa flattened her poodle skirt and reached up to touch the large bow holding her ponytail. Kellen, hair slicked, slouched beside her in dungarees and a white T-shirt. After their order arrived, Kellen parked under a tree. He was halfway through his French fries, when he gestured to her food and said, "Eat, Melissa, eat."

She scooted closer to the door. She wasn't touching anything he brought her. Kellen devoured his hamburger in three bites.

"I was working in the fields one day and saw what I perceived to be an angel," he said. "Never having seen a vision, and, naturally being a God-fearing man, I crossed myself three times and stole another glimpse. You sure you won't have any fries?"

A movement flitted in front of the car. A massive crow had landed in the tree. Was it the way the sun hit the bird's dark, coffee-colored eyes, or did the evil-looking creature return her stare? Kellen slid her fries to him and munched a fistful.

"At first, I thought perhaps I was mistaken. I sweltered in the sun, for the day was considerably hot and bright. With a scintillating flash of brilliancy, the vision was gone. Then a ray of light streaked across the sky, and I beheld a dazzling creature of immense beauty, completely nude, with skeins of the reddest hair I had ever seen. I fell to my knees, and the apparition vanished."

312

He picked up Melissa's abandoned hamburger, tossed the pickle out the window, and took a large bite.

"I hurried home to tell the wife, but she merely scoffed at me. 'Bah! Kellen! You stayed in the sun too long.' No words of mine induced her to believe my curious tale. I, for my part, never forgot it."

Kellen lit a stick of incense on the three-legged table across the room, settled onto the beanbag beside Melissa, and held her fast. Her tie- dyed T-shirt matched his. Red plastic beads hung from Kellen's neck and ceiling. A jasmine-scented cloud hovered over them. Kellen sneered through his beard and pushed long, snarled hair out of his eyes.

"I never saw my angel again, until the day I expired. Several of my children were already deceased, and I knew my last breath was imminent. Breathing was labored, and I soon observed the reason for it. My angel had positioned herself atop my chest."

He chortled. Melissa yawned. A wave of anger distorted Kellen's face, but he quickly regained sufficient composure to reward her disinterest with a leer. He gripped her neck and pried his fingers into her shoulder.

"With heavenly kisses and caresses, she comforted me in my final moments. I never fancied death would be so sweet. Between our murmurings, my angel asked me, 'Kellen, how would like to escape death?' Now that was an intriguing question, considering the moment was impending. 'Fair angel,' I sighed, 'not wishing to sound ungrateful, I desire only to acquiesce to my fate. For what in life shall I return? A nagging wife? Impudent children? An unyielding ground? Nay, angel, I accept my destiny.'"

The candle on the stool before them flickered and went out. With his free hand, Kellen reached under the beanbag chair for a lighter, talking as he rekindled the flame.

"The angel gazed ever so charmingly into my eyes and said, 'Kellen, I am your destiny.' 'Then, angel,' I said, 'I surrender to your will.' I closed my eyes and waited for death to overtake me. Paroxysms of pain seared through my neck as she clamped her fangs and liberally partook of my blood until I passed from life to the underworld. She was right. Death had not awaited me, after all."

Shadows of orange, lime green, and magenta illuminated Kellen's face from the dance floor's disco ball. Kellen's white shirt, under his powder blue jacket, was open almost to his navel. He briefly watched the spiraling couples, then stroked Melissa's feathered hair. She shrank from his touch.

"Oddly, as my blood passed away, my vitality returned," Kellen said, "and, with it, an ungovernable lust for blood and human flesh. Oh, how the spirit taunted my need, even as she smacked her lips, still dripping with my blood. 'Help me, oh my angel,' I implored, but she just shrieked in glee at my anguish. The shame and the craving were more than I could swallow."

Kellen's fingers twisted wound into Melissa's hair and bore into her scalp.

"My hands went round her neck intending to snap it, but she dissolved into air. I raged. Someone had to pay and pay they did. I embarked on a killing spree that day, beginning with my remaining family and not ceasing until half the village met their demise. Oh, what an inferno I created when I burned up their buildings, but that was only the beginning of my rebellion. My libido for blood was hardly satisfied."

He crushed his cigarette and swerved his desk chair away from Melissa. With gloved hands, she pulled down the jacket of her tailored suit and adjusted the slant of her hat. Kellen, in a beige and black pin striped suit, stared pensively out the shabby office window at the evening traffic. His matching Fedora hung on a wall hook.

"Of course, reason dictated the requirement of regular blood feedings. I also realized subtleness might insure my survival. My scheme was simple. I permitted my victims to continue their human state in return for consistent meals, money, and social favors. I readily destroyed those who betrayed me. Thus, I flourished."

Melissa was really angry now. "That's how you got John!"

"Ah, she speaks!" Kellen cried in exaggerated delight. "My spirit soars! Yet," his expression darkened, "they are words of the revolting John Simons. She crushes my heart!" He turned beseeching eyes toward Melissa. "Must we speak about John?"

Seething with contempt for him, Melissa said through tight lips, "We must."

314

"I initially encountered John at a small concert hall in Berlin. As a musician and as a man, he instantaneously bewitched me. The movement of his fingers manipulating the piano keys, the haunting music he composed, and the fine lines of his body made him an exquisite specimen for my collection. Still, I had to be certain. For several months, I trailed John ("Stalked, more like it," Melissa muttered under her breath), as he rendered a number of outstanding concerts. Such distinctive talent must be recognized and distributed to the world. I had the means to champion his cause, for a fee, of course."

"Of course," Melissa said. How she loathed him!

"I found John to be a reasonable man, and he willingly accepted my proposal. How lamentable for you, Melissa, that you will never know the intoxication of John's blood, none so delectable, mellow, full-bodied, with no lingering aftertaste."

Kellen's tongue grazed over his lips. Melissa shuddered and gagged. She desperately loved John, but she could never, never drink his blood.

"You're disgusting," were the only words she managed to sputter.

His rapturous countenance disappeared. "Then, a woman spoiled it all," he said. "Such is man's misfortune since the garden."

He turned the yellow, plastic mold upside down and patted it into shape. Only red swim trunks covered Kellen's deeply tanned form. He poured water over sand and scooped it into a wall. Melissa, in a purple bikini, knelt on a beach towel and shaded her eyes from the dazzling sun. The rays blistered her body, and the broiling-hot sand burned through the towel. She looked for covering and found none, more fearful of the gloating way Kellen contemplated her than the heat.

"Rub some suntan oil onto my back?" Kellen said with a seductive wave of the amber bottle before her eyes.

Melissa turned away, just as Kellen heaved the bottle far into the lake. Furiously, he tore into the sand and carved a trench around his castle. Only after he draped seaweed on its walls did Melissa realize the castle was Simons Mansion.

"After John's treachery, I never again serviced any person to that degree. My only hosts are women, since their wiles are less enamoring. I revel in them, extort their blood, and liquidate them in due time, but, as I previously said, you, Melissa, are different. You tricked John, and he will never forgive you. However, I relish your sporting demeanor. We will make a superior team."

Kellen leaned backward on his elbows, lowered his sunglasses, and smiled beseechingly at her, yet his countenance exulted in approaching victory, as he savored the lull and rejoiced at her discomfort. Why didn't the extreme heat bother him?

"I most certainly will not!" she shouted.

Somewhere above her, an animal screamed, a high-pitched, fading siren. Vultures circled above her head; thick, menacing thunder clouds rolled across the sky; and lightning careened from side to side. Kellen's fist smashed into the castle, and he laughed like a lunatic from some twisted, B-grade movie. They were back in the woods.

"Then, hurry to the fate you deserve!"

He exited in a raging blast of smoke. Melissa blinked against the flickering, crackling light from the library fireplace. John was sitting at his desk, shuffling through papers, and adding a signature here and there. His hair, draped over his black waistcoat, shimmered especially fair in the firelight. A lone candelabrum flickered at one end of John's desk, a sure sign Mildred was late lighting the lamps. Sharp desire violently stabbed her, and she flinched. She had missed him so much!

Henry, forehead creased in deep concentration, hunched in a chair across from John, sorting more papers into piles. For many days, Melissa had feared never seeing Henry again, and now here he was, wearing the same midnight blue suit she had admired on their date. How long ago that seemed!

"You!" she exclaimed in joy and relief. "I thought you had gone. I thought...."

Her voice trailed way at the sight of John, who paused in mid- signature, murderous eyes penetrating hers.

"Fooled again by the same pair," he said in a voice so calm Melissa knew only suppressed anger and bitterness produced it. "Well, almost the same pair." John glowered at Henry. "Eighty years later and still you soil all that is mine."

He turned back to her. "Melissa, you wanted to play Bryony, and you did it, my darling, right to the unfaithfulness. I salute you for a brilliant performance."

His words stunned her. John had known about Henry and Bryony? She looked for Henry's reaction, but his thin, sallow face had none. That's when Melissa noticed the baggy clothes, shrunken frame, and frail, bony fingers gripping the pen.

"Henry?" Melissa asked anxiously.

The house steward concentrated on his task and did not reply. Could John really hold a century-long grudge? Even so, why would he be mad at her? Many times John had sent Melissa home with Henry, insisted even. Besides, Melissa was not really married to John, not yet. It was all pretend, a fairy tale play for Melissa and a bit of blood for John.

A bit of blood.

Melissa tilted her head and looked at John. What was it Henry had said? He was forbidden to drink from Melissa's neck because her blood now belonged to John. Surely, John's intolerance would not extend to saving Henry's life!

"Oh, John, let me explain," Melissa began, then faltered at John's icy detachment.

"Go to your room, Bryony. I'll deal with you there."

His voice was terse and tinged with hatred, but he had called her Bryony! John was angry, but not too angry. He would listen to Melissa's explanation after he calmed down. Melissa would explain it all, later, when John came to her room.

To prove she understood him, Melissa kissed the top of John's head, but John only added his signature to another sheet of paper. She gently shut the library doors behind her. They obviously needed to finish their work.

With the lightest heart she'd had in days, Melissa happily climbed the stairs, gliding her fingers along the banister, feeling the heavy burden lifting. She almost started singing, so great was her relief, but caught herself. John did not, yet, share her mood, so why needlessly annoy him. Still...*John was back!*

Melissa sneezed twice, and she quickly covered her nose, which made her sneeze again. Through watering eyes, she beheld her dusty hand.

Dust! The servants were obviously slacking; she must speak to John.

The unexpected chill from Bryony's room stole Melissa's breath. Shivering hard, she grabbed the poker and stoked the nearly extinguished fire into comforting orange flames. She decided against lighting the gas lamp, for she didn't trust herself fiddling with kerosene, even though a candle wouldn't provide enough light for reading. Besides, she would have to sneak a book from Henry's study, which was certainly not worth incurring additional wrath from John. The fire was dreamy enough all by itself, and, very soon, John would share it with her. She settled on the couch under the window and remembered the first night John kissed her, under the moon at Albert Brumfeldt's house, away from the hideous guests. She relived the languid kisses in the morning room when John presented her with the garden party invitation and nearly cried at the love melting his eyes during their wedding ceremony. No, not their wedding ceremony, John and Bryony's wedding. One day John would be human. And then....

The clock ticked off the passing seconds, then chimed once. Melissa's eyes flew open. An entire hour had passed, and no John. The fire's easy warmth rippled her into drowsiness. She dozed and danced with John in the Rutherford's brilliant white ballroom. When the waltz ended, John jammed her close and pressed his cheek against hers. She shook with excitement of the anticipated kiss.

"Damn you, Melissa," he hissed in her ear.

She awoke with a start, teeth chattering. The fire burned low, and still no John. Where was he? Had he forgotten about her?

"Now, stop that," Melissa said aloud. "Be patient. John will come. He promised."

She yawned, reached for the pink and green quilt from the back of the couch, pulled it cozily to her neck, and drifted away to sleep under the faint scent of kerosene. Finally, Mildred is lighting the lamps, Melissa thought sleepily.

She paced back and forth until she made up her mind. She had to see what was delaying him. If she was careful, John would never know. She could just peek between the library doors. As Melissa tiptoed down the stairs, a mist from the first floor drifted up and over the staircase. It

cooled and thickened the closer Melissa came to the library, slowing her steps. Kellen? Her vision blurred, and she groped for the gap between the double doors until her fingers felt their gap. She peered inside. Henry rose to leave. Why, Melissa thought, feeling foolish, John would be upstairs in minutes.

As Melissa turned around, a slight movement captured her attention and held it. Henry shuffled away from John, so he did not see it, but Melissa did. The oak beam and silver sword no longer hung on the wall behind his desk.

"No!"

Soundless words dissipated into mist. She tugged and silently banged on the doors. The stake sailed into Henry's back and glinted through his chest; Henry's head bounced onto the floor before his bodiless frame fell. Through the haze, John glowered directly at her. Melissa shrank back; his eyes seared into hers; the mist spun her into a cocoon; and the candelabra hit the doors. Crackling flames choked Melissa awake, and she bolted upright, submerged in smoke. Springing to her feet, Melissa grabbed a bedpost, groped for the exit, and desperately swiped the air. *Where was that door?* Stay low, her first grade teacher had said, so Melissa dropped to the ground, smacked into the curved leg of the toilet table, and pawed through acrid smoke for the elusive doorknob *Think!*

"Wake up!" she wheezed aloud. *"Wake up! Wake up! Wake up!"*

Heart pounding, Melissa gasped for air and cried in exhaustion and despair. Above, the smoke condensed and curled until a translucent form emerged, the one person in the world Melissa was certain hated her.

It was Bryony.

CHAPTER 30: THE SECOND TIME IS HARDER

Transparent, ethereal, and swaddled in white garments, Bryony stepped from the pouring smoke and gazed unblinking at Melissa.

Was she angry or only sad? Did she resent Melissa's intrusion into her room, into her life? Her empty expression held no clue. She only stretched out thin, clear hands, but Melissa, even in the throes of a coughing fit, shrank away from the ghostly clutches.

A blast of cold air flew out as Bryony sprang into Melissa and hurled her at the window, slapping icicles across Melissa's face. She had passed through the glass! Melissa sucked the pure, cold night air into her lungs and breathed it, gratefully, out again, as she drifted onto the ground.

She landed with a gentle bump, then opened her eyes to thank her savior, but Bryony had vanished. Thick, black smoke poured from the upstairs windows. Someone pounded on the front door and shouted, "Melissa! Open up! Melissa!"

It was Steve, trapped inside.

Melissa scrambled to her feet and rushed up the porch steps to free him. A bang, and she bolted upright. Her bedroom door lay on the floor.

Steve grabbed her arm and yanked her to her feet. "Hurry up! We're leaving. The mansion is on fire."

On fire?

Melissa quickly threw jeans over pajama bottoms and slid her feet into shoes. Her mother and Brian stood in the living room, dressed and ready to go. She wrapped her arms around Melissa and hugged her.

"Thank heavens!" Darlene cried. "Melissa, how can you sleep so hard?"

Steve threw Melissa's jacket at her and hustled them all to the front door. Without warning, Brian broke free of Steve's grasp and ran to his bedroom.

"What in the world?" Darlene started to follow him.

"No!" Steve pushed her aside and beat Brian to the door.

"Where's Snowbell?" Brian cried. "I'm not going without her!"

Melissa had forgotten about Snowbell. "Oh, please find her Steve!"

Steve ran through the house shouting, "Snowbell!" but the cat did not appear.

"Let's go!" Steve flung open the front door.

"No! I won't!" Brian planted his feet on the floor and crossed his arms.

"Oh, yes, you will!"

Steve slung Brian over his shoulder. Brian kicked, punched, and screamed all the way to the car. "I'm not leaving without Snowbell! I'm not! I'm not! I'm not!"

Steve tossed him onto the front passenger seat. The bright orange flush eerily lit up the night sky. Brian braced his feet against the door, but Steve held the lock button down and started down the hill. Crackles popped and licked the air; Melissa's throat burned. Thick gray smoke overshadowed the moon; roaring, oscillating red and yellow tongues slit through the mansion and shot flares high into the sky.

Fire trucks and squad cars flew up the hill from Munsonville, Jenson, and even Evansville, which was almost an hour away. Brian stopped struggling, mouth hanging. An unfamiliar policeman approached Darlene's car and motioned Steve to stop.

"You have to leave the area, sir," he said.

"We are, officer," Steve said, trying to steady his voice. "This woman and her children live behind the mansion. I'm taking them off the property for the night." He paused and looked at the spectacle outside his window. "Can they save it?"

"It doesn't look good."

With a heavy sigh, Steve continued down the drive. "That mansion has always been a part of Munsonville," he said. There was real sorrow in his voice.

Tears ran down Melissa's face as watched the fire from the rear view window. "John," she barely breathed. "Oh, John!"

The loss of him was more than she could bear. Melissa would now flounder through life, alone, while John spent eternity with Bryony and his baby. Or was it Henry's baby? Did it even matter now? Henry! Who would take care of her now?

"Thank you," she whispered to the steamy glass, "for looking out for me." Wherever Henry was, she hoped he heard her.

Brian rubbed his eyes with the back of his hand and moaned, "Oh, Snowbell! I tried to save you."

In the fire's evil glow, Steve's face was drawn, but he reached out and ruffled Brian's head.

"Cats are pretty smart," he said. "Chances are, she's hiding in the woods and enjoying a nice, fat mouse."

They neared Main Street. The first few flakes of winter snow were falling. Melissa watched its silent appearance, with a sadness only a return to the past could alleviate. Thick, slippery slush soon buried the road.

Munsonville Inn's desk clerk clucked his tongue. "What a shame about the mansion," he said. "What a complete shame. No chance of salvaging the old place?"

"They don't think so," Steve said wearily, signing the register.

"Well, Munsonville won't be the same without it."

I won't be the same without it, Melissa thought.

Brian slipped his hand into Steve's larger one. "Don't go," Brian whispered.

"I won't, sport," Steve said. He squeezed Brian's hand in return.

No one said a word during the elevator ride to the third floor and down the narrow hallway. Just before Melissa followed her mother and Brian into the bedroom, she grabbed the hem of Steve's jacket. He turned around, startled, his eyes questioning.

322

"Thank you," she said, standing on her toes and kissing his cheek. "Really. For everything. I'm so glad you're back."

The worry lines abated. He warmly returned the hug, saying only, "Me, too." He started toward the elevator, but Melissa wasn't finished.

"Steve," she said. "Where do you live?"

He stopped again, baffled. "Why do you ask?"

"No reason. I just wondered."

"I have an apartment above Sue's Diner."

"Oh," Melissa said, wondering why he had never mentioned it. "Is it nice?" she added, doubtfully, recalling the diner's shabby appearance.

"It's not bad," Steve said. "I like it for sentimental reasons. Now, off to bed."

"Okay." What good was sleep without Bryony dreams? "Good- night, Steve."

"Good-night, Melissa."

The next morning, Steve treated them to breakfast at the diner. Brian whooped when they stepped outside the inn. Eight inches of snow had fallen during the night.

"Boy, oh, boy!" he yelled. "I wish we were home. What a snowman I'd build!"

With a steady eye on Melissa, Brian picked up two handfuls of snow and packed them together. As Brian started to throw, a second snowball knocked it to the ground. Brian spun around. Steve was chuckling.

"Well, I..." Brian was speechless.

"If you're going to play tricks, be prepared to play with the big boys," Steve said.

Melissa scarcely noticed. She had awakened crying into her pillow, still dreaming she and John were wrapped under blankets and gliding through the snow in an Arabian horse-drawn sleigh, with the sounds of the jingling bells filling the air.

The diner felt steamy after the cold walk. They placed their orders, and then Steve stepped outside. He soon returned, looking grim. Under his arm, he carried a folded copy of *The Munsonville Times*.

"I've got some bad news, I'm afraid," he said.

He handed the paper to Melissa. Wondering, she took it from him and opened it. The waitress poured more coffee. Melissa read the headline aloud, Remains of *Two Bodies Found in Mansion Ruins.*

Brian stopped drawing on his placemat, and her mother choked on her coffee. "Steve!" Darlene said.

Steve motioned for quiet. "Go ahead, Melissa," he said.

Why did Steve want *her* to read it? Melissa glanced at Steve, but he looked at her so oddly, she could only take a deep breath and plunge into the story.

Firefighters battling the fire at Simons Mansion early Sunday morning discovered the remains of two people.

They found the partially decomposed body of Kimberly Whitney, 17, of Grover's Park, Ill., at the bottom of the cellar stairs, despite police insistence that they had thoroughly searched the area.

Police Chief Tom Harper refused to comment, but Mayor Pete Rogers is demanding answers.

Darlene laid a soft hand on Melissa. "Oh, honey, I am so sorry."

Kimberly really *had* entered the mansion! Did she trip in the dark and tumble to her death, or had Kimberly encountered someone who hated trespassers, someone who ensured she would never reveal the mansion's secret? If so, why hadn't Melissa seen the body when she was in the basement with Henry? Were her time travels simply vivid dreams? Hot tears burned Melissa's eyes, but she continued.

Kimberly disappeared early Oct. 12 while visiting a home on the Simons' estate. An autopsy will be performed, but it appears Kimberly died from a broken neck.

A second body, a decapitated skeleton, was lying in a first floor room. Police are uncertain at this point of the body's identity, but the remains do not appear new. No missing people have been reported.

Melissa slowly closed the newspaper. Hope flickered once more. "They only found two bodies?"

Steve peered over the top of his coffee cup. "What do you mean, 'Only two?'" he said in a sharp voice. "Two bodies aren't enough for you?"

Her mother and Brian also stared at her, and Melissa felt her face grow hot as she stammered for words. "Maybe, homeless people had gotten trapped inside over the years?"

"Hmm," was all Steve said, but Melissa knew he didn't quite believe her. No matter. Steve couldn't prove anything.

Her mother reached for the newspaper and read the title at the bottom of the page: *Historic Mansion Burns to the Ground.*

A fire destroyed the 80-year-old mansion once belonging to internationally renowned composer and pianist John Simons. Firefighters fought for several hours to control the blaze. The cause of the fire is not yet determined.

Brian kept his head over his drawing, but Melissa knew he suspected the ghost.

The village acquired the property this summer. Officials had hoped to renovate the aging structure, formerly privately owned, into a major tourist attraction. Restoration was scheduled to begin this spring. The village board has called an emergency meeting for Monday evening to assess the damages and decide the feasibility of reconstruction.

Darlene set the paper down and shook her head ruefully. "Well, I'm out of a job."

"That makes two of us," Steve said, "although the village has plenty of other maintenance work to keep me busy, if I wanted it."

Darlene looked surprised. "You don't want it?"

"Not...sure."

Melissa blinked and sat up straight. Steve was a hard worker. Her mother said he needed the money. Why wouldn't he want it?

Her mother looked up at him, seeking his face for answers. "So, what do we do?"

A queer expression passed over Steve's face, as he reached into his pocket. "There's only one thing left to do," he said quietly.

He slid back his chair and lowered himself onto his knees. With a solemn face, Steve took her mother's hand and set a small, gift-wrapped package on her palm.

"Darlene, I love you so much." Steve's voice broke. "Will you marry me?"

Melissa was stunned. *Marry him?* Her mother had said Steve and her were just friends. When had they fallen in love? Where was the romance, like with John and Bryony? She glanced at Brian, but he was beaming from ear to ear. He didn't look at all surprised.

Her mother's face crumpled, and she softly said, "Oh, for Pete's
sake."

Laughing, crying, and shaking her head in pure bewilderment, her mother's trembling hands struggled to remove the paper. She paused, and then with a deep breath, opened the box. A tiny diamond ring nestled inside the red plush, its single stone flashing and sparkling in the diner's morning light.

"Ohhh," Darlene breathed, sounding more like Katie and less like the mother Melissa had known all her life. "I don't know what to say."

Before she could stop herself, Melissa quickly blurted out, "Say, 'yes,' Mom!"

"Yeah, Mom, say it," Brian echoed.

Darlene threw her arms around Steve's neck. "Yes!" she cried. "Yes! Yes! Yes!"

Melissa watched her mother, face shining with excitement, lean against her chair, take the ring from its box, and hold it before her face.

"It's so beautiful!" she said earnestly to Steve. "Oh, I hope it fits."

"It fits all right," Steve said, with a grin that reminded Melissa of Brian when he was up to something. "I borrowed your wedding ring." "You did what?"

"You left it on the windowsill."

326

Steve reached into his other pocket and returned the missing ring. Then he slid on the engagement ring, leaned up, and kissed her, the first time Melissa had seen him do it. The entire restaurant burst into applause, but Steve didn't stop. With a jubilant look, Brian dropped his pencil and high-fived an astonished Melissa.

That's why Steve was working the second job! He needed money to buy her mother a ring. He wasn't leaving; he was staying forever. Together, they would be a real family.

After breakfast, Steve and her mother went to the cottage to collect some clothes and her mother's typewriter. Melissa and Brian remained at the inn and played with a deck of cards Steve had brought from his apartment. They were halfway into their second game before Brian mentioned the fire.

"What happened, Liss?" he asked. "Do you think the ghost started it?"

Melissa set down a king. "No," she said.

Brian drew from the deck. "No, you don't think the ghost started it, or no, you don't think there's a ghost?"

What should she say to him? How would she make him understand what she herself did not comprehend?

Melissa played the last three cards. "I'm out." She looked at his glum face. "Oh come on, Brian. There's no such thing as a ghost."

Her brother stared at her, but said nothing, so she changed the subject. "Wow, Steve really surprised us today, didn't he?"

Brian picked up the cards and shuffled them. "What are you talking about?"

"You know, by asking Mom to marry him."

He stopped and looked at Melissa as if she had two heads. "Are you feeling okay? Steve's liked Mom ever since he met us."

"He has? It doesn't seem sudden to you?"

Shaking his head, Brian dealt out the cards. "Maybe, you should spend less time hiding in your room. What's so interesting in there, anyway?"

Melissa picked up her cards. "Nothing." It was the truth, now.

Brian gave her a suspicious look, then laid down a card. "Well, you should stop talking to yourself. It sounds creepy."

"Talking to myself?" Melissa felt uneasy. "When have I done that?"

"I heard you at night, sometimes, when I got a drink of water."

"Well, maybe, I talk in my sleep."

"Maybe," Brian conceded, but he didn't sound as if he believed it.

At noon, her mother and Steve returned from the Simons estate.

"Simons Mansion is gone," Darlene said. "I'm guessing the village won't rebuild it, either. It's too costly." "How'd the fire start?" Brian asked.

"I don't know," Steve said, pulling up a chair. "The police are investigating it." He looked at Melissa. "We saw the Whitneys downstairs."

"So soon? What's going to happen?"

"I imagine they'll want answers. Kimberly's parents don't look too happy."

"But we tried stopping her!"

"No one's blaming you, hon," Darlene quickly interjected. "They're more upset with the village board and the police."

Brian dealt a game of solitaire. "It was Kimberly's dumb fault for running off."

"I'm hungry," Steve quickly said. "Who wants pizza?"

Melissa didn't feel very hungry and, she guessed, neither did Steve. Brian, however, shouted, "Can I have extra pepperoni?"

"Sure," Steve said, reaching for the phone.

How strange to wake up in a motel room on a school day! With final exams completed, this last day consisted of refreshments and report card distribution. The school holiday parties of Melissa's past always were in classrooms, but because Munsonville School was so small, the teachers scheduled only one large party in the lunchroom, after the day's announcements, and after the students received their report cards. Even the school office closed for an hour, so all staff could participate, too.

This time, it was Brian's turn to shine. For the first time in his short life, he had straight A's. Melissa recalled the many hours Steve had invested into her brother, helping Brian study for tests and reviewing homework with him. She rapped knuckles with her little brother and said, "Way to go, Brian!"

Melissa wished her grades were higher. She received a B in every class except biology. Mr. Walczak had given her a C. She never had a C in her life and wondered what her father would say if he knew it? Frank blew up at B's. Then Sandy Rogers, the junior who had sat with Jack Cooper, approached Melissa with a large envelope.

"Hey, Melissa, could you do me a favor?" Sandy swayed on her platform shoes. "I'm supposed to give this to Mrs. Joyce, but I can't find her. My grandpa is really sick, and Mom is making me leave right now. Can you do it, please? I collected the report cards for all the kids who aren't here today, so Mrs. Joyce could mail them out."

Melissa bit into her cupcake and took the envelope. "Sure, no problem."

She tucked it inside her book bag, hoping she remembered to turn it in. The excited chatter of the younger students escalated into full-blown commotion. A certain man in a bright red suit had just entered the room. Behind her, Melissa heard three freshman girls talking.

"I hope I get a pet rock. That's what I told him last week."

"Not me. I want a mood ring."

"Have you seen my new autograph book?"

With round eyes and fingers in their mouths, the younger children inched their way to Santa. Two eighth grade boys, dressed like elves, had decorated a chair with red streamers and green balloons.

"Humph," Brian said. "Anyone can tell that's Mr. Walczak in a red suit."

"Well, you'd better not be the one telling," Melissa warned him. "I wonder how Mr. Walczak got the boys to wear those silly costumes, especially the tights."

"It was either that or detention for spit balls," Jack said, startling Melissa.

She hadn't seen him next to her. Several months ago, she would have fainted if Jack had stood this close to her. Now, Melissa scarcely noticed. She only wanted John back.

While Santa visited with the children, her friends finalized plans for Christmas break. Julie's mom would drive them into Jenson to see a movie. If the snow held, Katie's dad promised an afternoon of sledding in Simons Woods. Ann's parents said they could stay the night on New Year's Eve. Only Melissa didn't offer anything.

"I don't even know where I'll be living," she said, with sudden loneliness at the prospect of leaving, so different from her sentiments a few short months ago. What if John was still here, waiting for her? Would he find her in Grover's Park?

Santa now led the children in a few Christmas songs. They sang tunelessly, but enthusiastically: *Jingle bells, jingle bells, jingle all the way. Oh what fun it is to ride in a one horse open sleigh, ayyy!*

"Stupid song," Melissa scowled.

The party ended before she knew it. With choruses of, "Merry Christmas," enthusiastic hugs, and waving hands, the students burst out of school to the waiting bus. Steve and her mother, too, were outside, on their way to Jenson for last-minute Christmas shopping. Melissa dashed through the front door with her friends before she remembered the report cards.

"I forgot something," she called after them. "I'll talk to you guys later."

To Melissa's surprise, people swarmed the office. She thought everyone would be most anxious to go home. Melissa removed her stocking cap, untied her scarf, and tried not to squirm. After a very long while, she moved to the front of the line.

"Thanks, dear," Mrs. Joyce said, as she accepted the report cards. "I'm so sorry about the mansion. Will you be returning after Christmas?"

Melissa looked down and turned circles with her boot toe. "I don't know, yet."

"Well, if I don't see you again, good luck to you!"

Melissa nodded, glanced up, and tried to smile, but a mere, "Thanks," was all she could utter. Was this the end? Was it really over? Melissa plodded to the door and was halfway into the noisy hallway when Mrs. Joyce's voice called, "Oh, wait, Melissa!"

Puzzled, Melissa trudged back to the secretary.

"I almost forgot," Mrs. Joyce held up a padded, manila envelope. "Mr. Masters gave this to me last week. He said you left it in class."

Melissa took the envelope and stared hard at it. What was this?

"Oh yes, I did drop it," she fibbed and hurried toward the door. Stopping, hand on the knob, Melissa turned back. "Thank you! Merry Christmas and a Happy Year!"

"Merry Christmas to you too, dear. Hopefully, we'll see you in two weeks!"

Melissa sped out the door. The car was parked across the street, near the lake.

"Got everything?" Steve pushed back Darlene's seat.

I think so." Melissa climbed next to Brian and reached for the seat belt.

"What's that in your hand?" Brian asked through a mouthful of cupcake.

"Oh, nothing." Melissa swiftly slid the coveted envelope into her book bag. "It's just a Christmas card." She had no idea what Mr. Masters had sent her, but she wanted to be alone when she opened it, just in case.

"Only one more night at the inn," Darlene said, twisting in her seat to face them. "We go back to the cottage in the morning. The village decided to let us stay, until we make other arrangements."

"Which will be finalized before school begins," Steve said. "I have a job in Grover's Park."

"You're kidding!" Melissa said.

"He's not kidding," Darlene said, admiration creeping into her voice. "Steve contacted several janitorial companies near Chicago, and they all wanted to hire him."

"So when do we leave?" Brian bounced up and down on the seat, emphasizing each word. He landed on Melissa's lap, and she jabbed him in the ribs.

"Cut it out!" she hissed. "How many cupcakes have you eaten?"

"Your mother and I are driving to Grover's Park the day after Christmas to rent a house," Steve said. "You and Brian will spend a few days at the Daltons. When we return after the first of the year, it will be with a moving truck."

"As soon as the dust settles, we're getting married," Darlene said, sounding happier than she had in a long time.

The thought of returning to Grover's Park did not bring the ecstasy Melissa had expected. Amidst the happy babbling of her family, Melissa, hollow inside, miserably selected Christmas presents and tried to smile. Back at Munsonville Inn, Melissa trudged across the faded carpet to the elevator and wondered about the manila envelope. Brian frantically waved to make her hurry. Steve slid a hand between the doors and stepped out.

"You two go ahead," he said. "I want to talk to Melissa."

Steve led her to an easy chair near the lobby's largest window. He perched on the coffee table and looked straight at her.

"Melissa."

"I'm not upset about the ring, Steve, honest!" "Then, what?"

Melissa studied the carpet pattern, flowers with trailing vines. How could she explain her feelings to Steve without mentioning John?

"I don't want to move again," Melissa turned accusing eyes on him, "and I don't see how you can pack up and leave. You said Munsonville was your home."

If Steve didn't understand, no one would, but Steve rubbed his hands over his face, and said, "Well, now, I guess I did say that."

"Didn't you mean it?"

"Sure, I meant it, but...."

Steve stopped and sat erect, clenching and unclenching his hands, as he slowly formulated his thoughts.

"Since I've met your family, I've discovered home, for me, is not a place. It's being with your ma, you, and Brian. Your mother misses Grover's Park. Once I knew she'd have me, leaving Munsonville wasn't a hard choice to make."

Her eyes followed the carpet's winding stems under the coffee table and to a bubbling aquarium in the corner. Memories weren't sufficient for John; would they be enough for Melissa? She had no choice. They were moving, whether or not she liked it.

True, she was eighteen now, but, with no resources, she couldn't do much about it.

"Besides," Steve added with a happy grin, "I can't worry about being homesick when there's a wedding to plan."

A wedding! Now, that was something else. Melissa celebrated as heartily as everyone else over supper at Sue's Diner. More than once, Steve caught Melissa inspecting him, but she always covered it by asking him to pass the salt, the butter, or another napkin. Steve was not her father; he had none of her father's learning, culture, or charisma, nor could he ever could replace her father in their hearts. However, Steve was part of this village. Bringing him to Grover's Park meant Melissa would keep a tangible piece of Munsonville. With that, who knew what the future might hold?

After dinner, Steve took Brian back to his apartment for the night. Melissa considered opening Mr. Masters' envelope while her mother showered, then decided against it. What if it held bad news that made her cry? Private was safer.

"Bathroom's free," Darlene called.

Melissa unclasped her suitcase and removed her nightgown. Her mother settled into bed with a book. Melissa quietly unzipped her book bag, slipped out Mr. Masters' envelope, and tucked it between the folds of her nightgown.

"Mom, I'm getting ready for bed," Melissa said.

"Okay." Darlene said and turned a page.

She was surprised her mother could be so calm, but, maybe, getting married a second time wasn't nearly as stirring as the first.

Melissa locked the bathroom door and tossed her nightgown on the counter. The garment slid to the floor. Ignoring it, she closed the toilet lid and sat cross-legged on the stool. With a pounding heart and trembling hands, Melissa ripped open the envelope and peeked inside. She extracted a single sheet of paper, unfolded it, and read its few lines:

Twenty years from now, you will be more disappointed by the things you didn't do than by the ones you did do. So throw off the bowlines. Sail away from the safe harbor. Catch the trade winds in your sails. Explore. Dream. Discover. Mark Twain.

Henry knew all along he was leaving and not coming back! Longing, sadness, and loneliness washed over her all at once. Why, oh why, after introducing her to literature's greatest works; forcing her to see the travesty of the Bryony fantasy; and exhorting her to be herself, carve her own path, and live out her destiny, had he not even said goodbye?

Melissa's eyes misted as she slowly tilted the envelope upside down and shook out its remaining contents. A shower of dried, purple, rose petals released their fragrance and spilled onto her lap.

EPILOGUE

Melissa returned to Grover's Park two days before Christmas break ended, just enough time to unpack her suitcases before classes resumed. She had smuggled three souvenirs with her. Tucked amongst her clothes was the copy of, *Nocturnal Lore: The Collected Tales of Henry Matthews*, which must have slid down her bed that first night in the servant's cottage, another clue that Fr. Alexis had been right. Melissa's imagination was obviously on overdrive.

Keepsakes two and three really belonged to the Munsonville Public Library: *The Best-Loved Compositions of John Simons and Creatures of the Night: Witches, Werewolves, and Vampires*, neither of which could Melissa bear to return to their proper home.

After living inside a cottage for the last few months, the brown tri- level, down the street from her former ranch home, felt like a palace. Her spacious bedroom, with its white walls and tan shag carpet, seemed almost suite-like. She walked around the bare room, touching brass knobs on her closet and studying the swimming pool in the fenced back yard. How long before she stopped missing a wooded landscape?

Her sadness at leaving Munsonville contrasted sharply with the grandiose reception greeting her when she walked through the front doors of her old high school. Shelly and Laura decorated her locker in streamers and pinned long ribbons onto her. They had taped on assorted candies and gum, so a flustered Melissa had something to share with the other students when they saluted her return. She couldn't believe the attention. She had gained celebrity status.

Although none of her friends had heard of Munsonville until Melissa had moved there, Kimberly's disappearance and death, along with the devastating fire of the famous mansion, generated high interest in the village among her teachers and peers at Grover's Park High School. Everyone asked about it, but Melissa dodged the subject.

"The memories are just too painful," Melissa said.

Last semester, everyone at Munsonville School had assumed Melissa would write about John Simons because she lived near his mansion. This semester, her current English teacher assigned something similar: life on the Simons estate, from Melissa's perspective and experience. Melissa chuckled as she sat at her desk to write the first draft. Even if she could share the real story, no one would believe it.

Still, a canopy of sadness hung in the air. Shelly and Laura babbled constantly about Kimberly's death inside Simons Mansion, but it reminded Melissa of John, and it hurt her to chime in. It was bad enough she endured several awful rounds of questioning from the Grover's Park police before Kimberly's death was finally ruled an accident. So, when her friends started, Melissa insisted she would rather discuss something more interesting.

"Like Jason Frye," Melissa teased Laura.

Steve and her mother were married in their new home on Valentine's Day. An old college friend of her mother's, now a minister, performed the ceremony. They kept it small, just a few close friends of her mother's from Grover's Park, and no one from Munsonville. Melissa and Brian were the unofficial witnesses. Melissa wistfully wore the long, purple dress Darlene had bought her for the occasion, but Brian said he felt like a monkey in a tuxedo.

"Well, you are pretty cute," Melissa said, ruffling his hair.

336

To her surprise, Brian didn't get mad. He blushed and looked at his feet.

By rising extra early, Steve and Brian had proudly recreated their Thanksgiving feast for the wedding reception. Brian had convinced his mother that Steve's chocolate cake recipe was better than anything traditional the local bakery might produce. The family room eight-track stereo provided the music for the new couple's first dance, but neither seemed to mind the casual atmosphere or the fact Steve could not dance. Melissa even taught Steve a few steps, much to her mother's amazement.

"What happened to my daughter with the two left feet?" Darlene said when the song ended. "I didn't know you could dance."

"I saw it on television," Melissa said, avoiding Brian's skeptical look.

After a thorough check-up, Melissa's former pediatrician pronounced the anemia cured and discontinued the iron pills, adding to Melissa's anguish. She'd endure anemia a hundred times, if she could be close to John again, even if he drained away all her blood.

That last thought jolted her back to reality. What was she thinking? John, even if he had existed beyond her dreams, was gone. He would haunt her future only if she allowed it. She must forget him. She would have to be strong. Although it was hard, Melissa resolved to take Henry's advice. She had an entire life ahead of her. She would discover and explore, in ways that made her grow as Melissa, not Bryony's clone.

Brian cried every night the first week home, but he never saw Snowbell again. A co-worker's cat had a litter, and Steve brought home a tiny gray kitten. Charcoal soon filled the void in the boy's heart.

In March, Steve began a janitorial business. Her mother still wrote by night, but now accompanied Steve on job assignments during the day. Melissa and Brian, mostly Brian, assisted Steve on night and weekend jobs. Melissa used increasing amounts of homework as her excuse to decline family and social obligations, but, more often not, she abandoned her academic assignments in favor of curling up on her bed, cradling a silent music box, and gazing into the past. Her parents praised Melissa's

337

diligence, but worried about her falling grades. Brian avoided Melissa as much as possible.

Venturing into the past, however, meant encountering visions of Henry and his admonitions to forget Bryony. Since honoring Henry's memory also meant fulfilling his last request, Melissa would then bury the music box in the back of her closet, tackle homework with gusto, and relieve Brian of cleaning duties by vacuuming all weekend with Steve. When she brought home an A in typing, Steve allowed her to prepare his billing invoices. When she needed help in accounting, Steve let her practice on his books and corrected her mistakes. Her sensible side would prevail, as Fr. Alexis had promised.

By April, distance from Munsonville was easing her heartache, but it hadn't completely erased it. Her mother and Brian never mentioned it, but Melissa wondered if Steve ever felt wistful for his birthplace, or was she the only one with fondness for the rustic fishing village? If Steve ever looked back, he never showed it, for his world revolved around his new family. Despite her efforts, Melissa still dwelled on the magical autumn of 1975, especially when she heard piano notes on the radio.

This left Melissa at odds with Shelly and Laura, who both had solid goals for their lives. Shelly had a university scholarship; Laura would attend art school. Shelly hoped to open an accounting firm, marry, and raise one boy and one girl. Laura wanted to illustrate magazines. Both girls had boyfriends, and they were nice boyfriends, too, not controlling, domineering, older, imaginary men like John. Ironically, it was Laura who had delivered a huge lecture, after Jason had invited Melissa to the movies, and Melissa had declined.

"You wouldn't be upset if I went out with him?" Melissa had asked her.

"Of course not," Laura had said. "I won't lie to you, Melissa. I'll always have a place in my heart for Jason, but...."

"But what?"

"Life moves on. I don't know what happened in Munsonville, but you need to get past it already."

To prove she had "gotten past" John, Melissa agreeably went steady with Jason Frye, but just as agreeably let him break up with her the night of senior prom. Melissa pleasantly wished

Jason the best, and did not look back. Jason Frye was not John Simons.

Brian went on a growing streak that summer and stood two inches taller than Melissa did when she left for college in the fall. This time, packing up her possessions and moving away to another state was heart- breaking in a different way. She had not anticipated an adult life without John. Melissa's thoughts returned to the night of the fire. Surely, John, yearning for new life, would not torch his mansion, especially knowing Melissa, his redeemer, was inside. She had happily offered up her blood for him; he had no reason to hurt her. She considered Fr. Alexis's words. Through a series of unrelated events and by absorbing her grandmother's unusual coping methods, Melissa had spurred the vampire fantasies. The tragedies of the past were just that; she no longer needed the dreams. A future of her making was ahead of her, if she dared seize it. College would be that new beginning.

Orientation weekend was great fun. The upperclassmen planned a slew of activities for the freshmen. One was a scavenger hunt to acquaint the students with their new town. The freshmen and their mentors divided into teams and distributed a list of places to find. At each location, they snapped a picture with an instamatic camera, but the buildings blurred before Melissa's eyes, and she only saw Main Street.

On Saturday night, the school hosted a keg party in the gym. Melissa's roommate, Jill Eaton, had a good-looking brother, Bradley. He came to the dance that night with a few friends who were just as gorgeous as he, even though Bradley was twenty-three and too old for a college event.

"The lead singer is even hotter," Jill said with a giggle. "He's also a good friend of Brad's. That's why they're playing tonight for free."

"Cool," Melissa said, hoping she sounded enthusiastic.

The band *did* sound good. Melissa sipped her first beer, repulsed by its bitter taste. How did people drink the nasty stuff?

Melissa ditched her cup beneath a folding chair and remembered the punch glass she had hidden below a table, the night she had met Henry Matthews. Ignoring the sudden heaviness in her heart, she moved close to the stage area for a better look at the lead singer. Jill was right; he was much better looking than

Brad. Then Melissa saw the keyboard player, and her gut hit the floor.

It was John Simons.

Or, at least, it was someone who closely resembled John. She tried to sneak a decent look at him, but he kept his head bent over the keys. He did not contribute to any of the vocals. How odd to think of John Simons wearing jeans and a T-shirt! *Impossible!*

Hadn't he died in the fire? *Hadn't he?* Melissa needed to know for sure.

At intermission, Jill talked nonstop about the lead singer. "I told you he was hot."

Melissa tried to act nonchalant. "I like the keyboard player better. Who is he?"

"I don't know," Jill said. "Hey, Brad!" She stood on tiptoes and waved across several groups of people to catch his attention. "Brad!"

Brad gave her thumbs up and walked over to the girls. "What's up?"

"Melissa likes the keyboard player," Jill said. "Can she meet him?"

"No problem," Brad said. "I'll get him."

After he walked away, Melissa turned on Jill. "I can't believe you did that!"

"Well, you wanted to meet him, didn't you?"

"Not that way !"

Brad soon returned with him. The keyboard player, tall and broad, wore his blond hair very long. He had striking, almond-shaped blue eyes and wore his beard and mustache thinly trimmed, hardly noticeable at all.

"The ladies wanted to meet you," Brad said. "Jill, Melissa, this is Johnny."

A broad smile broke out on the keyboardist's face, as he extended his hand to Melissa. "How's it going?" he said. "Melissa, right?"

WORKS CITED

Calkins, Ed. Telephone Interview. 10 Mar. 2009

Hemmingway, Ernest. "Old Man at the Bridge." Full Poster Snips. n.p.
n.d. Web. 15 Feb. 2010.

Halm, Friedrich. "Love Quotes." Quotes, Quotes, Quotes. Cynthia Wells, 2002. Web. 15 Feb. 2010.

Longfellow, Henry Wadsworth. "A Psalm of Life." PoemHunter.com. n.p.
n.d. Web. 15 Feb. 2010.

Longfellow, Henry Wadsworth. "The Song of Hiawatha." FullBooks.com.
n.p. n.d. Web. 15 Feb. 2010.

"Mark Twain." Wisdom Quotes. Jone Johnson Lewis, 1995-2009. Web. 15 Feb. 2010.

Scott, Sir Walter. "Lochinvar." Old Poetry. n.p. n.d. Web. 01 Mar. 2010.

Stockton, Frank R. "The Lady, or the Tiger?" Page by Page Books. Page by Page Books, 2004.15 Feb. 2010.

"Tennessee Williams Quotes." Notable Quotes. n.p. n.d. Web. 15 Feb.
2010.

Van Dyke, Henry. "Gone From My Sight." The Ribbon. TheRibbon.com, 1998-2010. Web. 15 Feb. 2010.

Van Dyke, Henry. "The Mansion." Page by Page Books. Page by Page Books, 2004. Web. 15 Feb. 2010.

Whitman, Walt. "When Lilacs Last in the Dooryard Bloom'd."
Princeton University. Trustees of Princeton University, 2010. Web.
15 Feb. 2010.

WORKS CONSULTED

"1975 Monthly Calendars." ePrintableCAlendars.com. n.p. n.d. Web. 14 Feb. 2010.

"1975 – What Happened in 1975?" Spiritus-Temporis.com. n.p. 2005.
Web. 14 Feb. 2010.

Background Information for the Houston Ballet's World Premiere of
Dracula, March 13-23, 1997. n.p. n.d. Web. 27 Feb. 2010.

"Bathroom Basics – A Brief History of the Toilet." Victoria Plumb. n.p.
n.d. Web. 11 Feb. 2009.

"Biopharm Leeches: The Biting Edge of Science." Biopharm. Biopharm 1996-1995. Web. 17 May 2010.

"Bryony." Wikipedia, The Free Encyclopedia. Wikipedia Foundation, Inc.
09 Jan. 2010. Web. 14 Feb. 2010.

"Bubonic Plague." Wikipedia, The Free Encyclopedia. Wikipedia Foundation, Inc. 28 Feb. 2010. Web. 28, Feb. 2010.

"Bubonic Plague Symptoms." eMedTV.com. Clinaero, Inc. 2006-2010.
Web. 18 May 2010.

"Castles of Transcarpathia." The Tourist Guidebook: Transcarpathia. n.p.
n.d. 19 May 2010.

Col, Jeananda. "Inventors and Inventions from 1851-1900—the Second Half of the Nineteenth Century." Enchanted Learning. Enchanted Learning.com, 2000-2009. Web. 28. Jan. 2009.

"Croquet History." Maui Croquet Club. n.p. 13 Jan. 2010. Web. 15 Feb. 2010.

"Crustaceamorpha: Parasitism." University of California Museum of Paleontology. n.p.. n.d. Web 17 May 2010.

"Dandy." Wikipedia, The Free Encyclopedia. Wikipedia Foundation, Inc.
19 Feb. 2010. Web. 27 Feb. 2010.

Dandyism.net, n.p. n.d. Web. 27 Feb. 2010.

"Dinner-Parties." Cassells Household Guide, New and Revised Edition.
The Victorian Dictionary. n.d. Web. 12 Feb. 2009.

Dream Moods. Dream Moods, Inc., 2000-2009. Web. 28 Feb. 2010.

"Dressing then Part: A Victorian Gentleman's Personal Guide." Gentleman's Emporium.

Historical Emporium, Inc. n.d. Web. 24 Jan. 2009.

"Etiquette of the Victorian Era." n.p. n.d. Web. 07 Feb. 2009.

"Fast Growing Noxious Weed, White Bryony, Found in Bozeman." Montana State University. Montana State University, 28 July 2009. Web. 14 Feb. 2010.

Grieve, Mrs. M. "Bryony, White." A Modern Herbal. Botanical.com, 1995-2005. Web. 14 Feb. 2009.

"G. Schwechten." Wikipedia, The Free Encyclopedia. Wikipedia Foundation, Inc. 16 Jan. 2010. Web. 15 Feb. 2010.

Hannaby, Paul. "Creative Woodturning." Woodturning Home. Woodturning Home. n.d. Web. 27 Feb. 2010.

Harris, Kristina. "The Etiquette of Victorian Dress." The Vintage Connection. Kristina Seleshanko, 21 Apr. 2006. Web. 02 Feb. 2009.

Hoppe, M. "The Victorian Wedding Part One – Preparation." Literary Liaisons, Ltd., Literary Liaisons Ltd., 1997. Web. 31. Jan. 2009.

Hoppe, M. "The Victorian Wedding Part Two – The Ceremony and Reception." Literary Liaisons, Ltd. Literary Liaisons, Ltd., 1997. Web. 02 Feb. 2009.

"How to Steer a Rowboat." eHow, Inc. eHow, Inc., 1999-2010. Web. 17 Feb. 2009.

"Illustrated Glossary of Victorian Sartorial Terms." Nineteenth-Century Fashions: A Compendium. n.p. n.d. Web. 20 Jan. 2009.

Kelly, John. "Last Call to Dinner." Classic Trains Magazine. Kalmbach Publishing Company, 21 Feb. 2001. Web. 16 Feb. 2009

"Khust." Wikipedia, The Free Encyclopedia. Wikipedia Foundation, Inc. 03 Dec. 2009. Web. 29 Jan. 2009.

"Khust Castle." Primaria Municipiului Satu Mare. n.p. n.d. Web. 27 Feb. 2009.

"Khust District." tourinfo. n.p. n.d. 19 May 2010.

Lewandowski, Aleksandra. "Dinner at Eight: Victorian Dinner Parties." n.p. 2004. Web. 02 Feb. 2009.

McDonnell, Dr. John. Head Tilt in Cats (Vestibular Signs)." PetPlace.com. Intelligent Content Corp., 1999-2010. Web. 16 Feb. 2009.

McMath, Meredith Bean. "Inquire Within: A How-to Guide of Victorian Entertainment and Guide to the Civil War Ballroom."

Story root. Run, Rabbit, Run Productions, Inc., 2003. Web. 16 Feb. 2009.

"McVicker's Theater – Chicago, Illinois Lithograph." Old Chicago: History and Architecture in Vintage Postcards." Pat Sabin, 1999- 2010. Web. 29 Jan. 2009

"McVickers Theater." Cinema Treasures. Cinema Treasures, 2000-2009.
Web. 29 Jan. 2009.

Moniz, Emma. "The 'Net Guide to 19th Century Courtship and Manners." The Original Gone with the Wind Role Playing Game. n.p. n.d. Web. 29. Jan. 2009.

Mount, Harry. "Can Men Really Choose Home Furnishings?" Times Online. Times Newspaper, Ltd., 19 Oct. 2008. Web. 10 Feb. 2009.
"Newfoundlands: what's good about 'em; what's bad abut 'em." your Purebred puppy: advice You can Trust. Michele Welton. 2000- 2006. Web. 19 May 2010.

"Parasites Affecting Monarchs." n.p. n.d. Web. 17 May 2010.

"Plays of Dion Boucicault." Templeman Library Special Collections: Theatre Collections. The Calthrop Boucicault Collection. Templeman Library, University of Kent, Canterbury, 2005. Web. 14 Feb. 2010.

"Robert Emmet." Wikipedia, The Free Encyclopedia. Wikipedia Foundation, Inc. 12, Feb. 2010. Web. 29 Jan. 2009.

"Rose Color Symbolism." teleflora. Teleflora. 2010. Web. 19 May 2010.

"Schwechten." PianoGrands – Fine Antique Pianos. n.p. n.d. Web. 17 Feb. 2009.

Simplysupernatural-vampires.com, 2008-2009. Web. 27 Feb. 2010.

"Sound Advice." Long Island Stay lace Association. Coral Computer Consultants, 1996-2009. Web. 11 Feb. 2009.

"The Black Death: Bubonic Plague." The Middle Ages.net. n.p. n.d. Web.
18 May 2010.

"The Dandy." France in the Age of Les Misérables. Courtney Hopf, Leslie Kogan, and Rachel Brown for Mount Holyoke College History's 255: 'Les Miz and Les Media,' May 2001. Web. 27 Feb. 2010.

"The Supersizers Go—Victorian." Go Hungry. Makiko Itoh, 2003-2010. Web. 10 Feb. 2009.

"The Victorian Bedroom." Aunt May's Cottage. Aunt May's Cottage, 8 June 2007. Web. 08 Feb. 2009.

"The Victorian Picnic." The Judge's Lodging Victorian Museum. The Judge's Lodging Victorian Museum, n.d. Web. 17 Feb. 2009

"Traditional Rowing."Whitehall Rowing and Sail. Whitehall Reproductions. 1996-2005. Web. 18 May 2010.

"Ukraine/Tours." Pan Ukraine air service tourism. n.p. n.d. Web. 16 Feb. 2010.

"Vampire Bat." The Columbia Encyclopedia, Sixth Edition. Encyclopedia.com, 2008. Web. 01 Mar. 2010

Vampire Realm of Mist. Geocities. n.d. Web. 11 Feb. 2009.

"Victorian Architecture." Front Door. Scripps Networks, LLC, 2010. Web. 12 Feb. 2009.

"Victorian Domestic Servant Hierarchy and Wage Scale." This and That. Wayne Schmidt. n.d. Web. 26 Feb. 2009.

"Victorian Home in Historic District." Vacation Rentals by Owner. VRBO.com, 1995-2010. Web. 12 Feb. 2009.

Victorian Interiors and More – Victorian Life Wasn't Quite What You May Have Thought It Was. Atom. n.p. n.d. Web. 03. Feb. 2009.

Victoriana Magazine – Victorian Style Living. Victoriana.Com, 1996- 2010. Web. 31 Jan. 2009

VictoriasPast.com. n.p. n.d. Web. 16 Feb. 2009.

"Walleye Fishing Tips & Techniques." Twin Lakes Outfitters. n.p. n.d. Web. 14 May 2010.

Walsh, Townsend. "The Career of Dion Boucicault." Internet Archive, Internet Archive, 10 Mar. 2001. Web. 29 Jan. 2009.

Welcome to: The Dandy. n.p. n.d. Web. 27 Feb. 2010.

Wells, Richard A. "Victorian Dancing Etiquette." Manners Culture and Dress of the Best American Society. J.R. Burrows & Company. n.d. Web. 16 Feb. 2009.

"Welcome to our Victorian House.com." n.p. n.d. Web. 24 Dec. 2009. Web. 12 Feb. 2009.

White, Linda. "The Arabian Horse-A Brief History." Arabian Horse Times. Arabian Horse Times, 2010. Web. 15 Feb. 2010.

About the Author

Denise M. Baran-Unland is the author of the BryonySeries supernatural/literary trilogy for young and new adults, the Adventures of Cornell Dyer chapter book series for grade school children and the Bertrand the Mouse series for young children.

She has six adult children, three adult stepchildren, fourteen total grandchildren, six godchildren, and four cats.

She is the co-founder of WriteOn Joliet and previously taught features writing for a homeschool coop, with the students' work published in the co-op magazine and The Herald-News in Joliet.

Denise blogs daily and is currently the features editor at The Herald-News. To read her feature stories, visit theherald-news.com. For more information about Denise's fiction and to follow her on social media, visit bryonyseries.com.

About the Illustrator

Kathleen R. Van Pelt is a freelance illustrator who works mostly in oils and pen and ink mediums. She is originally from Chicago, where she received   her Bachelor of Fine Art from the University of Illinois at Chicago.

Kathleen now resides in Minnesota where its natural beauty and her "fur associates" (cats, dog, and mouse) inspire her to create "nature fantasy" images. Visit her at imaginarylinesstudio.com.

www.ingramcontent.com/pod-product-compliance
Lightning Source LLC
Chambersburg PA
CBHW031056260626
47172CB00001B/97